The Empress
Angelina's Quest

The Empress Angelina's Quest

A Beary Maxumus Adventure

CHARLES & IRENE NICKERSON

To order additional copies of this book, contact:
Xlibris
1-888-795-4274
www.Xlibris.com
Orders@Xlibris.com
550691

CONTENTS

Introduction..7
Prologue...11

Chapter 1   A Rude Awakening..................................15
Chapter 2   Candaris XII Shanghai.............................44
Chapter 3   Changes and Plans..................................69
Chapter 4   Lesser Anzico System..............................89
Chapter 5   Alfa Strike..112
Chapter 6   Revelations and Recovery 138
Chapter 7   Trouble from another Quarter:
              The Arrival of Admiral Astrid..................215
Chapter 8   Andapos System 270
Chapter 9   Effect..298
Chapter 10   Results...322
Chapter 11   Immigrants and a New Start....................336
Chapter 12   A Quiet Home Coming............................343
Chapter 13   Epilogue 363

INTRODUCTION

THANK YOU FOR READING *THE EMPRESS ANGELINA'S QUEST* THIS IS THE THIRD BOOK IN THE BEARY MAXUMUS SERIES THAT FOLLOWS THE ADVENTURES OF BEARY, POMPEY, ARTEMUS, CAESAR, AND BEN AND THEIR FAMILIES.

IRENE LIKES TO POINTS OUT THAT THIS IS A COMPANION VOLUME TO THE *CROSSROADS OF TIME AND SPACE,* A TIBERIUS MAXUMUS ADVENTURE. IN A WAY THAT IS TRUE, THEY TAKE PLACE DURING THE SAME TIME FRAME AFTER BOOK TWO.

TO PARENTS, MY 19 YEAR OLD DAUGHTER AND I PURPOSELY DISCUSES SOME TOPICS IN THIS BOOK ESPECIALLY ABOUT LOVE BETWEEN A HUSBAND AND A WIFE. IT HAS NOT BEEN OUR INTENTION TO OFFEND BUT TO PRESENT THESE TOPICS TASTEFULLY AND WITH HUMOR YET TO SPUR DISCUSSION BETWEEN TEENAGERS AND THEIR PARENTS.

I TAKE FULL RESPONSIBILITY FOR THE PRESENTATION OF MY CHARACTERS. IT IS EVERY WRITER'S HOPE THAT THE READER BEGINS TO SEE THESE BEINGS FOR WHO THEY HAVE BECOME IN THE WRITERS MIND.

AGAIN I WANT TO THANK YOU THE READER I HOPE YOU ENJOY THIS TALE.

SPECIAL THANKS TO MY WRITING PARTNER THAT SPECIAL LITTLE ANGEL IN MY LIFE, AND THE INSPIRATION FOR BOTH ERIN AND SHO-SHO MY DAUGHTER IRENE NICKERSON.

I WOULD ALSO LIKE TO THANK HARLEY MCCOY FOR HELPING ME EDIT THIS BOOK

AND LAST BUT NEVER LEAST THE CREATOR OF THE UNIVERSE AND HIS WORD, JESUS CHRIST WITHOUT WHOM ANY STORIES COULD NOT BE WRITTEN.

CHARLES L. NICKERSON

PROLOGUE

"LIEUTENANT MAXUMUS, ARTEMUS, and Captain Maritinus, Captain Gracchus asked that you join him in his wardroom if you please." MacIntosh said.

"Thank you Mac, we better get going." Beary said.

A few moments later they reported to the wardroom Gracchus was waiting. He was holding a message in his hands.

Gracchus motioned for them to take a seat, "Gentlebears, let's assume you have reported in for the duration. You three and the Commander have different status on this ship. Beary unless Artemus complains you are now the CAG and he is the ACAG, Your Executive officers have now moved up to your positions. It really doesn't change anything but I need you both to be in overall command of the Air Wing. Also you will both need to get in your flight time."

Artemus replied, "I like working for the Boss, besides he can fly both the daggers and the fighters. I am strictly back seat in a fighter."

Gracchus nodded, "Then that is settled. Also Ben a second Green Dagger was delivered did you order it?"

Ben shook his head, "No Sir, I don't have a crew for it."

Dr Vallen stepped in, "I can explain, The Shipyard felt we needed two the second was a gift."

Gracchus thought for a moment, "Then we will have to pick up a crew for it. We will be passing a Marine Air Base; will shanghai a crew if we can't find a crew to volunteer."

Ben looked at him, "Sir how . . .?"

Gracchus held up several forms signed by Admiral Starpaw, "These say it is legal. Now for the real reason I had you brought in. We will be leaving in four cycles no fanfare, were just slipping off. Our orders have changed we're going to the Pratis system first."

"Sir, don't get me wrong, but I thought other fleet ships were scheduled to go there." Beary said.

Gracchus nodded, "There were, but those units were from Strike Force Bravo and they are being sent to another border region. An Agricultural Colony was attacked. Luckily the new *BAF Broadsword* was nearby, it drove off the attacker. The problem is no one has ever seen this type of ship.

The Pratis people have a strong lobby. They want to go home and not just to Pratis V but to III, IV, and VI as well."

Beary called up the Star charts, "If we take the Dragon's Eye then we will be behind Carnes Drift. Then we could try and go through Haden's passage."

"Beary are you trying to scratch my new ship? While I know the Dragons Eye is stable Haden's Passage is a nightmare." Gracchus pointed out.

"Yes Sir, But if we take a conventional route it will take six months to get there, even with taking the Dragon's eye. Haden's passage cuts the time to a couple months." Beary said.

"You have been through it before?" Gracchus asked.

"Yes Sir, the *EAQ* is larger than what I was on but she should handle the passage." Beary said.

"Ok, we would have to pass by the passage anyway if we take the Dragon's Eye and it saves us three months. You have two weeks to convince me now get some rest." Gracchus said.

After Ben, Berry, Dr Vallen, and Artemus left, Jeanne stepped out. "You owe me twenty credits. I told you that is how I would go. Beary agrees with me."

Gracchus handed her the bill. "I knew you were going to be a problem as a First Officer."

"True, and a bigger one as a wife probable, but we make a good team Argus. Just trust your people." Jeanne said.

He smiled, "Hadn't you better get some rest?"

"Sorry Captain, duty calls. I'll be in Auxiliary control. We will be ready when you are."

Beary and Artemus informed Joe and Jane of their promotions both complained that left then short an administrative position.

Beary responded, "We might be able to fix that."

Artemus shook his head, "How do we know if the Bears we get are any good?"

Beary smiled, "Simple we hack the staff computer and look at their records."

Artemus sighed, "Beary that is against the rules you know that."

"Yes, that's why you have to be careful about whose codes you use." Beary said, as he pulled out a small black book.

Joe and Jane laughed; Artemus just dropped his head as they pulled out similar books.

"We are all going to be court marshaled aren't we?" Artemus asked.

Jane grinned, "No, Boss but you and Beary better let us get you the records; we just up dated our books twenty four cycles ago."

Beary nodded, "Ok they will be working for you anyway. Find a good Dagger crew."

Jane replied, "No problem you two better check on your families."

"Beary don't take this wrong but I think you would have made a good pirate." Artemus said.

"What can I say, it is in the blood." Beary said with a smile.

Beary and Artemus looked in on the family, only Shoshanna and Ice Song were awake. They headed for the engine room where Beary talked with the Chief Engineer then they headed to the Bridge. They had discovered they had two offices one off the Bridge and one down in the area that connected the two Hangers. A turbo lift connected their offices.

Commander Edwardian/Gracchus called Beary on his com unit. "Well, Beary how do you like your bridge office?"

He looked at it, "It's very functional Commander."

"And mostly for show Beary and ceremony, this is where you meet with the scientist and outsiders." Jeanne said, "Same with Artemus, your other offices are where I know you will do most your work and suggest it. They are more secure."

"Thank you Commander, I understand now." Beary said.

Artemus leaned against the door, "So we work for a couple also."

Beary smiled, "Isn't this ship all about deception, what you see, and what you don't"

Artemus just grinned.

Three cycles later Captain Gracchus walked on to the bridge. "Ensign Gorez, please inform Vandar Control that we are leaving without any fanfare."

Lieutenant Gorez did as he was instructed. "Vandar Control sends may the Creator go with us."

"Mr. Belows and Mr. Helios please take us to the Dragons Eye, full impulse power.

Lieutenant Maxumus if you please." Gracchus ordered.

Beary nodded, "Alfa flight, launch Cap."

With that order the mission and the adventure of the *Empress Angelina's Quest* begins.

CHAPTER 1

A Rude Awakening

BEARY AND ARTEMUS were setting in their new office on the flight deck when Flight Master Sergeant MacIntosh walked in. "Sir's we have a problem and I think we need to talk about it."

Beary and Artemus looked at him, "Shoot Mac what is it?"

Mac smiled these two didn't mind that he was a Non Com. they trusted him and weren't afraid to show it, good. "Do you plan to give up your gunner and WTO and your crafts?"

Beary looked at him, "No Mac, why?"

"Two things Sir, first if you don't we are short at least one fighter and one Dagger. The new executive officers will need a gunner and a WTO. Also Sirs, I need maintenance and logistics officer and we need an intelligence officer. Ensign Akhiok has some rudimentary knowledge of maintenance and logistics. Ensign We, is smart and speaks several languages. They would be good choices to be your S3 and S4. I can teach Ensign Akhiok everything he needs to know. I am sure Lady Maxumus would work with Ensign We." MacIntosh said.

"Alright Mac, take care of it we will be at Candaris XII for three days. Have Andreas Prime ship us another Fighter and Dagger they can give up one from the 12." Beary said. "By the way tell Pathfinder and Barbarous what you told us. Also have the ensigns' report to us will you."

MacIntosh saluted, "Yes Sir." Well that was that they listened then told him to fix it. Just like he knew they would. He had the two ensigns' report to the bosses and went to talk with the Squadron CO's.

Barbarous smiled when Mac was done explaining what Beary wanted. "Well Mac do you want me to make the call or do you."

"I can do it Sir. I am not sure the Captain of Twelve will be happy." Mac said.

Mac made the call.

Three cycles later two new Purple Daggers, a White Dagger, and two brand new Valkyrie fighters were loaded onto the Foil Claw. Its Captain took off in a mad dash to catch the *EAQ* which had a full days lead. He smiled to himself he would catch her after all he was a Fast Attack Destroyer.

Beary looked at the time. "Come on Savato, It is time to head home." He called the watch officer, "Ensign Banks we are heading to our quarters if you need us."

Banks answer back, "No problem Sir, Charlie Flight is flying CAP, and Delta Flight is on standby. Second squadron will take over in six cycles."

They rode the elevator up to the bridge. Commander Edwardian-Gracchus was setting in the Captain's chair. She turned to look at them, "What did you do put in a fifteen cycle day?"

Beary shrugged, "Just doing some paper work and filling some positions."

Jeanne ordered, "Go be with your families. Beary let your people do their jobs. You and Artemus put in one, eight cycle and split one, eight cycle shift per day. Have the squadron commanders, and your S3 and S4 cover the other eight. But no more fifteen or twenty cycle days, unless we are in combat is that understood?"

Beary and Artemus nodded, "Yes Mame."

They walked back and took the elevator down to the living quarter's deck. They walked past the civilian's quarters. A couple of the scientists were setting at a table playing chess they nodded as Beary and Artemus walked by.

As they pasted Dr. Sandra Orthandro's quarter's she stopped them, "You are Doctor Beary Maxumus are you not?" She asked.

Beary nodded, "Yes Doctor Orthandro I am."

She put her paws on her hips "Why would a gifted scientist like yourself, join the military?"

Artemus looked at her then at Beary, "If you will excuse me I need to get going."

Beary held him up and smiled, "Doctor Orthandro I enjoy being a soldier. I come from a long line of warriors, who have served their families and their clan. As a prince of that clan it is expected.

This vessel will allow me to both serve my clan and the creatures of the Federation, and pursue scientific research. Have a good evening Doctor."

Artemus looked at him "That was rude of her wasn't it."

Beary sighed, "A lot of them were thinking it. She just had the guts to say it. I don't care what they think Savato. This is who I am. My parents wanted me to be an astronomer, and an engineer. Don't get me wrong I enjoy doing both. But being a pilot a naval officer is all I ever wanted to be."

Artemus shrugged, "You don't have to convince me. The orphanage trained me to be an electrician, as you know I am pretty good. But I couldn't wait to get into the fleet. This life and the life you have given me is the life I have always wanted."

Beary looked at him, "But I haven't given . . ."

Artemus smiled, "Yes you have boss, even before Alexa found out who I was. You, Ben, and Caesar gave me a family, Pricilla too." Artemus leaned against the door leading into their family section. "Everything I have is because of you, your family, and Ben."

Beary shook his head, "No Savato, you made who you are. It was you who reached out to three lost cubs and gave them love. All we did was support you."

Artemus nodded, "That's the point Beary. You acted as family even before you became family. You reached out and saved me, that allowed me to save them and find love. For that my Prince I will always be grateful. I just want you to know it."

Beary nodded "Come on let's check on our families. Our wives are probable going to skin us."

Alexis was setting at a table working on a computer.

Beary walked over. "Alexis are you working on something interesting or just having fun?"

Alexis looked up and smiled, "Essay for a class I am taking on Bearilian military history. I was studying General Jordan's decision to send the 43rd infantry into Cortan's Pass to hold it against the Banta Horde."

Beary nodded, "What conclusion did you come up with in your essay?"

Alexis shook her head, "That's the problem Beary; General Jordan is a hero . . . But he made a mistake sending the 43rd to the pass. It was ill equipped for the cold and had no heavy fire power. They were just sacrificial lambs."

Beary nodded "You're right. If he hadn't what would have happened?"

Alexis looked down, "That's the problem. Don't you see by sending the 43rd he was able to win the day. But if he had sent another unit he might have also succeeded. The 181st was a mountain warfare unit. Why didn't he send them?"

Beary nodded, "Another good question. What did your research tell you?"

Alexis shook her head, "I just don't know. I didn't find anything but other bears analysis. None even discussed the decisions he made."

"Alexis when is your essay due?" Beary asked.

"Next week I just wanted to get it done early." Alexis said.

Beary wrote down a web address, "Go to this web site, and call up the archives list type in Jordan ///876-887 you will find your answers."

Alexis looked at him, "How did you know about these papers?"

Beary shrugged "Benjamin has been working on a complete history of General Jordan for a couple of years. He found the papers a few years ago and gave them to the archive with an understanding that access would be limited."

Alexis looked at Beary, "You sure he won't mind me looking at them?"

"No he won't mind. Just be sure to properly document your paper, and say it is from his personal collection of Jordan papers." Beary said with a wink.

Alexis nodded.

Artemus went in to his suite. Nikolaos was waiting for him. "Father everyone has went to bed but I wanted to talk with you."

Artemus asked, "What is it Nikolaos?"

"Father I was wondering could I train with Captain Maritinus and his marines. Lady Jessica and Alexis has taught me much. But I know I need to learn more before Ti takes me under his tutelage." Nikolaos said, "It will not interfere with my duties or my studies."

Artemus nodded, "I will discuss it with your mother and Lady Jessica. Then if they agree I will talk with Beary and Ben."

Nikolaos smiled. "Thank you, father goodnight."

Beary went in to his suite of rooms there was a note from Pricilla:

Check on Erin before you come to bed. Wake me I want to talk.

I love you; Pricilla

Beary read the note and smiled. Ok no more fifteen hour days. He walked into Erin's room.

"Daddy, Daddy you are home!" Erin squealed. "Look at our room Daddy that is Sho- Sho's bed and that is Mary- um's bed and this is my bed." She started bouncing up and down.

Maryam got up and walked over, "Yes Erin and we have a busy day tomorrow. So we need to go to sleep now lay down so your dad can tuck you in."

Erin smiled. "Ok Mary-um, Sho-Sho says you are right. She is, isn't she Daddy?"

Beary, put her down, "Yes Erin now let me kiss you goodnight." He did and tucked her in. He then kissed Sho-Sho and Maryam.

A connecting door opened and Artemus came in. "I guess we share this room."

Maryam smiled. "It works better for me and Shoshana."

Artemus smiled and kissed all three and waved to Beary who smiled.

Beary turned off the light and walked across the living room to his bed room. He turned on his light.

"Hi sailor you look tired have you had anything to eat?" Pompey asked

"Yeah Artemus and I had some sandwiches. The girls are bunking near one another?" Beary asked.

"Yes when Agathag gets older Andreios will move out of her room and they plan to open up the wall between the two rooms and make a big girl's room. So both dragons and all three girls will be together." Pricilla said.

"Is that fair to Maryam?" Beary asked.

"It was her idea. She pointed out that Andreios was a boar cub and there would come a point it would not be proper for him to go everywhere Agathag would have to go. Besides Agathag will be a protector also." Pricilla pointed out.

Beary slipped in next to her. "So what did you want to talk about?"

"How long will we be at Candaris XII?" Pricilla asked.

"If everything goes smoothly about three days," Beary said "why?"

"Do you know does the base have a good base exchange or is there a town nearby?" Pricilla asked.

"The town is off limits Pricilla. I had not thought about that. I'll bring it up to Captain Gracchus. Maybe we can get the base exchange opened for the entire crew not just military." Beary said.

Pricilla started snuggling into him when the com unit next to the bed went off.

On Andreas Prime, Samuel was setting in his office when two soft arms enveloped him and two lips kissed his neck. He turned and looked into the face of a beautiful Maxmimus female.

He wrapped his arms around her and swatted her tail. "Up to your old tricks again I see."

Isadora smiled, "You have never minded that I can take this form."

"No," Samuel said "but it always means you want something."

"Samuel your words . . ." Isadora started to say.

Issac looked at the female in Samuels's arms, "Madam who are you and why are you here?"

Isadora laughed, "I am sorry Issac. You have never seen me in this form have you? I can only do it when Samuel is near. It is I, your mother Isadora."

Issac looked at her eyes, "Mother is it really you?"

Isadora changed back. "You see my dear it is me. Samuel can transform into a dragon also but he only did it once. He did it to protect me."

Samuel shook his head, "A foolish stunt on my part also."

"Why you defeated him!" Isadora said with pride.

"Yes but I could have done it without transforming." Samuel pointed out.

"But he wouldn't face you as a Maxmimus, only as a dragon. I was worth it." Isadora said with her head held high.

Samuel replied softly, "Yes my love you were and still are."

Issac all of a sudden felt embarrassed, "I am sorry mother."

Isadora laughed, "Don't be it will keep. Besides he needs to call the young prince."

Samuel looked at her, "Oh yes!"

Beary looked at the com unit. "Maxumus, go."

"Ensign Verde, Sir you have a priority call on channel Delta 2." Ensign Verde said.

"Thank you Ensign Verde, I got it." Beary said

Beary switched to channel Delta 2. Samuel and Isadora's faces appeared. "Oh we are sorry Beary."

"No Samuel and Lady Isadora it is fine I just got in and we were talking." Beary said.

Isadora grinned, "Then I am really sorry."

Pricilla smiled, "Don't be my Lady. We had business to discuss before we could get down to business."

Samuel looked at Isadora, "Isadora, my Princess really! We have important . . ."

Beary laughed, "It is ok Samuel you will only make it worse trust me we can't win."

Samuel shook his head, "Beary I have dispatched the Seven. Annabelle Rosa and her cell are on the Dream in the Night as you requested. I told them not to make contact till after Candaris Prime."

Beary nodded "Thank you Samuel and you Lady Isadora and thank your Children for me."

Isadora bowed, "We live to serve my Prince."

Beary smiled. "It is just Beary my Lady Isadora. Good night."

Isadora shook her head, "We should have done more to protect him."

Samuel sighed, "It will be enough."

Issac lowered his head, "Is there anything I can do?"

Isadora kissed him, "Just grow strong my child."

Beary looked at Pricilla "Was there anything else you needed to talk about."

Pompey looked at her husband, "Not tonight just hold me. You are worried aren't you?"

Beary swung his legs out and sat on the edge of the bed, "I made a mistake, and I shouldn't have brought you and Erin along. I was just being selfish. If you had stayed on Andreas Prime, Gamey could have protected you both."

Pricilla sat up. "No! Beary you are wrong Gamey and Timothy and the others have proven that they would die to protect us. But only being with you . . . I would go crazy. So would Erin if you were out here without us especially now.

Look I have Night Wind and Night Song with me. Not to mention my Ladies and two dragons and the Artemus cubs. They are worth a company of Marines.

We are safe. Besides I helped design this ship. I know its capabilities."

Beary looked at her, "I couldn't stand sending you back either Pricilla but you have to know . . ."

Pricilla kissed him. "You my husband, need to be reminded what it is like to be married to a daughter of the Southern Continent."

Beary woke up and looked at his sleeping wife and smiled she knew how to chase away his fears alright.

His com unit flashed, "Maxumus go."

"Sir Ensign Reynolds, Captain Gracchus would like you to join him for breakfast in Ten Forward in one cycle if you could Sir." Ensign Reynolds reported.

"Thank you Ensign. Tell the Captain I will be there." Beary answered.

Pricilla smiled and rolled over, "I guess duty calls."

Beary nodded, "I will be home for supper tonight though, Commanders Gracchus's orders."

"Good now give me a kiss and get going." Pompey said.

Beary walked out of his quarters. Artemus was waiting for him along with Jessica.

Jessica stated, "Beary, Nikolaos wants to start training with the Marines. Ben said it would be alright. The truth is Alexis and I have taught him all we can. Well I could teach him some more about explosives but a spacecraft isn't the best place."

Beary asked. "Is he that good?"

Jessica nodded, "He really needs to be with Ti. His mind has matured fast as has his body due to the dragon blessings. Maryam and Andreios also need to be challenged more. Maryam is better with weapons than I am. Andreios has already introduced himself to the chief machinist mate and is studying under him a cycle and a half a day."

Beary shook his head, "Alright but what about Maryam?"

Jessica looked at both of them. "I want to start training her to use her body as a weapon. I want to train her in both Maxumus and Augustine techniques. Red Paw, also if Snow Flower or Ben can help me."

Artemus nodded. "Ok Jessica, if it is alright with Beary and their mother."

Beary nodded, "I just hope we aren't pushing them to fast."

Jessica nodded "Beary, Nikolaos, and the other two are already reading and doing math at a high school level. We need to challenge them."

"Alright do what you need to Jess for their best interest. They are your detail. Also Jess, do another review of the living quarters security setup for all sections." Beary said.

Jessica nodded, "Alright Beary."

As Beary and Artemus walked away Alexis walked up. "Why didn't you tell him Ben and we were scheduled to do that this morning?"

Jessica replied, "He is worried. Why let him know I am also."

Captain Gracchus and Commander Edwardian/Gracchus were waiting in Ten Forward. They waved Beary and Artemus over as Ben came through the other door.

Gracchus smiled, "Good you three are here." He signaled a steward who brought over a steam table with a small selection of breakfast dishes. "Fix your plates. Then we will get started."

Beary, Artemus, and Ben grabbed plates and filled them then grabbed tea and sat down.

Jeanne said, "Sorry to pull you away from your families. Of course Captain that's not a problem for you."

Ben replied, "No Mame, not yet anyway."

"Well maybe we should fix that." Jeanne teased.

"No Mame. That is not necessary." Ben said.

"You know what they say Captain, misery loves company." Captain Gracchus said.

Beary and Artemus just laughed.

Gracchus smiled; this was breaking all rules of command. However in away Beary and Ben were his equals their commands were separate from the ship. Artemus had been a separate command till, He and Beary was formed into a Composite Wing. "The Foil Claw is going to rendezvous with us in about two cycles they are bringing you more than you asked for two Purples, two Fighters, and a White Dagger. Each is loaded with a new module."

Beary nodded, "Ok that gives us a spare fighter."

Artemus thought, "They knew we had the room so they added the extra Daggers. Who knows the spare white might be for Caesar's personal use. The ship yard was upset he didn't ask for a command white."

Gracchus nodded, "So this isn't a problem."

Ben reported, "Sir, this morning Lady Jessica, Lady Alexis, and I are going over the security systems and protocols for the civilian and military living sections. Chief Flanagan is going to join us. Lady Jessica feels there may be some holes in our coverage."

Jeanne nodded, "Would you do a review of all areas especially the bridge and engineering. Think outside the box Ben if you were boarding this ship and wanted to cause maximum damage but couldn't reach normal critical areas where would you hit. Look for weak points we didn't think about."

"Yes Mame, I'll ask Nikolaos to aid us also then." Ben said.

"Why do you want the Artemus cub's input?" Jeanne asked.

Ben responded, "He has no preconceived notions about what is possible. You said to think outside the box. Nikolaos has a great analytical mind. He might see something we have been trained to miss."

Jeanne nodded, "Good enough Ben. That is the kind of thinking I was hoping for."

"We will be arriving at *Candaris XII* in two days do you think we could get them to open the Base Exchange for the entire crew?" Beary asked.

Gracchus smirked, "I have already put in the request with a note from the Good General. I don't think it will be a problem.

Gentlebears Admiral Starpaw and General Zantoran have given us a great deal of leeway and aid in this project. Partly because you three are heroes, but if we fall on our collective butts, they will hang all five of us."

Beary replied, "That's not a problem Captain, if that occurs, Artemus and I and probably Ben, will also be dead. If we are dead you and the Commander will probably be dead also."

Gracchus shook his head. "So in your view we either succeed or die."

Artemus nodded "It only makes since Captain doesn't it."

"Alright now I figure you Pirates can solve your own personnel problems but do me a favor and both of you get qualified in that spare Green dagger. It is supposed to be your Command post. Though you're getting a crew to fly it, it still would be good to have it on your flight certifications." Gracchus pointed out.

"Ben's pilot is taking us out this afternoon to certify us." Beary said.

Jeanne held out her paw and Captain Gracchus handed her a twenty credit note.

"You two are costing me a fortune." Gracchus said

After breakfast Ben met with Jessica and Alexis. "Do you have Lady Pompey and Erin covered if I take you two and Nikolaos with me?"

Jessica nodded. "Yes, I do, but why Nikolaos?"

Ben explained, "We are to evaluate the entire ship. We will think as we have been trained. How we would attack the ship. Nikolaos has no preconceived ideas he might see a weakness we have been trained to miss."

Jessica shook her head, "Ben you are one dangerous bear. You look for angles inside angles."

Ben got serious. "You both know that evil is coming for Beary, Pompey, and Erin. Along with Artemus, Snow Flower, and their children. They are my family. I will sacrifice my life and the lives of all my marines to protect them. Beary's Pilots and Artemus' feel the same way."

Jessica looked at him, "But what about the other scientists?"

Ben shrugged, "They are our job Jessica we will protect them. But Beary is one of us and as far as we are concerned so is Artemus. For a marine that means something. Besides, I am a Knight of the Dragon."

Jessica smiled, "Alright Ben. I understand. I'll call Nikolaos."

"Nikolaos, get your gear. You are with me." Jessica said.

Nikolaos answered. "I am here Lady Jessica."

Ben told him, "Cousin you are to help us evaluate the security of the ship. We are looking for holes in our coverage that might give an enemy a way to attack us."

"Yes Captain Ben. I understand." Nikolaos said.

Lieutenant Dan Mountain smiled as he took an evaluator's seat. The *Storm Cloud* was a beautiful green dagger. It was built to be an Air Wing Command Post. Some of the extra sensors were designed to aid fighters and Daggers. While his could do the same functions his had been designed as a Marine Attack Command Post. The differences were subtle but made both ships unique and extra deadly in their roles. "Sir, the Shipyard really knew how to build these babies. I thought mine was the best I had ever seen but for her purpose the *Storm Cloud* is the best green Dagger in the fleet."

Beary replied. "Well Dan let's see if she fly's as good as you say she looks."

Beary shot out of the launch bay and put her through her paces. When he was done Dan Mountain just shook his head and certified him.

It was Artemus turn next he launch next and put the Green through all the maneuvering movements in the book and a few that weren't. He then landed and the *Storm Cloud* was lowered into her bunker.

Lieutenant Dan mountain looked at Beary and Artemus, "Sirs, I didn't even know anyone could fly a dagger like that. Let alone a green. Needless to say you are both certified."

"Thanks Dan, tell Captain Maritinus thank you for letting us borrow you." Beary said.

Captain Gracchus looked at the clock and long range scan there was the Foil Claw she had taken two cycles more than anticipated but she was coming on fast.

Gracchus looked at his bridge crew, "Lt. Belows, quietly raise our shields to battle strength. Inform the CAP to land. Call, Maxumus and Artemus to the Bridge."

Beary and Artemus walked on to the Bridge, "What's going on Captain?"

"Something feels off." Gracchus said. "Would you know the power signal of one of your engines? By the way I ordered your Combat Air Patrol in they had been out there for six and a half cycles."

Beary nodded, "Echo Flight is ready to launch, however why don't we hold up for a moment."

Beary looked through the scanners hood and looked at the power signal coming from the other ships warp drive. "Those aren't VM engines we didn't design any with that power signature. In fact there isn't a ship in the fleet with that power signature."

Artemus looked at Beary and the Captain, "How do you want to play it?"

Gracchus shook his head, "They made their ship look like the Foil Claw how close do you think they plan to come before they fire on us."

Beary shrugged, "It depends on how we act. If we act friendly they might come in close."

Artemus shook his head, "Contact them. Play it by the book. They are late let them know we noticed."

Gracchus nodded, "Lieutenant Gorez, bring us to Red Alert. Tell all security personnel to report to stations."

Beary hit a button on his watch and a claxon went off in the ready room. Echo flight and five Purple Daggers launched. The other flights prepared for launch.

Gracchus looked at Beary and Artemus "Go you, are probable better off out there anyway."

Artemus called Chen We. "Head for the Storm Cloud. We are taking the Green Dagger."

Ensign Akhiok called Beary before he could call him, "Sir, Ghost is prepped and ready to go."

Beary smiled, "Thank you Ensign."

In less than five STU both Artemus and Beary had launched.

In the *Storm Cloud* a few barrowed technicians were turning on equipment. As Alfa and Bravo flight launched to back up Echo Flight which was now flying CAP. Harbinger fell in beside Beary.

"Harbinger, to Ghost we are on station," Barbarossa reported.

"Acknowledge. Valkyries take station over Talon. Gem Flight 1 take station ¼, click to starboard. Ghost is handing over control to Command 1."

All of a sudden telemetry data was feed into the fire control computers from The Storm Cloud.

Gracchus nodded to Ensign Gorez, "Sable Dragon this is Red Talon please Authenticate HWF."

After several moments, there was no answer. Then they received a garbled response."

Gracchus nodded "Captain Maritinus bring the ship to security condition 1 please."

Maryam looked at Erin, "Erin, go into your hiding hole now. Please keep Agathag safe for us ok."

Erin looked at her till Sho-Sho insisted. "Alright Mary-um I will take good care of Agathag I promise."

In the other room Andreios placed Agathag in a special basinet and placed her, in the hide. Erin pulled her deeper in as she had been taught.

Andreios opened the door, "I am going out into the hall. Mother is with Lady Pompey in the intelligence section. Lady Jessica and Alexis are not back yet with Nikolaos. Ice Song will guard this room."

Maryam nodded, "Sho-Sho and I can help cover it."

Gracchus watched as the unidentified ship got closer. "Sable Dragon, authenticate TTW."

Then a message came through, "Red Talon, Red Talon this is Sable Dragon we were diverted to *Candaris IIX* by red herring. We are not in your sector. Repeat not in your sector, Sable Dragon Authenticating HHU."

Gracchus watched as the other ship discarded panels designed to give it a fake appearance.

All of a sudden thirty fighters poured out of the other ship.

Artemus said "fire."

Eighty missiles from the five Daggers and thirty-six from the fighters leaped from their rails towards the enemy fighters.

The enemy fighters also launched but what they launched were not missiles but looked like insertion pods.

Beary realized immediately what they were. "Red Talon, they have launched boarding pods with transponders. Ghost out."

Soon the missiles arrived twenty of the enemy fighters died instantly along with twenty of the sixty pods they had launched. Other missiles bored into the enemy ship and exploded against its shields.

Artemus had the Purples launch again forty missiles streaked out. The other ten fighters died along with twenty more pods. The last twenty pods hit the *EAQ's* shields.

Two black clad figures materialized on the *EAQ's* bridge, and pointed their weapons at Captain Gracchus and fired. Only to have their energy bolts stopped by a force field that slowly collapsed around them. They were crushed and beamed out into space.

Jessica had sent Alexis to help protect Pompey as she ran to the living quarters.

Alexis was running down the hall when one of the black clad creatures materialized in front of her. It swung a weapon at her head. She dropped to her knees slide between its legs stabbing it in the lower abdomen as she passed through with one of her blades. Then she shot it in the back of the head as she came to a stop a few SMU behind it. The creature slumped over and died.

The Marines got into a firefight with ten of the creatures on the hanger deck. Ben grabbed one and snapped its neck as it tried to finish off one of his bears, which lay wounded on the hanger deck, shot in the back.

After five STU of fierce fighting, Ben had three Marines down and ten dead intruders on the hanger deck.

In the living quarters three materialized in Erin's and Agathag's rooms much to their horror they were facing two dragons. Ice Song and Sho-Sho engulf two in dragon's fire. The third fell to a well-placed blade thrown by Maryam. Who then walked up and shot the creature in the facemask.

Three more materialized out in the hallway. Andreios shot the first one with a wad of putty which exploded removing the side of his head. The other two fired at him. He dove to the floor.

That is when Jessica came in. She grabbed one of the creatures and shot him in the gut and then under the chin.

That is when the other one shot her in the side of the chest. He was going to finish her off. That is when Nikolaos grabbed a fallen weapon and hit the creature in the head with it, knocking it to the deck.

Nikolaos growled "You will not hurt her again!" and fired the rifle like weapon into the creature repeatedly.

Jessica weakly reached up and grabbed his arm. "That is enough Nikolaos check on Andreios."

Andreios got up a little blood on his forehead, "I hit my head when I dove for cover. I am sorry."

Nikolaos hit the com. "I have wounded in the Maxumus living quarters please send help."

Caesar looked at a medic as he worked on a wounded marine "Go!"

The creature had chased Dr. Vallen, till he had him trapped on a platform.

The Creature sneered at Dr. Vallen, "Surrender Doctor and I may let you live."

Dr. Vallen replied, "I think not. For I am not going to let you live." A force field formed around the creature and collapsed on him. Then Doctor Vallen beamed his remains out into space."

The enemy ship had damaged two of the Valkyrie fighters and one of the Purple Daggers. The fighting on the hanger bay had prevented the launch of other fighters or daggers.

Gracchus turned to Lieutenant Helios, "Enough, weapons free, tell the Air Wing to clear. Tear that ship apart."

The Fighters and Purples pealed out of the way as the *EAQ* turned broadside to the enemy ship. It started to launch more drones when over four hundred sixty missiles and fifteen rail gun shells started streaming towards it. Phasers and smaller rail guns started picking off the drones.

The strange ship didn't know how to respond its shields absorbed three hundred of the missiles and deflected ten of the large rail gun shells. Then their shields collapsed. The Captain on board the strange craft realized his ship was doomed and hit the self-destruct. The explosion damaged the electrical system on two of the fighters.

Beary had the damaged ships land first. One pilot and one WTO was injured and had to be taken to medical. None of the dagger crews were hurt but one of the daggers would need repairs as would the four fighters.

Ben was waiting for Beary and Artemus, "We have ten wounded besides your pilot and WTO. I have three Marines down, you have two flight line bears wounded. We also have two civilian scientists that were hurt. One of Captain Gracchus' people was also injured and two of our family. Andreios has a slight concussion, and Jessica."

Beary looked at him, "What happened?"

Ben shook his head, "I don't know. You'll have to ask Nikolaos. He probably saved her life, maybe Andreios also."

Caesar looked down at Jessica. Doctor Greenscales had strengthened her along with the other injured crew members. Still thank the Creator she had been wearing her vest. It had saved her life. Still the wound was severe. He finished cleaning away the shattered bone and closed up the wound. His fingers traced other scares long since healed.

Doctor Greenscales looked at Caesar, "She is a warrior. She will heal fine."

Caesar nodded, "How are the rest of the wounded?"

Greenscales shrugged, "Alive, a private Hopper was hurt bad. As you know but he will recover. It took more than the usual dragon medical practice. We had to give him a blessing. It has had minor side effects."

Caesar smiled, "He is alive and not crippled. I think he can live with the side effects."

Ben joined Beary and Artemus as they walked into the medical section. Pompey and Snow Flower were setting with Nikolaos.

Alexis walked over. "Andreios is fine a minor concussion. He dove under some protection, and hit his head. Jessica is still in surgery. Nikolaos saved her life. Beary, you need to talk to him."

Beary walked over and sat next to Nikolaos. "Are you alright?"

Nikolaos looked straight ahead, "Andreios is well. He will be able to return to his duties in a few days . . ."

"Squire Nikolaos that is not what I asked." Beary said gently.

Nikolaos started crying. "I failed her! I should have kept her from getting hurt."

Beary put his arms around him and waited. Then spoke, "Then it was my fault not yours Nikolaos. I failed to stop the drones before they reached the *EAQ*. We destroyed forty of them, but twenty got through. Tell me what happened."

Nikolaos looked at him trying to wipe away the tears, "Lady Jessica sent Alexis to be with Lady Pompey and took off on a dead run. I hesitated . . . I didn't know who to follow. Then I decided I should follow Lady Jessica. She had said earlier in the day you are with me. So I took off after her. But I couldn't catch her. I was twenty sub time units behind and could not close the gap. When I got there two creatures were down. Lady Jessica was down. One was standing over her. I don't know what happened after that till Andreios appeared. His head was bleeding so was Lady Jessica. I called for a Medic and tried to bandage Lady Jessica."

Beary nodded, "You saved Lady Jessica's life Nikolaos, and you killed the creature that attacked her."

One of the nurses came out, "Captain Maritinus, Lieutenants Maxumus, and Artemus your bears are in recovery and are doing fine. Could you let Commander Gracchus know that Ensign Domingo is also alright and out of danger? So is Dr. Francis. Dr. Hopkins is in serious but stable condition."

Ben gallantly walked up and kissed her paw, "Thank you Nurse?"

Nurse Aurora Blaze smiled, "My name is Aurora Blaze of the Red Star Clan, Ben Maritinus the Slayer of The Red Paw Clan. I know you are a great warrior Sire and the son of a Chief. I also know you are a charlatan when it comes to the ladies Sire." With that she walked off with just a slight swish of her hips.

Ben stood there with his mouth open. Pompey and Snow Flower wanted to laugh but somehow this seamed an inappropriate place to do it.

Alexis walked over, "It's alright Ben everybody gets shot down once in a while."

Next Caesar came out and knelt next to Nikolaos, "Thank you Nikolaos you bought her just enough time. We were able to save her. She is going to be alright in a week or two. In a month she will be able to return to full duty."

Caesar turned to Artemus and Snow Flower, "I want to keep Andreios overnight. It is just a very mild concussion but I want to play it safe."

Commander Gracchus came in, "Doctor how are the wounded?"

Caesar smiled a tired smile, "Most will recover in a few days. Lady Jessica and Doctor Hopkins will take longer. The dragon doctors made the difference. We may have lost a few if they hadn't been along."

"Why did they attack? What were they after?" Jeanne asked.

Beary looked at her. "They could have been after my family." Beary said.

Ben shook his head, "They might have been after something else, let's not jump to conclusions just yet. Paladin is already looking into it. We should have some answers soon. We do know they weren't Shape Shifters. We just don't know who they were."

Jeanne nodded. "Alright get things under control staff meeting in six cycles. We need to fix the hole in our defense they found. By the way Ben you had pointed it out as a possibility. But Fleet said no one used those old boarding drones anymore. That's why we didn't have the shielding you asked for. Once we get to Candaris XII that will be one of the first problems that gets fixed."

Beary looked at her, "I could give us some coverage now Commander."

"Alright Beary, but take care of your families first." Jeanne said.

Nikolaos stood up. "Commander Gracchus, it is our job. We will not fail Sire Maxumus. Father and he can return to duty. Lady Alexis is in temporary command. However, I give you my word Lady Pompey and Erin will be safe."

Beary looked at Nikolaos, he saw a look in his eyes that he had seen before. "Alright Nikolaos with Alexis' permission you are with Night song and Night Wind.

Alexis I want you in the family quarters." Beary said.

Alexis nodded, "Alright Beary."

Beary stopped and kissed her, "Tell Maryam, Ice Song, and Sho-Sho they did a good job."

Pompey grabbed his paw and walked him into the hall, "Are you alright?"

Beary looked at her, "No, I messed up. I knew their fighters were obsolete and couldn't really hurt ours. Even the Fighters that were damaged were damaged by fire from the *EAQ* except the two that had shock damage from when the other ship exploded. Mac was fit to be tied when he found that the shells that damaged the two fighters and wounded the pilot of 6 and the WTO of 18 were from the EAQ. I told him we would tell Captain Gracchus about it and let him handle it."

Pompey shook her head, "It happens, Beary. It might have even been your pilots fault you know that."

"That is why sensor logs are being studied. In any case it is my responsibility. This whole mess is probable my fault." Beary said.

Pompey kissed him then slapped him. "The kiss is because I love you. The slap is to wake you up Lieutenant Maxumus. Despite what some of the scientist might think this is a fleet ship. That makes it a warship and a target. So wake up and do your job and make it harder for someone to pull the stunt they pulled and stop feeling sorry for yourself."

Beary raised an eye brow, "Pompey?"

"I don't want to talk about it." Pompey turned and walked off.

Night Song smiled as she walked by.

Night Wind stopped, "At least yours doesn't bite."

Beary looked at him, "You want to bet?"

Night Wind laughed as he bound down the hall.

Beary looked at Snow Flower. "Is there something I should know?"

Snow Flower smiled, "Probably many things Beary." She said and walked right on by holding Nikolaos' paw.

Artemus looked at Beary. "Did I miss something?"

Beary shrugged, "You know our Pilot and WTO were hit by friendly fire."

Artemus tilted his head, "I was afraid of that. We need a dedicated crew aboard the Green. The scratch crew did alright. But Beary we made mistakes out there we shouldn't have made."

Paladin called Ben and told him what he had found.

Ben listened, "You are positive about this? Alright brief the Captain, John. No I don't need to be there. I want to check out a few things."

Ben saw two of his marines and signaled them, "You're with me."

They grabbed their gear and followed.

Paladin briefed Captain Gracchus and Commander Gracchus.

"Lieutenant Paladin you are sure about this?" Gracchus asked.

"Yes Sir. One was apparently an officer. He had a list of all the equipment and personnel they were after. You were to be assassinated. Doctor Vallen kidnaped. They planned to steal a dagger and if possible a fighter. They were also after this group of scientists. What I find interesting is Lieutenant Maxumus and his family is not on the list. Neither was Dr. Hopkins."

Jeanne looked at him, "Why then was he shot?"

Paladin shook his head "Until he wakes up, I might not be able to find out. One thing is clear this attack was directed at our mission. The *EAQ* was the target. The people on this list were considered important. But the map they used wasn't for the *EAQ* it was a concept map for the 14. The six that beamed into the Maxumus living quarters believed they were beaming into a weapons storage locker."

Gracchus shook his head, "Thanks Paladin, you better get back to your investigation."

"Yes Sir. The Captain won't be satisfied yet." Paladin said.

Doctor Greenscales came over to Caesar. "Shouldn't you get some sleep?"

Caesar smiled, "I just want to check on Doctor Hopkins. He was hurt bad."

"Yes, but I will set up with him. He is stable and healing. The antibiotics are helping prevent infection. I will wake you if need be." Greenscales said. "Besides, there are plenty of other Doctors, Caesar you are Chief Medical Officer not the only one."

Caesar nodded, "Yes, I know, herself has given that lecture often enough. Trust your team let them do their job."

Greenscales laughed, "True but if half the stories I have heard . . ."

Caesar shook his head. "No one knows, but I know some are. Especially the one concerning Mr. Maro. He told me that one himself.

I'll be in with Jessica on the chair."

Caesar walked in checked her vitals. He knelt down said a prayer to the Creator of the Universe. When he was done he pulled the chair closer kissed her and took her paw.

Ben found her hiding in a storage unit. She was crying. "Doctor Orthandro, it is Captain Maritinus. The fighting is over. The threat has been eliminated. You may come out now. I have two marines with me, they will protect you."

She saw his paw held out to her. She slowly took it. "They killed Robert he was trying to, to protect me." She said as she sobbed.

Ben replied in a gentle voice. "No Doctor Orthandro the good Doctor Hopkins is still alive. His is badly hurt but Doctor Greenscales and Doctor Vantanus was able to save his life."

"Robert is alive! You wouldn't lie to me would you?" She asked searching his face.

"No my Lady, we will take you to him. He is sedated and is still critical but he should live." Ben reassured her.

Ben brought her into sick bay. She saw the wounded marines and then saw Doctor Hopkins she broke down and started crying again.

Nurse Blaze looked at Ben and frowned.

Ben signaled her over, "Nurse Blaze this is Doctor Orthandro she was with Doctor Hopkins when he was shot. She was the one they were after. Please see to her and have one of the doctors examine her."

"Yes Captain immediately. Please Doctor, come with me." Nurse Blaze said.

In auxiliary control Beary started working on the shield emitter matrix. He studied the sensor log records of the attack. He saw how they used a pinpoint transport beam to transport the creatures in the drones into the ship. Each drone carried one passenger. As the drone was absorbed by the shield the drone opened a small divot in the shield that allowed a beam to enter. A blast would have been diverted by the shield but the beam was set at the same modulation as the shield. Why not, missiles with shield emitters did the same thing. Of course you could defeat missiles with shield emitters by having more than one level of shielding at two different modulations. But that extra layer of shielding required a lot of extra power most ships did not have.

Beary did some calculations, it would require three more APU's to be brought on line in engineering. These could be borrowed from the modules and replaced on Candaris XII even if he had to buy them off base. He wrote up his proposal and headed for the meeting.

Artemus looked at Captain Gracchus and the others in the room.

"The ship that attacked us was at best a sacrificial lamb. Its fighters were obsolete as was their ship. Their plan was to catch us napping. Kill the good Captain. Destroy the hanger bays. Steal a couple of daggers and if possible a fighter or two. Kidnap Doctor Vallen and other key scientist including Dr. Orthandro. Doctor Hopkins tried to rescue her when one of the creatures grabbed her. His, actions allowed her to escape and he was shot for his trouble."

Ben has more details but he is still searching the ship to insure we didn't miss anything. At this time all personnel are accounted for the last two scientists were found hiding in a white dagger module.

Two of our casualties were caused by friendly fire. One was caused by pilot error. The other was caused by a gunner, on the *EAQ*, over shooting his target and hitting a fighter. These are the type of losses we can never accept.

Having said that Lieutenant Maxumus and I take full responsibility for the incident, we should have requested joint training exercises and simulations. We just never expected this scenario. We underestimated an enemy that we took for being virtually harmless.

While we easily defeated them in space, they boarded our ship and injured bears we were sworn to protect. For us that is inexcusable. If you will permit us Captain Gracchus it won't happen again." Artemus concluded.

"Lieutenant Artemus and Maxumus, while I appreciate your willingness to take the blame for this one, the truth is you were not the only ones played. I was also. I looked at their ship and knew it couldn't pose a real threat. So I am as guilty as you two are." Gracchus said

Beary dropped his head, "Sir I can prevent a similar attack or at least limit its effectiveness. It would require stripping three APU's from spare modules and installing them in engineering. Using them would give us enough power to put up a second tighter force shield around the *EAQ*, giving her a layered defense. We would also need to use some spare emitters. These we would set on a slightly different modulation."

Gracchus nodded. "Alright bears we messed up and others got hurt. Let's learn from it and move on. Just remember it could have been much worse.

Beary do whatever you have to do. Get me that extra layer of shields."

Four cycles later the real Foil Claw delivered the fighters and daggers. The Captain of the Foil Claw offered to evacuate the wounded back to Andreas Prime. Caesar replied that they were probably better off in his sick bay since it was designed to operate as a hospital. Captain Gracchus concurred with his decision.

Ben sat down with Paladin. "I found thirty-six of these in supply crates throughout the ship. This one was in one of Doctor Orthandro's personal bags. I bet there is one in something that belongs to the Captain. Something he uses near the bridge. Something he would have had shipped to him."

Paladin scanned it. "They are all low level transponders."

Ben nodded, "Dial in your target and if it is attached to a personal item there is a good chance you will get in close.

Everything that these were attached to came through Darius V supply depot two weeks before we left and was delivered directly to the ship. It was all scanned but we were looking for Shape Shifters not electronic tags."

Paladin nodded, "That's why they didn't purposely go after Six's family. None of their stuff was shipped through Darius V."

Ben nodded, "Correct and the concept map did pass through there on its way to Captain Dumont the 14's Captain select."

After further investigation twenty-four more tags were found one was attached to the bottom of the coffee mug that had been sent to Captain Gracchus by his mother to commemorate his new command. The good Captain was not amused.

He sent a stern message to fleet security asking them to look into the situation.

He also read Doctor Franklin's autopsy reports on the creatures they had killed on the ship. They seemed to be feline in origin. But these were in particularly bad shape, half-starved at best. They also showed signs of self-mutilation. The Doctor said the last part was just a guess and what he took for self-inflicted wounds could be the result of severe physical labor also.

Gracchus passed this information on up to fleet also.

Jeanne looked at him, "Not much to go on is it."

"No and we haven't even left friendly space. What is really sad is we fought a space battle and used our main weapons. Most the civilians were so scared that we were boarded they didn't even notice. Did you read Ben's final report?" Gracchus asked.

"Yes, whoever is after this ship, wants its secrets. They also want you dead. I have buried one husband. Don't make me bury another one." Jeanne said.

Gracchus pulled her over and kissed her, as a young Ensign walked in. "Excuses me Captain and Commander, I thought this might be important."

Commander Gracchus got up off the Captain's lap. "It's alright Ensign Fa Lin. What do you have?"

"It is something strange . . . a series of numbers the other ship transmitted before it self-destructed. We almost missed it but Lieutenant Artemus had us combing through all the recordings. It doesn't make any sense." Ensign Fa Lin said.

"What is the series?" Captain Gracchus asked.

"That's just it sir it is just 3.141592654 it is the Numeric number for the mathematical symbol for π. That just doesn't make since. Why would they send that?" Fa Lin asked.

Gracchus looked at Jeanne, "Ask Beary to double the CAP. Tell sensors I want long range scan to double the range we are scanning around the ship."

Jeanne walked over to the Com unit "Lieutenant Maxumus the enemy sent π before it self-destructed, or at least the numeric equivalence. The Captain would like you to double the CAP."

Beary thought the circumference of a circle, πd, Area πr^2 so what were they trying to tell their friends? "Alright Commander but I think I am going to send out a flight of Daggers and two fights of Fighters plus two scouts."

"Alright, Beary it is your call." Jeanne said.

Beary called Barbarossa and Pathfinder, It was decided that one purple and one fighter would go out as scouts. Valkyrie 7 and the Amethyst were selected to act as scouts Golf and Hotel Flights launched as CAP along with Gem flight 2.

Gracchus looked at his watch. Fourteen cycles to go and they would reach Candaris XII.

In sick bay Jessica was waking up. She felt something in her paw. She tried to turn her head but something was preventing her from moving. She tried to talk but something was in her throat. She started to try and pull it out when a paw stopped her.

"Touch that and I will spank your tail." Caesar bent over and kissed her cheek, "I'll take it out in a few cycles. Once I am satisfied you are breathing well enough on your own. I need to wean you off the machine. Jess you were hit bad. Your vest only stopped 50% of the blast. You're going to make it and heal just fine, but you are going to have to let me do my job. Do you understand?"

Jessica looked up into his eyes and nodded.

"Nikolaos and Andreios are fine. So is the rest of the family. You scared us." Caesar added.

Tears started to form in Jessica's eyes.

Caesar kissed her, "Now none of that Jess no crying. You are alive the enemy is dead. Also for once, I can tell you something and you can't talk back. Jessica Jorgenson you are an impossible and infuriating female that is nothing but a paw full of trouble. You know what you want but every time you get close to having it you run away. Well you almost died this time. I am tired of you running away. So I am confining you to sick bay till you agree to marry me. Even, if I have to keep you in here for the entire cruise. You don't have to answer me now. I don't want you to. But in three cycles I am going to remove that tube. I will have your answer then. I have other patents to check on." Caesar walked out.

Jessica laid there. She didn't know what to do. She couldn't move. She couldn't talk and he had tied her paws down so she couldn't remove the hose in her throat so she could scream. Tears streamed down her face. He had asked her to marry him!

Nikolaos came to see Jessica. Nurse Blaze showed him in but only after Caesar explained that Squire Nikolaos had full access and was not to be questioned.

"Lady Jessica you have a visitor. I have told him you cannot talk yet due to the tube." Nurse Blaze said.

Nikolaos came over and kissed her paw. "I am sorry my Lady, it is my fault you were hurt."

Jessica shook her head no.

"I will never fail you again I promise. I love you Lady Jessica. You and Alexis are special to Andreios, Maryam and I. We made this necklace for you. You must get well so you can wear it." Nikolaos said.

Caesar smiled, "Do I have a challenger for her paw Squire Nikolaos."

Nikolaos turned and smiled, "Cousin Caesar if I was older or she was my age then yes, I would challenge you. But since she really only loves you and I am but a cub I cannot." Then he smiled "But if I did I do not think I would lose, but it might be close."

Caesar looked into those eyes. He had seen them before those hunter's eyes. "I was told that once before. We both wear a scar ever so slight from that encounter. It ended in a draw. You remind me of him."

Nikolaos asked, "Who, Sire Caesar?"

Caesar grinned, "Tiberius we were about your age. It was a good duel. Squire Nikolaos would you be my best bear, if Lady Jessica agrees to marry me?"

Jessica wanted to say something. She wanted to scream, yell, and hug both of them. She also wanted to bawl, but for some reason the tears wouldn't come.

Nikolaos bowed, "It will be my great honor Sire Vantanus to stand by your side. Also you should know despite the protest she is sure to make and the appeals to reason she will try to use. Her true heart's desire is to be your wife and lover."

Jessica almost gaged when she heard him say that. Even if it was true, he was too young to understand. She made some almost growling sounds in her throat.

Caesar scolded, "Enough of that young lady or I won't be able to remove it in forty-five STUs."

Nikolaos walked over, kissed her check, and walked out.

Nurse Blaze came in. "Doctor I need to change her bandages and bath her."

Caesar nodded, "Just let me, take a look at the incision, and then you can take over."

Jessica felt embarrassed as Caesar lifted the sheet. She realized for the first time, it was all that was on her. He cut away the bandage and checked the incision on the right side of her chest.

"Good it is healing very nicely. Use some wound soap on it." Caesar ordered as he replaced the sheet, and kissed Jessica's forehead.

Nurse Blaze came over and filed a basin with warm water. "Don't worry no one will walk in. I am going to bath you, change your sheets, and bandage your wound. The Doctor also said we can remove the catheter today.

It must be nice to have someone like him in love with you. Did you know he wouldn't leave your side except to treat the other wounded? Why he has slept in that chair for two nights.

That young cub was so gallant also. I bet he will break hearts all over the galaxy."

Jessica looked at Nurse Blaze and thought *if I had enough strength I would squeeze the air out of your throat. You know nothing about either one of them. But you are right I am lucky they love me.*

During the bath Nurse Blaze removed the catheter and brought in a night gown. "There that has to feel better. Once we get that tube out we will try and get you walking."

Caesar came in. "Alright let's get this done." He sprayed her throat with a numbing solution then slowly pulled out the tube. He checked her respiration and listened to her lungs. "Good everything sounds clear. Oxygen level is holding steady at 97% in your blood. We will keep monitoring it.

How do you feel Jessica?"

Jessica looked at him, "My throat is sore and I am hungry." she said in a hoarse voice. "Where is my necklace?"

Caesar placed it around her neck. "That is very pretty. I have ordered you some broth and tea to start with. I know it isn't what you want. But let's take it easy and see how your stomach does."

Jessica nodded, "Caesar you were just teasing . . ."

"No, Jess I wasn't and you can try and rationalize all you want. The reasons why you believe it would never work. But tell me this was Nikolaos right do you love me? Do you desire me?" Caesar asked.

Tears started falling from Jessica's eyes.

"If it hadn't been for Doctor Greenscales I would have lost you Jess. He strengthened you, which is why I was able to fix you up. It is also why in a couple of months your bone layer will be regrown. There I go being the doctor again." Caesar paused and looked at Jessica.

Jessica was biting her lower lip a habit she had, had since she was a cub.

"You are so beautiful, so irritating, so wonderful, and I can't live without you Jessica Jorgenson. So decide are you going to marry me or not." Caesar asked.

"You know that I love you but I . . ." Jessica started to say.

"Fine I will have you medevac off at Candaris XII and returned to Andreas Prime." Caesar said and got up to leave.

"You can't do that!" She cried hoarsely

"Yes Jessica I can. Nikolaos knows you're, lying to yourself and so do I. If you can't be honest about how you feel then you aren't fit for duty." Caesar said.

"This is blackmail!" Jessica screamed.

"Call it what you like. You walked away from me once. This time it is my turn and I will send you away." Caesar said.

"Why! You say you love me! Why are you doing this?" Jessica pleaded.

"Because I love you and it is time for you to start living, if not with me then with someone else." Caesar said.

"But I don't want anyone else; I have never wanted anyone else!" Jessica begged.

"Then marry me." Caesar said.

Jessica sat up tried to reach for him and almost fell but he caught her, "Don't leave me. Don't send me away Caesar please."

"Marry me." He said softly.

"Alright if you are sure you want me?" She whispered crying.

About that time Rubin Jorgenson walked in. "I have heard of a doctor having different types of bedside manners but groping my sister?"

Jessica turned bright red, "He asked me to marry him. I said yes."

Rubin laughed. "Then by all means Doctor grope away."

Caesar shook his head, "She fell trying to take a step and I caught her. It is not like that Rubin."

"Too bad," Rubin said, "it would have made a better story. Still could for that matter."

Caesar smiled, "Well I have other patients to look in on."

Rubin stopped him on his way out, "Thank you Caesar for loving her."

Caesar smiled and nodded then continued out.

"Well Sissy, you're going to final make an honest Boar out of him." Rubin said. "It wasn't right you running out on him the last time. We all understood why you did it. But you settled that score. He waited for you Jessica. Don't run again or I'll come after you myself."

Jessica sighed, "Alright Rubin, I understand. Can you do what I asked you to do before we left?"

"Partially, we get into Candaris XII in a few cycles. I can get what I need there to do the job properly. Give me four days and no one will be able to beam into our family section or the intelligence section without a family code. I'll make sure there are failsafe's but what happened the other day will not happen again. If I can get enough parts, I'll protect all the families, military living quarters, and critical areas with internal shielding." Rubin said.

Jessica sighed, "Tell Beary about our plans. Rubin call dad, tell him I am marrying Caesar."

"No problem Jessica. I'll tell him you'll call when you are feeling better." Rubin laughed, "I might tell him about the exam I witnessed also."

Jessica smiled "If you do tell him I placed Caesars paws there to show him where I still hurt. It will make a better story and Angelina will tell him it only made since. That will drive him nuts."

Rubin smiled, "Yeah it would at that."

CHAPTER 2

Candaris XII Shanghai

(Or do you want an Ensign with that Order)

"RED TALON, THIS Candaris XII Control welcome to MAB/ NAS Refuge. How may we be of assistance?"

"Candaris XII Control, we will be picking up supplies and additional crew members. Red Talon is taking up stationary orbit."

Colonel Fairbanks looked up at the message his communications officer handed him. "What do they mean by additional crew members?"

"I don't know sir." the young 2nd Lieutenant replied.

Colonel Fairbanks picked up his direct line to the fighter wings commander, Captain Jaspers. "Bill, Hank you know anything about the EAQ picking up crew members?"

Captain Jaspers was looking at a message from Admiral Starpaw. "They are headhunting Hank, and it has the blessing of both the Chief of Fleet Operations and the Commandant."

"Great and we are to let them have their pick of our people?" Colonel Fairbanks asked.

Captain Jaspers thought. "Well, there is giving them the pick, and then, there is giving them the pick, if you get my meaning."

"Yeah I do. Alright thanks." Fairbanks hung up.

Jeanne looked at Argus, "I told our three fine officers to show up in their Class A's fully decked out. I am having Pathfinder and Barbarossa, also go along. I would also like to suggest you take Lady Maxumus with you. Night Song, Alexis, and Nikolaos could accompany her."

Argus looked at her "Do you think that is wise?"

Jeanne nodded, "She should have some input on the Green's crew selection after all her section will be working with them. Also Macintosh and Flanagan should go."

"Alright tell them Class A's also. They might as well show up with two Bearilian Stars." Argus replied. "Mac can fly the Green Hills I don't want to take a dagger down."

Jeanne smoothed out his uniform and kissed him. "Alright my Captain, go get them."

"Get, some rest Commander you still have six cycles of rest coming before you go on duty." Captain Gracchus said as he smiled at his wife/first officer.

Beary looked at Pompey, "You sure about this?"

"Yes Beary. The Commander said I was to help you pick the crew for the Green Dagger. Alexis, Nikolaos, and Night Song are going with me." Pompey said.

Night Wind came over. "My Lady I will accompany you if you do not mind."

"No that will be alright." Pompey said.

Beary looked at him, "Marine vest and armor."

Night Wind nodded, "Yes Sire."

MacIntosh and Flanagan prepped the Green Hills for launch.

"Well cousin this should be fun." Flanagan said.

"No drinking Michael I warn you." Mac said.

"That's not a problem cousin. Not even if I wanted to I couldn't. That Big Lizard made it so I can't no more." Flanagan said. "I am permanently on the wagon. Besides I gave my word to Lady Morrow."

"Good enough Michael." Mac said.

Soon Artemus, Beary, Ben, and Pompey along with her escorts arrived and took their seats.

"Lieutenants, do you want to pilot the Green Hills?" Mac asked.

"No Mac you can handle her." Artemus said.

Captain Gracchus smiled as he and Pathfinder and Barbarossa came on board. "Alright let's go and see what we can dig up."

Mac lifted off, left the shuttle bay, and headed for MAS/NAS Refuge. He got landing instructions and put down on a landing pad not too far from the entry control point.

Captain Gracchus turned to Flanagan, "Get the shuttle secured then join us. We'll wait for you inside."

"Yes Captain." Flanagan said.

As they started going through the control point a Marine 2ⁿᵈ Lieutenant tried to prevent Night Wind from entering the base. Captain Gracchus started to say something but Ben was already talking.

"2ⁿᵈ Lieutenant Halverson is it? Well I am Captain Ben Maritinus. Why don't you call your boss and I'll call mine? Then yours can explain to General Zantoran why a Marine Working Canus assigned to my unit is being kept off a Marine base." Ben pointed out.

The 2ⁿᵈ Lieutenant started to wither.

Ben turned to Night Wind, "Sgt. Night Wind escort Lady Maxumus, and her personal protection detail through."

Night Wind saluted with his front paw. "It will be as you command, Captain."

The 2ⁿᵈ Lieutenant stared, "It can talk?"

Ben got right into the 2ⁿᵈ Lieutenants face and grinned an evil grin, "Yes and the fact that he has that ability is classified top secret, and if you reveal it to anyone you will be court marshaled. Do you understand?"

All the 2ⁿᵈ Lieutenant could do was nod as they walked by on to the base. The two Sergeants with him stared at one another. Things were not going well at all.

MacIntosh and Flanagan came in next. One of the MPs saw Flanagan. "What is a traitor doing walking around free?"

Mac looked at the Gunny Sergeant. "That is Chief Master Gunnery Sergeant to you."

Flanagan held up his paw, "Now Mac it is no big deal. I remember the Gunny and I can understand his animosity. I put him in the hospital after all."

The Gunny turned red, "You I should put you down right here and now!"

Flanagan shook his head, "Now there is no need for that. It just would cause problems for everyone."

The Gunny was getting even madder. He pulled his night stick and swung it at Flanagan. Beary had just came back out. Mac was moving as two more MPs started in.

Flanagan caught the MP's arm as Beary yell "Attention! What by the Moons of Bantine is going on here 2ⁿᵈ Lieutenant Halverson get control of your bears or I will."

The Gunny looked at Beary "Lieutenant, Do you know . . ."

"Yes Sergeant he is a recipient of the Bearilian Star for gallantry in the face of the Enemy. Have you ever even been in combat Gunnery Sergeant?" Beary asked.

"No Sir, have . . ." that's when he saw it the ribbon for the Bearilian Star, the Marine Infantry Badge, the Dagger Wings, the Jump Wings, the Naval Aviators Wings and all the other medals. "I guess you have Sir." the Gunny said.

"Gunny, tell your bears to back off and I'll tell you a little secret. There is only one bear in fleet history that has ever taken Flanagan in a fair fight. He is twice as mean as he is and that is Flight Chief Master Sergeant MacIntosh. If you and your friends really want to continue this, I'll give them permission to defend themselves. I am sure Admiral Starpaw and General Zantoran will be more than happy to ask why you were put up to this farce, when you get out of the hospital." Beary said

The Gunny just melted. "I apologize, Sir."

Beary nodded, "Flanagan, Mac let's go."

They followed Beary out, and joined the others.

MacIntosh said, "Thank you, boss."

Beary nodded, "It was just as you expected Captain Gracchus. They are trying to sand bag us."

Gracchus nodded, "I can't blame them, but I don't like their tactics."

"Colonel Fairbanks, this is 2nd Lieutenant Halverson sir. Your plan to intimidate the bears from the *EAQ* didn't work Sir. I am afraid they know what we were up to. They threatened to turn it over to General Zantoran. You didn't tell me the Captain was in charge of a MSD unit Sir. You know they report directly to the Commandant." Halverson reported.

"Alright Lieutenant, it was just a little joke that went bad. Don't worry they will use it as leverage against me, that's all. Just as I would have used it against them, if it would have worked." Colonel Fairbanks said.

Artemus looked at Captain Gracchus. "Sir Colonel Fairbanks is expecting us to see him first. Why don't we go and visit Captain Jaspers first. He will not be expecting us."

"Good idea, let's grab a transport." Gracchus flagged down a transport and commandeered it. He had the driver drive them over to Captain Jaspers' office.

Captain Gracchus walked in to the Headquarters building and into Captain Jaspers' office, "Sergeant, please inform Captain Jaspers that we are here."

"Sir, the Captain is not expecting you at this time." The Sergeant said.

"Sergeant, tell him I am here or I will tell him myself. I do not have time to be jerked around." Gracchus insisted.

The Sergeant relayed the message. Captain Jaspers was angry things were not going as planed and now he was going to have to deal with Gracchus from a position of weakness.

Jaspers walked out, "Captain Gracchus you have come at a very inopportune time. I must strongly protest . . ."

Captain Gracchus cut him off, "Captain Jaspers let's cut to the chase shall we. I have orders here that allow me to take anyone I want. However my CAG and ACAG are sympathetic to you. They understand that unit cohesiveness is important. However they have needs, they need a green dagger crew, an executive officer, and a WTO for the exec, for the fighter squadrons."

Beary added. "I would like to pick up an extra flight crew also."

MacIntosh, nodded, "I have a need for some extra maintenance bears also."

Captain Jaspers walked over to a chart, "Do you see my organization chart. Most of these pilots are green the few that would qualify for the job are my only combat veterans. I can't afford to lose them.

Look Maxumus you know how important it is to have good coordination in combat. Well my green daggers and my fighters are just starting to get dialed in. You have been in combat you know how important that can be." Jaspers pleaded.

Artemus looked at another board, "What about these pilots and this green dagger crew."

Jasper shook his head, "Transients waiting transport to the rear. The dagger crew is especially troublesome. It is an all-female crew. They attacked a pirate scout ship while bringing me my new green dagger. The two fighter crews are survivors from the BAF Fighter Frigate *Fast Paw* it was lost about three weeks ago, near the edge of the Pratis System. Only a third of the crew escaped."

Gracchus looked at him "Send all the information you have on their loss to the EAQ."

Jaspers looked at him, "Why?"

Pompey explained. "Because my dear Captain my intelligence section might find the information important since we are heading there."

The Captain looked at her, "Just who do you work for Lady Maxumus."

Pompey smiled, and opened her badge, "I work for both fleet Intelligence and Bearilian Secret Service Captain. I am a Zeno linguistics specialist and in charge of the Intelligence section on the *EAQ*."

That is when the Captain noticed Nikolaos, "Why is this Cub in here? We are discussing classified information."

Nikolaos introduced himself, "Sire I am Nikolaos Artemus. I am Lady Maxumus body guard. I have Top Secret ESI clearance and am also a member of the Bearilian Secret Service Protection Division." He then produced his badge.

Captain Jaspers shook his head. "But he is so young."

Alexis replied, "Which makes him effective at his duties others over looked him."

"Captain set up a room for us and we will interview the dagger crew first. Then the two pilot crews." Beary said.

Jaspers shook his head. "I'll bring you there personnel files."

Beary laid out the files, Captain Gracchus looked at him. "You don't need us. I'll take MacIntosh and Flanagan with me and we will find his maintenance Bears."

Beary nodded as they left.

Artemus sighed, "It is quite a group. The pilot is Lt. Jg. Gloria Romanov. Her file says she is an above average pilot. She is also a hot head. No one wants her or her crew because they are all to ruff for their Co.'s.

This is interesting the Technical Weapons Coordinator is a Maxmimus. Her name is Ensign Hannah Reuben"

Pompey looked up, "Did you say Rueben?"

Artemus nodded, "Yes why?"

"Her tribe comes from the deep desert of the Southern Continent. They are very proud bears." Pompey said.

Artemus continued, "Two are Red Pandarians a Rose King she is the Com Tactical Coordinator. Also a Debra Ni she is Tactical Plotting Officer.

The last three are Ensigns Fa Lo, Defensive Communications Coordinator, Jena Re, Long Range Scan Interpretation, and Sophia Kay Short Range Scan Interpretation."

Beary shook his head, "A lot of fancy titles."

"No," Pompey said, "highly trained specialist. Each one has gone beyond the normal Certification. It doesn't make since that they are a ferry crew."

Pathfinder dropped her head, "You know what the real problem is Beary, don't you?"

Beary nodded, "It is an all-female crew most Commanders don't want them."

"Precisely, Boss." Pathfinder said.

"Artemus you got a problem with it?" Beary asked.

"No." Artemus said.

"Does anyone?" Beary asked.

Everyone said "no."

"Alright call them in." Beary said.

Lieutenant JG Gloria Romanov led her crew in. She looked at the two naval Lieutenants and the Marine Captain and two civilians and Cub and what appeared to be a military working Canus. "Lieutenant, may I ask why my crew was sent for?"

"Yes Lt Romanov, we want to offer your crew a job. Flying the newest and best green dagger ever built." Beary said.

Ensign Rueben looked at him, "Why would we want to work for a northern clan dog, with his pretty trophy wife."

Pompey stood up and grabbed the hilt of her dagger, "Insult my Husband's Family again Sister and I will be more than happy to settle with you by the laws of the sand and the wind."

Ensign Rueben then saw her ring and also saw the scroll work on the top of her dagger. So "The Star" was a Daughter of the Southern Continent. But her blood was already boiling she couldn't stop. "Yes I will accept your challenge concubine to a pretender."

Nikolaos stepped forward before Alexis could say anything. "No my lady, this one is but a tiny yapping Canus allow your servant to teach it some manners."

Ensign Rueben laughed. "You would challenge me Cub! I will grind you into a little ball and spank you."

Nikolaos replied coldly, "Try."

Ensign Rueben swung a massive paw at him but Nikolaos wasn't there, Beary couldn't believe his eyes, as Nikolaos hit her in six locations on her body, with the tip of one digit on each paw.

Ensign Rueben laughed. "You think those little punches could hurt me."

Beary sighed, "You better grab your friend Ensign Rueben is going to fall in 3 . . . 2 . . . 1".

All of a sudden her knees gave out from under her and she couldn't move her arms.

Beary looked at her; two of her crew mates were holding her in a setting position. "I am Beary Maxumus; Guardian of Vandar, Squire Nikolaos is one of my squires. He used an old Augustin fighting technique called Point Attack. It shuts down parts of your central nervous system. If he had wanted to he could have killed you.

Nikolaos release her."

Nikolaos walked over and hit one spot on her back. She felt all her nerves catch fire.

Night Wind grinned, "Nikolaos, I am not sure I appreciate that yapping Canus comment none of our young ever yap."

Nikolaos bowed, "Yes Sire Night Wind, but your kind are not tiny."

He then turned to Ensign Rueben, "According to the laws of your own kind, I may demand tribute from you Lady Rueben."

Her eyes got big "You cannot mean?"

"No my Lady for I am but a Cub, but I do demand two things from you, first a kiss to satisfy the law and second that you show my Lady the respect she deserves." Nikolaos said.

Ensign Hannah Rueben smiled and kissed his cheek, "If you, were older it may have been worth giving you tribute, Sire Nikolaos Artemus." She then stood and bowed "Lady Maxumus and Prince Maxumus forgive me."

Pompey nodded "All is well between us sister."

Lieutenant Jg Romanov was staring at Night Wind, when he turned to her.

"Yes Mame I can talk. I am sure the good Captain will explain that my ability is classified." Night Wind explained.

Ben nodded, "He is correct."

Artemus shook his head, "Look all this has been entertaining, and my son has gotten some exercise. But we have work, to do Boss."

Beary nodded, "Well Romanov do you want the job or not?"

Romanov looked at him, "Why do you want us? No one wants us."

Beary shrugged, "Your crew is well trained, and aggressive I like that. I need a good green dagger crew to act as my mobile command post crew. I especially need a crew that can do its job whether I or Lieutenant Artemus are on board or not. A crew that can anticipate what Artemus or the Squadron Co.'s, want and get it done and keep our pilots alive. Are you that crew?"

Romanov looked at her females, "Sir we will be a royal pain in your tail. I'll be honest about that. I will expect your pilots to drill with my crew till they can do what we ask in their sleep. But if you want us to keep them alive then that is how it will need to be."

Beary nodded, "Alright Ladies, you work for me but understand this, I expect the best. Get your gear together; you will be leaving for the EAQ in six cycles. Go over to supply and pick up deep space equipment and weapon package 4 and 5 for each of you."

Ben handed them some forms, "Here are your signed orders all filled out and signed along with requisition forms. Oh here are a couple of blank ones Lieutenant if you think of any toys you, want that I forgot."

After they left the room she looked at Ensign Rueben "That wasn't real smart."

"I am sorry, but I had to know if the rumors were true. He really is the Guardian, Lieutenant. The one that destroyed the Devils Eye a lot of evil creatures are hunting for him and Our Lady, "The Star". I had to know." Rueben said.

Romanov looked at her, "What are you saying?"

Rueben explained, "We are heading into danger boss. They are going to need us."

"Great, alright ladies they say this green is better than any we have ever seen. We apparently, looking at these requisition forms, work for a bunch of pirates. So let's make good use of them. We might need Weapon package three and six also. I also want a squad weapon on board just in case we need to go planet side. We got six cycles get it done." Romanov said.

Barbarossa looked over the file of a Lieutenant Jg Patrick O' Haggerty; he had been passed over for promotion twice. But he also was the recipient of the Golden Claw with Clusters and the Golden Fang with palms along with other medals for bravery. He was an excellent pilot who couldn't keep his big mouth shut. Joe smiled well he could handle that.

Pathfinder looked over her copy of the file, "He won't want to go back out there."

"No but he will. There is nothing left for him back at Bearilia Prime. At best he is looking at a desk. With us he gets to keep flying." Barbarossa said.

"What about the three kids with him." Pathfinder asked.

"They survived combat. Their friends didn't that says something. We'll see what they say. If they don't want the job we send them home." Barbarossa said.

Pathfinder shook her head, "You know Joe we are a couple of low life's. You know that don't you?"

"Yeah Jane, I know but it goes with the job." Barbarossa said.

"You know these two are females?" Pathfinder said.

Barbarossa smiled, "You forget Jane I have flown with you. I don't care as long as they are good at what they do."

Pathfinder nodded, "Alright let's do this so I can go and get my bears."

Lieutenant Jg O' Haggerty came in. He looked at the two officers, "Just what is the meaning of all this?"

Barbarossa looked straight at him. "It is a job interview, this is Lieutenant Jg Jane Pathfinder she is the commander of the daggers on the EAQ. I am the fighter boss and I am looking for an executive officer. I also need another fighter crew."

O' Haggerty looked at him, "Are you crazy? Do you know where you are going? Do you know what these Cubs have been through?"

"Yes I do. The same thing a thousand pilots have been through. That makes them valuable to me. They survived combat. I have some green pilots that haven't seen the real thing yet." Barbarossa said.

"Why you dirty low life." O' Haggerty said.

"Good, we have that established I am a low life. I don't care. You're a loud mouth who doesn't know when to keep his big mouth shut. I don't care about that either. I just want to know if you can be a good executive officer and help me keep my pilots alive." Barbarossa said.

O' Haggerty sat down, "If I go back I am done forced out or a desk. You know that. But asking the Girls to go back . . ."

Ensign Katimai placed her paw on his shoulder, "Sir we will be happy to join your crew. I am Ensign Moon Flower Katimai my friends call me Kat. I am from the Red Circle Clan. My WTO is Ensign Paulette Mayotte."

"Sir, I am Ensign Billy Senna, I am Lieutenant Jg O'Haggerty's WTO I will go where he goes." Ensign Senna said.

"Well O' Haggerty, do you want the job?" Barbarossa said.

He looked at the three ensigns, "What will they be flying?"

Barbarossa replied, "Valkyrie III's".

O' Haggerty stood up, "Those old pieces of junk!"

"No brand new rebuilt armored warhorses that fly like nothing you have ever flown." Barbarossa said.

"Let me fly one and we will see." O' Haggerty said. "Who do we work for?"

"Lieutenants Beary Maxumus and Savato Artemus they are better known as Spirit 6 and Spirit Blade 2." Barbarossa said.

O' Haggerty looked at him, "The Ghost!"

"That's what the Arcrilians called him." Barbarossa said.

O' Haggerty looked at him, "What is your call sign?"

Barbarossa shrugged, "Harbinger 2, she is Venom 8"

O' Haggerty shook his head, "The Grim Reaper, and the Red Black Widow who are you bears?"

Pathfinder shrugged, "Just some tired old retreads thrown together by fate. Since you are so easily impressed I guess I should tell you are Marines are led By Captain Ben Maritinus the Slayer and 1st Lieutenant John Paladin Spirit 4."

"They called him the shade didn't they?" O' Haggerty asked.

"Well that is how we translated it. We don't have a word that comes any closer." Pathfinder said.

"Alright if the young ones are in so am I." O' Haggerty said.

"Get your gear we leave in five and a haft cycles. Here are requisition forms. Some are filled out some are blank get whatever you need new uniforms everything." Barbarossa said.

"Sir there are things we need we can't requisition and we have not been paid. They said our pay records would need to be . . ." Ensign Katimai tried to say.

Barbarossa pulled out his wallet, "Here Kat you three Ensigns split this and get whatever you need on Lieutenant Maxumus he will pay me back and he can afford it."

Ensign Katimai looked at the thousand credits, "But Sir this is a month's pay."

"No only a third there is three of you." Pathfinder said, "Here is another thousand credits I'll get it from Lieutenant Artemus he can afford it also. Now go time is wasting."

O' Haggerty smiled, "Thank you that is the first real kindness those three, have received since getting here."

"Do you need anything?" Barbarossa asked.

"No I was taught to always carry emergency credits in my vest and boots. I still have a healthy wad." O' Haggerty said.

Gracchus joined back up with them, "I sent The Chiefs back to the ship with the Maintenance bears. They found four that were shipping out. They jumped at the chance to join the crew of the *EAQ*."

Beary looked at him, "Which brig were they heading for?"

Gracchus laughed, "Well let's just say that they were all minor offenses and the Chiefs promised the Admiral that they would make exemplary enlisted bears of them or make them wish they had went to the brig.

The Admiral was very pleased with the change that Mac had worked in Flanagan so he said alright.

Let's catch lunch and wait for Caesar to join us." Captain Gracchus said?

As they were finishing lunch Caesar came in. He kissed Pompey and Alexis and touched Nikolaos's shoulder. "Do I have time to order something?"

Gracchus nodded "We can wait Doctor where are the Chief's".

Caesar replied. "NCO club they said they wanted to talk to some bears."

Pompey asked, "How is Jessica?"

Caesar smiled, "Good she should be able to return to her quarters in about three days."

Alexis looked at him. "Ours or yours doctor?"

Caesar almost bit through his spoon. "Well in a month or so I mean it depends on . . ."

Beary and Artemus laughed.

Captain Gracchus smiled, "At least you didn't wake up drugged in a priest's house son facing old nautical ecclesiastic laws."

Everybody laughed.

Caesar asked, "Pompey, are you done?"

Pompey nodded, "Yes Beary doesn't need me anymore."

"Could you and Alexis do some shopping for Jessica?" Caesar inquired.

Pompey smiled "I would love to."

Caesar handed her the list and saw her nails, "Pompey when you get back to the ship come and see me."

Pompey nodded, "Alright Caesar. Come on Alexa, Nikolaos, and Sgt Night Wind shopping a waits."

Beary watched as she walked away, "Caesar is she alright?"

Caesar thought, "Yeah Beary, I think she is just a little anemic. No big deal she, is do a checkup anyway."

Nikolaos looked at Pompey. "Lady Pompey Doctor Caesar knows."

"No Nikolaos he suspects. It is alright. I need to go and see him anyway." Pompey said.

Captain Gracchus smiled as he walked into Colonel Fairbanks office. "Hank that was a dirty trick you tried to pull. You're lucky my First officer wasn't with me."

Fairbanks shrugged, "Who was dumb enough to be your first, Argus?"

"Jeanne is my First." Gracchus said.

"How is that working out having your ex as your first?" Fairbanks asked

"Oh it is worse than you can imagine. She shanghaied me and made me marry her again." Gracchus smiled.

Fairbanks was shocked. "Congratulations Argus. Now why are you raiding me?"

"My dagger squadron needs an executive officer and a gunner and I want to pick up another dagger crew. I also need to pick up a pilot to fly a white dagger. If I can get them I would like to get a team of paramedic/rescue Specialists." Gracchus said.

"Who is in charge of your Air wing?" Fairbanks asked.

"Lieutenant Beary Maxumus is my CAG." Gracchus said.

"That name sounds familiar." Fairbanks said.

"He is Spirit 6 the one the Arcrilians called the Ghost. He is also the inventor of the Vallen/Maxumus warp drive system and the Maxumus APU's." Gracchus explained.

"So how old is this Lieutenant of yours?" Fairbanks asked.

"I think, he going to turned twenty-one years in a few months. Oh did I mention he is also a recipient of the Bearilian Star and the Rose medallion." Gracchus said.

"So what else is he royalty?" Fairbanks asked.

"Well our ship is named for his mother. Oh by the way his Father is Senator Octavious Maxumus." Gracchus smiled "The kid got where he is on his own merits. He never used his families influence. Although I'll admit I have.

Hank, I am heading out into danger with a bunch of pampered civilian scientist. That just learned that someone has targeted them personally. I get here and I learn a Frigate that was sent to scout our route was attacked and destroyed. On top of that my ship was boarded on the way here.

So yes Hank, I am going to take some of your bears and I want good ones."

Colonel Fairbanks nodded, "Alright Argus I have two Lieutenant that might give your people a choice. I also have two other crews that are due to rotate. They are good I have been trying to keep them. One has experience flying rescue missions. Have your bears check them out."

Gracchus nodded, "They don't work for me. They work for Admiral Starpaw directly. So do I."

"What about your, Marine Captain, who does he work for?" Fairbanks asked.

"He leads an MSD unit. You know who he works for." Gracchus answered.

"Zantoran directly I suppose." Fairbanks said.

"Yes and the General, has taken a personal interest in this one." Gracchus added.

"Alright Argus, I understand. No more games. I didn't realize you were really up against it." Fairbanks said.

Captain Gracchus gave Beary and Artemus the files. "Check these bears out. Doctor Vantanus, why don't you come with me?"

Beary handed the files to Pathfinder, "Here Jane you and Joe can handle this. I think Savato and Ben and I will go shopping."

Ben walked out into the sun shine "So where to first?"

Beary thought. "What do you need?"

"Better body armor if we can find some, we were issued mark II Armor. It is standard issue but I have wounded. Jessica was wearing mark II armor also." Ben said.

They walked over to the supply depot an old Gunnery Sergeant was setting behind a desk. He stood up and saluted "Sorry Lieutenant, you look like a snot nose Corporal I used to know."

"How are you doing Gunny Braddock? Gentlebears let me introduce Spirit 3." Beary said.

"I am good Cub . . . I am sorry Sir." Braddock said.

"It's ok Gunny there are some Bears that earned that right a long time ago. This is Lieutenant Savato Artemus my ACAG and Captain Ben Maritinus Commander of 981st MSD."

Braddock smirked, "I met another Captain Maritinus once."

"He is a Major now and my Brother." Ben said.

"If you're half the Marine, Sir he is your bears will be blessed." Braddock said.

"Thank you Gunny." Ben said.

"Alright Six what can I do for you." Braddock asked.

"On the way here we got boarded Maritinus' Marines were issued Mark II Armor it didn't stop the blast from the enemy's energy weapons." Beary said.

Braddock nodded "Mark II's are standard issue but they are not good for close combat. As a MSD Unit you should have been issued better equipment what depot did your equipment come from?"

"Darius V shipped the armor." Ben said.

"Alright Sir, I have some new armor that is unspoken for. It will equip a division. So I should be able to give you enough for your company, plus another twenty units." Braddock said.

"What is it called?" Beary asked.

"Dragon skin, it is supposed to be more flexible and stronger than the old Mark II armor." Braddock said.

Ben considered the name. "It is a good omen Dragon skin for the Red Paw Dragons."

Braddock nodded, "Why don't you look around and see what else you might need."

Gracchus walked over to the rescue squadron with Caesar "I don't know why we over looked a dedicated Paramedic rescue team."

"I was thinking about the problems I ran into on the hospital ship. It never occurred to me to look for unique problems we might face till we were attacked." Caesar explained.

"Well Doctor you were not alone in that. That is why we are trying to correct the problems now." Gracchus said.

As they walked in they heard an ensign pleading with his commanding officer. "Sir it is not fair or smart! Why break up the team just because I am being promoted. Where does it say that the team can't be led by a Lieutenant JG?"

The Commanding Officer shook his head, "You are a trained Doctor in a P.A. position. I am surprised they allowed you to get away with it this long."

"Ok Sir, but why split the team. It doesn't make since. Just give them a new ensign." The ensign pleaded.

"I tried. I don't want to lose any of you. But orders are orders." The Commander said.

"Commander Dalen I presume, I am Captain Gracchus, and this is my Chief Surgeon Dr. Caesar Vantanus. I understand you have a Paramedic Rescue team that is being reassigned and a doctor that is also being reassigned." Captain Gracchus said.

Commander Dalen blinked, "Yes this is Ensign soon to be Lieutenant JG Doctor Vern Kroller, and he is the current leader of Med Rescue Team 12."

"Well I am glad that they haven't shipped out. Doctor your orders have changed you are an emergency trauma surgeon are you not?" Gracchus asked.

"Yes Captain I am." Kroller said.

"Well you work for Dr. Vantanus also your team has been assigned to the *EAQ* starting immediately. Their new ensign is on board already. Would you collect your team and have them report to a Chief Gunnery Sergeant Flanagan. He will see to your transport to the *EAQ*.

Doctor Vantanus please make sure they have all the gear they need. Oh, don't forget to file their orders." Gracchus said.

Caesar nodded, "I'll take care of it Captain. Come on Ensign you can introduce me to your bears."

After they left the office "Lieutenant Vantanus is this legitimate?" Ensign Kroller asked.

Caesar explained, "Your orders are signed by Admiral Starpaw personally. Of course we are going to need to fill in a few minor details, like name, rank, and service number."

Kroller looked at him, "Who are you bears?"

Caesar shrugged, "A crew of a very special ship with a military and civilian crew. I need your team so I am shanghaiing you. I'll promise you two things; one your team will be kept together, two you will be in charge. But I will give you an Ensign P.A. to train. I personally believe in sending in combat trained surgeons. I have done it myself.

Oh, you will not need an insertion craft. You will be working with white daggers with dedicated rescue pods."

Kroller looked at him, "Medical Daggers I had heard rumors, but no one has seen one."

Caesar told him, "They were designed by the team that rescued the marines off of Dryden in a Red Dagger."

Kroller shook his head "I would give anything to meet them."

"Oh you will. All but one; he is still on the Saber Claw." Caesar said "Come on we have work to do."

In the meantime Pathfinder and Barbarossa were looking over the files. She looked at the first crews file they had worked with rescue teams and had, had good reviews from them.

"This crew is for Caesar. They have good flight records and have worked rescue. Fill out there orders and have them, called in." Pathfinder said.

Barbarossa handed her the other file. "These two are young and need some settling down. But they scored high on their last evaluation."

"Alright I'll take them and lay down the law." Pathfinder said. "Let's call them in."

The four Ensigns stood before them. Pathfinder looked at them "Who is Ensign Dale Black and Ensign Stan White."

The two Ensigns stepped forward, "We are Black and White they said in unison."

Pathfinder shook her head, "You two are being assigned to Dr. Vantanus as his personal pilot and defense coordinator on his White Dagger. It is a medical dagger. Dr. Vantanus will inform you of its capabilities. Here are your orders assigning you to the *EAQ*. Report to Chief Master Sergeant MacIntosh he will see you get transported to the ship. Pull all your gear and weapon packages three-six."

"Yes Lieutenant Pathfinder." They said in unison as they left.

Barbarossa looked at the other two. "Are they always like that?"

Ensign Gorky smiled, "Always but it makes them deadly. They can read each other's thoughts."

Pathfinder looked at these two. "What about you two?"

"Mame I am Mattathia Gorky and this is my gunner Eadweard O' Connor, were good in Reds as you know."

Pathfinder looked at them, "I will be the judge of that. As of right now you work for me here are your orders. Where we are going you better be as good as you think you are or you are going to end up dead. Do you understand?"

Ensign Gorky smiled, "Yes Mame, we will gather our gear grab the weapon packages and report to the Chief."

Barbarossa stopped them, "Ensign Gorky do you know a Lieutenant Jg Campbell and a Lieutenant Jg Muzorewa."

Gorky looked at him. "Yes sir why?"

Pathfinder responded, "I need a XO who would be a good pick?"

Gorky looked at his new Boss, "Permission to speak candidly Mame."

"That is the only kind I allow Gorky. If you ever hold back what you think is the truth. I will feed you out an air lock. My word is law once I give an order. Till then I want honest input." Pathfinder said.

Yeah this one could and would without blinking, "Campbell is a coward and an idiot. He will get Bears killed. Muzo is tough like you she takes no prisoners and she works till she drops. She expects excellence. She also takes care of her bears. The bears that have served under her would crawl through fire for her." Gorky said.

O'Conner just nodded.

The two ensigns left the room smiling.

Pathfinder looked at Campbell's file. "Well that answers that."

Barbarossa nodded, "Well call her in."

Lieutenant JG Sandra Muzorewa came into the room. "May I ask why I have been summoned?"

"Yes I am Jane Pathfinder the Commander of the Daggers on the EAQ this is Joe Barbarossa the Fighter Commander. We work For Lieutenants Beary Maxumus and Savato Artemus.

I am looking for a Xo for my daggers." Pathfinder said.

Muzorewa looked at them, "Why me?"

"First you are due to rotate. Second a dagger crew spoke highly of you." Pathfinder said.

Muzorewa looked at them, "I'll take the job on one condition. You take my gunner with me and keep her assigned to me."

Pathfinder looked at the file of ensign Honey Tajima. She was an average gunner. "Why?"

Muzorewa sighed, "I was a friend of her father. He was killed six years ago. She joined the fleet to carry on the tradition. Honey is an artist not . . ."

Pathfinder smiled, "Alright she can act as squadron S3 or some such job when you aren't flying."

Muzorewa held out her paw, "Everyone calls me Muzo."

Rubin Jorgenson finished his shopping including picking up replacement APU's. It was decided to purchase them from civilian venders than getting them through military channels. He docked the Green Valley and had crew members unload his ill-gotten gain.

The new Maxumus APU's were replaced in the pods that had theirs removed. He also had six more put in storage. The other equipment was taken to his laboratory in the intelligence section.

The new crew members started arriving Commander Gracchus found them empty berths. The paramedic rescue team was put in the medical section with the other medical staff.

The two new XO's and their WTO and Gunner were shown their offices. While the new pilots and crews were introduced to their Flights.

The new Purples were named, *Agate* and *Pearl*. The Pearl was to be the XO's new Dagger.

The New Medical Command post was named *Compassion's Hope*.

O' Haggerty looked at the Valkyrie III that was assigned to him it was brand new. He noticed most had nose art. "My call sign was Elf 4. I would like to paint one on the nose of my fighter"

Barbarossa nodded, "Go ahead have them put your design on the nose."

Pompey stopped by the sick bay, to bring in the packages she had picked up for Jessica. Nikolaos walked over and kissed Jessica's paw tenderly.

Jessica kissed him on the cheek, "I am fine Nikolaos, and from the report I have read, I would be dead if it hadn't been for your quick thinking. So no more guilty feelings Sir Squire, you did well."

A tear ran down Nikolaos face, "Alright Lady Jessica, but I will do even better."

Pompey showed her the dress they bought. "Is this alright?"

Jessica looked at it, "It is wonderful Pompey, was it expensive?"

Pompey replied. "That is none of your business. If you like it, then it is a gift from Beary and I."

"But my Lady, I know it had to be expensive!" Jessica said.

"Jessica would you deny me a little pleasure?" Pompey asked.

Jessica shook her head, "You have spent too much time with Lady Angelina. Thank you my Lady."

Pompey kissed her. "Thank you. That was the nicest complement I could have received. Well I have to go get a lecture from your future husband."

Alexis told her. "Jessica, get better quick. I don't like playing boss."

Jessica smiled and nodded.

Pompey walked in to the exam room. Caesar looked at her, "Do I need to do the pregnancy test?"

"No Caesar. I am carrying twins." Pompey said, "No I have not told Beary yet. I suppose you are going to make me."

Caesar shook his head, "Pricilla I should put you over my knee. Did Alexa know . . . Of course she did, wait till I get a hold of her."

"Caesar don't you see Beary needed us with him. What difference does it make if these cubs are born on this ship or on Andreas Prime? Do you think we would be any safer?" Pompey asked.

"I don't know Pricilla; I do see your point. But you are going to have to follow my directions implicitly.

Nurse Blaze, get in here. Pompey you know the drill put this on." Caesar then stepped out.

Alexis was waiting outside, "You knew didn't you?" Caesar asked.

Alexis nodded, "Of course cousin. However, her secrets are my secrets."

Caesar just kissed her, "If Jessica ever gets pregnant and keeps it from me you better tell me, or I'll ring your neck."

Alexis looked at him. "Are you going to tell Beary?"

Caesar shook his head. "I want to. But I can't. It would violate doctor patient privilege. Besides she can't keep it secret much longer."

He walked back in and examined Pompey, "Well my Lady as I am sure Alexa told you, you are pregnant with twins. I want you to start following up with one of the cub doctors on a weekly basis. Also take these supplements. Eat more protein and calcium. You are eating for three. I also want you in the gym for at least a cycle a day. Swim if you can, but exercise. One more thing, tell Beary now."

Pompey replied, "Just as soon as we leave orbit Caesar. Maybe this time I'll get to keep my promise."

"Get dress and go home you scamp." Caesar said.

Nurse Blaze looked at him, "Should you talk to an important patient like her, like that?"

Caesar looked at her, "Nurse Blaze, Lady Maxumus, is part of my family. Someone I would die for without a thought or care. The funny thing is she would do the same for me. That is what family is."

Pompey smiled, as Caesar walked out, "Caesar's family has been part of my Husband's Clan forever. We are family. He is correct I would give my life for him so would my husband. He is our friend and he is family. To my husband's clan family is important."

Nurse Blaze shook her head these Maxmimus were strange bears. Their relationships were strange. "May I ask Lady Artemus?"

"Lieutenant Artemus and Snow Flower joined our clan when they adopted their first three children. Ice Song was adopted when she agreed to become Agathag's protector and companion. She is also considered their daughter.

Shoshanna is my niece." Pompey said.

Nurse Blaze looked at her "The dragons are not pets?"

"Oh no they are family members. I guess Night Wind and Night Song consider themselves pets but I don't. They are family to me." Pompey said.

The *EAQ* quietly pulled away from Candaris XII, with its new crew members. Quietly new force fields started forming around parts of the ship as Rubin did his magic.

Ben was walking towards Beary's office when he bumped into a pilot carrying a load of equipment.

"I am sorry Ensign let me help you with this." Ben said.

Kat looked into his eyes, "Oh no Captain it was my fault. I was just going in here."

"Well then let me help you." Ben helped carry the equipment in.

"Sir, I am Moon Flower Katimai of the Red Circle Clan. But everyone calls me Kat." Kat said.

Ben smiled, "Ben Maritinus of Red Paw Clan."

"You are the Slayer!" Kat said. Then she kissed him full on the lips. "Oh I am sorry Sir that was inappropriate, it is just you helped save a member of our clan."

Ben looked at her, "Well Ensign no harm. I better a get going. I, ah, need to see Lieutenant Maxumus." Ben turned and ran into the wall then darted through the door.

Ensign Mayotte looked at her pilot. "You just can't help it can you."

"What Paulette?" Kat asked.

"You have to dance next to the flames just to see if you can get burned." Mayotte said.

Kat smiled, "You can't feel the heat if you aren't close to the flame and he is hot!"

Ben walked in to Beary's office and grabbed a cup of coffee and sat down. Artemus walked over.

Beary looked up. "Ben, are you alright?"

Ben looked at him, "I was just attacked by a Kat!"

Artemus looked at him "What?"

"One of Beary's, fighter pilots she kissed me! She said I helped rescue one of her clan off Dryden. Her name is Kat, she apologized, and I mean she really didn't need to apologize. It was a nice kiss but it's just . . ." Ben babbled on.

"Take a breath Ben. I have seen you have more composure with a knife in your leg." Artemus said.

Ben laughed "Combat is more calming than dealing with females."

"True and if we don't head home the Commander will have our ears." Beary said.

Artemus sighed, "Ben why don't you join Snow Flower, the kids and me for dinner."

"Alright Artemus I will join you. I forgot what I wanted to ask you two anyway." Ben said.

Beary got home Erin and Sho-Sho met him at the door and kissed him. "Daddy we are going to eat with Alexis tonight. She is fixing meat pie. You and Mommy are having a quiet dinner together." Erin squealed with glee.

Sho-Sho told him, "I will take care of my love. Maryam is with her family."

With that they walked across to, Alexis rooms. Alexis smiled and waved.

Beary turned to see Pricilla smiling at him. He started to say something when the com unit rang.

"Lieutenant Maxumus you have an incoming message on secure echo channel." Ensign Duran said.

"Thank you Ensign Duran." Beary said. He turned to Secure Echo his mother's face appeared.

"Hello, my loves." Angelina said. "I have some good news for you."

Beary asked. "What good news, Mom?"

"Well first Babs, is now Lady Babs Allis Maxumus she made an honest boar out of Ti a few cycles ago. It was a nice quiet ceremony.

Also Pompey Dear, I had Uncle Justinian spend some of your and Babs money. Octavious and I threw in a little also. So did Babs Uncle Max Harrah, Dee, and Bec. We brought the Dream Cruise Line. We are operating it under The Gem Corporation." Angelina explained.

Pompey nodded. "Sounds like a good investment."

Pompey took Beary's paw. "I guess this would be a good time to tell you and Beary that you are going to be grandparents again."

Angelina smiled as she watched Beary set down, "Are you alright, Dear."

"Yes Angelina, Caesar said I am going to have twins." Pompey said.

"Oh how wonderful. Stay safe my loves." Angelina said as she severed the link.

Beary looked at Pompey as she placed her paw on his lips.

"We can have a knock down drag-out fight. Which will do me and the cubs no good and leave you upset and settle nothing, because I will not leave the ship. Or you can kiss me tell me how happy you are and how much you love me, Erin, and our unborn cubs." Pompey said.

Beary wrapped his arms around her and gently placed his head on her stomach, "You southern witch you know I couldn't stand to be away from you now." Tears started flowing from his eyes.

She kissed the top of his head "Or me from you."

Ensign Kat walked in to Barbarossa office he was getting ready to call it a night.

"What is it Kat?" Barbarossa asked.

"Sir what are the rules on dating a Superior Officer?" Kat asked.

"Ensign is he in your chain of command?" Barbarossa asked concerned.

"Oh no Sir, he is a delicious Marine Captain I wish to pursue." Kat said.

Barbarossa sat down. "Kat I need a second opinion would you mind if we ask Pathfinder her opinion."

"No Sir if it is important to be sure it is alright." Kat said.

"Jane, come here. I have been asked a question and I need your opinion." Barbarossa said.

Pathfinder came in. "What do you need Joe? Oh hello, Kat why are you here?"

"Okay Kat, tell her what you told me." Barbarossa said.

"I just asked if it was permissible for me to pursue a delicious Marine Captain I wish to mate." Kat said.

Pathfinder turned her head, "Well Kat as long as he is not in your chain of Command it isn't against regulations."

"Thank you both." She said and bounced out of the room.

Pathfinder walked over and closed the door. Then they both started laughing till their sides hurt.

Finally Joe looked at Jane "Do we warn him?"

Jane shook her head. "NO."

Ben handed out the new armor Nighthunter and Blackpaw looked it over. "Thanks Skipper this is a lot better than the Mark II's we had."

Ben nodded. "How is it going?"

Nighthunter shrugged. "My Marines are mad boss, we got boarded, and we got caught flat footed. We cleared them out and they didn't accomplish their mission but civilians were hurt."

Blackpaw agreed, "It really sticks in their craw, Boss. We are better than that."

Ben nodded, "Talk to all the Gunny's and squad leaders come up with suggestions then take them to the first. I have the officers doing the same thing with the XO."

"Yes Sir." Nighthunter and Blackpaw said enthusiastically.

Artemus looked at his family. Dinner was over Nikolaos was deep in thought.

"What is it son?" Artemus asked.

"It doesn't make since father. Why did they go through with the attack they had to know it would not work?" Nikolaos asked.

"It depends on their main objective Nikolaos. They were after key scientist and planned to assassinate the Captain. We manage to stop most of their boarding party before they boarded." Artemus pointed out.

"Yes father, but still it was at best a suicide mission was it not? Would you not at least expect to gain something from such an attack even if it failed?" Nikolaos asked.

Artemus thought "You have a point son. Well enjoy your desert it is almost bed time.

A cycle latter Artemus couldn't shake Nikolaos words.

"Beary, Ben, Rubin meet me in the Captain's office." Artemus said in the com unit.

Captain Gracchus sat in his chair in his robe. "Lieutenant Artemus I was enjoying a few brief moments in my wife's arms what was so important you had to disturb that."

Artemus explained, "Sir I am sorry, but we missed something that's why I asked Rubin to join us. We didn't find any explosives the Canus and Marines have swept the ship. So what could they have done that could be so devastating that it could leave us helpless?"

Gracchus shrugged, "I don't know install a biological weapon or poison into one of our systems?"

Beary responded "Actually, Sir after Timothy was poisoned we thought that could be a possibility and put in detectors and filters to prevent that from happening."

Ben nodded "We checked anyway."

"So what is the threat?" Gracchus asked.

Rubin looked up. "This! It is a line of compressed codes tied into the communications network. He typed in some commands. Whoever designed this was good. It has quietly and benignly duplicated in several other systems. But they aren't as good as I am, or as smart as the builders of this ship. Beary, tell the Bridge to switch control to Auxiliary Control and the secure core."

Beary hit the com. "Bridge transfer control to Bravo, tell them we are going to secure."

Lieutenant Belows replied, "Transferring, control to Bravo in secure mode."

The secure core started up severing the connection of the main computer with the rest of the ship. It also released an anti-virus program that removed any unauthorized program from the secure system.

"The π signal they sent out was that to start the virus." Beary asked.

Rubin shook his head, "No maybe an arming key. Anyway I am isolating it now. This is going to take several cycles. The main computer is off line give me twelve cycles. I'll call Teddy. He can help me. Between the two of us we should be able to take care of this in less time."

Gracchus looked at Artemus, "Good catch. Tell Nikolaos at a boy for me."

CHAPTER 3

Changes and Plans

O N BEARILIA PRIME things were taking place that would affect all their lives.

Octavious and Angelina arrived back on Bearilia Prime. (From Candaris Prime and Ti and Babs wedding) The Senator from Pandarus VI's house had been fire bombed. Luckily no one had been home. However the Senate was in an uproar. Octavious was called into a meeting to find out what he was going to do about it.

Captain Bandar had been dressed down by fleet because Empress Maxumus had slipped off without him.

Also the hospital was starting to wonder if it wasn't time for her to move her practice to Andreas Prime, since they were having more and more security issues. The Board had hinted strongly that she should consider opening a branch of the Institute on Andreas Prime and setting up her practice there.

Angelina stormed into her office and slammed the door. "Bec, how would Jim feel about living on Andreas Prime? I could give him office space at the Castle."

Mrs. Maro smiled, "So they asked you to start an Institute on Andreas Prime?"

Angelina's eyes flared, "Yes!"

"And you didn't kill any of them. I am proud of you. Look Angelina my kids are moving there. De-De is working with Dave Johnson she has already asked Johnathan Augustus for a small piece of land. The others have also." Mrs. Maro said.

Angelina sighed, "I'll give you some from the Caesar/Maxumus land."

Mrs. Maro responded, "That's fine Angelina. You know I love you and Octavious."

Angelina kissed her. "I am going home. I need to think."

Strong Heart stood up, "I already called Sire Jorgenson my Lady. He is bringing the transport around."

"Dumb pet huh?" Angelina laughed.

He smiled a wolfish grin. "Mrs. Maro already knows my capabilities. I think I would like to hunt with her. She has the eyes of a hunter."

Angelina said, "Don't repeat that to anyone. But you are right."

Strong Heart nodded. He knew his Lady was one also. He kept that to himself.

Captain Bandar was waiting for her. "Empress may we talk?"

"Yes Captain what is it?" Angelina asked.

"Are you unhappy with us my Lady?" Captain Bandar asked.

"No Captain, Why," Angelina asked?

"Fleet has threatened to relieve us my Lady." Captain Bandar said.

Angelina was mad now. "It is alright Captain. I'll take care of it. Now I need some exercise before I kill someone. My family detail won't spare with me. Ti and Beary aren't home. Do you think you have twelve Marines that would be willing?"

"My lady they are all trained Marines. Some are combat veterans." Bandar said.

"That's ok Captain, have them wear protective gear. I won't hurt them." Angelina said.

Bandar brought the entire company down. Sgt. Fisher and Moon-Scare just sat down. They told their Lieutenant that they knew her son and were not about to go up against her. Twelve volunteers were selected including 2nd Lieutenants each were given a pugilist stick.

Angelina smiled, as she had Mr. Jorgenson tie a blind fold over her eyes. He then walked over next to Captain Bandar and threw her a stick which she caught.

Bandar looked at him, "What is she doing?"

Alexander Jorgenson laughed, "She is getting ready to beat your Marines. She is trying to make it fair."

Angelina taunted, "Come on Marines, I am one female and I am blind folded surly that is an easy enough target for you."

Two young marines charged in from different sides both went flying against the opposite wall.

Bandar looked at Alexander, "What happened? I didn't even see her move."

Alexander smiled, "Captain, your Marines are going to have to do better than that."

A 2nd Lieutenant organized a charge with five marines. She side stepped or blocked each blow. She then dropped the Lieutenant with a blow to his midsection followed by a blow to his head. She then sent two privates sprawling in opposite directions. The other three retreated. The first two pulled the lieutenant off the floor he was out cold. They and the other two rejoined the nine that were left.

They decided to attack in mass. In a matter of moments eleven Marines were laying around the work out mat. Six were unconscious and two had dislocated shoulders. The other three just refused to get up they had bruises they didn't even want to think about.

Alexander yelled, "Stop! Angelina you going to have to treat some wounded."

Angelina took off her blind fold, "Oh crap! I am sorry Captain."

She walked over to one young private he was holding his arm. She looked at it, "I am sorry son it is not broken but it is dislocated. I am going to put it back in. It is going to hurt but then it will be better in a few days." She looked into his eyes grabbed his arm and snapped it back in place.

"Thank you My Lady." The young private said just before he passed out.

She made sure there were no concussions. Then had the twelve tended to by other staffers.

"I am sorry Captain Bandar." Angelina said.

"No my Lady, that was the most amassing thing my Marines have ever seen. They said they would fight beside you anywhere any time." Bandar said.

"Thank you Captain and thank them. We will be leaving for home in about a week." Angelina said.

Octavious looked at Angelina, "Are you sure you want to do this?"

"No, I don't want this Octavious." Angelina said. "You can't spend all your time on Andreas prime either. You would lose your seat."

Octavious shrugged, "That might not matter. I might have to give up my seat anyway."

Angelina looked at him, "Why? Not because of me."

"No . . . Vice President Van Horn is very ill. He is going to have to resign. Coldbear asked if I would take his place. I told him I would have to talk to you about it. He gave me until the end of the weekend to decide." Octavious said.

Angelina looked at him. "What do you want to do?"

"I don't know. I would have more freedom and more responsibility. But I would also be seen as a lackey for Coldbear. David and I have been friends for a long time. He knows I am no one's yes bear." Octavious said.

"Who would take your place?" Angelina asked.

"Isaiah said he would like to try and run for the seat. He has Foreign Service experience. He also enjoys politics and the games involved. He also loves Bearilia Prime and has no intentions of going back to Andreas Prime. We could give him this house." Octavious said.

"What about Benjamin, Augustus, Maria, and Beany shouldn't they have a say?" Angelina asked.

Octavious shook his head, "You're their mother and the Empress and you don't know what is happening." he laughed

Angelina's eyes flared and she hit him with a pillow. "What do you mean by that?"

Octavious smiled, "Just that Benjamin has petitioned the council to start a University on Andreas Prime. Augustus sold his business here and has already started moving his family to Andreas Prime. Beany and her family are opening a law office in Saint Elaina's. She is moving into Grace Castle with Justinian, she pointed out he didn't need four hundred twenty rooms. Maria and Jim said that Andreas Prime needed more teachers. He passed his administrator exam. He will be a Principle at a new high school in Angel land."

Angelina looked at him "When did this all start?"

Octavious shrugged, "Alexa has been working on them for months. Isaiah complained. He said he didn't understand why she wanted everybody to follow her. Didn't she realize others might have other dreams? You know his usual speech."

Angelina smiled, "He was always compliant as a child. But in some ways he is most like Alexa and Beary."

"Just more devious, that's why he will make a great politician." Octavious said.

Angelina leaned back, "Ok, so we move to Andreas Prime. You tell David you'll take the job. De and your staff go with you and you're moving to Andreas Prime."

Octavious nodded, "Ok that settles that. Now what can this knight do for his Empress."

Angelina kissed him then smiled an impish smile, "Don't you mean to your Empress."

Octavious smiled. *Yes she still drove him crazy and he loved it.*

Angelina walked into the boardroom; the Directors of the Medical Institute were there. "Ladies and Gentlebears, I have decided that the Federation needs a second teaching Medical Institute. I will be opening one on Andreas Prime and moving my practice there. I ask that Dr. Torrance be made Chief of Nero-Surgery here. He was always my best student."

"Lady Maxumus we will be so sorry to see you leave but we are also glad that you will be starting another institute. With the Federation expanding Andreas Prime will be of great importance. Also we concur with your recommendation of Dr. Torrance." Mr. Greenbrier said.

Angelina nodded, "Good day." She then left without another word.

Dr. Torrance was waiting for Angelina, "But I wanted to go with you."

"No Tor, I need to leave someone here I trust. Besides if you need me you can always call. But the truth is your good enough, you won't" Angelina said.

"It won't be the same without you and Mrs. Maro." Dr. Torrance said.

Angelina just kissed him.

Rebecca handed her a coat, "Come on it is time. Take care, Dr. Torrance."

"You too Lady Maro" Dr. Torrance said as the two friends walked out the door.

Octavious looked at President Coldbear, "David, are you sure you want me. You know I am a pain in the tail."

President Coldbear smiled, "Octavious, Van Horn has to go under some risky treatment the Doctors only give him a 30% chance of surviving. He doesn't want to die in office. I will get Bob to appoint young Isaiah to finish your term. He owes me. I need you. I also want you to continue to run the Secret Service as Vice President. I will have

Bill Henderson report directly to you. That way your little agreements with him can stay in effect."

"Ok David I hope you know what you're doing." Octavious said.

"Octavious if I wanted a lackey or a yes bear I would have asked Simon from Darius V. I don't. I want you because I know you're honest and so is Angelina." Coldbear said.

Beary and Artemus was setting in Beary's office when an announcement came on the view screen in his office. "Stand-by for a ship wide broadcast from Bearilia Prime. Please stand-by."

On the screen was Vice President Van Horn he was standing before a joint meeting of the Bearilian Congress. Beary turned up the volume.

"My fellow Bearilians it has been my pleasure to serve my Federation since I was a young cub. Now I stand before you a sick and dying boar. I do not fear death. I am ready to go be with my Creator and his Word if it be their will. However I do not wish to die in servitude. So as of this moment I ask that you allow me that final promotion any servant of the general public may have the simple right to become an ordinary citizen.

So at this time I tender my resignation as Vice President. I nominate a Senator, who by his leadership and honesty has proven his worthiness, Octavious Maxumus."

The uproar was immediate, but the old bear just smiled and held up his paws. "Please my friends I ask only that you pray for me whether the doctors find a cure or the Creator takes me on the next great adventure, pray that I find peace. Thank you." With that Van Horn left the podium and walked down the aisle to the doors of the chamber and left.

Everyone stood in stunned silences.

Finally the Speaker of the House and the President of the Senate stood up. Mr. Freebear looked at the assembly. "It has been Three Hundred years since this body has had to replace a setting Vice President. One of our own has been nominated. A Senator we all know. Some like, some despise, but none question his integrity. I ask the House to Vote." Of six hundred Congressbears five hundred fifty voted yes, fifty voted no. Mr. Freebear looked at Senator Coldspring. "The Bearilian House recommends Senator Maxumus be confirmed as the next Vice President of the Federation."

Senator Coldspring bowed, "Thank you Mr. Speaker. The Senate will now vote." Of two hundred Senators, one hundred ninety voted yes, nine no and one abstained, Octavious.

Senator Coldspring called Octavious up. "Mr. Vice President."

Octavious looked at the gathered dignitaries and at the cameras. "My fellow Bearilians please join me in praying for Citizen Van Horn and please pray for me that I may never betray your trust."

Artemus looked at Beary "What just happened, Boss?"

Widja smiled, "No my Angelina that will not be a problem. I will ask the Council, I am sure they will agree. Having a major training hospital along with the new university they just approved will not only help our local population, but all of the races in the area including the Antilleans and others."

"Thank you Widja we will be home in about a week. I love you." Angelina said.

Beary got on the elevator and rode up to Captain Gracchus office. He knocked on the door. "Sir, did you know anything about this?"

Gracchus shook his head, "No Beary I didn't know anything. I was going to ask you the same thing. I guess we were all taken by surprise."

Beary just nodded, "Sir, about Haden's Passage. I still think it is our best bet. The *Fast Paw* was destroyed scouting the route we are supposed to take. While whoever attacked them may be trying to force us to try something drastic like taking Haden's Passage, the truth is there are at least five other more lengthy and standard routes we could take. The main drawback to taking Haden's Passage is that going through a wormhole leaves you defenseless for one STU."

Gracchus smiled, "Beary are you trying to convince me to take it or not to take it."

"The question is Sir, are we crazy enough to take one of the most dangerous wormholes in existence and does our enemy believe we are that crazy?" Beary asked.

"I take it you have a plan?" Gracchus asked.

"Almost, I have half a plan. It will depend on just how crazy you and the Commander are." Beary said.

Gracchus sighed, "Well, let me call her in and you can tell us your half a plan."

Commander Gracchus came in, "What do you need Captain?"

"Have a seat Jeanne, Beary has a plan he wants to explain to us." Gracchus said.

"Commander, it is just a concept. Half a plan at best but it may work . . ." Beary started explaining. Forty STU later he finished. "We have run some simulations. So far we have about a 50% success rate. Only about 25% are without massive casualties to my fighters."

Jeanne looked at him, "How massive Beary?"

Beary shrugged, "75 to 100% casualties depending on the attacking force, and the number the computer has us lose in the passage."

Gracchus shook his head, "So in actuality only 25% of our simulations worked out to our benefit."

"Sir, I don't trust simulations and all were based on worse case scenarios. We will not face the worst case or the best case. But I want to train my pilots and have Rubin work on solving the worst case problems." Beary said.

Jeanne nodded, "We reach the area around Haden's passage in two weeks. We can spend five to ten days flying the flag. The Lesser Anzico System only has three planets they formed an Independent Commonwealth within the Bearilian Federation. The Federation provides protection but they maintain their internal independence. We will be required to stop and offer aid medical etc."

"We also snoop around and make sure no one is sending information on us out?" Beary asked.

"Well, there is that also." Jeanne said. "Beary, call home find out what is going on, also what do you know about your mom's past?"

"She was a surgeon in the fleet for a short time. I guess that is where she met my dad. They never really talked about it. I know she saved Mrs. Maro's husband Jim. His fighter had been hit by a missile and he lost his legs. They say he died twice on the table but she refused to let him go. They say she had a fight with the head Doctor over it. But I don't know the details." Beary said.

"Anything else about her you could tell us?" Jeanne asked.

"Why?" Beary asked.

Jeanne smiled. "I just got a strange message from General Zantoran, Beary. He asked me to ask that is all I know."

Beary shrugged, "He should ask her, Mom is pretty open. It is Dad that has kept his past a mystery from us cubs."

That night Beary gathered the family together and called home. Caesar had allowed Jessica to come back down to her room. He sat next to the wheelchair he had her setting in.

76   CHARLES & IRENE NICKERSON

Beary called home and put it on the big screen. Octavious and Angelina appeared on the screen. She immediately saw Jessica in the wheelchair.

"Jessica, are you alright? Do I need to call your father in?" Angelina asked.

"No My lady, Caesar talked to him earlier today. I was injured but I will be fine. Caesar is taking good care of me though his bed side manners leave a little to be desired." Jessica said.

"Why is that Jessica?" Angelina asked.

"I wouldn't let her leave medical till she agreed to marry me." Caesar said.

Angelina laughed. "Caesar I am not sure I taught you that."

Caesar raised an eyebrow and smiled.

"Well anyway congratulations on your engagement may the Creator and his Word, bless you." Angelina said.

"Dad we all want to congratulate you on your appointment as Vice President." Beary said.

"Thank you. Isaiah is taking my seat and has asked Jenny to marry him finally." Octavious said.

"We are giving them the house. The rest of the family, have moved to Andreas Prime. We are moving their also. Caesar your family is also moving there." Octavious added.

Caesar nodded, "Thank you Octavious."

Erin smiled, "I love you Granddad and Grandma."

"We love you also Erin and you Sho-Sho." Angelina said.

Sho-Sho smiled "I love you both may you always feel my love for you."

Both felt something stir inside of them.

Beary told them. "Well we need to go. We all love you let us know when you get home. Oh Mom, why did General Zantoran have Commander Gracchus, ask me about your past?"

"Oh it is nothing dear probably for a background check. You know your father is the Vice President. You wouldn't want an assassin lying next to him." Angelina laughed with an angelic laugh.

Everyone else laughed to.

"Goodnight Mom, stay safe Dad, Beary out." Beary said.

Octavious looked at Angelina as he took her in his arms, "That was a little risky wasn't it."

"No, none of the family members with Beary know about the Banshee or her Heralds. Well Jessica and Alexis might have heard the names but they are just legends remember." Angelina said, "I wonder if I need to have another talk with the General?"

Octavious looked at her, "No let me take care of it."

The next day Octavious met General Starpaw and General Zantoran in orbit over Bearilia Prime aboard a new Dreadnought.

"Hello General, Admiral first I want to thank you for joining me." Octavious said.

"Mr. Vice President how can we help you?" Starpaw asked.

"First Gentlebears read and sign these documents." Octavious said.

Zantoran read the document and looked up. "Are you serious?"

"Yes General, I signed the same document seventy two years ago or was it seventy four it is hard to keep track. If you reveal what I am going to tell you, you will be killed." Octavious said.

Both officers signed the documents. "Alright what is this about?"

"It is about a specialized Secret Service Cell that was used to remove enemies of the Federation. It was a three bear cell that never existed. It was led by the Banshee. This agent was backed up by the two Heralds of Death. Their control agent was known as the Raven. It is important that you understand even these names are Ultra Top Secret." Octavious explained.

The General nodded "Alright I understand no more digging Vice President Maxumus. Are they still active?"

Octavious smiled "Who?"

Starpaw sighed, "Understood, Sir you know the old Banshee is being retired. I think the fleet needs a Banshee."

General Zantoran nodded. "Why don't we rename this one? It hasn't been officially named yet."

Octavious replied, "Alright Gentlebears."

Angelina looked at Mrs. Maro, "You sure Jim is ok with this?"

Mrs. Maro grinned, "Jim said he didn't know what took you so long. He actually has been talking to Octavious about letting him work out of Andreas Prime. Octavious said it would be ok but that we needed to move into the Castle for a while. I hope that alright with you."

"Bec, you even have to ask? You know I couldn't love you any more if you were my sister." Angelina said.

"I know my Angelina. I just hope Widja don't mind." Mrs. Maro said.

"She thinks it is great. Remember you are family. Widja is big on family." Angelina said. "Well that's everything. The house is packed except what we are leaving for Isaiah and Jenny."

"Come on everyone is waiting the Valorous needs to get back on patrol." Mrs. Maro said.

Angelina closed the door a single tear fell from her eye as she headed into a new future.

Romanov came in and slammed into a chair across from Beary. "Just how am I supposed to train that bunch of numb brained pilots how to stay alive?"

Beary looked at her.

"I know how important the mission in the wormhole is. But half your pilots couldn't find their lateral thrusters with their paws tied to it and the others have as much finesse as a meteorite. All they do is, slam the controls." Romanov ranted.

Beary sat quietly.

"There are maybe eight pilots not counting the XO and the CO and you that could pull this off. I guess if we start with them. I could train you up maybe two flights, which could pull off this stunt and survive the wormhole. I'll focus on them. Kat is about the best of the bunch maybe she could talk some of the others through it. By the way you need to go through the trainer to Boss. I need to know you will follow my instructions. You're going to be flying blind for part of it, if your stunt works." Romanov said.

Beary nodded.

"Alright, I know get back to work. You don't need to push so hard. I'll get it done Boss." Romanov said.

Beary smiled, "Thank you."

She looked at him, "It is ok Boss we'll get them through alive."

With that Romanov left.

Commander Gracchus was leaning against the other door. She looked at Beary, "You didn't say anything but thank you. Yet she felt that you gave her orders. At the same time you made her want to meet your expectations."

Beary shrugged. "I had a good teacher Commander, an old Gunny, who is now a fleet Chief Master Gunnery Sergeant. He said to pick good people who were driven to give their best. Listen to them when they need you to just listen. Help when they ask and stay out of the way as much as you can. But always support, encourage, instruct and be willing to learn. Romanov knows I am the Boss. She needs to know I trust her. That is why she came to see me. That simple thank you was all she needed."

Jeanne shook her head "Now she and her crew will fly through the Moons of Bantine for you. Beary it takes most officer years to learn the lessons you seem to already know."

Beary shrugged. "Commander, I started my squire training at the age of one. I made full Knight by the age of ten, which was young by most standards. Nikolaos may make knight at even a younger age."

Jeanne thought, "You were training to be an officer from the age of one. Plus you have a family tradition."

"Yes Mame. There is that also but it is more than that. We are trained to serve. That is the true key." Beary said. "What can I do for you Commander?"

"Nothing Beary, I just heard the news that Pompey is with cub." Jeanne said.

"That is what Caesar told her. Actually he said twins Commander. I am worried but she won't go home and the truth is she is probable as safe on the *EAQ* as she would be at home." Beary said.

Jeanne nodded, "Alright I just wondered if I needed to call in a referee."

Beary replied, "My father gave me some good advice. I decided to follow it."

Jeanne cocked her head, "What was that?"

"Just figure I had lost the argument and move on before we had it. It saves time and a lot of apologizing." Beary said with a smile.

Commander Gracchus started laughing and sat down. "No wonder your marriages last."

Three cycles later Beary and Akhiok arrived at the trainer, "Joshua just listen to their instructions and follow them it's just like blast training. I'll be flying but you'll need to handle some controls be gentle it is about finesse." Beary said.

"I will handle the controls as if they were a prickle berry." Joshua said.

The crew of Valkyrie 30 came out of the briefing room. Both Ensigns looked like they had been beaten. Ensign Nicene looked at Joshua, "Good luck Akhiok that one is just plain vicious."

Ensign Pratt looked at Beary, "I am sorry Sir. I can do better I promise."

Beary nodded, "Pratt if they were tough on you it is because they are trying to keep you alive, remember that. You are no good to me dead. Talk to Katimai if you don't believe how important this training is."

"No Sir, I understand but your right maybe Kat can help me. Thank you Sir." Ensign Pratt said.

Ensign Rueben came out, "Akhiok you're with me come on. He will rejoin you in the trainer Sir."

Ensigns King, Lo, Re, Kay, and Ni came out, "Sir come with us."

In a briefing room Ensign Rueben looked at Joshua, "So you are the Prince's WTO. You better be as good as he says you are, because if anything happens to him because of you I will hunt you down."

Joshua replied, "Hannah I fly with the Boss. I have for a while. Like most bears that know him. I would die for him. If you can make me better at what I do I will thank you. But understand I am his WTO and I run from no one."

In another room the others explained their role and how they would feed Beary information. While only Reuben would be talking to Joshua.

Beary nodded.

As they got in the trainer Romanov came on the com unit, "Sir, I will be evaluating you and be running the trainer."

Beary and Akhiok ran through their check list and simulated launch.

"Spirit 6, raise blast shield come to 122 correct to 122.6."

Beary, gentle corrected his course to 122.6.

Meanwhile Akhiok was told to adjust the x axis of the ship .5 SubSMU up. Then down X axis .25 SubSMU, which he did.

After two cycles of minute maneuvering exercising they moved on to combat maneuvering at high speed without weapon. It was at this point that Akhiok understood why they had spent two cycles doing the other exercises. After two more cycles the training was over.

"Sir, please have your crew meet us in the briefing room." Romanov said.

Akhiok shook his head, "Sorry Boss I almost blew it on that last maneuver I over corrected. I was getting tired. No excuse though."

Beary rolled his tired shoulders, "Joshua don't beat yourself up I think our trainers will do it for us."

Romanov looked at the scores they were phenomenal. Akhiok had scored a 99.5 and Beary a 99.6. No one ever scored a 100 it wasn't possible.

Reuben looked at Joshua, "Ensign Akhiok you over corrected toward the end of the combat run and at one point your reaction time was off by .0065 SubSTU, for a standard deduction of .5. You are receiving a Highly Qualified rating for this evaluation.

Lieutenant Maxumus Sir, you received a score of 99.6 with a .4 deduction. You anticipated two commands before they were actual given although you performed the command that was to be given."

Beary looked at Ensign Ni, "Were they commands from Ensign Ni?"

Romanov nodded, "Yes Sir. How did you know?"

Beary shook his head, "I thought it was a malfunction in the com unit. I heard a delayed echo in her commands after a while."

Ensign Ni dropped her head.

Beary asked, "Ensign Ni my family uses telepathic communication to communicate with the dragons in our families. Sometimes it even works between family members. You are a telepath or an empathic correct."

Ni looked at him, "Yes Sir, but it is not something my people approve of."

Beary smiled. "It is alright Ni. It was my ability that allowed me to use yours."

At that Ni smiled, "Thank you Sir."

Romanov smiled to herself. *So he took the guilt from her and told her she was valuable to him. But hasn't he did that to all of us? She looked at Reuben, Yes even Reuben was ready to fall at his feet and swear allegiance to the Prince of Andreas Prime.*

"Anyway Sir you also received a Highly Qualified Rating." Reuben said.

Beary smiled then replied, "Thank you Ladies."

Six cycles latter Artemus came home to the family section. Beary was setting at a table. Artemus came over and sat down. "You have another cup of that?"

Beary poured Artemus a cup of tea. "You look tired."

Artemus nodded, "That was the hardest evaluation ride I have ever taken. Lowest score I ever got also a 99.5. I also got out shot. I knew the kid was good when I picked him but he scored higher than I ever managed. He scored a199.6 out of 200. He beat my best score by .1. We, is a great gunner he scored a 99.9 on the evaluation. They had to work hard to find a tenth of a deduction."

Beary smiled as he sipped his tea. "Our wives said they would join us out here after they put the young ones to bed."

Caesar came out of his room, "You have another cup?"

Beary nodded and poured him a cup. "How is Jessica?"

Caesar responded. "I am returning her to limited duty. Teddy has Pompey covered in the intelligence section along with Rubin. She also has Night Wind with her. Night Song is about ready to have her pups, probably tomorrow."

Pompey and Snow Flower joined them. They sat next to their husbands. Beary poured two cups of tea.

Snow Flower kissed Artemus, "You look very tired husband."

Artemus smiled, "Long day but a good one. How about you? Are you ready for tomorrow?"

Snow Flower sighed, "Yes we are ready. Desks and all the classroom materials are in place. We start school on time. Rubin put in some extra security. He also built me a robot assistant. To help keep the cubs focused. He is called hoot. He looks like an owl type bird. Also Sho-Sho and Ice Song will assist me."

"Erin is looking forward to her first day. Maryam had to tell her that she needed to settle down so she could be ready for tomorrow." Pompey said.

Alexis smiled as she walked by, Beary saw her.

"How did your paper go?" Beary asked.

Alexis thought, "I got it turned in. My Professor asked how I got access to the Admirals personal papers. I told him I was related to Benjamin Maxumus. You would have thought he was going to have a stroke. By the way you were right the papers did discussed his feelings about the battle. He was tormented by the loss of the 43rd Infantry. But that they volunteered after the Commander of the 181st radioed that they had been ambushed and were pinned down."

Artemus nodded, "*The Fog of War*, lecture at the Academy the 181st was actually pinned down by the 33rd Highlanders."

Alexis shook her head, "That wasn't in my research either?"

Beary explained, "Most histories are written by the winners to glorify the winners or demonize them for political purposes. Some seek the facts in the hopes of coming close to the truth. Military histories try to do this in order to teach lessons. If you fail to learn from histories mistakes you repeat them."

"Is that what General Jordan meant by: "There is nothing more horrible than a battle won except a battle lost?" Alexis asked.

Beary nodded, "Yes and no. I think he meant that war itself is wasteful, necessary at times but always costly. That is why it should be avoided, but if it must be fought, fight to win. If you must pay the cost of war it is best to win."

Alexis smiled, "Well, I need to get to work."

Snow Flower took Artemus paw, "You, need bed and I need you. Come."

Artemus stood up. "Goodnight Beary, My lady."

Pompey leaned against Beary.

Caesar got up, "Well, I need to go cheek on Jessica."

Pompey grabbed Beary's paw "Come on you need sleep also."

Beary touched her stomach, "I am being selfish, and I should send you home. You would be safer back home. But I just can't stand the thought of not being with you."

Pompey kissed him very passionately, "Good."

Caesar knocked on Jessica's door he heard "Come in." So he walked in.

Jessica was lying in bed.

He looked at her, "You'll catch cold like that."

Jessica shrugged. "I just got out of the shower when you came to the door. Besides you're a doctor and you are here to remove the stiches aren't you?"

Caesar shook his head, "Jessica this isn't real smart I should . . ."

"No, Caesar don't you want me?" Jessica asks with pleading eyes.

Caesar wrapped the sheet around her, "More than you know my love. More than you know. But not like this. It would dishonor you. If you are that anxious to be my wife get dressed and we'll get married tonight."

Jessica kissed him, "Yes please, I need you."

Caesar walked across to Artemus suite and knocked.

Savato answered, "Caesar what is wrong?"

"I need Nikolaos." Caesar said.

Nikolaos appeared fully dressed. "She wishes to do it tonight?"

"Yes Nikolaos." Caesar smiled.

"We are ready Andreios, Maryam and I made this for her and you it is a wedding set." Nikolaos said.

Caesar looked at the golden bands and the ring with a white diamond with red star stones. "It is flawless."

"Andreios did the metal work. Maryam inscribed it and I polished the stones." Nikolaos said.

"You three honor us greatly." Caesar said.

"Wait," Ice Song said, "I need to bless them, μαψ τηειρ λοωε βε βλεσσσεδ. (May their love be blessed)

Caesar smiled, "Thank you Lady Ice Song."

Beary and Pompey came out. "What is this ruckus out here about?"

Caesar explained, "Jessica and I are getting married tonight."

"Did you call the Chaplain?" Beary asked.

"No, I forgot. She kind of sprang it on, me." Caesar said.

Beary nodded, "I am on it."

The Chaplin was waiting. "Good Doctor the next time I have a cold at midnight I am going to call you personally."

"Father John, please don't blame Caesar. It was my fault I love him so much that I offered myself to him as a concubine. I would have allowed him to take what was already promised to him. He has decided to spare my honor." Jessica said.

Father John looked at her. "I don't understand?"

Pompey explained, "It is the curse Father that our boars hold over us. It is a hunger that is never satisfied."

Beary thought, *doesn't that southern witch understand it works both ways. That is why I can't send her home and Caesar went half crazy when Jessica got hurt.*

"Father John according to our custom a female may offer herself up as a concubine. She is still legally the boar's wife but under our customs she has no rights of inheritance." Beary explained.

"Why is that?" Father John asked.

"Because Father a concubine has given up herself to her husband, she has become his property, either through conquest or desire." Pompey said.

"On Andreas Prime the Church stepped in and established ecclesiastic laws to protect females from unscrupulous boars. They tried to weaken the concubine traditions by making it a choice only the female could make. Also making it something a boar could change by marring the female before a priest." Beary added.

"Lady Jessica, why were you willing to offer yourself in that way?" Father John asked.

"It is simple Father I know my boar. I knew he would demand that we get married tonight. To save my tattered honor, and if not I had nothing to lose. I would still be his wife and be able to give him a cub, which is my desire." Jessica said.

Father John shook his head, "If I listen, too much more of this logic I will be corrupted by female thinking myself. You poor boars never have a chance do you?"

Beary, Artemus, and Caesar smiled, "No."

The Chaplin had them line up Nikolaos acted as best bear.

Jessica saw the rings that the cubs had made for her and Caesar and wept for joy. Caesar put them on her paw. She then placed the ring on Caesar's they had made for him.

Father John said. "You may kiss your wife."

Everyone kissed the bride and groom and promised to get them a gift the first chance they got.

Jessica kissed Andreios, Maryam, and Nikolaos and told them that their gift of the wedding set was the nicest that she had ever seen.

Then everyone returned to their quarters, Caesar took Jessica to his suite.

"I think I better look at those stitches now." Caesar said.

Jessica slipped off her wedding gown and hung it up. "Alright Caesar, If that is what you want."

Caesar laughed. "Well to start with Jess, my love, to start with."

The next morning Commander Gracchus came down to medical. "Doctor Vantanus, do you have a moment?"

"Yes Commander, Oh by the way I am sorry I didn't invite you and the Captain to the wedding last night. It was kind of spur of the moment." Caesar said.

"It is alright Doctor we were sleeping. You are planning to throw a party for the ship are you not?" She asked.

"Yes Mame, in a day or two when Jessica is a little stronger." Caesar said.

"Doctor does it come back?" Commander Gracchus asked.

"No Commander once your cured it can't re occur why?" Caesar asked.

"I am having symptoms." Jeanne said.

"Well, let me run some tests. Put on a gown. I'll call a nurse." Caesar said.

Nurse Blaze came in and helped the Commander, get ready, "Hello Commander Gracchus."

Caesar drew blood and ran some scans, "Nurse Blaze run this through the analyzer then bring me the results."

Jeanne sat up. "Well Doctor?"

"Commander it is not Treplots disease that is the good news. I won't be able to confirm my diagnoses till your blood test come back." Caesar said with a smile. "I do need to give you a few shots; he mixed a few vials together and gave her one shot then drew another and gave her another.

"What were those?" Jeanne asked.

"Oh you were due a couple of booster shots. Also you are low on iron so I gave you an iron shot. I am going to prescribe some vitamins." Caesar said.

Nurse Blaze came in. "Here Doctor." she said with a smile.

"Call Captain Gracchus, have him meet us in my private office." Caesar said.

"Please Doctor tell me." Jeanne said.

"No Commander you have a bad track record so he sets in on this." Caesar said.

Jeanne was almost in tears when the Captain arrived.

"Doctor what is going on?" Captain Gracchus asked.

"The Commander came to see me today. She was afraid of a relapse, I am happy to say that is not the case. However, she has a bad habit of hiding her condition from you and I didn't feel it was appropriate under the circumstances." Caesar said.

Jeanne grabbed Argus paws. "Go ahead Doctor give us the bad news."

Caesar laughed. "Oh I don't think it is bad news; you're going to have a cub."

Both Gracchus sat in total shock then asked, "How?"

Caesar shook his head, "Do I need to explain it to you?"

The Captain smiled. "No Doctor I guess I know how. I am just wondering when?"

Caesar explained, "A little over a month ago."

Jeanne blushed, "Oh, well thank you doctor."

Caesar looked at her, "You will see one of the cub doctors once a week Commander starting tomorrow do you understand?"

Captain Gracchus stood up "Yes Doctor she does and there won't be any argument."

Jeanne laughed nervously, "Dragon blessings have consequences I guess. I didn't believe you Doctor. I do now."

Caesar ordered, "You need to follow the medical directives we give you starting with taking those vitamins as I directed it is important."

Jeanne nodded. "Don't worry Doctor; Argus will see that I do it. Or he will have me keel hauled."

Captain Gracchus nodded, "Well maybe, turn her over my knee."

Caesar continued, "Ok be here tomorrow and we will set you up with a cub doctor."

Gracchus smiled as he left, "I am going to be a father."

CHAPTER 4

Lesser Anzico System

"MAYDAY, MAYDAY THIS is Sub Minister Sharon of Kalian of Anzico. We have thousands of injured and sick please send help Mayday, Mayday."

"Captain, report to the bridge. Lieutenant Maxumus, Artemus, Vantanus, and Captain Maritinus report to the Bridge." Lieutenant Gorez launched a signal booster probe.

The four friends arrived just as Captain and Commander Gracchus arrived.

Gracchus looked at Lieutenant Gorez "What do we have Mr. Gorez?"

"Sir, we have a weak mayday on an old Y band. I launched a signal booster probe. If they are using a repeater or are still broadcasting we should get another transmission."

Two STU latter, "Mayday, Mayday this is Sub Minister Sharon of Kalian of Anzico please someone answer we have thousands of injured and sick please contact the Bearilian fleet. Mayday, Mayday please someone answer."

"Beary, you, and Artemus better lead this one, along with Captain Maritinus." Gracchus said.

Caesar looked at them, "I'll grab my bags."

Gracchus shook his head, "No doctor. That is why you have a Paramedic Rescue Team. Besides you need to figure out how we deal with what they find."

Caesar nodded, "Right Chief Medical Officers don't do initial evaluations."

"Problems of command son, only CAGS and ACAGS are expendable."

Beary nodded, "Romanov, we have a mission. Two flights of fighters," Beary looked at Artemus, "One Purple and one medical flight and ten Roses."

Ben came on "Romanov coordinate with Mountain, *White Fire* is going also."

Romanov replied "Yes Sirs, we will be ready. Let's scramble ladies."

Barbarossa and O' Haggerty came running up "Where do you want us?"

Beary looked at them, "Protect the ship you two and Pathfinder and her new XO. Two of you run ops the other two fly with the CAP."

O' Haggerty looked at Beary, "Boss, Kat hasn't been assigned to a flight yet. Take her as your wingbear. She is good so is Mayotte."

"All right Patrick. I need to see how good she is." Beary said.

Beary turned to a com unit "Ensigns Katimai and Mayotte report to the ready room."

In the ready room Alpha and Delta flight were setting quietly. Kat and Mayotte were setting up front looking a little out of place. Gem flight one and Med flight 2 came in. and took their seats. Fifteen Marines filled in.

Akhiok and We sat down next to Kat and Mayotte.

Akhiok smiled, "So you're now our wingbear."

Kat looked at him, "What?"

Akhiok explained "You're flying the bosses wing Kat what number did they give you?"

"Valkyrie 38 we used to be Elf 12 and 13, but we were striped of our call sign by a communications officer on Candaris XII. His brother was lost on the ship. They were able to reestablish O' Haggerty's Elf 4 but not ours." Kat said.

Akhiok walked over and verified that Elf 12 and 13 had been deleted he then talked to Beary and walked back. "The Boss asked what call sing you want."

Kat replied, "Valkyrie 38 for me is fine."

Mayotte responded. "Valkyrie 38 sword is for me please."

Joshua nodded and called it in and came back, "Ladies you have your wish."

Team 12 came in along with Ensigns Black and White.

Artemus came in and nodded to Beary.

"Ladies and Gentlebears, we have received a distress call from the Lesser Anzico System. We are the closest Federation ship so we are responding. While the message was not clear, we believe hostile action was taken against this commonwealth by forces unknown.

This is a combat operation. Our job is to interdict the enemy. Then evaluate the situation, give aid and comfort to the populous." Beary explained.

On the bridge, Gracchus was reporting to fleet. "Sir that is all we know at this time. They are broadcasting on an old Y band transmitter. That in itself leads me to believe the situation is bad. If there are thousands of casualties, it will soon exhaust our supplies. Also we don't know the type or number of the enemy forces."

Admiral Starpaw nodded, "Alright Gracchus I'll send help. *Hope* is ten days away with Task Force 5. Try and contact them. Do what you can."

Gracchus called down, "Lieutenant Maxumus you have a go."

"Thank you Sir." Beary said. "Alright bears load up. We launch in five STU."

"Red talon this is *Storm Cloud* and *White Fire* launching." Romanov reported.

"Gem flight 1, ten Roses, and Med flight 2, launching at this time," We reported.

"Alfa and Delta flight launching," Akhiok reported.

"Alfa andValkyrie38 form up on me." Beary ordered.

"Delta Flight guard Med Flight 2. Spirit 6 transferring operational control over to *Storm Cloud*." Beary reported.

Pathfinder looked at her controls, "Red Talon, Venom 8 launching with CAP."

Muzo looked at Honey, "Monitor communications, Tajima."

"Yes Muzo." Honey said.

Tennyson flopped down on a cot. "If you need me Mame I am here. The Boss snores too much to sleep in the office."

O'Haggerty brought his ship over next to Pathfinder, "Venom 8 Elf 4 on station."

Pathfinder gave him two clicks, and turned to Ensign Cho, "We out shot Artemus's score."

Cho nodded, "Yes Mame I heard. I will strive to out shoot him." Lin Cho said. "If not I'll just have to marry him."

Pathfinder shook her head, "What is this becoming the love boat?"

Cho smiled, "Did I not tell you, Chen and I are betrothed. Our parents arranged the match when we were five years old."

"Kalian station, Kalian station broadcasting on Y this is Red Talon please respond."

"Sub Minister Sharon we are getting a response." An older bear told him.

Sub Minister Sharon jumped to his feet. "Red Talon this is Sub Minister Sharon can you help us?"

"Kalian station, be advised we are sending an advance team and we will arrive as fast as we can. We have limited abilities. But have contacted fleet. Red Talon out."

Sub Minister Sharon had tears streaming from his eyes. "Red Talon, be advised all planets were attacked by unknown warship. We have lost contact with other planets."

"Kalian station understood we will attempt to contact other planets. But, advance team will come there first because we know we have survivors there, Red Talon out."

"*Storm Cloud* to all units, we are launching orbital probes around all three planets. We are up linking data from all probes to sensors, at this time."

"Joshua, go check the sensor read out. Valkyrie 38 Sword, takeover threat assessment monitoring, Spirit 6 out"

Mayotte gave him two clicks.

Joshua started studying the data. "Boss all three planets are a mess. But we have survivors on all three planets. Most seem to be migrating to sheltered locations."

"*Storm Cloud* and *White Fire* analyze data. Split tasks and figure how best to handle this. Spirit 6 out."

"Red Talon to Kalian Station we have survivors on all planets. Red Talon out."

Sub Minister Sharon fell to his knees, "Praise the Creator!"

"Red Talon, can you help reestablish communication, Kalian station out."

"Advance team will attempt to aid in that endeavor, Red Talon out."

"Spirit 6, Spirit Blade 2, how you want to play it Boss." Artemus asked.

"*Storm Cloud,* take Alfa and Delta sweep system. Engage any Echo Victors. Spirit 6 out."

"Roger, Spirit 6 Alfa, and Delta flights formation Delta, cloak, and shields to max."

"Med 2 form up on Gem 1. Spirit Blade 2 let's put one medical supply and one equipment Rose on each of the other planets near the highest concentration of survivors. Then land on Kalian and proceed from there. Spirit 6 out."

"Slayer 1 to Spirit 6 I do have two teams of medics I could put one squad down with each team."

"Slayer 1, it is your call, but it would mean splitting one of your teams, Spirit 6 out."

"Slayer 1 one to Banshee 8, take your squad to Falian, RPD 3 take your squad to Galian take two Roses each one Medical one with equipment establish communications and aid station. Secure same do what you can and report."

On the *EAQ* Dancer and Nepos were pacing the floor when Paladin and Deerstalker came in. "First, don't we have something these two 2nd Lieutenants could be doing?"

Nepos retorted, "Sir we both have Marines out there guarding the daggers."

"Yes and the rest are supposed to be securing the ship?" Paladin pointed out.

"Yes Sir and they are. We just came in to check on the operation . . ." Dancer said.

"Look you two, you are the two more experienced platoon leaders, and I shouldn't have to hold your paws. Get back to work." Paladin said.

After Dancer and Nepos walked out, Deerstalker looked at Paladin. "How bad do you want to be out there?"

"Do you even have to ask?" Paladin smiled. "But like them our job is here."

Master Sergeant Red Tail came in, "Lieutenant Paladin I have my troops on standby if you need us."

"Thank you, Chief Gunny Red Tail." Paladin said absent mindedly.

Red Tail just smiled, "First you want to go for a walk?"

Deerstalker nodded.

They walked down one of the corridors, "Paladin still thinks of me as a Marine doesn't, he?"

Deerstalker nodded, "To us you will always be a member of the 981st MSD, Red."

The two friends continued on an informal inspection of the ships security and damage control stations.

Pompey was looking at signal intelligence that some of the hidden antennas were picking up. She picked up a weak signal coming from a point in space thirty thousand KSMU away.

She dialed it in "Mayday, Mayday this is the *Day traveler . . .*"

"Captain Gracchus we have a ship's mayday bearing 330, thirty thousand KSMU. I am picking it up on the Bugle Boy antenna."

Muzo and Barbarossa had just launched.

Gracchus looked at his screen "Doctor Vantanus, we have a small yacht in trouble."

"I'll take Doctor Greenbrier with me in Med 2 and 3 along with four Marines and two dragon Dragoons." Caesar said.

"Alright Doctor, Venom 8 and Elf 4 accompany Med 2 and 3 with your CAP.

Pathfinder smiled, "Charlie and Golf form up on me."

Med 2 and 3 shot out. O'Haggerty pulled up next to Pathfinder.

She just pointed he saluted.

"Elf 4 to Valkyrie 28 on me" with that he accelerated.

Valkyrie 28 fell in on his wing, as they pushed toward the location Pompey was feeding them.

The Day Traveler was a small space yacht. It had been attacked mercilessly and had been drifting for two days. Its life support was failing.

O'Haggerty did a quick fly by. His sensors told, him everything.

"Cutter 10, Elf 4: minimum life support on yacht, failure is imminent."

Caesar thought, "Can you attach a power pack and tow pack."

Ensign Senna was already down and putting on a Triple P (Personal Propulsion Pack) and grabbing a small emergency APU.

"Billy put on a safety line or I'll skin you." O' Haggerty ordered.

Ensign Senna smiled, "Yes Boss."

Then Senna was out the air lock he shot over to the yacht and found an undamaged external power port. He hit the shutdown button then attached external power and hit the restart button. Life support slowly increased. He then attached a towing hook to the yacht. And returned to the fighter and closed the air lock. He got on the com.

"Cutter 10, Elf Sword 4, I could not see real well but the outside of the yacht is a mess. Engines are shot out. APU is attached and life support is increasing. Tow hook is installed but I think it would be better if we remove any survivors first. The yacht might fall apart."

Caesar thought alright we do it the hard way, "Concur Elf 4, we will be there in less than five STUs.

"Elf 4 to Valkyrie 28; launch picket probes."

Valkyrie 28 launched six Class 5 probes establishing a sphere around them. The Class 5 probes started scanning the space around them. It picked up the rescue flight. He also thought he intermittently picked up a blip at the edge of the probes range.

"Elf 4 this is 28 Sword are you picking up an anomaly at 265-mark 200, range extreme."

O' Haggerty and Senna both looked at the data. "Valkyrie 28 Sword, send data to Red Talon. Keep an eye on it."

"Med 3 is docking." Two Marines and two dragons blew the air lock and entered the yacht. What met them made them angry. The pilot and copilot were dead.

A female steward was badly injured and was just barely holding on to life. The dragon dragoon forced some energy into her and picked her up and handed her into Doctor Greenbrier.

The two Marines forced the inner door. Inside they found a family; a boar, his wife, and two small cubs. The Marines checked their pulse all four were alive but barely. They were so cold to their touch. The sergeant picked up the little girl cub and passed her out to one of the dragons as his partner picked up the little boy and handed him out.

Doctor Greenbrier signaled the two Marines to get on board. "Med 3 is undocking,"

The two dragons brought the father and mother out and continued searching as Med 2 docked. The two Marines entered and loaded the father and the mother.

The dragons almost missed her. She was curled up in a ball the little maid was shivering and incoherent. She tried to scream at the sight of creatures she had never seen before. But they gentle lifted her out of bed and carried to the shuttle.

The Marines found an old boar in a butler's uniform. His breaths were labored. They picked up his limp body and carried him into the dagger.

The dragons moved past and opened up the engineering section. The devastation in here was complete. The bodies of the two crew members were impaled on pieces of equipment. They checked for signs of life both were gone.

They made one more careful sweep with scanners and left the ship.

Med 2 undocked and with half the CAP streaked to the *EAQ* with Med 3. Doctors and nurses were working feverously to save the lives of the survivors.

Pathfinder hooked a tow line to the yacht and started to tow it back to the *EAQ*.

O' Haggerty launched a cloaked Class 6 probe at the anomaly and headed for home.

Pathfinder had Cho shutdown the APU remotely. That is when Cho saw it a power signal that shouldn't be there.

"Golf Flight, execute emergency break, now!" Cho called into the com unit. With that she cut the tow and Pathfinder hit the thrusters.

Golf flight shot away from the yacht and cloaked. O'Haggerty and Valkyrie 28 saw the rest of Golf flight peel away from the yacht. Then it exploded magnificently.

He and 28 immediately cloaked. He started to turn back towards the anomaly but decided to wait for orders.

"Red Talon to all rescue units, return to base and launch cloaked Class 6 probes on axis 345 and 180 mark 200."

Pathfinder was furious with herself. "That was a good catch, Lin. I should have my tail kicked. I know better. Pick up survivors and then put a missile into the derelict, because it is always a trap."

"Harbinger 2 to Venom 8, Rule fifty-three over."

"Venom 8 to Harbinger 2, Roger Rule fifty-three and out."

Tennyson looked at Barbarossa "Rule fifty-three I don't understand, Sir?"

Joe smiled, "We were members of MSU units there are seventy-five rules. Rule fifty-three all derelict ships are a trap rigged to explode."

Tennyson nodded, "I think I will write that down."

Barbarossa smiled and tossed him a card. "Here I have a box of these."

On a strange ship approximately ninety thousand KSMU away a sensor officer looked at his Captain. "We must have destroyed the dagger and the fighters when the ship exploded. The probe showed them blink out just before it too was destroyed."

"So we got half of their fighters and one of those strange ships. This is good. We will wait and attack them when they least expect it, when they are dealing with the planets." The Captain said.

Beary landed near the point the signal was coming from. A couple of bears in dirty, blood soaked uniforms approached his fighter.

Beary stepped out and saluted, "I am Lieutenant Maxumus the CAG from the BAFRSV *Empress Angelina's Quest*. Are there any hostiles on the ground?"

"No Lieutenant. I am Colonel Mac Adams of the Home Guard. They didn't land any troops. They hit us from orbit and with drones and fighters. We shot down ten of their fighters."

Beary nodded, "I have a Paramedic Rescue Team coming in along with some supplies. One medic team was dispatched to the other two planets. Along with a squad of Marines, that will establish communications. Colonel we will do what we can, till a dedicated hospital ship arrives."

"What if that ship comes back?" Colonel Mac Adams asks.

Beary shrugged, "Then Sir, my wing will have to deal with it the best we can or die trying."

Med flight 2, landed along with six ROSES. *White Fire* also landed along with the rest of Gem flight 1. Ben and Artemus walked over.

"Colonel Mac Adams this is Captain Ben Maritinus of MSD 981. I will be leaving him in operational command while I check on the status of the other planets."

Doctor Kroller walked up, "Sir where do you want my team."

Beary looked at the Colonel, "Sir this is Doctor Kroller where can he set up his field hospital."

The Colonel shook his head. "Our hospitals were taken out . . ."

Kroller nodded. "That's alright Sir, I have emergency surgical suites and isolation wards. I can handle up to about two hundred patients with what I have. I can treat more. I just need a place to set up."

The Colonel asked, "Can you set up in a cave?"

Kroller nodded "All but the surgical suits. I can put those near the entrance and I have shield generators."

"Lieutenant Corry, show the good Doctor and his people to Shelter 15." Mac Adams said.

Lieutenant Cory bowed, "This way Doctor."

Kroller yelled over his shoulder, "Team12 grab your gear, this way."

Ben turned to 2nd Lt. Andropov. "Grab Blackpaw go relieve Archangel and have him join up with Nighthunter."

Andropov looked at him, "Sir won't that leave you exposed?"

Ben told him. "I have a squad with me. Get going."

Andropov saluted, "Yes Sir."

Blackpaw looked at his 2nd Lieutenant, "Don't worry Lieutenant the Skipper knows what he is doing."

Med 2 and 3 landed as did the rescue flight. Pathfinder was livid she wanted to launch an Alfa strike. They could see the mystery ship on the Class 6 probe.

"Captain Gracchus, I could hit them cloaked they wouldn't know what was hitting them!" She said.

Barbarossa shook his head, "Captain normally I would agree with Pathfinder. We might even have an advantage. They might think they got one of our flights when that yacht exploded. But we don't know the enemy's capabilities. If we launch an Alfa strike we could find ourselves without enough fighters and daggers to defend ourselves against an Alfa strike from the enemy."

Captain Gracchus looked at them. "If this was strictly a warship, I would go after them right now. However we are a research ship not a warship.

Yes, I know the EAQ has a battle cruiser under her outer hull. Still, we don't want to advertise that.

Keep a tight Combat Air Patrol around the ship and I'll have sensor control lay a series of cloaked sensor probes along approaches to both the ship and the system."

Gracchus hit his com unit, "Mr. Helios and Mr. Belows take us in. Lieutenant Gorez, notify Lieutenant Maxumus what has happened use Echo secure."

Beary looked at his com unit. "Understood, tell the Captain we will coordinate with Captain Maritinus."

"Spirit 6, to *Storm Cloud* return, to site Alfa 1 immediately."

Romanov nodded to her people. Who, sent out the necessary orders. "*Storm Cloud* to Spirit 6 understood."

Artemus walked up. "What do we have?"

"Trouble, we need to figure how we are going to deal with it." Beary said.

Ben walked over. "I just got a report from Archangel and Nighthunter things are bad on the other two planets also."

Beary nodded, "Pathfinder ran into rule fifty-three. They pulled a family and two servants off a space yacht. The crew was dead. They didn't find any traps on the ship. They didn't look on the outside. Luckily Cho picked up the power signal and everyone scattered and cloaked as it blew up."

Ben asked. "Did they land cloaked?"

"Yes, so there is a chance the enemy may think they destroyed the flight." Beary said.

Artemus smiled, since meeting Beary, him, and Ben had learned the seventy-five rules and lived to experience a few of them. "The Arcrilian Destroyer I finally pieced it together."

Beary corrected him. "That was rules sixteen, fifty-three, and sixty-five all wrapped in a nice neat package, but yes.

Romanov and the ladies should have managed to map the system and laid sensors. The EAQ is laying a net. So we should know where they are going to hit us from.

We just need to figure out how to ambush them."

Ben looked at Beary, "How can I help?"

Beary shrugged, "Defend the ship and the crew members on the planets. These bears are at their end Ben."

Ben nodded, "That goes without saying. But how do you want me to do it? Do we attack them or wait for them to hit us?"

Beary considered the situation. "We don't know what we are up against. So we are stuck reacting to them. Do you have a better idea how to deal with it?"

Ben thought, "No, I wish I did. With our cloaking ability we could put a team on a ship . . ., but getting them off. It would be almost a suicide mission."

Beary nodded, "A damaged ship, a planet, and a star base these are easy. But an operational warship, aren't so easy, not without better intelligence than we have."

Artemus looked at a map of the colonies, "Why didn't they land ground forces? If not here on one of the other planets; Kalian only has a population of thirty thousand bears it is the main planet. According to the Colonel, they can account for over twenty-eight thousand bears, of the population. The other two thousand live on remote farms. They have sent scouts out to contact them.

The other two planets Galian is a mining planet. It has a population of twenty-six hundred bears in four small towns, and a few farming and logging operations. Most of those ran with androids.

Falian is strictly agricultural maybe a thousand bears total perhaps less.

So why did they just do a bombardment of all three planets? Why not send in raiders?"

Beary nodded, "Ben why don't you go interview the good Colonel again. Have your lieutenants' talk to whoever is in charge on the other two planets and feed the information back to you. Find out what we are missing and join us on *Storm Cloud*. Romanov just got here."

Ben replied, "Alright Boss, by the way, do not worry, they haven't met us yet."

Romanov walked over, "Where do you want everyone?"

Beary thought, "How is the sensor net?"

"It will give us ten STU warning of an incoming raid. Red Talon is dropping a medical team on Falian. Then moving on to Galian then coming here. Three more cycles by my best estimation." Romanov said.

Beary and Artemus walked towards the *Storm Cloud* "Have the flights land, disperse, and cloak.

Romanov gave the necessary orders into her com unit.

Beary and Artemus walked into the *Storm Cloud*. Artemus turned to the crew as Beary sat down. "Alright ladies tell us what you found out."

Ensign Re stood up. "Sirs from what the probes are sending us the ship we are facing is a design we have never seen before. It is large possible a dreadnought in size with fighters. However there is one puzzling thing. The warp engines seem to be internal instead external. Lieutenant Maxumus this is a read out of their warp signal."

Beary looked at it. "Are you sure the engine is internal or is the aft section just one large shielded engine?"

Re looked at him, "I am not sure Sir. If that is the case . . . then this rear boom section is the engine and this front wing shaped section is the main body."

Beary nodded, "Then we need to determine what its capabilities could be."

Ensign Kay spoke up, "There seems to be launch tubs for the fighters, on two levels with twenty-five tubs on each level. The landing bays are on the back side lower level."

Artemus nodded, "So we are facing at least one hundred fighters."

Beary thought "Maybe a few less ten were destroyed here."

Romanov shook her head, "Let's assume they have spares say 10 to 20%."

Beary looked at her "Why?"

Romanov thought, "It is a raider. We haven't detected any support ships. So they expect losses. Where are they from? Where is their resupply point? You pointed out they didn't land a raiding party."

Ensign Reuben stamped her foot. "We are their resupply point if they can take us. What if they just recycle what they take or destroy?"

Just then Ben came in carrying a piece of metal, "Beary I thought you and Artemus should see this. It is off one of the fighter that was shot down."

Beary looked at the piece of metal it was black with a polished surface on the upper and lower sides. In between was a lattice of honey combed structures. "Do we know what part of the fighter this came from?"

Ben shrugged, "It was scattered over half a square KSMU. Left a long furrow when it hit then exploded. Two of my Marines found part of the cockpit the pilot was still in it. Doc is carefully removing it."

A sergeant came in "Lieutenant Maxumus, Doc Kroller wanted me to tell you he didn't have a lot of time to spend on the dead. The pilot was a feline type. Well feed and muscular, different from the earlier type, more predatory, and robust maybe sixty SWU heavier and two SMU taller."

Beary nodded, "Thank you Sergeant."

Romanov looked at Beary, Artemus, and Ben, "What does that tell us?"

Artemus frowned, "The other ship was a sacrificial lamb designed to test our capabilities. If they succeeded great, if not, even if they didn't get a message off, the enemy learns something."

"Romanov, send everything we have including an analysis of this piece of metal and the Doctors report to the *EAQ*. Captain Maritinus is taking over operational command on the planet. You are in charge of the air units here till we get back." Beary ordered.

Romanov looked at him and blinked "Yes Sir."

With that Beary and Artemus sprinted to their fighter and dagger and headed back to the *EAQ*. Kat sprinted to hers also.

She smiled at Beary, "You still need your wingbear, Sir, flight order six."

Beary nodded "Alright Kat even the Boss has to play by his own rules. We cover Spirit Blade 2."

"Yes Sir." Kat said.

On the *EAQ* the father from the *Day Traveler* was waking up. He saw a large creature bending over his little girl. It was gold in color with wings. He screamed.

Caesar came over, "It is alright you are on the *Empress Angelina's Quest*. We are a fleet research and survey ship. Your family is safe so is your maid, steward, and butler."

The bear looked at Caesar "What is that horrible creature doing to my daughter?"

Caesar shook his head, "Sir, Doctor Golden is a cub doctor and quite gifted. Your daughter was badly injured he is treating her injuries. He is a dragon from Andreas Prime and a member of my Clan and I believe my sixth cousin. So please do not call him names."

"I am George Cragon. I own the Dloper mine on Galian. The crew of the yacht, Captain Forest, Fred and young Tom . . ." Mr. Cragon started to ask.

"I am sorry they were all killed in the attack. The engineer and his assistant died trying to prevent the yacht's engines from exploding." Caesar said. "Your butler is very sick."

"Yes, Robert has Lymphoma a type of cancer. We were on our way back from Candaris XI, where he was receiving treatment from a Doctor Sebastian Dorel." Mr. Cragon said.

"That quack! He doesn't even have a medical license. He is wanted on Bearilia Prime for fraud!" Caesar exploded.

Mr. Cragon looked at him, "But the treatments have helped him. He told us that Robert was in remission."

Dr. Greenbrier came in, "He is not in remission, nor does he have Lymphoma. Never has had. He does have advanced Krovack's disease. The herbal medicine he was receiving masked the symptoms but did not cure them. If it had been Lymphoma even our dragon medicine at this advanced stage would not have been able to save him. Cancer is a disease that even we sometimes lose to. But Krovack's we can treat to a point it can be cured by Doctor Vantanus."

Mr. Cragon looked at the dragon. "Are you sure? Robert is very dear to me. He raised me more than my parents ever did."

Dr. Greenbrier smiled, "We have already started his treatments. But we must also treat his injuries and those I believe of his daughter your maid, Sally. The poor girl was very near death. She should recover in a week or two."

Dr. Frank Glacial, a squarely built Polarian, came in. "Mr. Cragon I am one of the two cub doctors working on your children. Dr. Golden is the other. Your son is awake and taking nourishment. He suffered a little oxygen deprivation and hypothermia. He is recovering. Your daughter suffered some flash burns. Dr. Golden has been healing these and her lungs, which also suffered some damage. I must tell you, dragon treatments also sometimes correct old injuries as a side effect. I just want you and your wife to be prepared and to help prepare your daughter, for her new world."

Mr. Cragon shook his head, "I don't understand?"

Dr. Greenbrier looked at the chart. "Oh I see. Caesar she was blind. The flash burn had burned her face and her eyes. Dr. Golden fixed the burn and regenerated the eyes and the damage to her optic nerve. Apparently she suffered from an older injury to the nerve."

Caesar nodded, "Did he wrap her eyes?"

"Yes, it will take a day or two for the new tissue to fully heal." Dr Glacial said.

Mr. Cragon was stunned, "He gave Tula her sight back?"

"Yes, Mr. Cragon." Caesar said.

"What about my wife?" Mr. Cragon asked "Is Lana alright?"

"She had some minor burns and also suffered some hyperthermia. She is recovering you can see her in about a cycle. You also need some more rest." Caesar said.

Mr. Cragon dropped his head. "Did you lose anyone saving us?"

Caesar thought, "We tried to tow your yacht in. It was rigged to explode when it was taken into tow after a specific time or distance. We're not sure."

Mr. Cragon started crying, "So that is why they attacked us. To turn us in to a Hazzax's Ram."

Caesar nodded, "Apparently. Perhaps it exploded prematurely. If it had gone off inside a ship it would have destroyed it. Do not let it concern you. It is our business to go into harm's way. Also your family is safe."

Beary, Artemus, and Kat arrived back at the *EAQ,* as it headed for Kalian.

Beary turned to Kat, "You and Mayotte get some food and rest, but be ready to go with a ten STU warning."

Kat looked at him, "Will be ready in five or less Boss."

Artemus replied, "Well I am going to need ten."

Beary responded, "He always was a little slow in the morning."

Kat smiled as her two Bosses walked away.

Akhiok and We walked up, "You two want to grab some food."

"Sure, but won't Cho mind We, you, having a meal with us, and not with your fiancé?" Mayotte asked.

"No, I already asked her to join us. I figured she could bring us up to date." We said.

Night Song whined just a little. However, Night Wind heard her and woke Pompey, "My Lady, Night Song has gone into seclusion, but she is crying."

Pompey got up. "It is alright. I will go to her. Go get Nikolaos."

Pompey went into the hiding room, that Erin uses and found Night Song. "It is alright my dear I am here to help."

Night Song growled then whimpered, "I am sorry my Lady it hurts."

"It is alright Night Song; I have been there with Erin. I have sent for Dr. Navarra, she will be here soon." Pompey said.

"I am here now my Lady. So we are having our pups tonight, yes." Dr. Navarra said with a smile. "Here let me examine you. Good, both pups are doing fine. Should not Nikolaos be here?"

"I am here Doctor." Nikolaos said from behind her.

The first pup that came out was a little female. She was pure white and very still. The doctor picked her up and stated rubbing her but the other pup started to come. "Nikolaos try and save her." Doctor Navarra said handing the small pup to Nikolaos.

Nikolaos took a small syringe and sucked out her nostrils. Then put a small puff of air into her little lungs and gently compressed her chest. He then gave her another breath he felt her chest. Yes there was a small beat. He then gentle bit her ear the young pup yelped and coughed a bunch of liquid out of her lungs. She then yipped again. Nikolaos put his finger near her mouth and she bit it. Nikolaos kissed her "You will live."

The little boy pup was born very healthy and immediately went to nurse.

Dr. Navarra reached for the little girl pup. She was expecting to receive a still born. Instead she found a live pup.

Nikolaos shrugged. "She had fluid in her lungs and nostrils. I cleared it."

Dr. Navarra scanned the pup. "She will need some tender care for a few days. Will you help Night Song Nikolaos?"

Nikolaos looked at the white pup, "Lady Night Song may she become my partner?"

Night Song looked at the white pup that had finally found a nipple and was eating her first meal. "Sir Nikolaos you saved her life. She is yours. You may name her if you wish."

Nikolaos bowed, "May she be Lady Ghost Wind, to honor the Prince and her father."

Night Wind stood with pride, "Thank you Sire Nikolaos. My Son will be Night Stalker to honor the one who saved his sister."

Nikolaos bowed, "You honor me, Sire."

Night Wind looked at Night Song, "May I enter my love?"

Night Song nodded, "Yes my mate, you may enter and greet your offspring."

Pompey came out and walked over to Sho-Sho, "The little white one is Ghost Wind a female. She had problems. The little black and gray one is Night Stalker. After the doctor leaves talk to the parents and see if you can bless the little pups."

Sho-Sho nodded, "Yes Aunt Pricilla."

Sho-Sho watched as the vet left. She then requested permission to enter. Night Song granted her permission.

Sho-Sho smiled at the two young pups. "Grow strong and intelligent and receive a dragon's blessing and love."

In the other room and around the ship, Ice Song and the other dragons felt a little power drain from them. Ice Song came in and asked to see the pups. She smiled at them.

"Sho-Sho may I talk with you?" Ice Song asked.

Sho-Sho nodded, "What is wrong Ice Song?"

"Did you bless the pups?" Ice Song asked.

"Yes Pompey asked me to." Sho-Sho said.

"Sho-Sho what words did you use? You drained power from me when you gave it." Ice Song said. "You have done it before, when you blessed Angelina and Octavious."

Sho-Sho looked at her. "What, but no dragon can take power from another?"

"My Princess you are wrong. Only the most powerful dragons can draw power to add to their blessings. But Sho-Sho even with the blessings we have received we should not be that powerful. I don't think I am." Ice Song said.

Sho-Sho sat down "What should I do?"

Ice Song shrugged, "I do not know. You should be careful. Such power is dangerous. Talk to Uncle Beary or my Father."

Erin stirred, "Sho-Sho it is ok. It only happens when you use the word love or you feel a strong feeling of love. I feel the power flow through us. It tingles."

"It doesn't hurt you, my love?" Sho-Sho asked.

Erin laughed, "Don't be silly my love. I am a Valkyrie. I am part of you, night, night."

Ice Song looked at Erin who had fallen back to sleep. "Is it hard to share yourself like that?"

Sho-Sho looked at her, "No, but we are just beginning to learn what we are capable of. Erin knew what the trigger was. I didn't, now I do. I will be more careful."

Dr. Greenbrier looked at Dr. Golden. "Did you feel that?"

"Yes, we gave a blessing or at least part of one. But who took the power from us. What dragon on board is so powerful they can draw power from other dragons at will?" Golden asked.

Greenbrier shook his head, "More important do they know they are doing it."

Other dragons were asking the same question of each other. None would have considered it was Shoshana.

Head Nurse Renee Apell called to Caesar, "Doctor Vantanus Team 1 is reporting from Falian."

"Thank you Nurse Apell, I'll be right there." Caesar responded.

He walked into the medical control center, and looked at the view screen; a young Surgeon looked back at him. "What do you have Dr. Hendrix?"

"Sir, several wounded are trickling in. Most are minor cases. The Marine medics had treated thirty cases of minor injuries before we got here. Their own doctors had treated some more severe cases. But they were low on supplies. We are assisting with some of the more critical cases. So far only seven hundred of the population has been accounted for. The Marines have sent out scouts and have reestablished the radio and video stations." Dr Hendrix reported.

"Alright Doctor if you need anything coordinate with the Marines and Nurse Apell." Caesar said.

"Yes, Sir team 1 out." Hendrix said.

The next to report was Doctor Janise Cooper from Galian.

"Caesar things here are a mess. The four towns were leveled. Most of the population made it to shelters. Their infrastructure was hit hard. Water pumping stations destroyed. Hospitals destroyed, only mine clinics survived. Only the Dloper mine was well stocked though.

Also there are a lot of damaged androids and robots. I am worried about reactivating them because of the potential of a virus or logic bomb." Cooper said.

"Alright, Janise, hold off take care of the bears. I'll see if I can get Teddy Maxumus and Rubin Jorgenson down there to take a look." Caesar said.

"Ok Caesar. Team 2 and 3 will take care of the rest. The Marines are trying to round everyone up. They say they can account for two thousand of the population." Cooper said.

Nurse Apell shook her head, "You should at least make her call you sir."

Caesar smiled, "Janise is a civilian. She doesn't understand military rank. She knows I am the chief surgeon to her that is enough. Also she is my friend. We both worked under Angelina. Next to Doctor Torrance she is one of the best Nero-surgeons Angelina ever trained."

Caesar looked at the situation board "How is Team 12 doing?"

"Team 4 and 5 just relieved them. Dr Kroller asked if he could see you, after he sees to his team." Apell reported.

"No problem, tell him I'll see him when he is ready." Caesar said.

"I told him to be here in less than a cycle or he could give his report to me or the night watch. Lieutenant, you have been on duty for sixteen cycles straight. You have a wife and you will not be sleeping here tonight." Apell said.

"Alright Renee, I get it the rules apply even to me." Caesar said.

Apell smiled, "Skipper you're one of the best doctors I have ever worked for. But you, like your friends push yourselves harder than you would push the bears under you. My job is to remind you that you don't have to do that."

Caesar sighed, "Thanks Renee, but remember you have put in just as many hours."

"No Skipper, I took a break and slept for five cycles, when I knew I had some dead time. Plus I have ten young nurses covering the control station and six on the ward. Like any good Marine I sleep when I can." Apell said with a smile.

About then Kroller came in and nodded to Captain Apell, "Sir, things on the planet was well organized. Still the enemy destroyed their hospitals and attacked their main infrastructure systems. If they hadn't had dedicated shelters it would have been worse. But the attacks themselves were not meant to be lethal. They wanted to inflict damage and they wanted to cause casualties . . . but they didn't want to kill their victims."

"Why, didn't you say they lost fighters?" Caesar asked.

"Ten they didn't care. They isolated them. They destroyed their means of communication, infrastructure, and hospitals. Nevertheless they didn't land troops. Not even on the less populated planets . . . That couldn't have resisted as well." Kroller said.

Caesar nodded, "Ok get some rest. Your team might be needed again."

"Oh Sir, they're feline. Except, they were different, from the bunch, that jumped you before. They were better feed and stronger built." Kroller said.

Caesar nodded, "Thanks, I'll pass it on."

Caesar started for his birth, but turned for Captain Gracchus office. Something Kroller said was bothering him. They purposely didn't kill any of the bears. They had intended to cripple them. Too set the population of the planets up for what? The attack on the *EAQ* couldn't have destroyed the ship, but it too, was designed to cripple . . . Caesar picked up his paces.

Beary and Artemus was in reporting to Captain Gracchus when Caesar barged in.

"They will land troops when they come back. They are planning to harvest the population for food or slaves." Caesar said.

Gracchus sat back in his chair. "I see my senior officers all think the same thing. Captain Maritinus just sent me the same message. So how will they hit?"

Beary looked at the map of the system, "They have at least one hundred fighters. Say three to five hundred raiders not more than that. It is a big ship. However, its engine is huge and takes up most of its back section. It is also inefficient. From what our probe is showing us. My best guess is that it has a maximum speed of warp 4. They have to know a task force is coming. They also probably know the nearest one is four days out."

Gracchus nodded, "So they hit us when?"

Artemus looked at Beary, "Tomorrow fighters will hit Kalian and Galian. They will land troops on Falian."

"Why, the small agricultural planet?" Commander Gracchus asked.

Beary responded, "It has the smallest population and no security force. Kalian proved they could fight. They destroyed ten fighters after the first wave attacked. Landing troops could be costly. Galian has a smaller population but it still might be able to resist.

But Falian the population was more spread out and is much smaller. Plus it has no organized militia."

"So how do you want to play it?" Captain Gracchus asked.

The staff of the *EAQ* continued their planning.

On the mysterious ship a feline, who resembled a black panther, smiled at his Captain, a large lion shaped feline, his huge mane standing out from his uniform. "The Bearilian ship is in orbit around Kalian. They have been sending down supplies to the planet."

The Captain looked at his intelligence officer, "The Gladiator ship what of it?"

The panther intelligence officer shrugged, "They were out matched. Their ship didn't have weaponry strong enough to penetrate the Bearilian ships shields. However, we knew that. Their purpose was to board the Bearilian ship and kill the Captain and other key members and to down load the virus. We know they succeeded in down loading the virus.

Unfortunately, the Captain of the gladiator's ship destroyed his ship too far away to damage the enemy ship."

The Captain waved his massive paw. "It doesn't matter. Just think of the panic that will be caused when we send the other half of the code and the virus attacks their systems. Especially when their life support shuts off and their air locks open. They will panic as they die. It will be glorious."

The intelligence officer nodded. Still he thought *what if something goes wrong*. "Captain, we should still show some caution. The Bearilians might pose a small threat."

The Captain smashed down his huge paw, "Nonsense they are no more than over grown rats. We are the predators. They are our prey. We shall hunt them down and smash their marrow. It will be glorious. Prepare the raiders for a feast tonight! We celebrate their victory. Then tomorrow we capture Falian and put the other two planets to the torch once again."

Rubin called up from Galian. "Pompey, tell the Captain that it was the same type of virus. If they would have rebooted the androids and robots they would have attacked the bears here on Galian. Teddy and I almost have it fixed. We are running a planet wide antivirus program through the control system which we isolated. Then we have it set up so that it will run as part of the boot up program. It will also prevent them from attacking the system again."

Pompey asked, "Are you sure Rubin?"

Rubin smirked, "Whoever wrote this virus was good Pompey, real good. However, Teddy and I are better. He, she, or it might be able to beat one of us but not both. Plus we had some help from Doctor Kanjorski from the Polanski Institute on Bearilia Prime. He was one of my professors. He makes Teddy and I look like kindergartens."

"Ok Rubin, just remember, a lot of what we do is classified." Pompey warned.

Rubin thought, "It is not a problem he works for your father –in –law."

Pompey nodded, "Alright get back here as fast as you can, both of you."

Jeanne asked, "Are they staying out of trouble Pricilla?"

Pompey shrugged, "Rubin is enjoying himself a little too much. I think Sire Jorgenson would not be pleased. How are you Commander?"

Jeanne sat down. "Tired, I was told to collect you it seems we are both late for an appointment with a good Doctor Golden. He is not pleased."

Pompey shook her head, "We are about to be attacked and he is worried about us being late for a prenatal exam?"

The Commander sighed, "Yes, and to quote my dear husband, while Lieutenant Maxumus doesn't work for him we do. So we better get our tails down there or he will have us carried down there."

Pompey laughed. "Well I guess we better go, shall we. Oh, they found a virus designed to make the androids attack the bears of Galian when they restarted them. They fixed it."

Jeanne replied, "I would expect nothing less."

They walked down to medical talking and laughing.

CHAPTER 5

Alfa Strike

B EARY AND ARTEMUS meet with Barbarossa and Pathfinder to discuss strategy. Ben had returned from Kalian and joined them along with Paladin.

It was decided that Paladin and Pathfinder would handle defense of the EAQ. While Artemus, would defend the planets along with the ladies from the *Storm Cloud*. Ben and 1st, 2nd, and 4th platoon would defend Falian. Artemus gave Ben six ROSES filled with air attack and ground attack missiles. The Mark 4 Death Hawk and Mark 8 Ground Attack missiles along with the mortars and other heavy equipment of 4th platoon, Ben felt would give him an edge. He also had the resources of the *White Fire* at his command.

Beary decided he would lead 1st squadron in with Kat acting as his Wingbear. Barbarossa and O'Haggerty would lead 2nd squadron. The time for the Alfa Strike was set for launch at 0630 Cycles. Daggers were rearmed and replaced the fighters that were on the planets.

That night Ben positioned his three platoons to protect the two main shelters on Falian. Only a small handful of bears that lived on Falian remained. Most had been evacuated to Kalian or the EAQ.

As preparations were made Beary and Artemus went to see their families.

Pompey smiled as Beary came in, "Do you have time to rest?"

"No, I need to get back to the hanger deck. I just wanted to kiss you and Erin before we head out." Beary said.

Pompey told him, "Don't worry, I doubt they know about our ships cloaking ability. They will be surprised when Rubin makes the EAQ wink out."

Beary shrugged, "A cloak has never worked on a large ship before. You sure Rubin can make it work on the EAQ?"

Pompey nodded, "He does, and if not it won't really matter the internal and external shield modifications will make a difference."

Beary swept her into his arms and kissed her, "You just make sure you stay safe."

Pompey leaned into his chest. "Don't worry Night Wind and Alexa will be with me. Jessica is going to stay close to Erin not that she needs to. Maryam and Sho-Sho would be enough. Nicholas is going to stay near Jessica. Ice Song and Andreios are going to protect little Agathag and Snow Flower. Plus Night Song will be near. She is taking care of her pups.

I am more worried about you."

Beary responded, "Don't be. I have Joshua as my WTO and a good wingbear. In fact since her crew is a spare. I think I am going to keep them, Katimai and Mayotte are a good team."

Pompey kissed him again, "When this is over invite them over for dinner, along with Joshua, Ben and maybe a few others. I should at least get to meet the new members of the unit."

Beary dropped his head "You know we could lose some . . ."

Pompey put her paw on his lips, "Yes, more the reason, I need to know them. The burden cannot be yours alone."

Next door Artemus kissed Snow Flower, "You sure you're going to be alright?"

Snow Flower nodded, "I would be better if you could lie in my arms tonight."

Artemus whispered, "When this is over . . . I am going to try and get the boss to let us take a day or two off.

Snow Flower kissed him, "I think Pompey would like that also. I know the children would love it."

Artemus went in and kissed his children.

Nikolaos promised to protect everyone as did the other two.

Artemus then smiled at Agathag. She reached up at him and "Squealed Daddy, I love you Daddy."

"I love you also Agathag. Obey Ice Song and your brother Andreios." Artemus said.

"O tay Daddy." Agathag whispered.

Artemus then turned to Ice Song. "A kiss my daughter."

Ice Song kissed him "I love you father Artemus."

"I love you Ice Song." Artemus said.

Beary went in and kissed Erin, "You mind Maryam and Sho-Sho and do as they tell you."

Erin nodded, "Yes Daddy, I will. Don't worry no harm will come to us. We are strong aren't we Sho-Sho?"

Sho-Sho grinned, "Yes my love, but you must mind your father."

Beary came over and kissed Sho-Sho, "I love you too Sho-Sho."

Sho-Sho heart swelled and a small amount of power flowed from her as she gave Beary an unintentional blessing. She smiled and said "προτεχτ."

Beary felt the blessing, "Sho-Sho what did you just do?"

Sho-Sho shrugged. "Nothing Uncle, I love you."

Artemus finished briefing his dagger teams. Then he turned the briefing over to Romanov.

Romanov looked at the dagger crews. "Gem Flight 3 will be controlled by the *EAQ* you will be flying CAP and under the Command of Lt. Pathfinder. The *Storm Cloud* will provide tactical control for Gem Flights 1 and 2. We will also help control fifteen Missile armed ROSES. Gem Flights will be on Echo.

We will also be providing telemetry for the Alfa Strike on Delta through the sensor and probe net.

All units are to remain cloaked unless Spirit Blade 2 or Spirit 6, orders otherwise."

Romanov then moved over to a projection of the system. "The *EAQ* is going to try and cloak then move to position XS. Gem Flight 1 will proceed to TS and patrol this section. While Gem flight 2 will proceed to FD and patrol this section.

We feel we will be facing at least one hundred enemy fighters plus drop ships. Our mission is the fighters. I know it will be tempting to try and take out the drop ships. But the fighters must be stopped first."

Beary stood up. "Valkyries listen up. If while we are out bound we see their attack inbound we will not. I repeat will not attack. Our job is to destroy their ship."

Ensign Franks said, "Sir, you mean we won't engage there attack force?"

Beary looked at him, "That is exactly what I mean. Our job is to destroy or at least incapacitate the mother ship. You will maintain radio silence and remain cloaked no matter what happens. Is that understood?"

All the pilots said "Yes Sir."

Beary looked at them. "Board your crafts. Send them to the Moons of Bantine."

Dr. Kroller and Team 12 were heading out of medical, when Nurse Blaze stopped him, "Dr. Kroller would you give this note to Captain Maritinus for me?"

Dr. Kroller looked at her, "If I get the opportunity Nurse Blaze."

"Thank you Doctor." Nurse Blaze said.

Dr. Kroller hurried on down to The *Compassions Hope* just as he arrived, Kat ran up.

"Dr. Kroller you and Team 12 are going to Falian, are you not?" Kat asked.

Dr. Kroller nodded.

"Please Dr. Kroller; give this note to Captain Maritinus for me. Tell him I will protect Lieutenant Maxumus and ask him to stay safe for me." Kat said. As she ran off to board her fighter.

One of his sergeants came out, "What gives Skipper?"

"Just a couple of letters for Captain Maritinus, I was asked to give them to him." Kroller said.

The sergeant whistled, "From two different Polarian females?"

Kroller smiled, "Yep."

"I feel sorry for him. He will have an easier time with the enemy than two females of his race." The sergeant said as he climbed on board.

On Falian, Ben was talking to his First Sergeant. "Chief Deerstalker, I want you to handle things here at the command post. I am going to go forward and check on the defenses."

Deerstalker looked at him, "Skipper, you should stay here."

Ben smiled, "I can't see what is happening from here Chief. Besides you're as good a tactician as any of us. I'll take Private Halberd and Sergeant Whitepaw with me. Halberd, grab your com equipment."

Halberd looked at him, "Yes Skipper."

Sergeant Whitepaw grabbed a SARG (Squad Automatic Rail Gun). "Don't worry First Sargent. I'll take care of the Skipper."

Ben grabbed a case filled with claymores and a phaser rifle, "Let's go Marines."

The three took off on a trot towards 1st platoons position.

Deerstalker looked at Lt. Jg. Mountain. "Sir, have one of your bears keep track of the Skipper for me."

"No problem First, We are here to support you." Dan Mountain said with a smile.

Ben and the two Marines traveled for half a cycle before they reached 1st Platoons position. 2nd LT. Archangel was looking over his Marines' fighting positions as was Gunny Nighthunter.

Ben slipped into 1st Platoon's headquarters position; Sergeant Travis was manning the plot. "How is it going sergeant?"

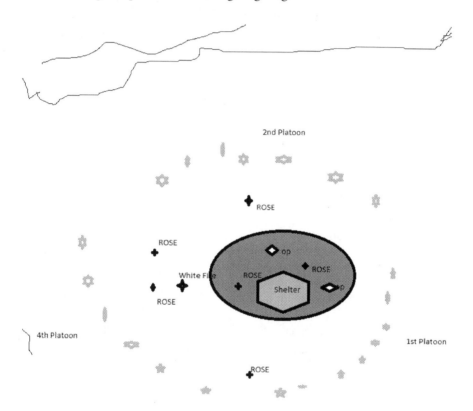

"Hi Skipper. The LT. and Gunny our out checking the fighting positions. We are in good shape here. The shelter is in that hill behind us. We have two fire teams with two ROSE hidden on top. 2nd Platoon is on the far side, with a ROSE behind. 4th Platoon is on our right. We have the hill and the shelter surrounded and fighting positions prepared so we can fall back on the hill." Sergeant Travis said.

Ben looked at the map. "We have two large gaps."

The Sergeant nodded. "Yes Sir. Those are covered by claymores and sensors. The terrain is steep and inhospitable. They could attack through there. However, we could shift Marines over there and block their advance or hit them with the ROSES. OP 1 is looking straight down this one and OP 2 is looking straight down this other one."

Ben nodded "Ok, tell everyone to use land lines only."

"Yes, Skipper." just then the land line rang the Sergeant answered it. "Yes First Sargent, he is here. Alright I'll tell him. Skipper, Dr. Kroller is about to land. He says he has a couple of messages for you."

Ben nodded. "Alright Sgt. Travis, tell Archangel I'll be back. Let's go you two."

Ben, Whitepaw, and Halberd took off on a trot towards the shelter where the *Compassions Hope* was going to land.

Dr. Kroller instructed his team to establish their field hospital inside the shelter and to pull the dagger inside the large cam shell doors. He then stepped outside and waved at Ben.

"Good to see you Captain Maritinus, we'll be set up in half a cycle. I noticed the civilians are all armed." Kroller said.

Ben shrugged, "If they get past my Marines and get inside the shelter, I wanted to at least give the civilians a chance to fight back. The ones that stayed behind are frontiers' bears. Most have some military experience and a whole lot of life experience."

Kroller nodded, "By the way I have a couple of letters for you, here."

Ben looked at them, "Who are they from?"

Kroller smiled. "Nurse Blaze and Ensign Katimai both seem sweet on you. Kat said to tell you she would protect Lieutenant Maxumus and asked that you stay safe."

Ben shook his head. "I don't need this distraction right now."

Sergeant Whitepaw smiled at Halberd. "Our Captain has a weakness."

Halberd looked at him, "What?"

"Females disconcert him." Whitepaw laughed.

Ben thought "Stay in contact with my First, I'll be on the line."

Ben then trotted over to the 4th's command post. Lt. Dancer was double checking his range estimates to known landmarks.

Ben looked at him "How is it going?"

Dancer looked at him and smiled, "We are ready Skipper. I just was triple checking my figures. I can hit them. Are you sure they will take the bait?"

Ben thought, and looked at one of the transmitter towers half a KSMU from their front line. "Yes they will take the bait and we will be facing a force three to four times our strength."

Dance shrugged, "It's alright Skipper. We are an MSD unit we are supposed to be out numbered."

Ben nodded, "Just make sure your Marines wear their armor. I don't care how hot it gets."

"Understood Skipper, they know this Dragon Armor is a lot better than the old stuff." Dancer said.

"Alright, I am heading over to 2nd platoon stay loose." Ben said.

Blackpaw saw him coming over the rise, "Skipper over this way."

Ben veered over. "Hi, Gunny, what's up?"

Blackpaw replied. "This is a safer route Skipper. That ground over there is loose, plus we have claymores in there. They should be safe but no point in taking any chances."

Ben nodded, "It would be embarrassing to be blown up by one of our own mines."

Ben looked at Blackpaw, "How is it going Gunny?"

Blackpaw responded, "My Marines are a bit nervous Skipper. So is the LT. but that's normal."

Ben nodded, "Ok let's get over there. So I can talk to Andropov."

Blackpaw nodded, "He'll be fine Skipper."

Ben smiled both Blackpaw and Nighthunter had been running interference for their platoon leaders. Trying to teach and move them in the right direction. Yet here he was just as young as they were and he was the Company Commander and was supposed to know it all.

"Do you need anything?" Ben asked.

"No Skipper, we're set as far as supplies are concern. My Marines will stop them." Blackpaw said.

They arrived at the Command Post. Andropov looked relieved. "Good to see you Captain. Do you know what we will be facing?"

Ben shook his head. "Best guess is two hundred to four hundred Raiders plus whatever fighters get through to us."

Andropov looked almost ill. "Sir, would you care to look over my fire plan?"

Ben shook his head, "No, Andropov you and Gunny Blackpaw I know went over it probable a dozen times. I am not here to second guess you.

I just wanted to make sure everyone has on their body armor and that the shield generators are on standby."

Andropov nodded, "Yes Sir, As soon as we get the word we can bring them on line."

"Good," Ben placed his paw on Andropov's shoulder, "You're doing a great job Sergei, just keep trusting Blackpaw and your other NCOs. You have done your job text book perfect."

"Yes Sir, but will it be good enough." Andropov asked.

Ben shrugged. "That is in the hands of Providence. All we can do is prepare, then do our best, and trust in the Creator of the Universe."

Andropov looked at the young Polarian Captain. *Was that his secret? He just put everything in the hands of Providence.* "Yes Skipper."

Ben waved at his two Marines and headed up the hill.

Andropov turned to Blackpaw. "He seems so calm."

Blackpaw answered, "He is LT. where he comes from death is just part of everyday life. The things they hunt for food hunt them for food. Every day is a hunt where life and death is on the line. To him combat is just another hunt."

"Spirit 6 to Red Talon Alfa Strike launching."

"Red Talon Control to all Valkyrie Creator's speed."

Beary and Kat launch followed by both First and Second Squadrons.

Joshua light signaled Ensign Tennyson "First Squadron will hit the engine section Second Squadron try and hit launch bays and weapon areas."

Tennyson signaled back. "Message understood, good hunting, good luck, and Creator's blessings."

With that the two squadrons cloaked and split up and went to warp.

"Spirit Blade 2 to all Gem Flights cloak and launch. Venom 8, take care of the EAQ."

Venom 8 to Spirit Blade 2, try and stay safe boss. Gem 2; watch your back out there a good exec is hard to find."

"Gem 2 to Venom 8 so are good bosses."

"Red Talon to Gem Flights, clear to launch. Creators speed."

With Beary in the Ghost, and Kat in Valkyrie 38 forming the point of the spear Alfa, Bravo, Charlie, and Delta flights formed up on either side.

Barbarossa and O'Haggerty formed the point of the spear for second squadron with Echo, Foxtrot, Golf, and Hotel flights forming up on them.

The two squadrons separated by twenty KSMU, cloaked, and flying under radio silence, were linked by data streams that were being feed to them through an up link from the *Storm Cloud*.

As they got within thirty thousand KSMU of the mystery spacecraft Joshua's threat receiver started going off.

"Boss we have inbound fighters. It looks like around one hundred twenty five fighters and twenty larger ships." Joshua reported.

Beary nodded, "Joshua down loaded the information to the link and send it to the *Storm Cloud*. Have them remind everyone to maintain radio silence and to let them pass. They are not our target."

"Roger Boss. Message sent on sensor link." Joshua said.

On the *Storm Cloud*, Ensign Reuben picked up the message and relayed it to the other fighters then to the Gem Flights, the EAQ, and the Marines.

Romanov smiled, "Alright Ladies, Ensign Akhiok gave us a good warning. I want tracking and I want to know when they get within range. We get the honor of firing the first shot."

Aboard one of the jump ships a leopard looking Centurion looked up from his instruments "Commander, I picked up an intermittent blip on my screen."

The Commander, a large lion looking creature, came over and looked, "I see nothing. It was probable a glitch or our own reflection off one of these small asteroids."

The Centurion thought again. "Yes Commander perhaps."

"Come on we were told that these bears are not all that advanced. Did you see the plans for their research vessel? It only proves they are lazy and creatures who value comfort. Did we not crush one of their warships?" The Commander said.

"Yes, Commander we did." The Centurion agreed. Then he thought *a small scout frigate.*

Beary maneuvered his squadron away from the track of the inbound raid, as did Barbarossa with Second Squadron. It was hard even for them not to engage the inbound force. They were Artemus' and Pathfinder's problem not theirs. Their target was the massive warship now fifteen thousand KSMU away and closing.

Storm Cloud feed the shield frequencies directly into their missiles shield emitters. On each of the fighters targeting systems were turned to standby as they bore in on the enemy ship.

Beary watched as the distance dropped away. Even with their cloaking ability he expected to be discovered at any time or to start picking up the enemy's combat patrol.

However, the enemy was so sure that the EAQ would be no threat. They had sent all there fighters, to attack her and the planets.

The enemy strike force hit the first marker and started splitting up. The twenty large ships and twenty five fighters separated and headed for Falian. The other one hundred peeled off and headed for the EAQ and the other two planets.

Romanov smiled, "Send Act 1 commencing. Empty ROSES 8, 9, and 10, hold our missiles in reserve."

Ensign Reuben smiled, "Missiles away."

One hundred eight Mark 4's missiles leaped from their launchers on the ROSES. The ROSES then turned and headed back to Kalian.

The missiles were programed to uncloak when they were within one hundred SMU.

The Feline pilots didn't have time to react. Their threat receiver went off as the missiles started to arrive. Each fighter and drop ship had two missiles targeted against it. All but two of the drop ships had three missiles targeted at it.

The Mark 4's hit. Some were defeated by the fighters' shields and the shields and armor of the drop ships. Still when it was done five fighters were destroyed and ten suffered some damage. One drop ship was drifting. Its pilot compartment ripped open to space and a large hole in its troop compartment. Another was leaking plasma from a damaged engine. Still they proceed on towards Falian.

Romanov swore under her breath. "Tell the flights that the Mark 4's didn't stop them. It's going to take more than three missiles per fighter."

Reuben retargeted her last thirty six missiles. She targeted five on the wounded drop ship, four on seven of the wounded fighters, and three on an eighth. "Launching, our second missile strike on the attacking force Commander, thirty six missiles away."

Romanov nodded, "Understood. We are moving to the rearming point."

The thirty six missiles bore in on the damaged fighters and drop ship. This time the missiles stayed cloaked all the way in. The first fighter was just ripped apart as the Mark 4's slammed through its weakened shields and battered armor. Soon seven more fighters were either just gone or were drifting lifeless in space.

The drop ship was the last to die. The five missiles hit it near its weakened rear side shield near its leaking plasma engine. The warhead from one of the missiles ignited the plasma. The resulting explosion disintegrated the drop ship in a blue haze.

The Panther Intelligence Officer looked at the message from the strike commanded. "Commander our fighters and drop ships have been attacked. Two drop ships and thirteen fighters have been destroyed by an unknown enemy force."

The Lion Ships Captain slammed his massive paw on his command chair. "Tell them to send the rest of the code now!"

Ruben looked up from his scope. "They are sending a numeric signal. That is our cue Captain Gracchus."

Gracchus smiled, "If this works Ruben, you'll be worth your keep. Mr. Belows cloak the ship.

Mr. Helios, if it works take us to warp towards the enemy ship. No point, in letting Lt. Maxumus and his pilots have all the fun."

All of a sudden the EAQ winked off the enemy sensors and scanners. It did it in such a fashion that it looked like it exploded or disintegrated.

The Panther looked up from his com Unit. "Captain our units report the code was sent and the enemy's research ship was destroyed."

The Lion Captain smirked "The code worked to well."

That is when the first alarms went off on his ship.

Beary and Kat launched first, followed, by the rest of first squadron. They each carried eight, Mark 4's on each wing. These they launched on the rear warp engine of the Feline ship. Three hundred twenty four missiles left their launchers cloaked and with shield emitters tuned to the Feline's shield frequency.

About the same time second squadron launched on the main body of the Feline ship. Again Barbarossa and O'Haggerty launched first, with the rest of the squadron ripple firing after them. Another three hundred twenty four missiles streaked at the Feline warship.

The first missiles struck the engine section of the Feline warship. Despite the shield emitters over one hundred twenty of the missiles

CHARLES & IRENE NICKERSON

were stopped by the shields. The armor plating defeated another two hundred missiles although the armor was severely damaged in places it held. Only four missiles burned through and did minor damage to the warp cells.

The results on the battle section of the ship were similar. Almost half of the missiles exploded on or inside the shield. The rest were stopped by the armor plating. Except, two missiles exploded inside empty launch bays.

Alarms were going off on the bridge of the Feline Warship. The Captain roared at his bridge crew "Turn off those alarms and find the enemy!"

That is when the second wave of missiles arrived. This time the missiles burned through the weakened shields only sixty four were stopped by the shields around the engines. The armor plating still stopped over two hundred of the Mark 4's but this time some of the armor plating was blown off into space. Sixty, Mark 4's burned into what proved to be the actual warp nacelles. They managed to damage two of the four nacelles that were held inside the structure at the back of the enemy's warship.

At the front of the ship the missiles defeated the weakened shields better but still smashed themselves against the thick armor plating. Only twenty scored any real damage knocking out a couple small weapons areas and two more, empty launch bays.

Beary was dreading the next order. He realized the Mark 4's had done very little damage and was sure the Mark 10 bombs would do even less. He was also sure his 40 SUBSMU rail guns weren't going to do much damage either.

That's when the *EAQ* materialized not far away.

"Red Talon, to all units, break off contact, return to TS and aid Spirit Blade 2."

"Spirit 6 to all units, break, break."

With that the Valkyrie fighters peeled off and went to warp.

Pathfinder and her flight of Purple Daggers had been left behind by Captain Gracchus. She decided to join the *Storm Cloud*.

Near Galian, Artemus was waiting with his five daggers, and five ROSES. Fifty enemy fighters started their run on the planet. Artemus smiled and launched a full barrage from the five ROSES and commanded them to land on the surface of Galian.

One hundred eighty missiles raced at the incoming fifty fighters. Artemus however had only targeted twenty five of the fighters that meant that at least six missiles were targeted on those fighters.

The Feline fighters' threat indicators went off just as the Mark 4's arrived. Soon fighters started dying. Even with their armor. Six, Mark 4's proved too much for the Feline fighters. Still only twenty were destroyed. Four suffered severe damage. One was only moderately damaged.

Still, the thirty remaining fighter, speed towards Galian. The Feline Squadron Commander had survived the first missile strike. He had his surviving fighters spread out. The undamaged ones speed up. Leaving, the five damaged fighters to defend, themselves.

Artemus looked at the information he was receiving from *Storm Cloud,* from all the probes, and sensors. "Gem Flight 1 launch Alfa package. We take out the damaged fighters; we'll let the others stop the healthy ones."

We smiled, "I have targeted six missiles on the healthiest of the stragglers and three on each of the others. Also guns are hot. Launching on targets; Tango 20, Tango 30, Tango 40, Tango 15, and Tango 7."

Eighteen missiles speed towards the damaged Feline fighters while ninety missiles reached out towards the other thirty again only fifteen were actually targeted.

The damaged fighters started dying first as the missiles started arriving. Soon all five were either disintegrated or left drifting dead in space.

The other thirty started to be struck. Again fighters started to be damaged or destroyed by the missile volley that slammed into them. When it was over ten fighters were destroyed. Three were showing some battle damage. Still twenty fighters pressed on towards Galian.

The Strike Commander was struggling to control his damaged fighter. He tried to report in, but his com equipment was out. He cursed as he saw another volley of missiles approach his remaining squadron's fighters.

One hundred eight Mark 4's reached out towards the remaining twenty fighters. Two of the damaged fighters seem to die almost immediately. The Squadron Commander just barely managed to avoid the two missiles that come towards him. Other fighters started exploding. It was all over in just a matter of a few SUBSTU. When it was over nine fighters still remained.

The Squadron Commander tried to signal the remaining fighters, but he couldn't raise them. That's when he saw the strange crafts materialize among the survivors. Three of his fighters died before anyone could react, as phasers smashed through their weakened shields and armor. Three of his fighters turned to try and run back to their ship. The other three reached the edge of the planet. Only to be met by a shower of missiles that blotted them out of the atmosphere.

The Squadron Commander found himself surrounded by three of the strange crafts. That is when he heard. "Feline Pilot, this is Lieutenant Savato Artemus of The Bearilian Federation you have no hope of escape. Surrender or die!"

The Lion did the only thing he could do. He fired his cannon.

The shell exploded against the *Star of Vardar's* shield.

We fired his Gatling phaser, as did the other two daggers. The Feline fighter started to be torn apart, as the phasers ripped it and the squadron commander apart.

While this was going on Gem Flight 2 was tangling with the other squadron of Feline fighters near Kalian.

Muzorewa had positioned her ROSES with each of her daggers. When she detected the fifty fighters coming in and heard that it took at least five missiles to kill a single fighter she decided on two massive volleys. They targeted the first twenty five fighters. One hundred ninety eight missiles reached out at the Feline Second Squadron.

The Second Squadron's Commander a nervous Leopard type heard a garbled transmission from the first squadron and the raider group about missile attacks when the fighter next to him exploded.

He looked back just in time to see the first two missiles explode against his shield. Then much to his horror the next three passed through and tore into his ship. He tried to scream as his fighter disintegrated around him. When it was over twenty fighters were either totally gone or drifting dead in space. Five others were showing some damage.

This squadron was in total disarray. Not only was the Squadron Commander killed in this first strike. So were the Executive Officer and the two Flight Commanders, along with several senior and experienced pilots.

Without leadership, the survivors broke formation and headed in several directions.

Muzo smiled and directed her second strike. One hundred ninety eight more missiles reached out. The first to die were the previously damaged fighters. In the end only fifteen more were totally destroyed including those five that had been damaged. The other fifteen warped out of the system heading back to their mother ship.

Pathfinder had reported her situation to Romanov who directed her to Falian immediately. It was Romanov's hope that Pathfinder might be able to take some of the heat off of the Marines.

Pathfinder and Gem Flight 3 arrived just as the twelve fighters and eighteen Drop Ships reached the outer Atmosphere of Falian.

"Venom 8 to all GEM 3 units, take them down."

Three hundred ninety six missiles launched from the six Purple Daggers and five ROSES towards the thirty enemy ships. While the Daggers and ROSES were cloaked Pathfinder wanted the enemy to see the missiles. They reacted just as she thought they would. The fighters who were in the lead fell back to try and deal with the threat.

A few launch their own missiles intercepting about forty of the incoming missiles. Still three hundred fifty six missiles fell on the twelve remaining fighters and the last two drop ships that were just entering the atmosphere. With over twenty five missiles targeted against each ship the fighters were quickly blotted from space. The two drop ships were sent spinning through the upper atmosphere like two burning meteorites.

On the planet Ben steadied his Marines. A few of the dragon Civil Engineers had joined them and had helped reinforce some of the fighting positions. They were now helping to protect the Medics of Team 12.

Ben looked at Halberd, "Let everyone know that they are coming through the atmosphere now."

Private Halberd nodded, and sent the coded message. He looked a little green.

Ben smiled, "It is ok to be scared Son, it shows good since. They are dangerous prey and should not be underestimated. However, you are also dangerous and well trained. You will do well."

The Private looked at his Captain who was watching the sky. "Thank you Skipper."

Sergeant Whitepaw whispered, "Skipper, if you don't mind could you not show yourself like that."

Ben dropped down, "No point in giving one of their pilots an easy shot."

Soon sixteen drop ships could be seen heading towards the three transmitter towers and the dummy defensive positions. That was set up around them.

Ben picked up the land line, "Target the drop ships. Fire the Mark 4's."

Dan Mountain smiled, as he targeted the sixteen drop ships with ninety, Mark 4's. The missiles launched cloaked and headed for the drop ships.

On the first drop ship the Raider Commander gave the order to open the bay doors to drop the deployment sled. This freed the drop ship to become an attack craft.

Just as the sled released the missiles arrived. The missiles missed the first sled, but passed into the interior of the first drop ship. They exploded killing its gun crews and knocking out its engines. The Raiders Commander ejected as the first drop ship spun into the ground and exploded.

Two of the sleds were hit as they dropped free. The Raiders on board were blown off. A few survived and floated to the ground on emergency parachutes.

One drop ship was hit in its flight deck and crashed into the ground. Three of the crew and ten of the raiders escaped, before it exploded in a ball of flames.

All the drop ships suffered damage. A few were unable discharge their raiders so they landed. The others also landed to supply covering fire. Only six still had main guns that worked these they turned on the first communications tower and its defense's. They opened up. Soon shells started falling all around the tower.

The Feline Commander grimaced as he nursed a broken arm. "Captain, gather up your Raiders and the Survivors from 8, 10, and 5 join them to your company."

The Jaguar Captain saluted and bounded off. He found the ten Raiders from 5 and the three crew members. He pressed them into service as Raiders. He had them follow him. He found two survivors from 8, and six from 10. All the rest were dead. Yet he now had a force of forty-one Raiders under his command.

Two of the drop ships, that were shelling the communication tower, still had their Raiders on board. The drop ship's doors had been jammed by the Mark 4's. The aft doors were also warped by damage to the armor plating.

Dan targeted the six drop ships, with the main guns, and launched ninety, Mark 8 Ground Attack Missiles, at them. Fifteen missiles fell on each of the six drop ships. Three exploded almost at the same time. Another had its main gun blown off by three missiles. While the rest ripped off its wings and left it smoldering.

The Raiders, trapped on the other two, could hear the explosions of the first missiles, which landed near their drop ship. They started working harder to get out. Then a missile hit, ripping the end off, one of the drop ships. It killed six Raiders as the others poured out. Three more were killed as a missile exploded near them. Still eleven managed to escape before the drop ship exploded.

On the other drop ship, the missiles tore through the top of the Drop Ship. It killed the crew and killed five of the Raiders. The others finally escaped out a hole in the side. The fifteen survivors ran for a rocky ravine and started climbing. The lead Raider didn't see the trip wire. All of a sudden ten canisters popped up out of the rocks and exploded. One hundred thousand small round balls pierced the air. The Raiders were caught in the middle of the canisters and were ripped apart. When it was over all fifteen were dead.

The Panther Raider Commander snarled he had started out with twenty drop ships and four hundred Raiders. His drop ships were burning, badly damaged or gone. He had also lost half of his attacking force.

"Captains gather your troops and attack!" The Commander roared.

The Jaguar Captain and his forty-one Raiders fell on the first tower's defenses. Only to find them empty.

A Lion Captain with thirty four Raiders fell on the second tower's defenses. He also found them empty.

The leopard Captain leading two groups of raiders also found the Third tower's defenses empty.

The other five groups of raiders were spread out in an arch with two groups in support of the Lion's and Leopard's forces and one with the Jaguar's.

Ben looked through his field glasses and whispered now.

As if on cue Lt. Jg. Dan Mountain and 2nd Lt. Dancer launched their attacks.

The eighteen Mark 8's exited the left missile launcher of the *White Fire* and flew in three different directions. He had six missiles targeted at each of the tower locations.

Lt. Dancer also had his mortar crews open up. The explosives shells started falling among the feline Raiders.

The Panther Commander screamed, as he saw his Raiders being torn apart. He ordered them to withdraw and regroup.

The feline Raiders orderly withdrew from the towers. They fell back to beyond their drop ships.

Ben could see the mangled bodies of several Raiders around the fake defenses of the towers. He was also amazed by how orderly they withdrew. "They didn't panic. Spread the word they are going to be coming. These are professional troops. Battle hardened, don't give them a chance. They won't give any of you one." Ben said as he grabbed his gear and headed for 1st platoon.

The Jaguar Captain was angry. He looked at his surviving Raiders. A few were wounded but those still alive could still fight. He had only lost fifteen Raiders in the attack. He gathered up his twenty six survivors.

A leopard lieutenant staggered over "Sir, my captain is dead, along with seven of my raiders."

The Jaguar nodded "Join your Raiders with mine, Lieutenant. Have them dig in, till the Commander decides our next move."

The Lieutenant saluted and moved off.

Two Raiders carried the body of their Lion Captain back to the rally point. He had died half way back. They had refused to leave him. Twelve of their comrades lay dead in the trap, which had been set for them.

A Lynx Captain came over, "After you see to him, join your Raiders with my survivors."

The NCO looked up. "Yes Captain, we have twenty two Raiders."

The Lynx nodded. "We have another thirty from the other two units. The other Captain was also killed."

The Leopard Captain looked at his mangled arm or at least what was left of it, but he was one of the lucky ones, he was still alive. He smiled. It appeared he would stay that way for at least a few time units. He had started out with forty raiders, now he had twenty eight left.

He was the only officer still alive. The other two unites had lost their captains, lieutenants, and almost eighteen Raiders. That left twenty two raiders to join his command.

The Panther Commander looked at the three captains and the one lieutenant. "Where are the other officers?"

The Leopard shrugged. "Dead, I imagine we will be joining them soon."

The Leopard Lieutenant looked at him, "But, the air wing and the *Pride's Home!*"

The Panther Commander shook his head, "The air wing is gone at least I cannot contact them. The *Pride's Home* is under attack by unknown forces."

The Jaguar looked at the Commander, "I figure our enemy has to be around that hill we landed around."

The Panther nodded, "It is the only defensible position. How many do we have left?"

The Lynx answered. "1st has thirty nine, 2nd has an even fifty, and I have fifty two Raiders."

The Panther nodded, "Transfer one of your Raiders over to 1st to give him an even forty. I will join him in his attack. We will hit from the north while you hit from the west and 2nd hits from the East. We will attack in two time lengths."

Archangel was getting nervous. "Sir, what do you thing they are waiting for?"

Ben sat down. He took out a small pocket knife, grabbed a stick, and started carving it. "Gabriel, you need to relax and calm down. Stay vigilant, but relax. You cannot control what the enemy will do next. We have executed our plan effectively. It is now their move. They are out of range of our mortars at the moment. When they come they will hit fast. Speed is their only ally at this time."

Nighthunter came in, "Skipper the out post reports movement. They have figured out where we are."

Ben nodded, "Turn on overhead shields. Just in case they have anything left that can lob shells. I wish we could have set a barrier shield."

Nighthunter shook his head, "Skipper a friend of mine lost Marines to one of those during a fire fight. We'll trust our armor and take the risk."

Ben sighed, "Ok Gunny, tell everyone to stay sharp. Make sure they stay hydrated."

"Don't worry Skipper. My NCOs' and I have been kicking tail." Nighthunter said.

Ben looked at the figure he was carving, "They are trapped and wounded. They, by now, know that their air wing is gone. We destroyed their drop ships. They know they have nothing to lose, because they are already dead. All they have is a desire to kill as many of us as they can before they die. They will show no mercy. Make sure our bears understand."

Nighthunter nodded, "I'll pass it on Skipper." With that he left.

Archangel looked at him, "Sir, are you worried . . ."

Ben smiled, "Gabriel you are a good platoon leader. I am here because my gut tells me this is where I should be. I might take off and head over to another point, if my gut tells me to. Here Beary says they are an intelligent creature." Ben handed him a carved Unicorn Whale. With that he walked out and found a fox hole on the line. Private Halberd and Sgt. Whitepaw jumped in after him.

Sgt. Whitepaw set up his weapon. As Halberd insured his land line was working. He then took up his phaser rifle.

Sgt. Whitepaw looked at his Captain, "Skipper not that I am complaining but should you be this close to the line."

Ben smiled, as he looked through his field glasses. "We could try, and get a closer look Sergeant."

Whitepaw laughed, "Skipper, I am willing. However, I think the kid might faint."

Halberd gulped, "No Skipper. I'll go wherever you go . . ."

Ben smiled, "I think we better wait. I think they are coming."

With a massive roar, the Raiders launched their attack. The Marines were fast to respond. Lt. Dancer's mortars started launching. However, the Raiders were coming faster than the shells could fall. Only a few in each group were killed by the barrage.

The Marines started firing from their prepared positions. Still the Raiders kept coming. Soon they hit the lines.

Ben and Whitepaw shot one, as he dove into their fox hole. That is when Ben saw one of his young marines go down, with a blow to his head. Ben jumped out of the fox hole and tackled the large lion Raider, who was preparing to shoot the Marine again.

The Lion lost his weapon. He recovered and pulled his knife. Ben pulled his. The Lion swung a massive paw and caught Ben across the face. The lion started to move in, when Ben hit him square in the nose, with a jab of his own, knocking the lion back.

Ben told him, "You'll have to do better, than that little swat."

The lion roared and leaped at Ben. Ben pushed his knife deep into the Lion's chest and twisted it. The Lion Raider stiffened and drove his knife in to Ben's arm.

A Jaguar Raider fired. His slug hit Ben in the back. The blow of the slug knocked the air out of his lungs and threw him to the ground.

Sgt. Whitepaw fired a sustained burst cutting the Jaguar in half.

Ten Raiders had run right pass the Marine positions. They headed for the position of Team 12. As they neared it the Dragoons rose up. The feline Raiders had never seen dragons before. Three of their numbers were in gulfed in flame. Then the dragons were among them. In a matter of moment the remaining seven were dead. Two of the Dragoons were bleeding, from minor wounds.

Private Halberd helped Ben up. "It is alright private. I am alive." Ben said.

"Yes Sir. But you're bleeding. Besides, the fighting is over here." Halberd said.

Sgt. Whitepaw came over. "Skipper, ah heck, medic over here."

The medic came over. He bandaged the knife wound, and then removed the Dragon Armor gentle. "Get a gurney over here now! Captain, don't move till I can get you laid down. You have a penetrator in your back, near your spine. If you hadn't been wearing the Dragon Armor . . . you would have been dead. As it is if you move wrong you could be crippled for life."

Ben nodded, "Alright how is Private Harpeth?"

The Medic shook his head. "Sir he is bad. It is a nasty head wound . . . I just don't know."

Ben looked out at the carnage a Leopard officer, who was missing the lower part of his left arm, was laying just a few SMU away. A hole drilled just above his left eye, where a large caliber rail gun rifle slug had passed through his brain. "How many did we lose?"

The medic shook his head, "We have over twenty wounded Sir. Some are very critical. Some like the private might not make it, but most will. You need to lie on your stomach and not move Sir. Ok let's go."

At the field hospital Doctor Kroller was working feverously stabilizing the wounded. He looked at private Harpeth and moved over to Ben.

Ben looked at him. "I'll keep. Work on the kid."

Kroller shook his head, "He is a loss cause. I can't save him. He isn't strong enough and I don't have the time."

Ben looked at him, "Doctor Kroller he is one of my Marines. Get a dragon, have them, help you, and you try or I will kill you."

Kroller looked at him. "If you move you will be crippled. You could even die."

Ben looked at him. "Then I'll die."

Just then one of the Dragoons came over. "Captain Maritinus, I am Slow Tooth. I am not a medic. However, I can try and help. My brothers and I are metal working dragons. Still we will pray for him and try and give him some of our strength. It may not be enough."

Ben nodded, "Thank you Sergeant."

Kroller looked at the three dragons. "But you're wounded."

A silver dragon smiled, "These are just scratches doctor. We are dragons. It takes more than this to hurt us."

They prayed over Private Harpeth. His blood pressure and other vitals seamed to strengthen. Doctor Kroller hooked up a bottle of blood and started working on the damage to his head. He closed it up and bandaged it.

Ben looked at him, "Well?"

Kroller looked at him, "I don't know. He has a 40% chance of surviving. He had zero. We need to get him to Kalian and a Nero-surgeon. You also, I have looked at you back. I don't want to touch you. I am just not good enough."

Dancer came over, "Skipper how are you?"

Ben smiled, "Alive, for now anyway. How bad is it?"

"Twenty wounded. Five critical, including you and Archangel, he will live Skipper. He is hurt. He has a punctured lung. Andropov took one through the leg clean. He is ok, might limp some for a while. The First, Gunnies, and I have things under control, along with Mountain. You just get better Skipper. You set us up right boss. They were tough and had nothing to lose. Our Marines never ran and took them head on. These creatures were battle hardened. Most of ours were green. They did good Sir." Dancer said.

Nighthunter and Blackpaw came in and walked over and talked to Dr. Kroller. Then nodded and walked over.

"Skipper, we have Whites and Purples coming in to evacuate the wounded. You, Lt. Archangel, and Private Harpeth are going out first, along with the other two, Corporal Tindal and Sergeant Fowler." Blackpaw said.

Pathfinder came in. "Where is he?" She saw Ben and turned almost white.

"Jane, it is alright. There are others hurt worse than me." Ben said.

One look at Kroller told her different.

Med teams from the White Daggers swept in and gentle moved the five critical wounded to the *Mercy* and took off. Pathfinder followed with five walking wounded in her Purple.

Ben tried to look at the others but he was trust up and strapped down. So he constantly asked for updates. Harpeth was still stable which was a miracle. The nurse told him. The dragons had somehow repaired some of the damage. Kroller had slowed the bleeding, but not stopped it. Still he only needed a little blood to keep up with what was draining. Archangel was also in bad shape. The tube in his chest was helping but the lung needed to be repaired. The other two also needed neurological surgery.

Dr. Janise Cooper was waiting on the *Mercy* when it landed on Kalian. She had directed Dr. Hanson and his team into operating room three. She wished Caesar was here. She didn't like playing boss. She didn't think Hanson liked taking orders from a Civilian either. However, Caesar had made it clear she was in charge.

Archangel was rushed into surgery. The others were taken into triage. Dr. Cooper looked at each one. She checked over private Harpeth made some notes, called a nurse, and had him, wheeled into an isolation ward. She did the same with the other two then came to Ben.

"Prep the Captain for surgery." Janise said.

"No," Ben screamed, "take care of my Marines first I can wait."

Janise looked at him, "Do you want to kill them Captain? I am administering medicine that will help with the swelling in Private Harpeth's brain. That will allow me to better assess the damage and to treat it. Cutting on it may not be the best approach unless, you want him to die. The other two have spinal cord injuries that may or may not be repairable. While they are stable, they are also weak. I need them to be strengthened and to fight the infection that is trying to set in. Then there is, you. You have a needle shaped projectile trying to enter your spine, to sever your spinal cord. If I don't remove it you will be paralyzed and probably die. I have maybe a cycle to start the operation before I lose the race. It is your choice."

Ben looked down, "Alright Doctor do what you need to."

Dan Mountain moved the dead Panther away from the door of the *White Fire*. He could tell this had been a high ranking officer. He saw the body of a Jaguar Captain nearby. Both had been killed when a grenade had gone off near them, as they approached the Green Dagger. Dan shook his head. He thought *they had almost made it*. Another five SMU and the Panther would have breached the door.

Gunny Killinger found the Lynx Captain he was severely wounded. "Kill me!" He roared in pain.

"I could call a doctor." Killinger said.

The Lynx grimaced in pain, "No, it is not our way. Please kill me so I die with honor."

Killinger nodded and shot him.

While this was going on Beary, and the fighter wing picked up the eighteen enemy fighters racing back to the Feline Warship. They moved to intercept them.

"Boss we are down to guns and phasers." Joshua said.

Beary nodded, "First Squadron, Delta Attack Formation. Second Squadron, back stop our attack. Ghost out."

Beary was shocked by the fact that there seemed to be no order in the enemy's fighter formation. In fact they seemed to be flying independently of one another.

First Squadron dove into them with phaser and rail gun fire. Three of the enemy fighters exploded. Others tried to fire back.

Beary dove between two fighters. Akhiok blasted both with rail gun fire and Gatling phasers. The one on the right exploded. The one on the left turned away. It was blown in half by a well-placed bomb that Mayotte had lobed at it.

Then the threat receiver went off in Beary's and Akhiok's helmets. Joshua launcher flares and chaff. Beary twisted down. Joshua tried to find the missiles. Just then Kat's fighter cut behind them and twisted left. Two missiles broke off and followed her. She headed straight at a Feline fighter and dove underneath it. The first missile exploded destroying the other fighter. The second followed her and exploded behind her. Luckily her shield absorbed most of the blast and deflected most of the fragments. A few did penetrate the shield but not the Vandar platting.

Beary was furious. "That little idiot could have got herself and Mayotte killed!"

Joshua responded, "Yes Sir, sure saved our tails though. Whoever fired those caught us looking the wrong way Boss."

Beary sighed, "Alright, I won't court martial her. Make sure you write them up for a Bronze Fang."

Joshua smiled. "You got it Boss."

Beary looked around two of his fighters were drifting. He could see that the crew was communicating with light signals. Two other fighters were heading over to assist. The enemy was gone.

"Harbinger, to Ghost, we intercepted six that slipped through. All enemy forces destroyed, waiting orders."

"Ghost to Harbinger, lets return to Red Talon. This might not be all of them."

While all this was going on Gracchus had announced his presence. "Mr. Belows and Mr. Helios, if you please, bring us to bear on the enemy warship. Mr. Vance, give me a full spread of weapons."

Four hundred, Mark 4s leaped from their launchers, as did twelve large, and forty small caliber rail gun shells. Class I and Gatling Class IV phasers lashed out at the Feline Warship.

The lion Captain responded by launching his own attack and defensive missiles. Three hundred missiles launched at the EAQ, as did phaser fire and a few smaller caliber rail guns.

The problem for the *Prides Home* was it was already damaged. Its warp nacelles were also damaged. Its defensive missiles stopped one hundred fifty of the Mark 4s. The shields stopped another one hundred. Still one hundred fifty burned through smashing the already damaged armor plating. The phasers smashed the shields, allowing the rail gun shells to smash through. Three of the twelve hit the weakened armor plating of the warp boom further damaging the warp nacelles. Others smashed into the hanger bays and outer weapons areas. Soon, fires were starting in the now empty hanger bays.

On the EAQ defensive systems destroyed almost two hundred of the incoming missiles. The shields absorbed the rest. One rail gun shell past through a weakened point and hit a Gatling phaser putting it out of commission. It was withdrawn into the ship and replaced by the spare unit.

The Lion Captain was screaming. He was trying to get his crew to move faster. However, his warship was slow to respond. Critical systems had been damaged. He watched as the strange ship seamed to spin on its axis and bring its other side to bear. As he tried to turn towards it, he realized it was too late. His ship was moving too slow. The other captain was dancing around him in a deadly ballet. He watched as another four hundred missiles came in, as more rail gun shells were launched, and as more phasers lashed out. He responded with the last of his defensive missiles. They managed to stop two hundred of the inbound missiles. The others attacked a single location on his ship. He could feel his ship almost cry in pain, as the engine boom was tore loose, by the effect of being smashed, by the missiles, rail gun shells, and phasers.

Power started failing around the ship. The engineer not waiting for orders jettisoned the warp core. Some of the crew manned fast life boats and jettisoned away from the *EAQ*. They hoped to escape to a nearby wormhole. A few made it. Others killed themselves. A few others, including the Captain and the intelligence officer jettisoned in life pods among the ships debris, as it self-destructed.

Five of the large life boats made it to a small wormhole, before the fighters returned. Two tried to shoot it out with Delta and Echo Flights and died as a result. Ten life pods were picked up and transported aboard the *EAQ*. The lion Captain and intelligence officer were among them. They were thrown into holding cells. Dragon guards were put on them.

CHAPTER 6

Revelations and Recovery

BEARY AND KATIMAI was the last to land. Beary was still fuming when he got out of the fighter. Two of his fighters had suffered complete power failures. Luckily, it was after the enemy had either been destroyed or had moved past them. Then there was Kat.

Beary marched over to her. "Ensign, just what by the Moons of Bantine, was you doing out there? You could have got your tail blown off!"

Kat shrugged, "Better ours than yours Boss. That's a wingbear's job to protect the lead."

Beary looked at her, "You ever pull a stunt like that again and I'll ground your tail. Both of you, that goes for you too Mayotte. You're just as guilty of that stunt as she is."

Mayotte nodded "Yes Boss."

Beary just shook his head, "Get cleaned up, and write up your reports. Make sure you take credit for all your kills. Including the one you feed his, own missile to." With that Beary walked off. Pompey was waiting for him. She looked shook.

Pompey looked at him. "It's Ben, he is hurt bad. He is on Kalian. Dr. Cooper is operating. Caesar says she is real good. Archangel is hit badly also. They have twenty wounded. Three others are critical."

Kat leaned against the door. "Captain Maritinus?"

Beary looked at her, "Kat snap out of it! You could have been killed out there today. It is the risk we take. Ben is tougher than most. You can check on him when he gets on board. Right now, you have work, to do."

Kat blinked back the tears, "Yes Boss, you are right. We do not cry for the living." She walked over and kissed Beary then Pompey. "He is a good Boss Mrs." With that she walked off.

Beary shook his head. "What am I going to do with her?"

Pompey looked at him. "Keep her. She would die for you."

Beary sat down, "She almost did today. One, of the enemy got the drop on us. We didn't see the missiles coming in till it was too late. She and Mayotte pulled in front of them breaking their lock on us. They got them chasing them. She feed one to the ship that launch on us. Then out ran the other for the most part."

Pompey kissed him. "Then I owe her a great deal."

Beary shrugged, "We might have survived the hit."

Pompey sat on his lap and kissed him again.

Akhiok walked in, "I am glad we didn't have to find out Boss. Hello my Lady."

"Joshua it is just Pompey you know that." Pompey said.

"Boss, I heard about Captain Maritinus and the others. We are starting a blood drive just in case. Lieutenant Barbarossa said that Hotel is flying CAP. Golf is on stand-by The Captain wants you." Joshua said.

Beary nodded, "Thanks Joshua."

Captain Gracchus was waiting for Beary "You heard about young Ben?"

Beary nodded, "What can I do for you Sir?"

"We captured the ship's Captain and a Centurion who seems to be their intelligence officer. He keeps trying to tell the Captain to settle down and shut up. But the Captain just keeps getting shriller. The other fifteen crew members are just that, lowly crew members. They are scared to death of our dragon crew members.

After you get cleaned up, I want you to go with me to deal with the Captain and the other officer." Gracchus said.

Beary hit the shower. As he did the Gem flights landed. Most of the wounded were transported to the *EAQ's* sick bay, including Archangel. Who was awake but still on oxygen and inhaled medicine to help his lungs heal.

Ben was still in surgery on Kalian. Artemus had returned to the *EAQ*, picked up Snow Flower, and went back to the planet. Five angry Marines went with him to protect Snow Flower.

Private Harpeth had been returned to the *EAQ*. Two dragon doctors went to work on him. After a cycle they came out to talk to Caesar.

Dr. Golden looked at Caesar, "He is hurt very bad. We were able to repair some of the damage. It is good that Dr. Cooper did not operate. He probably would have died. We have repaired the vascular damage to the brain. But the tissue damage is beyond us."

Caesar nodded. "Angelina developed a treatment we can try. But we need to wait a few more days. You have probable increased his chances to 50%."

Dr. Golden shook his head. "We can regenerate optic nerves. Repair thousands of injuries. Still some are beyond our abilities. There are cancers we can't cure . . ."

Caesar smiled, "We are doctors not the Creator of the Universe or his Word. Even dragons are limited by what He allows you to do."

Dr. Golden smiled, "You should have been an Augustine."

Caesar shrugged, "Angelina was, and she taught me."

"I wish she was here." Janise Cooper said.

"Caesar that penetrator was a pain . . . I got it out. He is going to be laid up a few weeks. Probable need a couple of weeks of physical therapy also.

How is Harpeth?" Janise asked.

Caesar shrugged, "Dr Golden and his staff fixed the vascular damage, but there is tissue damage. The swelling is under control so is the infection."

Janise nodded. "Seventy two more cycles and we should know if we can try her M1 Treatment. If not then I might have to go in and remove the damage tissue. I don't want to do that if I don't have to.

The other two also suffered spinal cord damage. I know that dragon medicine might be able to help in this area. Since both were hurt in the lower part of their spine."

Dr. Golden nodded, "If there is still some connecting nerve tissue, we can regenerate the cord. If the gap is small, we might still be able to do it. Our medicine has its delicacies Dr. Cooper. Still with your help we will do our best."

"They will be bringing Captain Maritinus up soon. I want a low gravity bed made up for him. We need as little pressure on his back and front as possible. I almost lost my race with the penetrator. It was still moving toward his spine. The Dragon Armor had damaged it.

But it still managed to try and work its way towards his spine. When I went after it, it moved away from me. It had a small Nano Processor in it." Dr. Cooper said.

Caesar shook his head, "A smart projectile that small. Using Nano Technology that is bad news, make sure you write up a report for fleet about it. Include how you dealt with it; make suggestions how to beat it."

"Caesar I am a Civilian." Janise pointed out. "Fleet won't . . ."

"Janise you are a member of my staff and a member of this ship's crew. Fleet will listen. The good Admiral and Angelina will see to that." Caesar pointed out.

Janise smiled, *was this the shy med student she had known a few years ago.* "Alright Boss I'll do it up right."

On Kalian, Ben was waking up.

"Captain, please try and lay very still. Don't thrash around. You are coming out of anesthesia. You were badly hurt do you remember?" Nurse Harland asked.

Ben's mouth was very dry. "My Marines . . . how are my Marines?"

Nurse Harland gave him a sip of water. "Do you know where you are? Do you know what happened?"

Ben was confused. He knew he had been drugged, "Maritinus Ben, Captain Bearilian Marines 765659."

Artemus came in. "It is alright Ben. You're safe so are your Marines. Harpeth and the others are already on the EAQ. You will be the last to Med-evacuated out."

Ben took a breath. "Sorry nurse. I was momentarily confused. I take it I am on Kalian. I was stabbed in the arm and shot in the back. I believe."

Snow Flower came in. "You had better live Ben Maritinus; I do not plan to have to wail over you and sing death songs for several hundred years." With that tears started to fall.

Ben smiled, "Then Snow Flower, do not water the ground now with your tears. I will live."

Ice Song came in she saw Ben and growled, "Where is the coward that did this?"

Ben said. "Dead, Sergeant Whitepaw killed him."

Ice Song nodded and walked over. With tears flowing from her eyes, "Ben Maritinus Knight of the Dragon, Warrior of the Red Paw, and my cousin forgive me. Except a dragon's blessing,

Ι Ιχε Σονγ Προτεχτορ οφ τηε μοον ασκ τηατ ψου βε ηεαλεδ ανδ προτεχτεδ ωιτη α δραγονσ λοπε ανδ σηελδ. (I Ice Song Protector of the Moon ask that you be healed and protected with a dragon's love and shield.)" Ice Song spoke in the ancient language of the dragons.

Three of the Dragons nearby felt power flow from them, not much but some. They looked at each other it had happened again.

Ice Song felt power flow from her and through her. Some of the power was not her own. She realized she had done what she had scolded Sho-Sho for, and it scared her.

Ben winched in pain as his injury started to heal, as did older injuries. He smiled *dragon blessings were not always pleasant.*

Beary came out of the shower, he wanted to take a nap. Pompey kissed him.

"I know your day isn't over. The Captain wants you to talk to the Captain of the Enemy ship. However, your niece says she needs to talk with you. She says it is important." Pompey said.

Beary looked at her, "Do you know what it is about?"

Pompey looked down, "Maryam told me about the situation. Then Sho- Sho explained it. I have mixed feelings about it."

"You're not going to tell me are you?" Beary asked.

"No Beary, just do not over react and hear Shoshanna out fully. Remember, we cannot change who our daughter is." Pompey said.

Beary nodded and walked in to the nursery. Over in the corner, of the room, stood a young teenage Maxmimus, in a gold and silver dress.

The teenage girl slowly turned around and knelt before him, lowering her dragon eyes. "My Prince, I hope this form does not offend you?"

About that time a small pink dragon, with a golden crest on her head, flew into Beary's arms squealing "Daddy."

Beary looked at Erin, "Sweet heart change back and go play with Maryam."

"Ok Daddy, but don't be cross with Sho-Sho. I learned to do this on my own." Erin changed back and scampered back to Maryam. She looked back at Sho-Sho "Do not kneel, Shoshana. You are a Princess of Andreas Prime as am I. We kneel only before the Creator and his Word. That is right isn't it Daddy?" Erin said.

Beary smiled, "You are correct Erin." He reached down and helped Sho-Sho to her feet."

"Come Sho-Sho let's talk." Beary said. He led her into the living room. "You are stunning in this form but how is it possible?"

Sho-Sho looked at him, "Do you wish me to change back?"

Beary shook his head "No, not yet unless it causes you pain or problems."

Sho-Sho shrugged, "No, it is a side effect of our bonding. Erin discovered she could change into a dragon and that I could take the form of a Maxmimus. Not all Valkyries could do it. It requires a rare genetic code. Very few dragons can. I do not know if I can because it is genetic or if it is because she touched me.

Ice Song may be able to also. Agathag has a quasi-bond with her. They are able to share thoughts, but not see through each other's eyes."

Beary nodded. "What else are you not telling me?"

Sho-Sho dropped her head. "Ice Song just discovered she also has the ability. We seem to be able to unintentionally draw power from other dragons, to strengthen blessings. Without their consent, it is a terrible violation of dragon law."

Beary looked at her, "Shoshana, that should not be possible without some form of trick like the others used."

Sho-Sho sighed, "We have been . . . set apart. Just as you uncle are more than a pure Maxmimus. You have, as does Ti, some dragon DNA. If you would have been a female, you two could have become Valkyrie like Erin."

Beary looked at her, "What?"

"Do you not understand uncle? Samuel is in your lineage." Sho-Sho said. "Why do you think he has watched over your family as he has? He was not Constance's uncle but her father. Lady Ann was her mother."

Beary looked puzzled then nodded, "The bonding it changed Samuel's DNA. The gene was prevalent in the Caesar, Maxumus, and Augustine Clans because we were descendants of the three brothers who were Constance's children."

"Yes. We the descendants of Star Firerena have certain abilities, because her mother was Lady Valorous." Sho-Sho said.

Beary shook his head, "Sho-Sho, who knows this?"

Sho-Sho shrugged, "Sire and Lady Valorous, Star Firerena, and us."

Beary nodded, "Let's keep it that way. Sho-Sho, tell Erin, to hide this information deep in her mind.

Now change back. I might make use of this ability of yours latter, if that would not offend you.

Also, you need to explain to the other dragons what happened, both you and Ice Song."

Sho-Sho changed back into a dragon and kissed Beary. "Thank you, uncle, for being so loving and understanding about everything."

Sho-Sho walked into her room.

Pompey smiled, "Is everything alright?"

Beary shrugged, "What can you do? It is a gift or a curse. I would rather treat it as a gift."

The medical shuttle arrived with Ben. He was taken directly to sick bay.

"I tell you I am fine. My back is totally healed. You can unstrap me from this contraption!" Ben growled.

Caesar came over. "That is enough Ben. You were hurt real bad. It takes weeks to heal from that kind of surgery."

Ben smiled, "You want to bet?"

Dr. Cooper came over. "I'll take that bet Captain. You'll be lucky if you can walk in a month."

Ben looked at her. "Doc, I'll walk right now, if you'll let me out of this contraption."

Caesar grabbed a scanner. Ben's injuries were healing, including old childhood injuries. "Not today Ben, you're not done cooking yet. You should still feel it in your spine."

Ben nodded "A little. It itches and I can't reach it."

Caesar ordered "Well don't. Let me put you in the low gravity bed, but I won't restrain you. As long as you stay in bed, until we tell you different."

Ben looked at him "How long?"

Caesar shrugged "Give me two days. I'll even let you work up here, as long as you stay lying down."

"Ok Caesar. How are Harpeth and my other Marines?" Ben asked as they put him in the low gravity bed.

Janise answered for Caesar. "Captain Maritinus, Corporal Tindal, and Sergeant Fowler were both hit by the same type of penetrator you were, but lower in the back. Their spinal cords were damaged just above the tail bone. Their legs are currently paralyzed. We hope to fix their spinal cords. First, we had to stop the infection that tried to start.

Private Harpeth is alive. He is in a drug induced coma. I do not want him to wake up yet. Dr. Golden and one of his dragons, a Vascular doctor, repaired most of the vascular damage in his brain.

But he still has massive tissue damage. There is a treatment developed by Dr. Maxumus that might help. It has its risks, but it is at the moment our best option."

Ben nodded, "Caesar, set me up a com link also. How is Archangel?"

Caesar reported, "Much better, give me a month, and you can have him back to full duty."

Ben nodded.

The First Sergeant looked at him. "Skipper, don't give the Doc any trouble. Don't worry, Paladin and I can handle most problems."

"It's ok Master Chief, there are a few things I need to take care of personally." Ben said.

The First looked at him "Sir, I could handle the calls . . ."

"No Chief, my responsibility." Was all Ben, could say.

First Ben called his parents, "Hail Father, it is I your Son."

Sire Maritinus looked at his youngest son, "Ben, you have been injured?"

Ben shrugged, "It is just a scratch. I will be back to duty in a day or two. Do not worry father. It is almost fully healed. I just did not want you or mother to worry unnecessarily. Stay safe father."

"Stay safe my Son." Sire Maritinus said, as the com link dissolved.

Ben straightened a little he made other calls to the families of his wounded Marines. He praised their dedication to duty and their bravery.

He expressed concern over Corporal Tindal and Sergeant Fowler's wounds. He assured their families that the *EAQ* had the finest medical staff in the universe. Including two surgeons, that had been trained by Angelina Maxumus. Ben explained that he had been told personally by her Highness, that they were her best students.

He final come to the last phone call. An older Bear and his wife answered the communication unit. "Sire and Sirena Harpeth please forgive me. I am Captain Ben Maritinus of the 981ˢᵗ Red Paw Dragons. I am your Son's Commanding officer . . ."

The old Bear smiled. "You are the young captain that attempted to save and may have saved our son. You are also the one, through your quite devotion, that led him back to the Creator and his Word. We, Captain Maritinus, will forever be in your debt. Whether our son lives or the Creator takes him, for he can now return home."

Ben looked at him, "Sire I pray, that I can return your son home to you alive. We have excellent doctors on board. I promise that no matter what his unit will return your son to you, one way, or the other, as is your custom."

The older Female nodded. "May, the Creator bless you, Captain Maritinus. As for our son, we will accept His will."

"I will keep you informed about your son, or one of my officers. Please feel free to contact us if you need anything. Or a Sir Gamey Maxumus on Andreas Prime. He will see that your needs are taken care of." Ben said "Thank you." with that he cut off the communication unit.

He took a breath and called Gamey. "Sir Gamey I need to ask . . ."

"Ben you have been hurt!" Gamey said.

"It is just a scratch. Ice Song did something that is healing it and all my previous scratches." Ben smiled weakly "Gamey some of my Marines were hurt worse . . . One a young private may not make it. His family is struggling. I have an account with my uncle an investment. I would like to cash in and send to his family . . ."

"Sir Maritinus, you are a Knight of the Caesar/Maxumus Clan, a Knight of the order of the Dragon. Just tell me the names of your wounded Marines families and all will be cared for." Gamey said.

Ben looked at him "But . . ."

Gamey smiled "Ben you are family. We take care of family. Your crest is on my wife's wall Sir Knight. Also, my Empress loves you. Just send me the names and I will take care of everything."

Ben copied his list and sent it, "Thank you Gamey."

Gamey nodded, "Rest Ben Maritinus the Slayer, Knight of the Dragon." With that Gamey's face faded.

Ben sat there he was a warrior of the Red Paw. Warriors didn't cry. Yet there he sat sobbing uncontrollably.

Kat walked in and saw him. She walked over and covered his head and shoulders with a blanket. She then placed his head on her chest. She sat there and didn't utter a word, till her wrist com went off.

"Kat where are you? We're going to be late for our debriefing!" Mayotte said.

Kat looked at Ben, whose sobbing had stopped. He was sleeping. "Take the meeting, I'll call the Boss."

Beary looked at his com unit. "What is it Kat?"

"Sir, I need to stay with Captain Maritinus. I cannot go to my debriefing. It is important that I stay Sir; it has to do with our culture. If I don't he will be dishonored." Kat said her voice was shaking.

"Alright Kat, Ben is now your responsibility till you can tell me what this is about, which you will do." Beary said.

"Yes Boss, he is your friend you will understand." Kat said.

Kat gentle bent down and nipped his shoulder. "Ben, please wake up. We need to talk."

Ben opened his eyes and realized he was staring at female breast. He slowly sat up. "Ensign Katimai . . ." then he realized what had happened and he started to turn away.

But she grabbed his face, turned him back to her. She kissed him passionately. "Do not turn away from me Ben Maritinus of the Red Paw. I am Moon Flower Katimai of the Red Circle Clan, daughter of High Chief Alakanuk Katimai, of the Seventy Tribes of the Red Circle Clan. There is no shame between you and me. You are a great warrior of your people and the son of a great chief."

Ben looked at her "You saw . . ."

"I saw nothing. Only that you were exhausted from your wounds and from the energy to heal them. I gave you a place to rest your head. Which I would gladly do anytime, I would offer you even more if you wish to claim it." Kat said with a smile.

"Why? After seeing . . ." Ben was almost shaking.

Kat smiled, "Do you not understand? I am in love with you. I have claimed you for my own. You can resist if you wish. But in the end you are destined to be mine. I have seen it. Besides, I will give you strong cubs, love you harder, and stronger than anyone else ever could."

Ben looked at her, "Kat, I . . . You don't know . . . but . . ."

She took his face and kissed him again.

At this point Nurse Blaze walked in. "What are you doing in here?"

Kat looked at her, "What does it look like? I am seducing Captain Maritinus. I have marked him and claimed him for my own. Before, you could change your mind, and try to move in. After all a chief's son should be with a chief's daughter."

Nurse Blaze almost turned pink. "Get out of here right now!"

Kat smiled. "I can't Lieutenant Maxumus ordered me to stay. I am to take care of Captain Maritinus. I plan to do just that."

Caesar heard the commotion and walked in. "What is going on in here?"

Kat looked at him "Doctor, can I talk to you in private? It is important."

They stepped out of the room. A few minutes later Caesar came in with an evil grin. Two corps bears followed.

"Ben, we are transferring you to a private room. You cause too much trouble up here." Caesar said with a smile.

Kat had a big grin on her face, as she had the two medics follow her out.

Ben looked at her. "Where are we going?"

Kat replied "A recently vacated room in the Maxumus family section. I am to take care of you."

Ice Song saw them as they arrived "What is going on?"

Kat looked at the Frigorific Dragoon. "You are Ice Song, Ben's cousin, and Lieutenant Artemus daughter?"

Ice Song looked at the attractive female Polarian. "Yes, but who are you?"

"I am Moon Flower Katimai, of the Red Circle Clan and the Captain's temporary nurse. Though you're healing of him means he will not need me for long."

Ice Song looked at her. "But you are Kat, Prince Maxumus' wing bear?"

"Yes, Ice Song." The medics finished wheeling Ben in to the empty room. Kat let the door close. "There are some wounds your blessing did not heal. Those I will try and heal tonight. Do you understand young one."

Ice Song blushed, "Only a little."

Kat sighed. "Me too, I will not go too far or he will be forced to marry me. I want him to. Yet it must be his choice . . . not forced on him. Tonight, I will sing to him and make him more comfortable.

When the Boss gets home, have him come and see me."

Ice Song nodded, "Alright Kat. I will tell Sho-Sho and Maryam also."

Beary looked at the Captain. "Well Sir, that is about it. I'll have Kat finish her debriefing tomorrow."

"Beary, it may be none of my business, but what is going on?" Captain Gracchus asked.

Beary dropped his head. "Ben called all the families of his wounded Marines. I don't know maybe to reassure them. Maybe to give them a chance to blame him for their son's getting hurt. It didn't happen they all thanked him for being their son's captain, including Private Harpeth's parents.

After the calls Ben called Gamey. I am not sure why. Then Kat called me and said something had happened. That she would explain later but that it was important that she stay with Ben.

Ben's culture has some different rules. Kat will explain what she needs too."

Gracchus nodded, "I should have been there for him Beary. It is devastating the first time you have to do it. He did it from a hospital bed."

Beary shook his head, "He wouldn't have let you. Kat has been there also. She is better equipped to help him."

Gracchus grimaced. "Poor Ben, It just doesn't seem fair throwing him to Kat."

There was a knock at the door. "Excuse me Captain. I am looking for Lieutenant Maxumus."

"I am here Mayotte. What do you need?" Beary said.

"Boss, I can't find Kat anywhere." Mayotte said.

Beary smiled, "Paulette, get changed. My wife is inviting you for supper. As for Kat she is on temporary reassignment. You'll be flying a desk for a day or two as S3 or S6. Whatever job we figure out you're, a staff grunt, when you're not flying, now. You and Kat work for me full time now."

Mayotte responded, "Already figured that out Boss. No one else would put up with us. Well maybe O'Haggerty. Don't worry boss Kat may be a pain in the tail. But she is a great pilot and she has a heart of pure gold."

Beary smiled, "She is not in trouble Paulette, at least not yet."

Mayotte saluted and left. *What was Kat up to now?*

Kat walked over to a bag containing some of Ben's cloths she pulled out a pair of swimming shorts. She walked over to him.

"I noticed this room has a mineral hot tub. I have turned it on. You may put these on or not it is your choice. Get undressed. I will be back to help you into the water." Kat said as she walked over to another bag, took out a thin rob, and a small bathing suit. She walked into another room.

Ben felt the heat razing through his fur. He quickly put on his swim suit. She was over powering. She meant to bathe him. It was customary for females to do that, but always in threes. It prevented, well misunderstandings.

Kat came out with the robe loosely tied around her. Underneath was a bright red bikini. It stood out as a bright contrast to her pure white fur.

Ben's mouth felt dry. He knew he was staring as she walked over.

"Do you like the view Captain Maritinus?" Kat asked.

Ben looked into her deep blue eyes, "Why, when I dishonored myself in front of you? Why . . ."

At that point Kat slapped him hard across the face. "Ben Maritinus, don't you ever let those words ever leave your mouth again! What dishonor was there in your tears? No one else saw them, only me. Do you think you are the first warrior to shed such tears?

Now come let me help you into the water."

Ben realized Kat was strong, as she half carried him to the hot tub and lowered him into the warm water. "Kat you still didn't answer my question."

Kat half whispered, "My best friend, someone I grew up with, was killed on the *Fast Claw*. It was our job to protect them. We were overwhelmed. My lead, who I was supposed to protect, was killed right before my eyes, before I could react. We were outnumbered. We killed twenty of their fighters. It wasn't enough they just kept coming . . . till we had no munitions left. Only O'Haggerty and my fighter were left. Both were shot up bad. Yet we survived. Lieutenant O'Hanlon and his WTO Langer were gone. So were Ensigns Henning and Pell. They were good crews, there wasn't even anything left to recover." Tears weld up in Kats eyes.

"So don't tell me that tears are dishonorable, Ben Maritinus. I have been there. I will probably be there again someday or someone will shed a tear over me. It is part of our job. Just as it is part of yours.

If you cannot shed a tear for your Marines, that are hurt or killed in private or with one that loves you, what good are you?"

Ben looked at her and kissed her eyes gentle "Forgive me Kat. I . . ."

Kat kissed him very passionately, and then laid his head on her chest. "Ben just rest and let the water relax you."

Ben looked up at her. *How could he relax she was so over powering?*

Kat started singing an old song. Her voice had an almost angelic quality.

Ben sighed, *an angelic voice and a body to tempt a Saint. Oh boy this Kat is pure trouble.* He thought as he drifted off to sleep.

After a few moments there was a knock at the door. Kat eased Ben over and put a pillow under his head. Put on her Robe. Then she answered the door.

Beary and Pompey looked at Kat. Whose robe was just barely closed.

Beary smirked, "Pompey, this is Ensign Moon Flower Katimai my wingbear. We call her Kat.

Kat, this is my wife, Pompey Maxumus."

Kat responded shyly, "It is a pleasure to meet you Lady Maxumus. Forgive my state of dress. I was attending to Captain Maritinus. His physical wounds were healed by Ice Song. Others were not."

Pompey smirked. "When we are alone Kat, you may call me Pricilla. It is my secret name. I understand about such wounds." Pompey looked at Beary. "I also understand the cure. Just how far are you willing to go?"

Kat blushed, "My Lady, I will not compromise his honor. Well not yet anyway. However, I do want him as my mate. Is that wrong?"

Pompey replied. "I personally approve. Still, Lady Artemus is his family, you should approach her."

Kat responded. "Yes, my Lady. Sir, you understand what has happened?"

Beary shrugged, "I have an idea Kat. I have been there. I had someone to help me. Also, I wasn't wounded at the time."

Kat nodded. "I must get back to him." With that, Kat went back in. She climbed back into the hot tub and placed his head back on her chest.

Ben woke up and looked into Kat's eyes "You really don't need to do this for me? I am fine now."

Kat shook her head, "No. Dr. Vantanus will be here in the morning to talk to you. Are you hungry?"

Ben shook his head. "Just tired I guess."

Kat nodded. "Alright, I will help you over to the bed. So you can put on your pajamas or do you sleep without them?"

Ben looked at her. "With pajamas, well, I wear work out pants, to be exact."

"I thought so. They are on the bed. Get changed. I'll be back." Kat said.

Ben changed quickly and got under the covers. She would leave now and the torture would be over. He was wrong.

Kat came out, in a not so revealing nightgown. Yet it fit her very well. "Move over Captain. I need a nap also. I intend to sleep in your arms, not on the floor."

"Kat, it is not proper, for a single boar and female, to sleep alone." Ben said.

Kat kissed him. "Ben Maritinus, I have not known a boar. If you wish to take me, I will not resist. If afterwards you reject me, then by our customs, the shame is mine, not yours. I have placed myself in this situation of my own free will. I have told you that I love you. Without you saying anything or pursuing me. The decision of what you do to or with me is yours."

Ben looked at her. "I will protect your virtue and honor Kat. I swear."

Kat grinned, "Then I will not damage your virtue too much either Ben." With that she crawled in next to him and held him close to her and kissed him. Then she wrapped her arms around him. Again she started singing.

Ben's eyes closed as sleep took him. His dreams were confused. Nightmares would try to start but were interrupted by dreams of swimming in a warm lake with Kat. When he woke up he was embarrassed. As the night wore on his dreams had grown more daring. He rolled over away from Kat. She just pressed her body harder against his back and pulled him closer to her.

Mayotte returned to her berth. She had been totally enchanted by both Lady Maxumus and Lady Artemus. Still, she was worried about Kat. She hadn't returned to her quarters. Yet some of her things were gone. It wasn't like Kat, unless she had done something . . . Well, it was Kat. Kat did dance to close to the flame.

In the holding cells the lion Captain was still throwing a tantrum. One of the dragon guards asked the other what he thought the lion would taste like barbequed. That quieted him down for a while.

The Panther intelligence officer was trying to figure out how they had failed. He realized that their intelligence was faulty. Still they shouldn't have failed so horribly. Some blame belonged to the Captain, but not all.

He looked at the dragons. These creatures were not mentioned either.

The next morning Ben woke up and went into the bathroom. He looked in the mirror, as he washed his face, and paws. His paws were still shaking, but not quite as bad.

He walked out and looked at Kat. She slept like an angel also. He walked over and touched her face. She smiled.

"Good morning Moon Flower. I hope I wasn't a burden to you last night." Ben said.

Kat responded by kissing him and pulling him back into bed. "The doctor didn't give you permission to get up without assistance you know. So get back in bed." She leaned over him and kissed him again. He noticed a couple of buttons had come loose and he tried to close them.

"What is wrong, don't you like the view?" Kat asked.

Ben blushed, "No, it is breath taking but I just . . ."

Kat kissed him again and snuggled against him. "I have embarrassed you. Mayotte, always says I dance too close to the flame. My father wanted sons. He got twelve daughters, eleven very proper ones and one hellion. You can guess which one I am. I wanted to be a Warrior. I broke several of our taboos proving I was as skilled as any boar. Finally I joined the fleet to save my father further embarrassment."

Ben responded "You are no boar. But you are a brave warrior, your father should be proud."

Kat kissed him very passionately, and then wept in his arms. "My father disowned me. He said a female was for birthing warriors not for being warriors."

Ben lifted up her head. "Then your father is wrong. In our clan females are warriors. They must be, for they must protect the home while the boars hunt. Doesn't my cousin were the mark of a warrior of the Red Paw, a gift from a dragon?"

Kat looked at him, "Ben, it is unfair of me to ask, but do you think you could learn to love me?"

Ben looked into her eyes again, those deep sea blue eyes. "Kat you are impossible. Do you know that? You devour me, drive me insane, and then ask me if I could learn to love you?"

Kat's eyes started to brim with tears.

Ben sighed, "Give me a couple hundred years to work on it. With you taking care of me, and will see."

Kat let out a war hoop and started to peel off her night gown when Ben stopped her.

"Kat slow down. There are proprieties. We are in Maxumus territory and I technically belong to their clan. If you do what you started to do, you would become my property, under their law, it is not what either of us wants." Ben said.

Kat looked at him and replied. "I told you, I was willing to bear the shame."

Ben kissed her. "However, I am not willing for you to."

Kat looked at him "Then you do care for me?"

Ben kissed her again, "Love it is a strange emotion for me Kat. I think I might be falling in love with you, is that fair enough?"

Caesar looked at Jessica and slapped her on her tail. "I want you in the pool today, at least forty laps, and then a light work out."

Jessica rolled over "Is that my husband or my doctor talking?"

Caesar kissed her, "Your doctor. Your husband just has better knowledge of the subject."

"Where are you off to so early?" Jessica asked.

"Across, to your old room, so I can check on Ben's wounds. Kat is taking care of him. Ben's wounds are healed but his mental wounds . . . well Kat is working on those." Caesar said.

"Well, I have to get back to work also. Young Nikolaos needs his training advanced again." Jessica said.

Caesar shook his head "Is he really that good?"

Jessica laughed. "He is going to surpass my skills soon and I am real good. He is going to be on Ti's level. He really needs to be with him."

Caesar shook his head, "Not yet, let him learn some compassion first, that he can learn from you."

Jessica kissed him. "Go see your patients."

Caesar crossed the hall and knocked on the door.

Kat looked at Ben. "Oh the doctor is here." She put on her robe and walked to the door. "Come in Doctor Vantanus. Your patient is over there, if you will excuse me." She turned walked into the other room and closed the door.

Caesar smiled, *cool as a breeze*. He turned to Ben, "Alright, you know the drill."

Ben, laid on his stomach as Caesar examined his back.

"Is there any pain or soreness in your back?" Caesar asked.

Ben shook his head, "No Caesar. I am completely healed. Ice Song's blessing was very powerful. I think it was more powerful than she intended."

Caesar nodded, "She is young, you're lucky you didn't sprout wings."

Ben smiled, "True." Then the smile faded.

Caesar closed his bag. "You are confined to quarters, Captain till further notice."

Ben looked at him "Caesar I am healthy, I am fit for duty!" Ben's paws were clinched.

Caesar touched his friends shoulder. "Ben look at yourself, you were ready to hit me, to lash out in anger. You're right physically you are ready. Look at it objectively are you really ready?"

Ben sat down. "I can't let my Marines down."

Caesar shook his head, "That is bull and you know it. You have two weeks of rehab, do to your injuries. Well, Ice Song shortened one type. Kat can work on another. Get your head on straight. Ben, I have been there remember. So has Beary. It never gets easy. If you don't learn to deal with it, it will destroy you. Do you understand?"

Ben looked at him and nodded.

"That female has offered to help you. Let her. She knows the pain. Ben, she is strong and good. I am not sure you deserve her. You're still one of the luckiest bears I know." Caesar said.

Ben dropped his head. "She says she loves me."

Caesar grabbed his shoulder and squeezed, "Then don't be an idiot, love her back. Life, the way we live it, can be too short to throw love away. I almost lost the only female I ever loved."

Ben looked at his friend, Caesar was right. "Alright, Caesar, I'll take a day or two to get my head on straight."

Caesar sighed, "You better, or I'll turn you over to Angelina."

Ben shook his head. "Not even you could be that cruel." Then he laughed.

Kat came out in her uniform. "I guess I better report for duty."

Caesar looked at her. "Ensign Katimai, you still work for me. He is still your patient. You, young lady, are on 24/7 duty till I say otherwise." With that Caesar closed his bag, "I'll check on him again tonight. Make him talk more."

Kat looked at him. "But, doctor what about Lieutenant Maxumus."

Caesar handed her signed orders, "This makes it official. He said he would leave it up to you how you accomplished your objective."

Kat nodded then whispered, "You all love him?"

Caesar shrugged, "He is a stubborn idiot at times, but he is family. We take care of our family." Caesar touched Kat's face and walked out.

She looked at Ben, tears streaming from her eyes, "What is it like to be loved by so many creatures?"

Ben looked at her and smiled, "Overpowering Kat. When their kind accepts you as one of them, they envelope you in a flood of love that just sweeps you away. The three oldest Artemus cubs were orphans survivors from a pirate attack. Artemus wanted to adopt them but he was single. Beary's sister contacted my cousin who was in love with Artemus. She came and married him on the spot. So they could adopt the three cubs. Gamey and Widja his wife the Empress Dragon supported them in the name of the Clan. Now those orphans belong to the Maxumus Clan."

Kat sat beside him "How about your own father? How does he feel about your relationship with the Maxumus Clan?"

Ben looked at her, "Has not our two clans been joined by marriage? Is not the Artemus Family both Red Paw and Maxumus? Has not my Clan's seal been placed on the Empress's wall? We have been greatly honored by our relationship with them."

Kat thought "I bet they would say it was the other way around."

Ben nodded, "Yes, you see you do understand the truth of their greatness."

Kat dropped her head, "I have dishonored you. I spoke boldly to Nurse Blaze. Yet I am a disowned daughter of a chief."

Ben kissed her. "Tell me the whole story Kat. Please, if I am to talk to your father I need to know everything."

Kat looked at him. "Why . . . Why would you contact my father?"

Ben kissed her and nibbled her neck and opened her shirt and pulled it down to reveal her shoulder. "So you were given the Mark of your Clan."

Kat pulled away and cowered. "Please forgive me!"

Ben pulled her over, "Why, did you have it put there falsely?"

Kat sat up "No two elders of our clan approved it, after I and Mayotte destroyed two Arcrilian fighters during a scout mission. It was right before the peace treaty of Carnise Drift. They attacked us, but we out maneuvered them. Then we destroyed them. I figured that the destruction of our accursed enemy earned me the right to the mark. The elders agreed." She looked at Ben for approval.

Ben responded "I would say it qualified you as a warrior under my clan's rules, and deserving of the mark. So?"

Kat dropped her head, "My father didn't see it that way. He said I disgraced him. He then disowned me."

Ben turned her to him, "Then he is an idiot Kat. We shall call my father first. Would you bring me a uniform please? Just a casual one, father might be worried otherwise. Your father does not deserve better."

Kat did as he said. Then she went in and re arranged her uniform, which Ben had messed up, while he changed.

Kat sat in fear as Ben called up the com unit. Lunara's face appeared, "Hail Son, I was told you were gravely injured."

Ben waved off the statement, "A gifted surgeon and a dragon's love has returned me to perfect health mother. I am well I swear."

Lunara smiled "Who is she beside you?"

"Mother, this is Moon Flower Katimai of the Red Circle Clan a brave and compassionate warrior." Ben said.

"She is strikingly beautiful my son. Are you bringing more honors to us my son?" Lunara asked.

Kat almost turned pink. "My lady, I am not worthy of a warrior as great as your son."

Lunara laughed. "Nonsense he is the one that must work to be worthy of you. I will call Aleut."

Aleut came on the com. "My son why did you not tell me . . . Oh hello who is this ravishing young female?"

"First father like I told mother, I am fully healed father. Ice Song healed what the doctor repaired. Her blessing was so strong even old injuries were healed. That is not why I called father . . ."

Aleut listened for ten STU he nodded and stroked his chin. "You are a very bold female, child. Just the kind I would choose for my youngest and a warrior to boot. I know your father. He is an idiot. Forgive me child, perhaps I speak to frank. I do not like him nor him me.

Even if you do not choose my son, I will give you a place of honor in our clan."

Tears flowed from Kats eyes, "Thank you Sire Maritinus I . . ."

"It is alright my dear. Just put up with my son. He always dances to close to the fire." Aleut said. "Ben you know what to say. If he dishonors her in anyway, defend her honor, or I will skin your hide."

Ben nodded, "It will be as you commanded father."

Kat looked at him as the com link dissolved, "Why?"

Ben smiled, "His sense of honor has been challenged, because your honor has been denied by your own father. I will rectify that and reestablish your honor Moon Flower Katimai."

Ben next called Kat's father. She wanted to hide. Ben refused to let her. Her father's face appeared.

"Hail, High Chief Alakanuk Katimai, I am Captain Ben Maritinus the Slayer, of the Red Paw Clan, son of Aleut and Lunara Maritinus Chiefs of the Red Paw." Ben introduced himself.

"What do you want? What is that dog doing next to you?" Alakanuk said.

"Sire," Ben said with an even voice, "Your daughter is a highly decorated fleet officer and a fine pilot. I wish to ask your permission . . ." Ben tried to say.

"That dog is no daughter of mine . . ." Alakanuk started to say.

Ben started to see red, "Sire, I have tried to be civil. I wish to court your daughter."

"I told you Red Paw slug that she is no daughter of mine anymore! She is refuse. Do with her as you please!" Alakanuk screamed.

Ben looked at him "Then hear this Alakanuk! I claim her as a lost one and take her as my own. I give her to the Red Paw and establish my father as her regent."

"I care not what you do. Make her a slave for all I care." Alakanuk said.

Ben's temper flared. "Know this pig. If you ever speak such to her again, I will cut the warrior's mark from your shoulder and hang it from my hut. No true warrior would do what you have done. You are no chief. You are a pig, a swine. If I ever see you in person, I will gladly show you what a true warrior is made of."

Before her father could answer, Ben cut off the Com.

Kat looked at him. "You didn't mean what you said? You couldn't I . . ."

Ben looked at her he was mad. "Moon Flower Katimai your last name is offensive to me. After meeting your father, I cannot nor could my father allow it to stand."

Ben opened his door. Night Wind was standing there, "Sergeant, go bring Lady Maxumus, and my cousin here. Also tell Beary and Artemus I need them."

Night Wind nodded, "As you wish Ben."

Ben bowed "Sorry."

Night Wind just smiled a wolfish grin and took off.

Kat looked at him "What are you doing?"

Ben looked at her. "You heard him. You now belong to me Kat, by our own laws. So I am claiming what is mine. May, he go to the Moons of Bantine."

Snow Flower and Pompey arrived. "What is wrong Ben?"

Ben looked at his cousin. "Kat is salvage. Prepare her. She is now mine, by our law. Call a priest so Maxumus laws may be met."

Snow Flower bowed. "It will be as you say Ben. Come Moon Flower we must get you dressed."

Pompey stopped "Ben Maritinus what . . ."

Ben came over and kissed Pompey "Her father dishonored her Pricilla. This is the only way I can restore it, Short of killing her father. That is something I might have to do someday. I must give her a new name, a new clan. He called her a dog, refuse, worthy of only being a slave. If I could, have reached him I would have killed him right then and there."

Pompey nodded, "I'll get the Chaplin."

Kat was crying. "Why, after what my father said? Why would he want me?"

Snow Flower kissed her, "Cousin, he takes after his father. Just promise me that you will love him hard for the rest of his and your life."

Kat nodded through her tears.

Beary called Pompey. "What is going on?"

"Grab Father John, Caesar, and Artemus and get down here now. Paper work is already done." Pompey said.

"What paper work?" Beary asked.

"Marriage license, etc., you know the usual paper work." Pompey said.

"Pompey what have you done?" Beary asked.

"Not me. Ben, and is he hot under his collar. He said something about regaining Kat's honor and him killing her father." Pompey said.

Beary called Artemus told him to grab the priest. He then called Aleut they talked for five STU. He then called Mayotte and Commander Gracchus. Mayotte went to join her pilot. Commander Gracchus just said about time and laughed.

Father John just shook his head. "Of course I'll perform the ceremony. If I didn't I might have to answer to one of Empress Angelina's relatives or friends. She is an Augustine you know. Do you know how many Cardinals belong to her family?

What kind do you want Kat?"

Kat looked at him, "Just simple father. Whatever would please the Creator and his Word?"

Father John replied, "True love given freely pleases the Creator and his Word. Do you love Captain Maritinus, Kat?"

Kat looked at him. "I cannot live without him father. I must have him. I must give him my love."

Father John looked at the females in the room. They all had the same smile. "You females are going to corrupt me, I know it."

Pompey laughed, "It is alright Father John it is an illness I am sure you are immune to."

Mayotte came in. "So you finally fell into the flame."

Kat shrugged "No not yet. Tonight I will dance in the fire."

Ben was still fuming when Artemus walked in with Caesar.

Caesar looked at him "I didn't mean tonight . . ."

Ben tried to smile, "It is necessary for Kat's sake. I can't explain anymore."

Artemus looked at him. "Ben?"

"No, but you know what will be required tomorrow Artemus, to meet our laws." Ben said.

"Of course Ben, Snow Flower and I will see to it." Artemus said.

Beary walked in. "Could you two step out for a moment?"

Artemus and Caesar did.

"I talked to Aleut. He told me if it went bad, he had instructed you to marry Kat." Beary said.

Ben nodded.

Beary looked at him. "I could give her a name without you having to do this."

"NO!" Ben screamed. "I am sorry Beary. I wanted to kill . . . no I want to kill him. How could he be so petty? How could he treat someone so kind, so sweet, and so loving with that kind of cruelty?

Don't you see I have to do this?"

Beary looked at him, "You love her?"

Ben dropped his head "Yes. I don't know how it happened or when. But listening to that pig speaking to her like that set my blood to boiling."

Beary nodded. "Need any help?"

Ben shook his head, "No, I can handle it. Getting it off might be harder."

Beary smirked. "Someone else will help you then."

Ben blushed.

"Too bad I have to give this suite up. It is nicer than what I have in Marine Country. I mean my old room is really just my office with a cot." Ben said.

Beary thought. "Move in, your family. Jessica doesn't need it anymore."

"What about Kat?" Ben asked.

"She is still my wingbear, Ben. She is just too good for me to loose, unless you say so right now." Beary said.

Ben shook his head. "I couldn't do that to her Beary. She loves to fly. She loves flying your wing. Is she good?"

Beary nodded "The best Ben."

Ben sat down to put on his shoes "It really doesn't change anything does it. Family or not, we all risk our lives for one another. It is our connection the blood we shed and the blood we spill."

Beary nodded, "Something like that Ben. Yet, it is more than that. It is the faith and love we share as well."

Ben smiled *did Beary know that he would follow him anywhere even to the Gates of the Halls of the Moons of Bantine. But then so would anyone that ever had been touched by this Cub.* "Ok Beary I am ready."

Artemus produced a ring set. "Andreios said he wished he could have done a better job, but he had so little time."

Ben stared at the blue diamond circled by white diamonds held by two Frigorific Dragons, and two simple gold bands.

Ice Song and Sho-Sho came over and blessed them with the ancient words; HONOP HOПE LOçE, (HONOR, HOPE, LOVE) which was engraved in them.

Ben bowed and kissed both of them, "Thank you, I love both of you."

Kat knelt before him in her veil. He placed the engagement ring on her finger. "This female is by our laws a lost one. By this ring I claim her, and pledge to protect her with my life and with the Red Paw Clan," He looked at Beary who nodded "and with the Caesar/Maxumus Clan. All who agree say aye."

The gathered assembly all said aye including the dragons.

"Moon Flower of the Red Paw and Caesar/Maxumus Clan will you be my mate." Ben asked.

Kat looked into his eyes, "I am yours my Sire. However you choose, as wife, concubine, or slave."

Ben lifted her face. "No Red Paw or Caesar/Maxumus is a slave. I would be boiled in oil by the wives of the Clan if I did not marry you my love."

Father John conducted a brief wedding in the Maxumus living area. He hoped he was done marring these bears. At least this one wasn't in the middle of the night.

Kat placed the ring on Ben's Paw. "I am now yours?"

"Yes, Kat Maritinus you are." Ben said.

A small celebration was held. A larger one for the ship was planned. But this one was just to meet certain requirements. Mayotte kissed Ben and thanked him.

Snow Flower, Pompey, and Jessica made discrete suggestions which caused Kat to blush bright pink.

Ben took it all in. *How had four friends, thrown together by fate become a family? How did an unassuming now twenty-one year old become its head? Yet even he looked up to Beary. Like what a brother? That was the only word that fit. He owed Beary a debt he could never repay. Yet Beary, would just twist it to say that it was he who owed the debt.* As he pondered these things Kat came over and took his paw.

"Husband, I am told it is time." Kat said.

Ben looked at her as she went in and put on a night gown that had been given to her.

He had managed to kick off his shoes, when she came out. The gown left little to the imagination, but what it left was devastating.

CHARLES & IRENE NICKERSON

"You are beautiful Moon Flower." Ben said.

"Ben, I know my father's name displeases you. It was him that named me Moon Flower. It displeases me. My true friends named me Kat. Can I not be Kat Maritinus?"

She sat next to him and undid his Jacket.

Ben looked at her, "Kat it is, my Kat." Ben said kissing her.

She smile and got up and hung up his jacket. "Where are we to live?"

"Beary offered us this set of rooms Kat." Ben said.

"But this area is for his family!" Kat said.

"Yes Kat. You are now part of that family." Ben said.

Kat took off his shirt and hung it up. "These are nice rooms. Are you sure it is permissible? Will I still be his wingbear?"

Ben smiled as he slipped off his pants which she hung up. "Beary said you were too valuable to him too lose, unless I told him so, before we got married. I know you love to fly too much. I can't ask you to give it up."

Kat looked at her husband he was gorgeous, "I like working for the Boss. He is tough but fair."

She kissed him again, "I can make this a good home for you. One you can be proud of. I will bring honor to your father also. I promise."

Ben wrapped his arms around her waist. "I do love you Kat."

She turned in his arms and faced him. "I know you do, Ben. Still, tonight does your blood boil out of hate for my father or desire for me?"

Ben looked at her sea blue eyes. "Both, Kat, if I am to tell you the truth."

She untied her gown and let it drop. "Then decide which is stronger husband, desire, or hate. If it is desire then you may have what is yours. If not take what you must."

Ben placed his head on her stomach, "I will never take from you."

She laid him down. "Then hate cannot live in your heart. My father only took from my mother. He only knows how to hate. I will show you that I can learn to give."

Ben woke up in the middle of the night. He went in and washed his face. Then came in and knelt by his bed. He prayed that he would never fail this female or his Marines again. He sat on the bed when two arms enfolded him.

"Come husband you need to be comforted some more. I think I will try what Snow Flower suggested this time." Kat purred.

Ben woke up to Kat singing. Her robe draped over her as she fixed his breakfast. "Don't tell me you cook also?"

Kat shrugged, "Better than some. Not as good as others. I am still learning. It is a hobby."

Ben slipped on his bottoms. She pouted.

"I guess you should." Kat said.

Ben walked over and kissed her. "Female, I am still recuperating remember?"

He patted her tail, "We need to get dressed. There are proprieties we must take care of."

Kat beamed "Breakfast first, then shower. Then we will get dressed husband."

Ben marveled at the aroma of the sausage, egg, and potato scrambler that she had prepared. He realized the citrus juice he was drinking had been freshly squeezed. Everything was delicious and carefully proportioned. "I take it there will be no seconds."

Kat shook her head "Not till you are back to training Ben."

Ben nodded. "The food is excellent Kat, all of it."

She got up and sat on his lap. "Then my husband is pleased?"

"Yes, Kat Maritinus, your husband is very pleased." Ben said.

Kat smiled and whispered into his ear.

Ben looked at her. "Kat you are insatiable."

She smiled and kissed him. "If you don't think we have time now promise me later."

Ben told her. "Come let's get cleaned up."

After they got showered and dressed she kissed him again. "Let's do that every morning."

Ben looked at her "Which part?"

Kat smiled, "Why not all of it?" She giggled.

"Kat what am I going to do with you?" Ben asked.

"Love me hard and give me a dozen cubs to love. So I can honor you, boy cubs." Kat said.

Ben grinned "Or daughters like their mother."

Kat looked at him and wept "You would see that as an honor?"

Ben responded "Yes Kat, and so would their future husbands."

Charles & Irene Nickerson

As they opened their door, Artemus and Snow Flower placed a wreath of flowers on Kat's head. Then Artemus placed a garland around Ben's neck. They then tied their wrists with ribbons of flowers.

Kat's eyes flowed with tears as Snow Flower and Artemus kissed her and Ben. "Thank you, you have honored our traditions."

Snow Flower winked, "Did you honor ours?"

Kat smiled "Four or five times. I think the first time I wasn't very good, but I think I got better."

Ben just turned bright pink.

"From Ben's reaction I think you did quite well Kat." Snow Flower said.

Ben had called earlier to let everyone know Moon Flower was no more. She was to be known as Lady Kat Maritinus.

Pompey came out "Ben; Caesar and Beary had to go on ahead. You have an appointment with Captain and Commander Gracchus there are all the required forms. I am going to follow discretely."

"Why are you going Pompey?" Ben asked he knew there was a problem.

"Kat's Father has filed a complaint with Fleet. We will deal with it." Pompey said.

Kat looked at her "Lady Maxumus . . ."

"It is Pompey dear or when surrounded by family Pricilla is fine. In this case however I am acting as her Majesties representative, in my capacity as, the Star of Vandar, Princess of Andreas Prime." Pompey said.

Ben had looked at the paper work. Even the name change all had the Imperial Seal of Andreas Prime. There was even a letter from Ben's father explaining their law and how it applied and their treaty with Andreas Prime, which gave Empress Angelina jurisdiction in this matter for him. Everything was presented in a ton of legalese.

Ben presented it to Captain Gracchus.

Captain Gracchus looked it over. Then he looked at Ben, "How much of this is forged or just plain Mount excrement son? Not that I personally care but Fleet wants answers. Kat's father has some influential friends."

Pompey came in. "Captain, I am here in my capacity as the Star of Vandar, Princess of Andreas Prime. Angelina told me if there was a problem you could call her. She was sure you would accept my word that those documents are ethnic.

She also said that she doubts that Admiral Starpaw or General Zantoran would question there validity. However, if they wish to ask her personally, she would be more than happy to discuss it with them."

Commander Gracchus almost laughed at that. "Pompey, I am sure Argus will not question the validity of these documents. Since as the Star of Vandar you could produce them, place the Imperial Seal on them and they would have the same status. The addition of Angelina's name only strengthens the Red Paws' claim."

Pompey smiled that smile. "Then I guess I am no longer needed."

Captain Gracchus shook his head, "Pompey did anyone ever tell you, you are devious."

Pompey grinned, "Yes Captain, thank you."

Jeanne started laughing as she left. "I thought Beary was dangerous. Compared to the females in his life he is an amateur."

Kat didn't care for that comment till Ben started laughing.

"I never thought about it Commander, but I think you are correct." Ben said.

Gracchus looked at both of them. "Ok so the marriage is legal and binding. No problem. Billeting is taken care of and no change in duty assignments. Neither one of you belong to me anyway.

This situation with your father is a problem Kat. I can't make it go away. I will tell fleet it is a Clan situation and to contact Empress Angelina. Try and let her handle it."

Commander Gracchus came over and kissed both of them. "Ben you are still on sick leave. Why don't you take some time and go planet side.

We are giving shore leave to the crew. A resupply ship will be here in six days so take a few."

Ben smiled, "I'll check with Caesar. Thank you Commander."

Jeanne watched them leave, "What are you going to tell fleet?"

"What I should of told them to begin with go to the Moons of Bantine and on the way talk to Angelina Maxumus. She'll probable offer to help them get there." Argus said as his wife kissed him.

As Ben and Kat entered medical, he saw the section with his wounded marines. He walked over to Sergeant Fowler and Corporal Tindal. "How are you two doing?"

Both sat up "Were doing great Skipper." They both moved their legs. "Give us a couple of weeks and we will be walking. A month and we will be back on duty."

Ben nodded, "Thank you both."

"Skipper, thank you for what you did for all our families." Sergeant Fowler said. "It wasn't necessary, but it helped. It especially helped the young privates'. There isn't a Marine in the unit that wouldn't follow you to the Moons of Bantine." Sergeant Fowler said.

Ben touched his shoulder. "Thank you Sergeant."

Kat kissed them both on the cheek.

Tindal smiled as they walked on "Wasn't that Ensign Katimai?"

Fowler replied "Name tag said Maritinus."

Tindal reclined back on the bed. "Good, the Skipper needed her."

Ben walked into Harpeth's room. Dr. Cooper looked up.

"He is better Captain. The treatment is helping but it will take time. We could still lose him." Dr. Cooper said. "Every day he gets stronger."

Ben nodded, "Thank you doctor."

Kat took his arm. "Come husband let the doctor work."

Caesar looked at him, "Well?"

Kat replied. "I need permission to take him planet side for two days."

"Not alone Kat, at least one armed escort, and I would prefer two." Caesar said

"Why?" Ben asked.

"Just my gut Ben, I can't say more than that." Caesar said.

"Mayotte will go. Maybe you can find a young 2Lt. to go with us." Kat said.

Ben looked at Caesar. "How about Archangel he is still recovering?"

"It might do him good to get off the ship and take it easy. That will put more responsibility on Mayotte. He won't be 100%." Caesar said. "But alright he goes with you, if he agrees."

Archangel heard the conversation, "When do we leave Skipper?"

Ben told him. "Have someone pack you a kit and a weapons pack 2 one for me also. We will leave in two cycles, if, I can clear it with Lieutenant Maxumus."

"All right Skipper. Oh by the way, congratulations on your marriage, Skipper and to you also my Lady." Archangel said.

"I am just Kat, Gabriel." Kat said.

"No Mame, you are now Ensign Lady Kat Maritinus a great pilot and the Captain's Lady. To the Marines of this ship that means a lot." Archangel said.

Ben smiled, "Will see you in two cycles."

Kat walked over to a com unit. "Paulette, grab weapons package 2, 3, and 6, your swimming suit, and some other cloths. Meet me at the 38 in two cycles. I'll clear it with the Boss."

Kat and Ben took the turbo lift to Beary's office. Kat smiled as she saluted, "Sir, Doctor Vantanus, and Commander Gracchus have suggested I transport Captain Maritinus and 2Lt. Archangel to the surface of Kalian. They require a few days of R&R. Doctor Vantanus required that I take an armed escort with us. I was hoping to take Mayotte with me."

Beary sighed, "So, Ensign Maritinus, you are planning to use 38 as your mode of transport."

"Yes Sir, I am." Kat said.

"Alright Kat just be careful. A good wingbear is hard to find." Beary said.

"Boss, I'll have a com unit. Don't go anywhere without us." Kat said.

"No problem Kat. Ben, have fun but call home before you take off." Beary said.

Ben nodded "Next stop Beary."

With that Ben and Kat headed back to their new rooms. Jessica and Alexis met them and gave them a kiss. "Here are a few credits as a wedding present. Buy yourself something for your room."

Kat looked at the twelve thousand credits "This is . . ."

"A gift," Jessica said, "We didn't have time to prepare Ben a proper dowry."

Alexis laughed. "You deserve something to compensate you for how we spirited you into a quick marriage to our Ben."

Kat smiled and kissed them. *So this is family. Maybe not sisters but loving cousins,* "Thank you." she whispered.

Ben just kissed them. "I need to call home."

Jessica thought, "Oh that reminds me forty laps! Nikolaos we need to go swimming."

Nikolaos appeared, "Yes my lady, Caesar just called to remind you."

Ben called his father. "Hail father. It is I your son."

Aleut looked at Kat, who sat with her head on his son's shoulder. The old bear smiled. "I see you have brought honor to your tribe and clan."

Ben replied. "Her name is now Kat Maritinus father. Her old name is no more. It was done at her request. Father, I ask if I may have our mark placed on her shoulder."

Aleut howled with joy. "I Aleut Maritinus, so bestow the mark of a Warrior of the Red Paw on my daughter, Lunara do you concur as Mother of the Tribe?"

Lunara responded, "I as her mother as well as Mother of the Clan and tribe do concur. Kat you have brought honor to our Clan we will celebrate your wedding tonight. Then when you and our son come home we will throw a feast."

Kat bowed. "Thank you and thank you Lunara for your son. He is a great boar and a great bear. His cubs will sing of how blessed they are to be his children."

Lunara wept. "Your words bring me great joy and honor daughter." With that Lunara left.

Aleut's chest had swelled, "May the Creator bless you both. Son you have done very well, goodbye."

Ben looked in her eyes, "You are trouble. They will now pester me for grand cubs night and day."

Kat looked at him with tears in her eyes, "I love you Ben."

Ben looked at the clock. Oh well they had a cycle. He undid her uniform.

Kat smiled. "Oh well, I guess we have a little time."

Archangel was looking at Paulette Mayotte. She looked fine in her flight suit. "What do you think is taking so long?"

"She is probable dancing in the flames." Paulette said.

"What?" Archangel asked.

"Nothing it is just a joke between us. We were both known as flirts. Pushing the envelope dancing close to the flame so to speak, Kat always said that was the only way to feel the heat. She also said she always wanted to dance in the flames. To find out what it felt like to truly be loved. I guess she is dancing in that flame." Paulette said.

"If that's the case, then the Skipper is truly lucky. She will be honored by all our Marines. She will be our Lady." Archangel said.

"Pedestals are too easy to fall off of." Paulette said.

"That is why we don't put are ladies up on them." Archangel smiled.

Ben and Kat arrived, "Sorry thought we should figure out where we were going. The good Colonel suggested a cabin by a small lake and hot spring. It is north of the main settlement about sixty KSMU. He said it was nice, secluded, and had a good landing field."

Archangel looked at the Valkyrie III fighter, "It is a little small isn't it."

Mayotte laughed, "No, it has all the comforts of home. Besides it is a short hop. We'll put down the drop seats. They're a little small but you'll be fine."

Kat jumped into the pilot's seat and rode it up to the flight deck. Paulette strapped Ben and Archangel in. Then she set some dials.

"If we have to eject you drop out the bottom. Capsules come out of the wall behind you. Kat and I will come and find you if we are still alive in the pod. Have fun." With that Paulette strapped in and rode up to the flight deck.

Archangel looked at Ben, "It is a lot smaller than a dagger."

Ben nodded, "Not really meant for carrying passengers is it."

"Skipper, excuse me for saying this but your lady is really something." Archangel said.

"It does make you appreciate what they do, doesn't it?" Ben said as they felt the G force of a high speed launch.

Archangel fought the urge to empty his stomach. "Doesn't feel like that in a dagger either."

Ben tried to smile "Dampening fields on the daggers keep you from feeling it."

Kat got on the intercom. "You two put on your helmets and pressurize your suits"

They did as told then Ben asked "Why?"

"Two reasons husband. First in this fighter I am the Boss, no one else. Flight regulations will be followed. Second, I don't wish to be a widow, due to a silly electrical failure or accident." Kat said. "Do either of you have any questions?"

Ben and Archangel both said "No Mame."

Kat dialed in the coordinates they had been given and headed for Kalian's surface. Mayotte scanned the surface.

Thirty STU's latter they started the landing sequence. Kat sat the 38 down on the landing pad near the cabin. Then they started shutting down the fighter.

Mayotte came down, told Ben and Archangel they could now unstrap and move around. She then grabbed a phaser rifle and went out the door.

Archangel grabbed another and followed her.

Mayotte signaled him to circle the other way.

After a few STU they met by the shore of the lake.

"It looked clear to me. How did it look to you?" Archangel asked.

"It is quiet. There is some wild game but none near the cabin. We should check it out." Mayotte said.

Archangel and Mayotte cleared the cabin. To Archangel it felt good. He was in his element this was what Marines did. Mayotte followed his lead. The cabin was clean and neat. No traps no problems. It even had three bed rooms.

Mayotte said, "Ok so we bring them in."

Ben and Kat brought the gear in. "What rooms do you two want?"

Archangel thought. "Back right, that way I can watch forest and lake approaches."

Mayotte replied. "I'll take the loft, gives me good overall coverage."

Kat smiled. "That gives us the front left bed room."

Beary and Artemus walked into Captain Gracchus office. "You wanted to see us Sir."

Commander Gracchus got up off her husband's lap. "Beary your timing is horrible."

Beary asked, "Is the cub kicking yet?"

Argus smiled, "I think I can feel a small flutter."

Artemus nodded "Soon it will get more noticeable."

"Gentlebears, you are not here to discuss the state of my pregnancy." The Commander fumed.

The Captain sighed, "Mood swings, probable not taking her vitamins properly. Maybe I should call Dr. Golden?"

"You know very well he said we are doing fine . . . Oh. We have work to do. Beary and Artemus the good Captain does not wish me to interrogate the prisoners. Nor does he want them near Pompey. A sentiment I feel is ridiculous. We are both capable of doing our jobs." Commander Gracchus stated somewhat miffed.

Beary nodded "Yes Mame. However, I think the Captain is correct. Also I would like to have Shoshanna and Ice Song, take part in the interrogations, along with Romanov and her ladies."

"Why?" Captain Gracchus asked.

Beary pondered his answer, "Shoshanna has a new ability that may be useful. Ice Song may or may not also have the ability. Both have telepathic abilities. So do at least two of Romanov's crew members. Plus they have tactical knowledge."

Gracchus got up. "I see the new abilities first hand. I also want Nikolaos and Andreios with them?"

Artemus looked confused. "Why?"

Gracchus handed him a report from an assistant engineer on the ship. "Andreios is a quick learner. Beary you need or Dr. Vallen needs to spend more time with the cub. Nikolaos is just, well Nikolaos."

Sho-Sho looked at Beary and then at Captain Gracchus. "Are you sure uncle?"

"I will not force you Sho-Sho. It is your decision." Beary said gently.

Sho- Sho bowed her head "Please Captain, do not be offended." She shimmered then standing before him was a strikingly beautiful young Maxmimus with dragon eyes in a silver and gold gown.

Gracchus's mouth about dropped, "Shoshanna you are a stunning young dragon but as a young Maxmimus you are breath taking."

Artemus just smiled, "Nice illusion my dear."

He then turned to Ice Song "Give it a try daughter."

Ice song looked at him, "I . . ."

Artemus kissed her. "If you cannot it is alright. If you can it may be useful my daughter. You and I are not what we were."

Ice Song nodded, she also shimmered standing there was a young Polarian with some Maxmimus features. She was dressed in a long silver gown.

Artemus and Snow Flower stared "It is a good thing Gisfrid is not here. He would be trying to transform so he could challenge all the young bears for your paw." Snow Flower said.

Ice Song's cheeks turned pink, "But he already has my heart."

Artemus kissed her, "Daughter you are beautiful, but it is just an illusion that reflects your inner beauty."

Maryam grinned. "Sister you are gorgeous. But then you always were."

Nikolaos and Andreios just shook their heads, "If she stays in this form we will have to threaten the young Marines."

Ice Song smiled, "If you two keep growing I will have to be chasing the females from you."

"Maryam, you have the small ones. I have need of the boys. Beary said.

"Alright, Beary, they will be safe. I need to work with Erin on some basic self-defense. Agathag should watch."

Beary and Gracchus followed by Sho-Sho, Ice Song, Nikolaos and Andreios headed for the holding cells.

Two dragon NCOs were talking when they spotted Sho-Sho and Ice Song in their Maxmimus form. They both dropped to one knee and bowed. "Your Highness and our Lady."

Shoshana walk over and kissed them "No dragon kneels except before the Creator and his Word. My Grandmother and Mother have so decreed."

They both stood. "It will be as you wish Princess Shoshana and you Lady Ice Song."

Ice Song nodded, "You are to kind."

The older of the two bowed "Not at all Lady Knight."

Beary nodded "Sergeant, we do need to proceed."

The older of the two smiled "Oh yes Prince Maxumus." Then they stepped aside.

Beary, heard one of them, say, "It is good that our Princess and her handmaiden are so powerful."

"Yes it is a good omen for our race." The other said.

Beary smiled, just the reaction he had hoped for. Shoshana and Ice Song had played it perfectly.

The Captain whispered to Beary. "What was that about?"

Beary explained, "It is rare for a dragon to be able to do this. Only the most powerful have this ability. I know of only one other living dragon that can, the First Lady, Samuel's wife, Isadora."

Captain Gracchus eye brows went up "Oh, I didn't realize."

Beary dropped the other shoe, "Erin can turn into a dragon."

"What?" Gracchus said staring at Beary. "But how is that possible?"

Beary shrugged, "She is a Royal Valkyrie. She and Sho-Sho share common ancestry. I'll explain it someday when I understand it better myself."

The lion was again raving. The bear guards were getting annoyed.

Captain Gracchus came in "What is all the noise about?"

The lion looked at Gracchus. "Who lead the cowardly first attack on my ship?"

Beary stepped forward. "I lead the Alfa Strike on your ship."

"What is your name?" The lion growled.

"I am Lieutenant Beary Maxumus." Beary said.

The lion almost screamed. "Maxumus! You are too young to be the one that help rescue the She Devil herself!"

Beary looked at him, "When was that?"

The panther thought "Seventy-four years or so ago. Our emperor was assassinated by three females. We captured the She Devil, the other two escaped. But then this Maxumus rescued her. He killed the Captain's older brother. You look like he did."

Beary thought, "It could have been my father. He was a pilot back then."

The lion screamed "Then I challenge you. If I can't kill him give me a chance to kill his son!"

Nikolaos looked at the lion. "Let me accept his challenge Sire. I could kill him."

"Or I." said Andreios.

"My Prince." said Ice Song

Reuben smiled, "It would be my pleasure to serve you, also my Prince."

Artemus just shook his head, "First, I am next in line, no one else. Well I might have to flip Shoshana for it."

Shoshana looked at the lion. "He would not be worth the effort. If my uncle doesn't want him you may have him Sire Artemus."

The lion snarled, "After I kill him. I will take you as a prize." He said to Shoshana.

Shoshana smiled and bore her thoughts into his mind "Know this lion. If I wished I could kill you with just a thought. I could stop your heart or just destroy your mind."

The lion's eyes got big. He was trying to scream.

Beary turned to Shoshana, "Sho-Sho enough. You know it is not an honorable way."

Sho-Sho nodded, "You are correct my uncle. Besides, he is not worthy of such a death."

The lion recovered. "I'll kill you all."

Beary's eyes turned cold. "But you will have to kill me first."

The lion scoffed. "Then let's get on with it."

Captain Gracchus looked at Beary. "Are you sure about this Lieutenant?"

Beary nodded, "I have to except the challenge Captain, especially if there is a threat to my father."

Gracchus nodded "No one is to interfere."

Beary took off his top. "No weapons. You will have to kill me with your bare paws."

The Lion Captain grinned, "So much the better. You will die more slowly."

Beary had the lion released into a small area and a force field erected around them.

The lion told him. "You have sealed your death Maxumus." The lion bared eight SubSMU metallic claws on each paw.

Beary took a fighting stance. "Let's dance you and me."

The lion charged. He hit Beary across the face and slashed his chest with a set of claws.

He turned only to have Beary land two blows to the side of his head. That sent him sprawling to the floor.

Beary looked at him, "You will have to do better than that?"

The lion looked at his paws two of his claws were broken off and lying on the floor. He got up and charged. This time he tried to sink all his claws into Beary's stomach. He even twisted them and pulled them away.

Beary just smiled and hit him across the face, then threw him across the space.

The lion looked, no blood, no entrails hanging only, his claws bent back on themselves.

Beary sneered "Now you understand. The Arcrilians call me the Ghost. They claim they have killed me a dozen times. But I always come back. Now I am going to kill you."

The lion got up and charged again.

Beary hit him twelve times, as he side stepped the lion's mad rush.

The lion stopped. His arms fell to his side. His knees buckled as he slumped to the floor.

Beary walked in front of him.

The lion looked at him "What did you do to me?"

Beary looked at him, "I have killed you. You have only a few moments to live."

The lion looked at him "How?"

Beary smiled "An old technique past down by my mother's family for centuries. It was she who taught it to me."

As the Lion's eyes dimmed, "The She Devil was your mother . . ."

Beary was bothered by the dead lion's words.

The panther looked at Beary, "You have killed him?"

"Yes." Beary said.

Artemus looked at him. "Do you wish to challenge me?"

"No, I wish to live and someday return home." The panther said.

Shoshana looked at him. "You will come with me. We shall talk."

The panther looked at the young Maxumus. "Would you not be afraid to be in a room with me?"

"No, Centurion Exelon, for you have some honor. Besides you would be no match for me. I am more powerful than you can even imagine and twice as deadly." Shoshanna said.

As she lead the panther into an interrogation room. Beary walked over to Ensign Ni. "Debra, I would like you to use your ability to monitor what is going on. You may refuse."

"I will do it for you, Sir." Ensign Ni said.

Beary explained "Debra, do nothing that offends your belief, you always have the right to say no."

Ensign Ni smiled, "It is alright Lieutenant. There are exceptions, this is one of them."

Beary nodded. "Thank you."

He looked at Romanov "You know what to do."

Romanov nodded. "Yes Boss. Are you sure she will be alright?"

Beary answered, "Sho-Sho can handle him, plus Ice Song is near. But you have the option to do what you deem necessary."

The panther sat down. He did not understand he was not chained. He was sure that there were armed guards near, but he was sure he could over power this young Maxumus female, if he wanted to.

"You are wondering why there isn't an armed guard in with us. I told you. I have nothing to fear from you. She stood before the one way mirror. The truth is my handmaiden is near. She is very formable a Knight of our Clan. But even if she were not here, you are no threat to me in this form or my true form." Sho-Sho said.

The panther looked at her. "True form, I don't understand."

Sho-Sho smiled, "Oh, forgive me. I haven't properly introduced myself. I am Shoshana Maxumus, Daughter of Sir Gamey Maxumus, Knight of Vandar, and her Highness Widja Caesar/Maxumus Empress of all Dragons and Andreas Prime, Handmaiden of Empress Angelina of Andreas Prime my Grandmother."

She placed an image in his mind. "You see in your mind my true form. My uncle felt it would be easier for you to talk to me in this form." She sat primly in front of him.

The Centurion was afraid. "You are a dragon?"

"Yes Centurion Exelon, I am. I am one of the most powerful of my kind. I could take from you the information I want, tearing apart your mind to get it. You could not stop me. I know from my encounter with your captain he would not have hesitated to order such a thing." She watched the fear in the panthers eyes rise. "However, my uncle would be displeased and I would have fallen into a trap, I do not wish to fall into." Sho-Sho said. "You should know though, I will do anything to protect my family, even if it means tarnishing my soul."

The Centurion nodded. "I believe you Lady Maxumus. We are a race known as the Korats. We once had a large empire but it is no longer. We are now surrogates of a larger Empire. The Klingon Empire, They have not turned their attention this way yet, but they were contacted by parties that asked for assistance to solve a problem. The hated name Maxumus was mentioned. My Captain volunteered."

Sho-Sho nodded, "How far away is your Empire."

The panther replied "Farther, than it used to be. The She Devil killed our Emperor on our nearest old out post. When the Maxumus rescued her he started a rebellion that cost us five systems. They now are known as the core of the Gorn Federation."

"Where are your other ships?" Sho-Sho asked.

He looked at her. "You destroyed our slave ship and ours."

"Centurion Exelon, please do not make me force you to give me the information." Sho-Sho said.

He dropped his head, "When we left, two other sets of ships, left for Bearilian territory. We have not been in contact."

Sho-Sho gently probed his mind "You may return to your cell Centurion Exelon. Sleep in peace, we may talk again."

Sho-Sho explained everything she had learned.

Gracchus looked around the table "Ok, we tell fleet we have four more rouge ships from the Korats Empire, in our territory. Golden Dragon 1 is a possible target."

Beary nodded. "So are we, but they don't know why."

Pompey looked at Beary, "Notify General Flame Heart. Andreas Prime could be targeted."

"Ok, bears get to work. Admiral Astrid and his task force will be here in forty eight cycles. I need to know what I can and can't tell him." Gracchus said.

Beary looked at Shoshana, "You and Ice Song can return to yourselves if you wish."

Ice Song changed back "That feels better."

Sho-Sho paused "After we talk to grandfather."

Beary first called General Flame Heart and explained as much as he could. He also called Gamey who notified Brigadoon and the Palisades.

Beary then called his Parents, who he learned was at the Caesar/Maxumus Castle. "Mom and Dad we are on an ultra-secure line. I need to ask a few questions."

Angelina nodded. "Is that our dear Shoshana setting with you? You are lovely dear. Isadora would be proud."

"Thank you Grandmother. I must ask. Are you the She Devil that killed the Korats Emperor seventy-four years ago?" Sho-Sho asked.

Angelina smiled, "That was not my code name, dear, but it will do for this discussion. Yes, my cell conducted that operation."

Beary stared at her, "Mom?"

"Really, Beary, don't look so shocked. I can't go into details; I would have to kill you. The only reason your father is still alive is because he is too good in bed." Angelina said.

Beary, face blushed "Mother!"

Sho–Sho laughed.

Beary composed himself. "We were attacked by two warships from the Korats Empire or what is left of it. There are two pairs of ships still at large."

Octavious nodded, "Beary, our involvement with that Empire is classified so far above everybody's pay grade that it never happened. Do you understand son. Your mother and her ladies never existed, ever! Those that even have a slight knowledge have literally signed their own death warrants, if they ever divulge what they know. You and Sho-Sho have just added your names to that list."

Beary looked at his father. "I understand Sir. What do I tell Captain Gracchus and my intelligence team?"

Octavious looked at him. "Son, do you trust them?"

"Yes, with my life father." Beary said.

"Then tell them what you must. Sho-Sho can you erase the prisoners memories without hurting them." Octavious asked.

Sho-Sho looked at him. "Grandfather, what you ask is dishonorable?"

Octavious nodded. "You only have to alter the part about Angelina and me. If you cannot then they all must be killed, before Admiral Astrid arrives."

Tears fell from her eyes. "Power is a horrible burden."

"Sho-Sho you do not have to do this! We can take our chances." Angelina said.

Sho-Sho shook her head, "No Grandmother. Grandfather is correct. I can do it without doing harm."

Angelina looked at Beary. "Do not let her be burdened."

Beary nodded. "I love you both." He turned off the com unit.

"Sho-Sho, he had no right to ask you to do this." Beary said.

Sho-Sho shook her head, "No Beary he is right! We do not know who are enemies are. Ice Song and I can do this. We will be gentle. The other option is murder."

That night while the prisoners slept, Sho-Sho and Ice Song moved among them like wraths. Entering their dreams and giving them sweet and peaceful dreams. Then they slowly rewrote the memories of their old Emperors death and the Gorn uprising. Utterly removing any memory of the She Devil or the name Maxumus accept hers and Beary's.

Beary explained the situation to the intelligence team and Captain Gracchus.

Captain Gracchus looked at him. "Couldn't Sho-Sho erase my memory also?"

"No Sir, she won't do it." Beary said.

Captain Gracchus shook his head. "I have to lie to an Admiral?"

Beary explained. "Those are the Vice Presidents orders Captain."

"Beary, I hope he can get us a pardon before we get court marshaled" Captain Gracchus said.

Beary responded, "I am not worried about a One Star, I work directly for a Five Star."

Gracchus smiled "Come to think about it so do I."

Sho-Sho came in; in dragon form she looked tired.

Beary kissed her "I am sorry Shoshana."

"So much sadness, life for them was hard. The average crew member was little more than a slave. These Klingons treat their race as little more than armed slaves. They allow them the allusion of autonomy. But control all commerce and trade." Sho-Sho said.

Beary dropped his head. "Like my race treated yours."

Sho-Sho kissed him. "No my uncle, no dragon ever saw it that way. We each gave a life to end the war, and had two lives joined together. Now our lives are inseparable."

Gracchus responded. "I hope our young Captain is having fun.

Well go home get some rest.

Lady Shoshana, can I ask you to be here tomorrow, when Admiral Astrid comes to visit. Also can you come in your other form?"

Sho-Sho nodded. "If you wish Captain, I am at your disposal."

Gracchus nodded, "No Princess, but I need you to make sure I don't get trapped into saying anything I shouldn't."

Sho-Sho walked over and kissed him. "I will come then as a Princess of Andreas Prime and a representative of my Grandmother."

Gracchus smiled as she walked out. "Smart and beautiful, I am not sure I want to be in Gamey's shoes or whatever."

Beary replied, "You don't know the half of it."

While all this was going on Ben and his party had been exploring. They had found the mineral hot springs. Kat put on a one piece, somewhat conservative swimsuit.

Ben looked at her. "You look great, but what no bikini?"

Kat kissed him, "I am married. I need to be more proper. Don't worry I will put on a show for you later."

Mayotte on the other hand came out in a dangerous blue bikini.

Archangel's mouth fell open.

"Gabriel, you can look all you like. You try and touch and I'll break your arms." Paulette said.

"Yes Paulette, but if you're going to dress like that I am definitely going to look." Archangel said.

Paulette smiled, "Well you better. I wore this for your benefit after all."

Kat slapped her on the tail. "Now, who is dancing near the flame?"

Paulette smiled. "Sometimes one needs a little heat."

Paulette walked up next to Gabriel and traced the scare on his back where the penetrator had exited. She then stood in front of him and traced the entry scare, as she touched his hard chest. "Of course the rules don't apply to me. I am responsible for ensuring you are healing properly." She then turned slowly and walked in front of him.

Ben smiled, "Lieutenant, keep your mind on your job."

Gabriel looked at him "Yes Skipper."

Ben laughed.

Kat squeezed his paw. "You are evil. You know that?"

They got to the hot springs Ben and Gabriel climbed in, as Kat and Paulette placed food and drinks on the edge of the spring, before climbing in. Paulette pulled a small phaser rifle with a folding stock from the bottom of the basket and placed it on a hidden ledge out of sight.

"It is water proof, designed for under water operations." She whispered into Gabriel's ear.

He whispered back "A Marines dream, a gorgeous girl who knows weapons."

Paulette smiled, "You are a silver tonged one aren't you."

Kat washed Ben's back and front.

"Ah, when I was single three pretty maidens would do this and see to my comfort." Ben sighed loudly.

Kat kissed him as her paw disappeared below the bubbling water. "But they could not care for you the way I can or keep you nearly as warm as I."

Ben's eyes got big. "Kat I . . . know I will be the happiest of boars."

Paulette turned brushing her body against Gabriel. She looked at him and whispered "Kiss me and look behind me in the trees fifty SMU. Go ahead and make it look believable just get a good scan of the area."

Gabriel slowly guided his paw across her stomach and kissed her hard and full on the lips. Then down her neck, across her shoulders, and back to her mouth. Then back to her other shoulder and back to her mouth. Then up to her ear. "I count five figures maybe six."

Paulette kissed him "I thought I counted seven."

Gabriel kissed her neck. "Figure ten, now slap me and swim over to Kat.

Paulette slapped him, "Beast!" She then swam over to Kat.

"We have company." Paulette whispered.

Kat looked mad. "Ben, talk to that Lieutenant of yours."

Ben moved over looking angry "How many?"

Archangel looking defensive whispered "We are sure of seven probable ten that is our best guess."

Ben frowned, "Good acting."

Archangel whispered, "Great leading Lady, Skipper."

"Ok, gather everything up we are heading back. Paulette you are in the lead. Gabriel you got the tail, where all dirty dogs, belong. Look thoroughly chewed out." Ben said.

They gathered everything up and headed for the cabin.

Kat took Ben's paw. "We could head for the 38; I could have us airborne in a few moments."

Ben whispered back as they walked. "No, you have it cloaked don't you?"

Kat replied quietly. "Of course, and running on a small APU. Strictly SOP."

Ben squeezed her paw and whispered, "We go to the cabin and see what happens."

They reached the cabin and went inside. Ben barred the door, while the girls closed the inside shutters.

Archangel found the door to the cellar. He opened it and went down and checked it out. As he suspected there was another door he opened it and followed the tunnel for several SMU. He then returned, locked the door and barred it.

He went upstairs. "We have an escape tunnel."

Ben nodded. "Good, as long as they don't know about it also."

Ben looked at the ladies. "You better get dressed."

Archangel came out of the back, "We have two coming around to the front."

Ben nodded. "Do you have armor on?"

"Yes Skipper, by the way they are locals." Archangel said.

Ben nodded, "Play it loose. It might be just a local militia or bandits trying to shake us down. No point in a large body count."

"You in the cabin come out!" a voice shouted.

"Back me from inside." Ben opened the door and stepped out.

Ben asked. "What can we do for you?"

The bigger of the two sneered at Ben. "We said for you all to come out."

Ben lowered his voice. "Do you think we are idiots? If anyone tries anything, your fault, my fault it doesn't matter. You two will be dead. Now what do you want? What right do you have to ask these questions?"

The other two looked at the Polarian in front of them. "Just who are you to ask?"

Ben replied "Captain Ben Maritinus of the 981st MSD aboard the *BAFSRV EAQ.* I am renting this property from its owner Colonel Mac Adams. Here is a letter of agreement. Now who are you?"

The two looked at each other. They were nervous. "We're just . . . local Militia. Just making sure everything is secure. How did you get here?"

"The old transport in the shed. It runs ruff but it runs. Do you have any other questions?" Ben asked

The older of the two nodded. "You have females with you?"

Ben looked at him with penetrating eyes. "My wife and her weapons officer, we are all on leave, some R&R, after defending this sector. But you don't want to bother them right now. It would make them cranky."

The youngest one smiled, "You know it might not be safe here by yourselves. Maybe we should camp nearby."

Ben looked at him. "Oh, I think we are perfectly safe. My Lieutenant and I are trained combat Marine Officers. Our ladies are experienced combat pilots. We have all killed more than our share of vermin. I am not worried about a few bandits."

The older one grabbed the sleeve of the younger, "We need to get back on our patrol. Be careful now ya hear."

Ben nodded and turned to walk back in.

As he did Archangel came out and fired twice.

Ben saw movement, at the left front corner of the cabin; he dove, pulled his weapon, and fired.

The bandit's shot passed just over him while Ben's exploded his head just above his right eye. The shooter fell dead.

Ben got up. "Get inside!" That was when he heard two rail gun rifles cough from upstairs.

The bandit leader knew things had gone wrong. He watched as two of his bears started running from an area near the shed, across the field. Then he saw a flash and heard something just in time to watch his two bears be picked up and thrown to the ground like rag dolls.

Then a branch near his head exploded. He dropped to the ground.

"Pull back farther into the woods. We need to rethink this! It has already cost us more bears than it should have." The leader ordered.

Once they were back behind a hill one of his Lieutenants came over. "What do you want to do now?"

"I don't know what we should do. We have already lost five bears." The leader said.

"But they have females with them! Do you know how much they could bring on the black market?" The lieutenant said.

"They are Fleet Officers; do you think the fleet wouldn't hunt for them?" The leader asked.

"So, we sell them fast, and then they will become someone else's problem." The Lieutenant said.

The leader shook his head. "We cannot take them with the five we have left."

"So we leave two bears behind, go back, and bring back the rest of our band." The Lieutenant said.

"How many are you willing to bury?" The leader asked.

"Those females are worth one hundred thousand credits each or more. Plus their weapons and gear could also fetch a good price." The Lieutenant said.

"We will go back and put it up to a vote. If they agree then we will try and take them. Leave two bears behind to watch." The leader said.

Archangel looked at Ben. "What do you think Skipper?"

"I think they will be back with reinforcements. If I was them I would leave a couple of watchers. I think I need to kill them. Then we can decide what we want to do." Ben said.

"But why, they have to know we can kill them?" Archangel said.

"Because, they figure they could sell our ladies for a small fortune on the black market." Ben said.

Archangel fumed, "Over my dead body."

Ben nodded. "That is their general idea."

Ben put on some forest camouflage.

Kat looked at him, "Where are you going?"

"To eliminate the bandits watching us and to leave a message to the ones that will be coming back." Ben said kissing her.

Kat said "It is . . ."

Archangel explained. "Kat he killed over one hundred Arcrilians by himself. Two bandits in the woods won't have a chance."

Ben looked at him. "You know what to do."

Paulette responded curtly. "We're not helpless Boss."

Ben nodded. "I know Paulette."

Ben took off down the cellar. He followed the tunnel it seemed to go on forever. Then he came to a metal ladder, he climbed up it. It came out into a hollow tree. He slipped out the door.

He could smell one off to the left smoking. The other off to the right had just relieved himself. The odor was almost over powering.

Ben moved to the left. He fitted a spear point on a strait branch he picked up from the ground. The bandit was watching the cabin he lit another smoke. As the match flared Ben hit him in the back with the spear.

The bandit wanted to scream, but he couldn't. He slowly fell to the ground as his eyes grew dark.

Ben put out the small fire that started where the match and smoke fell. He then pinned the bandit's body to a tree.

He then started stalking the other bandit. It didn't take him long to find him. This bandit however was large and muscular. Ben launched two spears at him. The bandit turned just before they hit. One caught him in the shoulder. The other caught him in the arm.

The Bandit glared at Ben and pulled the spears out of his body. He pulled a knife and charged Ben.

Ben fitted two more spear points and started moving. He dodged a knife blow and drove a spear into the bandit's midsection. He also drove the second one into his back.

The bandit staggered then pulled the spears out of his body. He threw them to the ground. He was bleeding heavily. "I am going to kill you!" He screamed.

The bandit swung his knife at Ben. Again Ben slipped under him and stabbed him twice in the chest with his knife. Still the bandit kept coming.

The bandit threw his knife at Ben. It missed, but it distracted Ben, long enough for him to grab Ben in a death hug.

Ben could feel the air being crushed out of his lungs. Ben stabbed with his knife over and over. He finally brought the top of his forehead down on the top of the other bear's snout as hard as he could.

This blow loosened the other bear's grip. Ben slipped out and hip threw him to the ground. He then drove his knife through the bandit's neck. The bandit twitched then died. Blood was everywhere. Then Ben saw the yellow stain dust capsules in his pocket.

"He was a dope addict!" Ben said to the trees. "I was almost killed by a dope addict!" It was then that Ben realized *that it was his vest that had saved his life or at least extended it.*

Ben pinned this bandit to the tree upside down. He did it in a way to leave a clear message, that trying to hurt their females, meant only death and possible a horrible one at that.

Ben went back to the tree. He slipped in, closed the hatches, locked them tight, and returned down the tunnel.

Archangel was waiting. "Skipper, are you alright?"

Ben grimaced. "I have a couple of bruised ribs. One was hopped up on yellow stain dust. Couldn't feel any pain, he almost squeezed me to death. The vest saved me."

"You better get up stairs. Let Kat have a look." Archangel said.

Ben replied. "She might finish what he started." Ben climbed the stairs, as Archangel, secured the tunnel.

Kat looked at him. "How bad are you hurt?"

Ben shrugged. "I am fine, just a couple of bruised ribs."

"Take off your shirt. Let me have a look." Kat ordered.

She touched his ribs on the left side he winced a little. She probed not to gentle on both sides. Then thumped his chest, again he winced a little. "Mostly bruised muscles, maybe a rib or two, you're lucky. Whoever he was didn't cave in your chest."

Ben whispered. "I wore my vest. He was on yellow stain dust couldn't feel pain."

Kat looked at him. "So, if they take us, we can expect the worse."

Ben looked at her. "They are not taking anyone. We are four trained combat soldiers, against a bunch of undisciplined bandits. We have a good defensible position and an escape route or two."

Paulette looked at him. "Boss, could you tell how long they had been gone?"

Ben thought "Half a cycle the smoker was a chain smoker. He had smoked four smokes was starting a fifth."

Archangel thought, "The younger bandit said maybe they should camp nearby."

Kat nodded, "We could cover what five KSMU a cycle with full gear, more if lightly outfitted."

Ben nodded. "Figure three for them. They plan to be back tonight. So their main group is no more than nine KSMU away."

Paulette looked at Ben, "What do we do?"

Archangel answered for him, "We move extra food and water into the cellar. Build a fort inside near the cellar door and one in the cellar while they rest."

Kat thought. "Two cycles, then you two sleep."

Kat took Ben's paw and lead him into the bedroom. "You aren't going to sleep. I am going to punish you for playing hero."

A cycle later she was sleeping peacefully beside Ben. He looked down at her. Ben thought *here they were facing death and she was sleeping like an Angel. But wasn't that their life?* Ben smiled *Kat didn't fear death or life. She just lived. She danced first near the fire now in life's flames never afraid of getting burned.* Oh how he loved her.

Paulette looked at Gabriel. "How will they come at us?"

Gabriel thought about it. "If it was me, I would hit us at twilight or dawn from the lake or the buildings by the shed. We have a blind spot there. They still would have to cover open ground but not as much. Plus there is cover to fire on us from. This cabin was designed to deal with bandits. They can't starve us out or wait till we run out of water. We have plenty. Besides, they know if we don't check in someone will come looking."

Paulette looked at him. "So, you're not worried?"

Gabriel looked into her eyes. "If it was just me and the Skipper then, no," He saw her getting mad "Look Paulette I know you and Kat are tough. You are two of the most competent and dangerous females I have ever met. That fighter of yours scares me half to death. But if we fail, they will kill the Skipper and me. They won't kill you. I have seen what slavers do to female captives . . ." he turned away from her.

Paulette looked at him then turned him towards her and kissed him. "When we rest, I want you to hold me in your arms. Nothing else, no funny business, but I want to feel your heat."

Gabriel looked at her "Paulette it . . ."

"Gabriel, I have never known a boar. You would have to take me and you wouldn't like that. Neither would I. Can't you just show me some tenderness?" Paulette asked.

Gabriel sat down. "Paulette you're safe with me. I have a secret no one knows. Before I become a Marine, I was a novice Priest. I had taken a vow of celibacy. The Church I belonged to didn't believe priest should marry. When I was sixteen our church was raided by Brigands and Orion slavers, I saw what they did to the young nuns.

After six months I escaped from my captives and made my way back to Bearilian space. I changed my name to Gabriel Archangel and joined up.

I was well educated they put me into OTS and I became an officer. The priest was dead the avenging angel was born."

Paulette put her head in his lap, "Then how many females have you kissed?"

Gabriel told her. "One, you were my first. Like that, if you know what I mean."

Paulette sighed. "Then, I will be safe in your arms Gabriel. Perhaps you will be safe in mine."

At the encampment of the bandits, the head bandit was listening as the raid leader and his lieutenant argued.

He looked at the Lieutenant. "You are foolish enough to want to go back. They will have communication equipment. That Marine Captain is playing with you."

"You are as old a female as our raid leader was. At least put it up for a vote. Let those that want to follow me, go." The Lieutenant said.

The head bandit gave in. "Fine if there are those who want to follow you to their death, then they can go. But do not return. I do not want the fleet hunting me."

The Lieutenant responded with a little speech of his own. "You heard him. He is afraid of the Bearilian fleet and four of their officers'. Two of which are females. Who will follow me to relieve the two boar officers of their equipment and females?"

Twenty young bandits rallied to him. Some had come with him when he had joined this band. It was soon apparent no others were going to join him. Well his welcome had been worn out and his hopes of overthrowing the leader of this group weren't going to happen. Yet he had picked up replacements for those he had lost plus a couple more.

"Let's go, fortune awaits us." The Lieutenant said.

With that twenty bandits followed him out of camp.

When they were well out of sight, the head bandit called his raid leaders together. "Pack up camp. I want to head northwest into the mountains as far away from here as we can get. Whether that idiot fails or succeeds he will bring ruin onto all of us. Especially, if they find us anywhere near that cabin."

Kat woke up, stretched, and looked at Ben. Then sat up "We have a com unit with us, you could have called for help several cycles ago!"

Ben nodded. "Still could, if I thought we were in any real danger."

Kat looked at him. "You mean you don't think they are coming back?"

Ben kissed her neck, chest, and then her lips. "Oh no, my love, they are coming back. I am just not sure how many."

She looked at him. "You were expecting this weren't you?"

Ben shrugged. "The good Colonel mentioned that was why he wanted us to use this cabin. It is a trap Kat we are the bait."

Kat looked at him, "You couldn't have told me or the others?"

Ben shrugged, "Would you have acted different? Would have Paulette? I know Gabriel would have." He already tried his com unit, it was jammed." Ben pointed to a small jammer.

Kat looked at him. "Why? You have to have a reason. The bear I love couldn't be this evil without a reason."

Ben dropped his head, "I am doing it for Archangel . . . Kat I can't tell you anymore, and it is his story. There is a good reason for everything I do. I always weigh my honor against my actions. I only ask that you withhold judgment. If you find me unworthy, I'll understand."

Kat was mad and touched by the total absurdity of what he said. "Ben Maritinus, what am I supposed to do setting here naked in bed? Throw up my arms and denounce you. Storm out of the room nude? You are my husband for better or worse. It just makes me mad you felt a need to keep a secret from me."

"Kat, I am sorry. I was wrong. Can you forgive me?" Ben asked.

Kat dropped her head tears flowing. "Now you went and did it. You broke all the rules. If you would have been my father you would have beaten me, the way he does my mother, for talking to you like that. But you asked me to forgive you."

Ben wrapped his arms around her. "Kat, I might not be a very good husband yet. But I will never be your father."

Kat kissed him. "I will give you lots of sons."

Ben held her tight. "Daughters are fine, whatever the Creator wishes."

Paulette pounded on the door. "Your nap time is up. You need to give someone else a chance to do it."

Archangel smiled and looked at her, as she realized what she said.

"I meant sleep! You don't think I meant . . . Gabriel you know better!" Paulette stammered.

Ben came out. "Kat needs a moment. You two can go ahead."

Paulette grabbed Gabriel's paw. "Well come on Lieutenant you heard him it is our turn." She stopped looked at the both of them. "We're just going to share a room. You need the loft to watch for bandits. We're not going to do any . . . I mean we will leave the door . . ."

Gabriel pushed her into the room. "Her purity is safe with me Skipper."

Kat smiled. "But is his with her?"

Ben laughed. "That is his problem Kat not ours."

Paulette looked at him. "I sounded like an idiot, didn't I?"

Gabriel replied with a smirk. "Perhaps, look I'll sleep on the floor. You take the bed."

Paulette looked at him. "No," she laid down "You come and rest beside me. The bed is big enough. Besides if you can't trust a boar who was a priest. Who can you trust?"

Gabriel shook his head. "The young priest is dead and buried Paulette. I am not sure what or who I am anymore. I just have a burning desire for revenge against . . . What if I am becoming just like them?"

Paulette looked into his green eyes, "Then you aren't an Angel but a demon and you will take what you desire. Gabriel, I believe you are an angel. I hope someday to fall in love perhaps with you. It is your choice who or what you are."

He laid down with his back to her and she wrapped herself around him, and snuggled in close.

Paulette whispered right before she dozed off "I told you I needed to feel your heat . . ."

Gabriel closed his eyes. "Please, my Creator let me be the Angel she expects, for I fear becoming a demon from the hate that still burns in my heart. Is it possible for love to bloom among the thorns of hate that live in my soul?"

Kat looked in. Gabriel opened his eyes and held a paw to his mouth then mouthed "She is already asleep."

Kat nodded and walked on up the stairs.

Ben was looking out a window. "It will be awhile before they get back. Then we will activate the cabin's defenses."

Kat wrapped her arms around Ben, "Are you sorry . . . I know your father pushed you into . . . I mean you probably . . ."

Ben looked at her. "Still testing me Kat? Should I ask for leave, so I can kill your father? I am not him Kat. I have my faults. I have many. I never really planned to marry, I never figured I would live that long. The Creator has blessed me with you, an Angel, but one with a broken heart. I cannot replace what he broke, Kat. All I can do is give you the love, I have."

Kat sat down. "Is that what I have been doing this morning? Looking at you and trying to see my father. Expecting you to be like him, Acting gentile at first, then turning mean. My mother said it was just the way things were."

Ben shook his head. "Kat, I can be vicious, when it comes to protecting the ones I love. But my father taught me better than that. Besides if my father had ever hit my mom. She would have cut him to little pieces.

I could never be like him Kat. My Dad taught me a lesson about honor and love, when I was about Nikolaos's age. I have never forgotten." Ben took a deep breath. "I was just a wild cub not thinking. I saw some fish lines set on a river bank. They had fish on them. I thought what the harm. I could take the fish and replace the bait no one would be the wiser."

Ben paused again Kat looked at him and nodded.

"I sold the fish at the market, pocketed the coins, and made up a reasonable story. I thought about catching the fish." Ben paused again, pain showing in his eyes.

Kat nodded again.

"The Polarian that owned the lines spotted my tracks and followed them into the market. He caught up to me before I made it home. He took me before the council.

I tried to make an excuse; I gave him the money I had received. But steeling fish in our village is a major crime. The council however was worried about the sentence of twenty-five lashes. That was what the law required and in public. After all I was the Chief's son."

Tears were flowing in Ben's eyes. "My father said the law had to be satisfied. I had brought dishonor on the village. The debt had to be paid. The full twenty-five lashes were to be given.

I was taken out and tied to a skinning post. My shirt striped from my back. I heard the whip master limber up his whip. A member of the council put a piece of soft wood in my mouth and told me not to scream out.

I prepared for the first strike when a shadow fell over me. I saw two strong arms bending over me. Then I heard the whip strike and tear flesh. I felt blood and sweat fall on my fur as each strike fell harder than the first. Yet, no other sound was heard.

On the last strike two large boars came over and pulled the paws away from the post. They lowered my father to the ground. He never said a word as they carried him into our hut.

My mother grabbed my paw and told me not to dishonor my father with a tear till we were inside.

I wanted to turn away, to hide, but she made me stand there and study every mark the whip made. She said my dishonorable act had placed each stripe there. They were not as deep as the ones I had put on his heart. It was my duty in life to erase those marks of dishonor, by bringing honor to my father and my clan."

Ben paused again. "My father has never mentioned that day or what he did. Yet, it is burned into my soul."

Kat fell at his knees crying, "So much love. How, could a father have so much love for his children?"

Ben looked at her. "My father says it pales in comparison to the love the Creator has for all of his Creations and all his children. He told me once as a father we are to live by the standard the Creator sets."

Kat looked at him, "You truly believe this don't you Ben?"

"Kat it is the way my father has lived his life and the way he rules as Chief and as a father. He has been a good teacher." Ben said.

"I am sorry Ben. I will stop crying. I will stop testing you, and I will be the wife you deserve I promise." Kat said.

Ben picked her up. "Kat just be Kat. She is plenty good enough for anyone."

Kat picked up a pair of field glasses. "Two more cycles?"

Ben nodded, "Give or take, we'll turn things on soon. Even if they get back they won't try anything before dusk."

Kat shook her head, "03:00 cycles in the morning, if, it is a moonless night. They will try and catch us in a low REM time."

Ben nodded. "Even if it isn't, either that or they will come at dawn."

Archangel was getting stiff. He rolled over on to his back and looked at his watch. They had been a sleep for three cycles.

Paulette rolled half on top of him, hooked his leg, and buried her face into his chest.

"Paulette, they let us over sleep, wake up. Come on we need to get up." Gabriel urged.

Paulette's eyes opened, "Oh, hi Gabriel, umm you smell good. Did anyone tell you that?"

"Paulette, wake up we have work to do!" Gabriel prompted.

"I was having such a nice dream. You and me, a sunny beach . . ." She smiled "You aren't a priest any more are you?" Paulette asked.

Gabriel sat up. "Paulette I . . ."

Paulette sat up. "Gabriel, what was the young nun's name?"

Gabriel looked at her. "It wasn't just one they tortured all . . ."

Paulette shook her head. "No, they may all haunt you a little but you only called out one name in your dreams . . . Sister Anna Louisa."

Gabriel stood up and walked to the window. He was shaking. "You say . . . I called her name . . . in . . . my . . . sleep?"

Paulette walked over to him. "Yes, who was she?"

Gabriel tried to shake the memory from his brain. He could still see her laughing face. "She was my friend . . . We may have even loved one another within the strict rules we lived in. I don't know. We were young. Both brought up to serve in the capacity that was chosen for us, she as a teacher and I as a priest."

Paulette wrapper her arms around his waist, "Please Gabriel I know you are fighting your own demons. But you need to talk about this. I am your friend . . ."

Gabriel looked at her. "I don't know that I could tell you even if you were my lover."

Paulette looked at him. "Is that what you want Lieutenant Archangel, just a throw away lover? Do you think that will kill your demons . . .?" She walked away from him and sat on the bed.

"Fine, then come and take what you want. I won't resist. I won't give it to you either. Better you than one of them out there." Paulette said.

Gabriel's eyes flashed he walked over and started to slap her. Then he just slid to his knees, in front of her. "Why . . . Why did you say those things?"

Paulette shrugged, "It wouldn't have been the first time I have been knocked around, if you had hit me. I have been slapped around before. You're just the first boar who stopped themselves. You need to talk about it Gabriel. It is eating you alive. I know. I have been there. I have lost bears I cared about. Including the boar I was planning on marrying. He was killed on the Fast Claw."

Gabriel looked at the tears in her eyes. "They had hurt her bad. I got to her cell. I found a way out and I carried her. They trailed us for days. Finally, I snuck us onto a freighter heading for Bearilian space. It was dirty but warm. I was able to steal some food and water to keep us alive. But her injuries were bad. Worse her spirit was broken. She said she was no longer fit to serve the Creator or fit for any decent boar. I told her the Creator would not hold the evils committed against her as sins she committed. That she was blameless. She was lost in her own despair and nothing I said or did seem to matter. The night we arrived in Bearilian space she just stopped living. The autopsy was inconclusive. The doctor didn't feel she died of her injuries. It was like she just stopped living . . ."

Paulette looked at him. "You blame yourself?"

Gabriel glared at her. "Shouldn't I? I was a priest. I should have been able to help her! I was her friend. I loved her!"

Paulette sighed, "You aren't the Creator. You didn't set the stars in motion. I bet he tried to reach her also. We are given free will Gabriel good, bad, or ugly. She had a choice. You gave her those choices; forgive herself, and live or hate herself, and die. She chose death.

You also made a choice. You gave up the cloth, changed your name, and put on this uniform. You can live and die with your hate. Or you can live with the things that uniform stands for. Yes, you could still die. We all can. It is part of the job. Hate doesn't leave room for love or honor. So what is it you want?"

Gabriel looked at her. "Just what are you offering me Paulette?"

Paulette shrugged, "A choice I guess, between what I believe you need, and what the demon in you says you need. I can't stand to see you suffering. So you can choose, take from me what the bandits would take and feed the demon or take my paw, hold me, and talk to me. Perhaps take a chance that something wonderful could grow."

Gabriel looked at her, "So, I can either give up my hate and guilt. Then pursue a possible love affair with you. Or I can just take you further feeding that hate and guilt."

Paulette dropped her head, "Yes." and unbuttoned a button.

Gabriel reached up and stopped her. "Don't, Paulette I wouldn't know what to do anyway. Besides all you would accomplish is scaring me half to death. Tell me why you would do this."

Paulette shrugged. "I told you why, at least part of it. You and I aren't so different. I lost the boar I loved. He was kind and gentle most of the time, unless he had been drinking. He was getting help. Especially, after Kat almost killed him one night. But when he was sober he was a very good and kind boar. He treated me good and he never tried to take liberties even when he slapped me round. To be fair I probably deserved it a couple of times."

"So were both damaged goods is that what you're saying?" Gabriel asked.

"No, I am saying that we are two bears with hard life experiences. That might find comfort in each other's arms. At least some understanding when the coldness and loneliness creeps in." Paulette said.

Gabriel kissed her. "Hi my Lady, I am Gabriel Archangel Marine 2nd Lieutenant and I think you are beautiful."

Paulette smiled, "It is my pleasure Sir to meet you. I am Ensign Paulette Mayotte. I hope to get to know you much better over a life time."

Gabriel looked at her. "You never deserved it Paulette, Kat would tell you the same thing. I don't want to speak ill of the dead, but he was a coward. You deserve better."

Paulette asked. "Are you applying for the position?"

Gabriel stopped at the door. "If I can prove worthy of you, both, to you and myself then, yes." With that he headed out and upstairs.

Paulette stopped and fell to her knees and started crying. She didn't understand why. Nor could she stop.

Kat came down and found her. She helped her to the bed. "Paulette did he hurt you?"

"No!" Paulette sobbed

Kat looked at her "He didn't . . ."

"No he said he wouldn't know how . . ." Paulette sobbed some more.

Kat was now confused, "Paulette what is wrong?"

"He was hurting so bad . . . Girl just gave up on living . . . He couldn't help her . . . They tortured her and hurt her . . . He rescued her but she . . . just died . . . It hurt him so bad . . . now he said . . . He might . . . want to be . . . with me . . . if he can prove . . . worthy." Paulette sobbed out.

Kat looked at her. "You want him!"

Paulette looked at her with tears streaming "No . . . Yes . . . OH KAT, I have made a mess of everything!"

Kat just laughed. "You fell into the flames and got burned. Oh baby, get your act together. We are going to have company. Also if you want him go for it. If not tell him now!"

Paulette looked at Kat and whispered. "Is it wrong for me to want him so soon after . . .?"

Kat looked at her. "That worm was no good. I would never have let you marry him. He would have gone out an airlock by accident. Archangel might be alright if you want him go for it. I need to go help my husband. Now get your act together Mayotte there is work to do."

Paulette sighed *that was Kat make a decision then get it done period.*

The bandit group made their way to where they had left the two lookouts. It had taken longer than the ex-bandit Lieutenant had liked. He smiled well he was a small band leader again. He was sure these two would join him.

One of the younger bandits screamed. He ran back then threw up. He couldn't talk all he did was point up the hill.

Three of the group climbed the hill with their new leader. They stared in horror at the smoker. He was pinned to the tree with a spear through his throat and several smokes shoved in his mouth.

The leader looked at him and turned to two of the bandits, "Take him down please. We need to find Zorda perhaps he is still alive."

One of the other bandits looked at him, "No one could take Zorda he is invincible."

Another agreed "If he attacked Zorda we will find one less Marine and Zorda probable eating him."

They pilled rocks over the smoker and started working their way towards the point Zorda should be.

The Leader was the first to spot him. His mind refused to believe what he was seeing. The big bear was hanging pinned by his feet between two trees. His body had been slit from groin to neck and a sign was pinned to him.

This is what happens to all that Threaten Our Ladies!

The other Bandits were visibly shaken by the sight of him. Who could have been strong enough to have killed Zorda? They asked among themselves.

Some thought of sneaking off. All of a sudden this did not seem like a good idea.

The Leader knew he was going to lose bears if he didn't do something. "Look at what he did to our friend! Does it not make your blood boil? He even challenged all of you! There are only two boars in that group. I have seen the females they are exquisite. There is no reason we couldn't sample them before we sell them!"

All of a sudden he had regained their interest.

"Plus, who knows what other treasures they might have with them. They are all four fleet officers. You all know how well paid and pampered they are. They are also arrogant. They will not expect us to return. We will hit them tonight while they are asleep, get some rest." The leader said.

He then called over one of his old followers. "Jocko pass out some chemical courage to those that need it."

Jocko nodded. "You know what you told them was pure bull. We should walk away find easier prey. If we attack these bears we will die."

The leader looked at him. "Are you deserting me?"

Jocko shook his head, "It matters not to me. I have been a dead bear since that raid on the church, all those years ago. What we did there was wrong and evil. That young priest escaped. Someday he will find us and send us to the Moons of Bantine. So if I die here or elsewhere it does not matter."

The leader looked at him. "You are daft, he is dead has been for years. Are you afraid of a ghost?"

Jocko shook his head, "No, but you will look into his eyes before you die." With that Jocko went off, to do what he was told.

The leader laughed. "Then I am safe, because, I will not die today."

Archangel watched as Ben walked over to a cabinet and flipped a switch. All of a sudden a wall opened up and monitors turned on. He heard a metal door slide across the front door.

"Skipper what is going on?" Archangel asked.

"Sorry Gabriel, the good Colonel asked if I would help him with a small problem. I wasn't sure how good an actor you were, so I couldn't tell you till now." Ben said.

"Alright Skipper, if you say so then it is so." Gabriel said.

Ben looked at him. "That isn't what Kat said. I couldn't tell her all of it either. Just before things got interesting fleet sent me an inquiry. It seems that your records didn't quite checkout. You cleared your security clearance but a recheck turned up problems. In fact no records exist of a Gabriel Archangel except an obscure entry in a birth record. It was above the name of a James Havilland. It is funny they were born the same day at almost the same time.

Havilland's record was amended to show that he died about six years ago. He was a young priest. He was living at a colonial outpost convent, with a group of teaching nuns and fifteen older priests. It was attacked by Brigands and Orion slavers.

The older priests were butchered on the spot. The nuns and the younger priests were carried off. The report says they were tortured.

This Havilland and a young nun escaped and made it back to Bearilian space. She died but the cause was unclear.

The record doesn't say how he died. In fact all there is a line entry in the record with a date."

Ben looked at Gabriel. "How did he die Gabriel?"

Gabriel sat down and looked at his Captain. "Skipper . . ."

"Gabriel how did the young Priest James Havilland cease to exist and Gabriel Archangel come to be." Ben asked.

Gabriel shrugged, "He died of a broken heart and of hate. What good was he? A priest that couldn't even comfort his friend, someone he loved. He failed. He hated himself; maybe he even hated the Creator for a while. I don't know. In the end the priest died Skipper. All that was left was revenge, hate, and purpose. Archangel was born."

Ben nodded. "Go on Gabriel."

Gabriel nodded. "I had friends in the church they helped change the records. Gabriel was born James died, it was that simple. Then I found the Marines. I found something I could believe in again. I was well educated, they sent me to OTS. That is about it Skipper.

Now what happens to me Sir?"

Ben shrugged. "Seems to me fleet just messed up. Those birth records are from a small back water planet. That is where you were born and lived."

Gabriel nodded.

"Then it seems to me other records were probably lost in fires or such. I am sure a Baptismal Record could show up in an old Bible or something now couldn't it?" Ben said.

Gabriel looked at him, "Skipper?"

"Gabriel, are you planning on ever going back to being who you were?" Ben asked with penetrating eyes.

"No Sir, James Havilland is dead and buried." Gabriel said.

Ben nodded. "Then I tell fleet they messed up. You are you Gabriel Archangel. That Father James Havilland is truly dead. Which means Gabriel you live this life the Creator has given you. If he sends blessings your way, you hold on to them."

"Paulette?" Gabriel asked.

Ben smiled, "Well son, you could do a lot worse."

Gabriel wanted to laugh he was older than his Captain but perhaps only in years. "Thank you Skipper."

Ben looked at him "Are you back on good terms again with the Creator?"

Gabriel nodded, "I went to a sermon at a Dragon Chapel. I listened to him preach a sermon from a passage, I had taught from many times. He took the passage farther. He talked about redemption and how the Creator gave his son, the Word, as a sacrifice to sin. So, that all the Cosmos, all of Creation could be redeemed. How his act of love shows us how we should love. That forgiveness starts in our own heart. That we had to forgive ourselves, and then ask the Creator to forgive us, but we had to be willing to give up all our hate and lust for revenge.

I haven't quite succeeded completely, but I am trying. If I succeed then maybe I can become worthy of Paulette's love, Skipper."

Ben nodded. "Good enough for me Gabriel. I think we have movement. The Colonel wanted us to look for these five especially. They aren't locals but were reported in the area."

Gabriel stiffened as he looked at the five pictures.

Ben looked at his eyes. "You recognize them?"

"They were part of the group that attacked the chapel. This is the one that . . . He kept hurting the nuns over and over then he . . ." Gabriel was crying.

Ben's fur was almost crimson "He took them?"

Gabriel nodded. "Ben, if he is among them he is mine, please."

Ben nodded, "He is your kill."

Kat and Paulette were standing in the door.

Ben looked at them. "You heard?"

Paulette nodded. "Some Sir, some I already knew. These were some of those that hurt her."

Gabriel nodded.

Paulette grabbed a rail gun. "Then they die."

Gabriel looked at her, "Not this one. He is mine Paulette."

She looked at him, "All right the rest are mine."

Kat grabbed the other rifle, "I guess I pick up strays."

Gabriel looked at them as they walked out to cover the back windows. "I don't think I would want them mad at me."

Ben replied. "Kat and Mayotte are dangerous. You confided in Paulette?"

"Yes Skipper, seemed like I needed to." Gabriel said.

Gabriel checked the monitors. "They're bedding down Skipper. They are planning on hitting us at night."

Ben nodded, "I think Kat called it, sometime after midnight, before dawn."

Gabriel looked at Ben. "Why don't you and your lady get something to eat and grab some sleep? Say three hours that would be say 22:00 cycles. Then Paulette and I could rest for a couple say till 01:00 cycles. You could use the back room down stairs. It covers the lake."

Ben frowned. "Gabriel, I am not sleepy."

Gabriel reasoned. "It is her honeymoon Skipper. Do you think she wants to be doing this or being with you?"

Ben shrugged. "I'll ask her. Kat, Gabriel thinks we need to take a break."

Kat came in and smiled. "Either that or let's go hunt them."

Ben grabbed her paw. "Come on I'll make you a sandwich."

Kat winked at Paulette as she walked by.

Paulette sighed. "I don't think it is a sandwich she is wanting."

Gabriel laughed. "Him either, he wants her as bad as she wants him."

Paulette shook her head. "No, she needs him. I have never seen her like this. Kat is happy and sad . . . She wants a cub growing inside her, his cub."

Gabriel asked. "Is that so wrong?"

Paulette shook her head, "Of course not, but so soon?"

Gabriel wrapped his arm around her. "Have I messed us up, Paulette?"

Paulette looked at him. "Who are us, Gabriel? Or is it James the priest who took a vow of celibacy?"

Gabriel kissed her hard on the mouth. "Did I kiss you like a celibate priest?"

Paulette smiled. "No, like a silly twelve year old cub, I can work with that."

Gabriel sighed, "James Havilland is dead and buried Paulette. There is even a headstone and grave. With him died the young confused priest. A dragon priest accidently taught me that I didn't even understand what it meant to be a priest. The Skipper is teaching me to be a better Marine, but that is his job."

Paulette turned away. "Then the question comes back to us?"

Gabriel shrugged. "I guess I want that to mean whatever you want it to mean Paulette. If you don't want there to be us, then I will understand. I might not be worthy of you."

Paulette looked at him. "Your right, you might not be worthy of me. I know some wet nosed priest wouldn't have been. I know a boar living on hate wouldn't have been. However, a Marine Officer, living by the code and willing to love, might be worthy of the gifts I have to give."

Gabriel looked at her "Paulette . . ."

"We have movement." She looked at the monitor. "It is this one." Paulette handed him the wanted poster.

Gabriel looked at it. "He is the one they called the Laughing Boy. He was a sadist. He loved torturing the nuns."

Paulette picked up his poster. "You said that only that one was yours. He is mine. He is my present to Sister Anna Louisa's poor soul, may it rest in peace." Paulette saw a list of monitors "Good I can use that."

Paulette went to a window facing the approach the bandit was taking. She hit a switch and a monitor popped up out of a table. She opened a firing port and attached a cable from her scope to the monitor. A red circular pip appeared on the screen. She focused it in on the slow moving figure, which was trying not to be noticed. He was crouched behind a rock.

Paulette aimed at his right foot, which was sticking out from the rock. She fired.

The bullet tore through his foot. It ripped the side of his foot off.

The bandit screamed. He tried to crawl away from the rock, dragging his injured foot behind.

Paulette aimed again. This time the bullet took out his left knee.

The bandit was rolled by the power of the bullet. He held his leg his lower leg was just barely holding on. He held up his right paw when the third bullet tore it off at the wrist.

The bandit sat there looking at the stub where his paw had been. He looked at his mangled foot and his destroyed knee. He was bleeding to death and he knew it. He turned to the cabin and screamed obscenities at it when another bullet tore through his brain.

Paulette came back in, threw the poster down with an x over his face. "He is dead he will never hurt anyone again."

Gabriel looked at her, "Thank you . . . can I do anything for you?"

Paulette looked at him. "Give up some of your hate."

Gabriel nodded, "I'll try Paulette, for you."

Paulette sat on his lap. "What are you waiting for?"

Gabriel looked at her. "I don't understand?"

"Kiss me Gabriel." Paulette said.

"You said I did it badly. Maybe you can teach me how you like it." Gabriel said.

Paulette smiled and pulled his arms closer around her and kissed his lips gently but firmly. "Umm that was so much better. Maybe I can teach you a few things."

Ben had turned on a monitor next to the bed. "We can still help monitor security while we rest."

Kat smiled "Rest? Is that what you want to do? Well alright but I think I will take off this uniform and lie down." She took it off and crawled into bed and looked at him. "Well are you going to just set there or come and keep me warm?"

Ben just shook his head, he took off his shirt and started to lie down, but she shook her head.

"No husband those are scratchy, off." She pointed down.

Ben just complied and jumped into bed. "You sure those two are alright up there."

Kat frowned, "Off now Ben Maritinus."

Ben looked at her. "But Kat what . . ." that is when he heard a ripping sound of fabric "Oh Kat, why did you do that?"

Kat told him. "If I can't fix them, I'll buy you new ones I like better. Like Gabriel said this is our honeymoon and you put a hunt in it. I want equal time." Then she whispered "I want a cub so you better get busy Captain Maritinus. Mayotte will be watching the clock."

Ben looked at her "But Kat . . ."

The leader couldn't figure what was taking Laughing Boy so long. He should have figured out by now if they were still there. "You go and see if can see Laughing Boy."

"Ok Boss, no problem." The young bandit said.

Jocko came over. "You know that Laughing Boy is dead or he would have been back by now."

"Jocko, you don't know that!" The leader screamed.

Jocko just got up, walked over, and stirred a fire.

The bandit moved to the edge of the trees. He saw a body spread out on the field. He took out his spy glass. He saw the shot up body of Laughing Boy. He took off to report.

He stopped in front of the leader trying to catch his breath. "He was blown apart Boss. He is lying in the field just torn part. Half his foot, one knee, his right paw is gone, and the right side of his face."

The leader looked at Jocko who looked back and said "Well you got your answer. They are still there."

The leader looked around "We will hit them at around 02:30 cycles. They will be asleep by then."

Paulette looked at Gabriel. "I still need your heat Gabriel."

Gabriel looked at her. "Paulette don't you think it is a slippery slope."

Paulette got up and walked over to a wall map. "It could be Gabriel. I won't deny it. I probably wouldn't even resist. You could probable do whatever you wanted Gabriel. Kat understands I am jealous of her. She is feeling alive for the first time in a long time. Maybe, I want to feel that way also. Don't you want to feel alive also, Gabriel?"

Gabriel looked at her. "Paulette, just being around you makes me, feel alive, for the first time in years. Like I told you I wouldn't even know where to start. If you want someone to love you Paulette, I could easily become that boar. As for the other I am probably worse than useless."

Paulette laughed. "It is just my luck, to fall for a resurrected dead celibate priest."

Gabriel put his arms around her." However, I am no longer celibate. I am just without knowledge. Also I don't want to bring dishonor to the female that may one day bear my cubs. Besides, Kat would kill me if I hurt you."

Paulette smiled and looked into his eyes. "Then you will have to be strong for both of us Gabriel. Because I am going to dance just as close to your flame as I can till I get burned up or you turn me away for good."

"Why, Paulette?" Gabriel asked.

"Because I want you Gabriel Archangel, it is ridicules I know. Still Kat said to make up my mind. So I did." Paulette said.

Gabriel dropped his head. "Can we take it just a little slow? Paulette, I am just a back water boy . . ."

Paulette kissed him. "Did you say the female that . . . may . . . one . . . day . . . bear . . . your . . . cubs?"

Gabriel nodded. "Well, I might have thrown that in a moment ago . . ."

Paulette flew into his arms and kissed him. "Did you mean it Gabriel? Don't tease me. Please tell me the truth?"

Gabriel looked at her. "Paulette, would you let me court you, do it properly. Then once you are sure I am really worthy of you. Then let me ask you properly, with honor that you deserve."

Paulette pulled away from him and walked away. She ringed her paws, *Kat told her to go for it, get it done. Well that was that*! "No Gabriel Archangel that just won't do. Who are you to decide what I deserve? What I believe would bring me honor? You boars and your crazy ideas of what honor is. I'll tell you what I want from you, Gabriel Archangel. I want a ring on my finger, you lying in my arms against me, and your cub growing inside me. I personally don't care what order you make that happen!"

Gabriel sat down she looked mad. "Is that your final word on the subject?"

Tears were welling up in her eyes. "I guess I am done."

Gabriel dropped to one knee. "Then Paulette Mayotte is there someone I need to approach, before I ask you to become my wife?"

Paulette shook her head no.

Gabriel nodded. "Then marry me Paulette. If you are sure you really want me."

Paulette let out a war hoop and pounced on him.

Ben looked up. "What was that?"

Kat replied. "Paulette scored a kill or a Gabriel." Then she looked at him "Why you scheming scoundrel, you underhanded . . . Ben Maritinus how? Did you plan this? Did you purposely throw those two together?"

Ben looked at her, "Kat come on. How could I possible plan for a romance between a young 2nd Lieutenant, that I had to prove to fleet wasn't a celibate priest in hiding, and a young WTO that just happened to be my young bride's partner."

Kat sat up on him. "If you have a set of marriage license in your briefcase, with their names on them, and medical forms, you are in trouble Captain."

Ben dropped his head. "Does that mean I have to sleep on the couch?"

Kat looked at him, "How many copies?"

Ben shrugged. "I had to cover contingencies. Paulette worked fast."

Kat looked at him. "This is going to cost you Ben Maritinus. I promise I will punish you. First your pajamas are gone."

"Kat come on, I didn't force anyone I just . . ." Ben tried to say.

"Ben Maritinus you are a cad. You are a well-meaning, loving, and delicious cad, who I can't get enough of. You're a cad none the less. Come on get dressed. We have to rescue your Lieutenant from Paulette before he has to marry her." Kat said.

Kat walked in to the control room. "Ensign, go get some rest."

Paulette looked at Kat. "Kat he asked me . . ."

"Mayotte, go now." Kat ordered.

"Yes, Ensign Maritinus." Paulette left the room crying.

Ben saw her and grabbed her. "Paulette, I think I am in trouble. I think I need to ask your forgiveness also." Ben sat her down and explained everything.

Paulette looked at him. "Kat and Gabriel knew nothing of your plan?"

Ben explained, "No, only Beary and Artemus knew my plans."

"Still, you couldn't cause it. You just put us together. It was still our choice, wasn't it?" Paulette asked searching his eyes.

Ben nodded. "Yes Paulette, but I was betting it would happen. The odds were in my favor. Kat is really mad because I used you."

"No Captain, you have given me a gift. Kat will see that. Thank you Sir, but we can't get married, no license." Paulette said tears still in her eyes.

"Paulette, my best friends come from a long line of seafaring collectors of valuable goods. I already have the necessary forms." Ben said.

Paulette kissed him and ran off to cry some more.

Kat looked at Archangel. "Is this the way you do guard duty?"

Archangel looked at Kat. "No, it isn't my Lady. We killed their scout and I set the automatic alarm. Paulette wanted to talk."

Kat looked at him. "I know exactly what Paulette wanted and it wasn't to talk! So you promised to marry her to take advantage of her, didn't you?"

"No Kat, I didn't. I tried to get her to let me court her properly. She said no. She threw down the gauntlet. She said she wanted three things a ring, me against her and a cub inside her and she didn't care about the order it happened." Gabriel said. "She frightened me half to death, I knew she meant it."

"So you plan to take her up on it don't you?" Kat said.

"I plan to marry her and love her Kat, is that wrong?" Gabriel asked.

"You know what I meant Gabriel don't act dumb!" Kat said

Gabriel dropped his head. "Don't you understand Kat? That is the problem. I haven't got a clue. The order that trained me believed that anything dealing with the flesh was evil. That kind of love was not just forbidden, it was strictly taboo. We didn't even conduct marriages because the Father Abbot felt it would dilute our piety."

Kat sat down and laughed. "Then answer me this. Do you really love her Gabriel?"

"Yes Kat, she has given me life." Gabriel said.

"Then you may marry her Gabriel. Know this; if you hurt her I will kill you. Believe me Gabriel, when I say after I am done even my husband will swear he is an amateur compared to me." Kat said.

Gabriel bowed. "My Lady Maritinus if I fail to honor her, may you use my own knife."

Kat nodded. "Spoken like a true Marine Lieutenant Archangel."

Ben looked at Archangel "Well?"

Gabriel shrugged. "She said I can marry her, Sir. But she is mad, Sir."

Ben grinned. "It is alright Gabriel, Polarian females are fiery. That's why Polarian boars have no fear of the flames. Go to your lady she needs you."

"Alright Skipper." Gabriel said.

Kat looked at Ben. "Ok, your scam might work out alright. However, you and your friends will pay. I don't know how, but, I will get even Ben Maritinus, on you, and them also. The whole bunch of you will pay, that I promise. You're on guard duty Captain Maritinus."

"Ensign Maritinus, I still out rank you." Ben said.

Kat looked at him with fire in her eyes. "Do you really want to go there, Sir?"

"No Kat, I don't." Ben said.

Kat came over and sat on his lap "You know you are in big trouble don't you."

"Yup, I figure it is going to cost me." Ben said.

"Our berth, is it really ours to decorate the way I want?" Kat asked.

"Yes it is," Ben said.

Kat looked at him. "What about Archangel and Mayotte where will they live?"

"If, the plan goes well, then a contingence has been worked out for them, in officer country." Ben said.

"They will need things also." Kat said. "Ben, he doesn't have much, neither does Mayotte. Her pay is still messed up so is mine. We have the twelve thousand credits. I can do a lot . . ."

Ben kissed her. "Kat, I am a Combat Captain plus I have investments. Also, Sir Gamey just told me about an account the Empress opened in my name. Even after the money he sent to help the wounded Marines' families this is what I have left."

Kat looked at him. "That can't be correct!"

Ben shrugged. "You my love can help them out. Be frugal. I don't think Paulette would understand."

Kat shook her head. "My father will hate you Ben. Thank you for loving me. I know none of this means anything to you. But your willingness to use it to help others brings honor to your father, your clan, and your wife, even if you are still a cad husband."

Gabriel heard Paulette crying. He knocked on the door. It opened slightly. She was curled up on the bed, "Paulette, may I come in?"

She sat up and looked at him. She picked her uniform pants up from the floor and hung them and straightened her shirt. Then she flew into his arms. "Gabriel, what did Ensign Maritinus say?"

Gabriel was confused, "Kat said if I ever hurt you she would kill me in a fashion that would surpass even the Skipper's abilities. But if you were dumb enough to want me, then you could keep me. She did hint that the order did matter to her Paulette. Also, that I better keep things in the right order.

I am not sure she would approve of your current state of dress."

Paulette laughed. "I have more on than I did in my Bikini you ogled me in. Besides, these shorts can be worn as outer wear in the flight area. There not our underwear, those are underneath. You want to see?"

Gabriel shook his head. "When Kat feels it is appropriate. I want to live to marry you."

Paulette kissed him, "Ben, sent you here didn't he?"

Gabriel nodded. "He said you were upset."

Paulette nodded. "Kat was mad at me and Ben. She felt he was using me to protect you. He was betting if he threw us together . . . Well he knew I had been watching you since I got onboard the EAQ.

The fleet is looking for a celibate priest hiding as a Marine 2nd Lieutenant. If he got us romantically involved or better married off. Then there was no way you could be that dead Priest James Havilland."

Gabriel sat down she came over, sat on his lap, and put her head on his shoulder. "So Paulette, now that you know he planned this, what do you want to do?

Paulette kissed his cheek. "Do you still want me Gabriel?"

Gabriel wrapped his arms around her and held her closer. "I just don't want you to think I am using you to . . . Live a lie."

Paulette kissed him "Then let me have your cubs' lots of them. Fill me with your love every day for as long as we live."

Gabriel kissed her. "You'll have to teach me."

Paulette snuggled against him. "We will figure it out together, come on let's get some rest."

Gabriel shook his head. "No, you go ahead. I'll sleep in the chair. I'll stay in the room, but Kat might misunderstand."

Paulette nodded. "Then can you just hold me like this for a little while?"

Gabriel kissed her gentle, "Alright Paulette. I don't think Kat would mind." He looked and she was asleep.

Kat looked at the clock. "They will be coming soon."

Ben patted her tail. "You really are good at this aren't you?"

Kat shrugged, "A hunt is a hunt Ben. I am a good mate for you."

    CHARLES & IRENE NICKERSON

Ben nodded, "Full gear we leave here alive. They don't."

Kat saluted. "Yes, Captain Maritinus. Sir, I'll go wake up the kids."

Kat looked in the door. Paulette was asleep on Gabriel's lap. She was in her alert shorts. Kat shook her head. *Paulette what were you planning?* "Ok, you two, get up, full gear, it is show time."

Gabriel almost dropped Paulette as he stood up. Instead he just held her in his arms.

"Lieutenant, the Ensign has two good legs. She can stand on them." Kat said.

Gabriel stuttered, "Yes my Lady."

Kat smirked, "Alright Paulette, we got work to do come on."

Paulette responded. "Alright Boss."

Kat swatted her tail "I better marry you off. You are becoming shameless."

Paulette kissed her. "Thank you, Mommy."

Gabriel grabbed a scoped rail gun and moved to a shooting port with a monitor. He plugged in his scope.

The ladies were set up. Ben hit the master control. Mine fields activated. The trap was set.

The leader split his group into two groups. He would lead the first group with Jocko and eight others. Snakes would lead the other with Dice and seven others along the edge of the lake.

"Ok, let's go. Remember we want the females alive. Kill the boars." The leader said.

Jocko looked at him. "He is here. He is waiting for you and me and the other two."

The leader looked at him "Who, Jocko?"

Jocko smiled. "The Priest, Omak. He is waiting for you."

The leader looked at Jocko who had walked on. Then brushed off the fear he felt and pressed on.

Ben picked up the group coming in by the lake. He saw the nine moving slowly along a rock out cropping. He activated a small mine field and pressed the button. The first two bandits had passed beyond the area on the display. Then two more cleared. Then four small canisters sprung from the ground and burst open. Two of the bandits dove behind rocks. But three were caught flat footed and were torn apart by the explosion as ball bearings ripped through their flesh.

Ben shook his head, Bouncing Betty mines, nasty. Still there had been a delay in the system. Yet this force had been cut by a third. Then he saw another one flip side ways, as the side of his head exploded. The others took to the ground again.

Gabriel shook his head. "Skipper, I missed."

Ben said. "I saw one go down."

"Just dumb luck, the one I targeted moved at the last second. His friend was standing in the line of fire." Gabriel said.

Ben shrugged. "One down is one down. Stay sharp Gabriel. Maybe, I can move them back into a kill zone for you."

Ben was getting ready to set off a couple more mines, when he heard the ladies rail guns discharge.

The other group of bandits was moving, in the tall grass. They were spread out trying to move to the out building. So they could fire on the cabin from cover.

Two of them had raised their heads at the same time just to get a better idea where they were. That was when Kat and Paulette spotted them. They fired simultaneously. Four hundred grain 50 caliber rail gun slugs slammed into the heads of the two bandits, flipping them into the air like rag dolls.

Ben saw the approximant line they had been in and set off a line of mines in the general location.

Sixteen Bouncing Bettys sprang from the ground and mowed down the grass ten SMU in front and behind of where they popped up.

Two more dead bandits could be seen in the cameras.

The leader looked at his six survivors "Run for the buildings it is your only chance."

He and Jocko ran together. He heard more explosions. He felt something tear at his coat that was flapping behind him. When he reached the shed he looked around. Only Jocko and one other were with him.

"Where are the others?" He asked.

Jocko shook his head. "They are all dead."

Dice and Snake crawled over next to them. Dice was holding his arm.

Snake looked at him. "They are all dead. Dice is hit in the arm it missed him. Still it almost took his arm off."

The kid looked at them. "I have this. I can blow a hole in the cabin. I know how to use it good. I climb up into that window. Shoot, and then boom. We go in cut and kill."

The leader answered "Sure Kid that is a great Idea."

The kid climbed up to a small ledge and the upper window in the shed. He opened the window and was aiming the grenade launcher when Gabriel spotted him.

Gabriel snapshot his rail gun.

The slug caught the kid just above his left eye. Throwing him back, as he fell he triggered the launcher. The grenade exploded against the rafters of the shed raining debris down on the surviving bandits.

Ben grabbed his phaser and combat knife. "Come on let's take them."

Kat grabbed her rifle. "Paulette, stay here and call Colonel Mac Adams. Watch our backs."

Ben and Gabriel were the first out the door. Ben saw Snake trying to make it to the lake. He took off after him.

Gabriel saw a figure enter a small barn.

Kat went to the shed. She saw figure just standing there. "Freeze" she ordered. He seemed to be complying then she felt movement, then a knife was in the air, she fired. A body fell behind her. The other body slumped slowly to its knees.

She looked behind her. A bandit, with a garret in its paws, lay dead behind her, with a knife in his throat.

She ran over to the other figure. He was bleeding from a stomach wound. She tried to steam the blood. "I am sorry"

Jocko grimaced in pain. "Don't be my Lady. I deserve to die. I knew I would die tonight. You have released me from the torment I have suffered for over six years." He saw here necklace, "Do you believe that the Creator could really forgive a murder and a thief, my Lady?"

Kat looked at him. "The Creator sent his Word to redeem all of Creation of our sins. If you trust in him and truly ask for grace and forgiveness then yes."

Jocko nodded. "Pray for my soul my Lady. Pray that he will receive me . . ." with that Jocko the thief died.

Kat cried. She took off her necklace and wrapped it in his paw. Then she prayed over the bandit that had saved her life at the cost of his own.

Snake reached the edge of the water when he realized he was being followed. He turned around to see Ben standing there.

Ben told him. "You're under arrest."

Snake shook his head. "No, I am going to kill you or you are going to kill me Marine. Those are the only choices." With that he pulled out a wicked curved knife.

Ben pulled his marine fighting knife, "Well come on."

About that time Ben heard a crack and saw Snake pitch backwards into the sand with the top of his head gone.

"Captain what is it with all this boar to boar knife crap? You had a phaser shoot the so-in-so. Then move on. That paw to paw stuff can get you killed." Paulette said into his ear piece.

Ben looked up and waved. He turned back.

Gabriel started searching the small barn. Omak jumped him from above. Gabriel threw him.

Omak sprang up to faced him. Fear crept across Omak's face "You, but your dead!"

Gabriel sneered "That's right I am. However, I was resurrected. I am now an avenging Angel. I am here to take your life Omak."

Omak pulled a knife and swung it at Gabriel.

Gabriel blocked it and broke his wrist making him drop the knife. He then hit him knocking him back.

Omak picked up a hammer and charged at Gabriel.

Gabriel caught his arm as it made its downward ark. He pulled his whole body through the ark and slammed him into the floor then twisted his shoulder till it broke.

Omak screamed out in pain. "Why don't you kill me?"

Gabriel looked at him. "You are under arrest."

Omak spit at him. "You know they will never hold me!"

Gabriel picked him up and hung him on a hook. He did it so his feet couldn't touch the ground. Behind his back was a large round nob.

Omak was squirming. "I'll get loose, I'll find you. I'll kill that pretty thing with you. Then I'll kill you!"

Gabriel spun around and shot out with his right foot catching Omak in the center of his body mass, driving his back against that large nob.

Omak felt his back break, felt his legs grow numb, and cold. "What have you done?" He screamed.

Gabriel walked over and whispered into his ears. "I have broken your back. Hopefully I severed your spinal cord. When they tie the rope around your neck they will have you strapped to a wheelchair so its weight will help snap your neck. I hope they will send me a video."

Ben came in. "Gabriel, are you alright?"

Gabriel nodded. "He is under arrest Skipper. He'll need medical attention. His back got broken."

Ben nodded. He walked over to the bandit. "He is letting you face justice. If it was up to me I would finish the hunt."

Paulette opened the door. "Ben, Gabriel, Kat needs you!"

Ben and Gabriel ran over to the shed. They found Kat crying over a bandit's body.

Kat jumped up into Bens arms "He saved my life. I thought he was attacking me. I shot him . . . I didn't know. He thanked me. He said I stopped his torment."

Gabriel bent down. "He was the one that helped us escape."

Gabriel took out a prayer book. Prayed over Jocko and placed the Prayer book in is right paw.

Ben looked at them. "Gabriel what do you want to do."

Gabriel looked at him. "Ben, ask that he be buried in hollow ground, no mention of his crimes. Just put down his name Jocko, a lost soul that in the end asked for redemption and grace."

Ben nodded. "It is my debt of honor. I will see that it is done."

Soon Colonel Mac Adams arrived. "Were any of you injured?"

Ben looked at him. "Colonel, we are Bearilian Marine and Naval Combat Officers. We have an injured bandit in the barn. He will need a back board. His spine is broken. Colonel I do have a favor though."

Mac Adams looks at him. "What is it Captain?"

Ben looked at him. "This bandit his name was Jocko he died saving my wife's life. Would you not put him with the others? Have him receive a proper burial in hallowed ground. I will pay all his expenses."

Kat looked at the Colonel. "Also please do not let your bears remove those items from his paws. Insure they are buried with him as they are."

The Colonel looked at them. "Why would you do this for him a bandit?"

Ben answered. "Colonel, for us this is a sacred debt of honor that must be paid. Can you understand, Sir?"

Mac Adams nodded. "Since, I now am in debt to you for solving this problem . . ."

"During my one and only honeymoon, I would like to point out." Kat injected.

"Oh, I see. Lady Maritinus. I give you my word. Your wishes will be followed." Mac Adams said.

CHAPTER 7

Trouble from another Quarter: The Arrival of Admiral Astrid

"RED TALON, THIS is White Dragon control, we are entering the Lesser Anzico system."

"White Dragon, please authenticate GGU."

"Red Talon, we authenticate UUG."

"We are glad to see you White Dragon, and all your friends." Red Talon out.

"Red Talon this is White Dragon 6 can you patch me through to your first officer."

"White Dragon 6 patching you through to Red Talon 2."

Jeanne turned on her com unit. "Hi Cathy, what gives?"

"Whoa Jeanne, are you ok. You have really let yourself go." Cathy said.

"Oh, it is worse than that Cathy. I am pregnant." Jeanne said.

Cathy's mouth fell open, "But how?"

Jeanne shrugged. "I got sick. The cure returned my ability to have a cub. Well a night of passion with my husband . . . Well here I am."

"So it is true, you are married to Argus!" Cathy said.

"Yes Cathy and we had Admiral Starpaw's blessing. It was all legal. Well mostly." Jeanne laughed at her own joke.

"Jeanne that is why I called . . . I am sticking my neck out. Astrid is coming head hunting. He is after you and Argus's heads. He is also after a Marine Lieutenant Maritinus and an Ensign Katimai."

"That is Ensign Maritinus, Cathy." Jeanne said.

"Jeanne, what are you running a floating love boat?" Cathy asked.

"No Cathy, I am operating a Scientific Research Ship with a half civilian crew and three separate commands. Two of which that don't answer to Argus or I. If you want to know the truth, we are just glorified bus drivers. Oh, excuse me, I forgot. Make that, four separate commands. I forgot one; he is a kingdom on to himself." Jeanne said.

"Look Jeanne, he plans on court marshaling Maritinus and a few others. I just wanted to warn you." Cathy said.

Jeanne looked at her. "Cathy is he a flaming idiot? Who does he think he is?"

Cathy looked at her. "He is an Admiral, Jeanne, a Task Force Commander."

Jeanne shook her head. "Cathy, do you know who we work for? Who our lieutenants report directly to? Who Captain Maritinus has a direct com line to? Who also just sent him a wedding present?"

Cathy just shook her head, "No, Jeanne I don't. He is just a simple Marine Captain."

"Cathy, he is the commander of a MSD Unit. Maritinus works directly for Zantoran, personally. He also helped save the Vice President's son. He is considered a Knight and part of his family. Do you think if Golden Dragon 1 gets pissed, your Admiral will make his next board?" Jeanne asked. "This ship is named for our CAG's Mom. Do you get the picture Cathy? He might cause trouble, but in the end he will pay a heavy price."

Cathy Ellis, First Officer of the Dreadnaught *Castles Gate*, heave a sigh. "Alright, Jeanne, I wish you good luck. I just didn't want you to get blindsided."

Jeanne nodded, "Thanks Cathy. I owe you."

Cathy thought. "He is also going to demand answers about a 2nd Lt. Archangel and a James Havilland. I couldn't find out what that what that was about."

Jeanne shrugged, "Shoddy book keeping, on a backwater colony."

Cathy looked over her shoulder. "I got to go."

Jeanne got up and walked in to Argus's office "We got trouble."

Captain Gracchus listened. "We don't need them to come back to this." He called Beary and explained the situation.

Beary thought. "I don't need Kat or Paulette back till we leave the system. Technically, Ben and Archangel are on medical leave. Except for that little problem, they helped the good Colonel with."

Gracchus thought. "You have a problem with Ben's solution with our other problem?"

Beary laughed, "Sir, I am too deep in the conspiracy. No, we just greased the wheels. It was their decision.

Sir, have Sho-Sho with you when Astrid comes to visit. She can protect you."

Gracchus smiled. "Alright, contact Ben. Give him another couple of days. Tell him Plan B, before they get back to the ship, consummated Beary."

"Understood, Sir, I'll tell him." Beary said.

Artemus looked at him. "Where is our honor?"

Beary laughed. "I told you, I come from a long line of seafaring collectors of valuable goods."

"Valkyrie 38 this is Spirit 6. Extend maintenance flight on Marine components, two days. Do you copy?"

"Spirit 6, Valkyrie 38 Sword, understood we are to extend maintenance flight two days."

"Valkyrie 38 Sword, paper work on second Marine component must be validated. Unit must be verified functional. Do you understand?"

Paulette looked at Kat. "What do I say boss?"

Kat sighed. "You want him. We'll find a preacher. The rest is up to you."

Paulette smiled. "Spirit 6, 38 Sword will insure all requirements are met over."

Gabriel looked at Ben. "Just how much trouble, am I causing and how deep is the . . ."

"The word is conspiracy Gabriel. Don't, worry about it. Just be a good husband, love Paulette, and treat her properly. If not you won't be the only one that dies." Ben said.

"Well the good Colonel said we couldn't stay here. But he told me about a nice little artist village. It also has a nice little church up in the mountains. It is a tourist trap for intellectuals and art collectors. Paw made wood furniture shops and old book stores." Kat said. "It has a small air field."

Ben nodded. "Let's go. Maybe it has a nice hotel."

They got strapped in and Kat took off.

Gabriel looked at Ben. "Sir, please next time grab a dagger."

Kat laughed. "Big tough Marines, they act like little cubs if you ask me."

Ben replied. "Just keep it up Kat and I'll sleep on the floor."

Kat laughed "It might be a little hard on your back, but I am game, if you are."

Paulette laughed *poor Ben he could not win.*

They landed at a small airfield. The airfield manager came out. He looked at the fighter as Kat and Ben got out.

He looked at Kat, "Young Lady, you the pilot of that there fighter?"

Kat responded sweetly. "Yes Sire, I am Ensign Kat Maritinus of the EAQ. This is my husband Captain Maritinus of the 981ˢᵗ MSD."

"You one of the pilots, that kicked their tails up there?" He pointed into space.

Kat nodded. "I only nailed four. I should have done better."

The old bear whistled. "She is a keeper son."

Ben replied. "Sire, you wouldn't have a hanger we could rent for two days? We are on our honeymoon. Our friends are looking to get married."

The old bear raised an eyebrow. "Sure, you can put it in hanger number 3. It is good, tight and you can secure it.

You got the proper paper work for your friends. You know his CO; will have to have signed a permission slip for him to be married by a civilian pastor?"

Ben nodded. "That's not a problem. I am his CO."

The old bear grinned wider. "Well, that makes it easier. I can rent you a transport to get you down to the village."

Ben replied. "Thank you, Sire."

"Well Captain, you come with me and do the paper work. Your lady can put her fighter away." The old bear said.

Ben walked in to his office. He saw an old ragged patch of a Silver Dragon throwing two bombs. "Sire which one were you?"

The old bear smiled. "Silver Dragon 22, I wasn't one of the originals. I was a replacement. Not many of the originals survived. Shoot, not many of us replacements did either."

Ben nodded, as he paid the rental fees.

The old bear looked at him "You're young for a MSD Captain, son you must really impressed someone."

Ben shrugged, "I was just in the wrong place at the wrong time, and survived for someone to tell about it."

The old bear nodded, "There is a hotel in town. It's called the Green Horn. It has the best rooms . . . but the owner is a little particular about renting rooms. You tell him Zeck said he better give you all the best he has."

Ben held out his paw. "Thank you, Sir.

"Zeck Hammerhead, son, it is a pleasure to meet you, Captain Ben Maritinus the slayer." Zeck said. "Oh, by the way if you see Golden Dragon 1 and his Lady, tell them hello for me."

Ben walked out and pulled the transport over. Kat and the other two loaded their bags into the trunk and got in. "We ready to go?"

Kat nodded. "I cloaked it and put a lock on the door.

He was a nice old boar."

Ben told them. "He used to be one of you. He was a member of the old *Silver Dragon Squadron*. He said he was Silver Dragon 22, a Zeck Hammerhead."

Paulette and Kat both looked at him with a blank stare.

"What?" Ben asked.

"You said Zeck Hammerhead, as in Admiral Zeck Hammerhead. One of the greatest fighter bomber pilots, whoever lived!" Kat said.

Paulette's eyes shinned. "They are still using his books to teach bombing tactics at advanced training!"

Ben thought. "Well, maybe you two can buy him dinner or something."

Paulette looked at Ben. "Do you think we could?"

Ben shrugged. "Let's check in. Then go find the church."

Paulette dropped her head, as they passed a dress shop.

Kat looked at her. "What is it Mayotte?"

"It's nothing Boss." Paulette said.

"Ben, how much cash you got on you?" Kat asked.

Ben thought, "Fifty."

Kat said "Ok, with the twelve thousand, that should do what we need. That will give us twelve thousand fifty credits."

Ben responded. "Ah, no Kat, fifty thousand credits. Here just take it. Do what you need. I'll stop at that bank and get some more."

Kat just looked at him, then at the wallet. *Ok, this was not the way her dad ever did things.* "You two get us checked in . . . at what is it called?"

"The hotel Green Horn is the name he gave me." Ben said.

"Right, then you two, go talk to the priest or pastor at the church. Don't let him give you any trouble." Kat said.

Ben nodded "Have fun Kat."

She came around and kissed him then whispered. "How much may I spend?"

Ben looked at her. "Kat, it is your's to spend. If, you need more, just tell me. Beany, hasn't had the time to get all the legal and financial paper work done."

Kat looked at him "Beany?"

Ben smiled. "She is Beary's sister and our lawyer."

With that, a stunned Paulette stood looking at Kat. Ben and Gabriel pulled off to go find the Green Horn.

"Kat what is going on?" Paulette asked.

Kat giggled. "Shopping Paulette, come we are going to find you a wedding dress."

Paulette looked at her. "But, Kat I can't afford . . ."

Kat gently pushed her towards the shop. "Now Ensign Mayotte, move your tail, there is the dress shop."

Paulette dropped her head. "Yes Mommy."

Kat swung into the dress shop. The owner came out. "Yes?"

Kat told her, "She needs a wedding dress. With her figure you shouldn't have trouble fitting her."

The owner looked at Kat. "When is the wedding?"

"Tonight Madam, please outfit her with everything she needs." Kat said.

"My Lady, what you ask is quite unusual!" The owner said.

Kat laid down twenty thousand credits. "Will this cover the unusual?"

The owner looked at the cash, and then looked at Paulette. "As you say with her tight petite body, she could be a model. Yes, I have several dresses that would fit almost perfectly."

"Then I will leave her in your paws. Give her, anything she needs. Throw in something for the wedding night." Kat said "Is that a good book store?"

The owner shrugged. "If, you like old and rare books, most are too intellectual for my tastes. You, young female come with me. We have work to do. Your lady must think you are special."

Paulette put on an evil grin. "Oh, my lady, it is a shotgun wedding. I defiled one of her husband's bears. Now, I must marry him, to save his honor."

The old female looked at her in shock. Then she smiled. She was not sure how much was said in jest and how much was true. Still twenty thousand credits made it to where she didn't care.

Ben walked in to the Green Horn. An old boar was behind the counter. "Sire, we would like to rent a couple of rooms, for two nights."

"Why?" The old boar asked.

"Well Sire, it is my honeymoon. Also my lieutenant is getting married this evening . . ." Ben started to explain.

"No dag-burn it, why should I rent to a couple of bums like you two?" the old boar asked.

Ben looked at him and leaned on the counter. "Because, Zeck said you better. He also said you better give my wife and her WTO the best two rooms you have. Also the best service they ever got."

The old boar looked at him. "Marine, you married to a female fighter pilot. Is she any good?"

Ben smiled an evil grin. "Golden Dragon1's son is our CAG. He is as good a pilot as his father was. He picked her to be his wingbear. Does that answer your question?"

The old boar sat back. "Well in that case. I'll give you suites two and four. Only, because of the ladies, I don't care for knuckle draggers, even MSD knuckle draggers."

Ben held out his paw. "Captain Ben Maritinus 981st MSD. That is 2nd LT. Gabriel Archangel."

"Retired, Flight Chief Bosons Mate, Vern Radcliff, it is nice to meet you." Radcliff said.

Ben asked about the church. Radcliff told them Father Henderson should be there. He was new. Their regular minister was on sabbatical.

They drove up to the church. Gabriel was nervous. "Skipper there is no way this is going to fly."

Ben explained. "The paper work is legal. I have signed your permission paper work."

"What about Paulette's papers?" Gabriel asked.

Ben pulled them out, already signed, and showed him.

"Come on, will talk to the priest." Ben said.

They walked into a nice small chapel. At the front was a Maxmimus Priest in bishops robs praying.

Ben and Gabriel sat in a pew.

The Bishop got up and turned around. "You must be Ben. I have been expecting you."

Ben looked at him and smiled. "Father, I am Ben Maritinus this is Gabriel Archangel.

Bishop Henderson looked at Gabriel, with penetrating eyes. "So Gabriel, you are the lucky groom. Where are your ladies?"

Ben explained. "Kat, my wife, felt that Paulette needed to be properly equipped Bishop."

"Oh, enough of that Bishop nonsense my name is Augustus Henderson. Bishop is just my administrative position in the church. I do not think the Creator much cares. As my wife Anna says a priest is a priest whether he is a pastor or a cardinal. The job is the same to serve the Creator and his Word." Bishop Henderson said.

Ben nodded.

"Now, forgive me Gabriel, but I must ask this question. Do you love Paulette Mayotte? Also, are you doing this of your own free will?" Bishop Henderson asked.

"Yes, Bishop I am." Gabriel said.

"Gabriel, just call me Augustus." The Bishop said.

"Ben, I take it you are acting as Paulette's father- at-litem, in this instance? Since she is an orphan and was a ward of the church." The bishop asked.

"Yes Sire, I will accept that responsibility." Ben said.

The bishop pulled out some papers. "Then you will have to sign these. So will Kat. You understand they give Paulette legal standing as your true daughter."

Ben nodded. "My Father will receive great honor from this."

Gabriel looked at Ben. "Sir, I don't understand . . ."

Ben explained. "It means Paulette is legally my daughter, once Kat signs the papers. Which means you will be my son-in-law, Gabriel. May, the Creator help you."

The bishop looked over all the other papers. "Well that female Empress Pirate cousin of mine seemed to cover everything else. So, now all we need to do is the service. Also Kat needs to sign this paper work.

Why don't you two grab some lunch. Bring the ladies back here for tea at 3:00. The wedding will be at 6:00 tonight."

Ben replied, "Thank you, Augustus."

Gabriel bowed and kissed his ring "Thank you, Bishop Augustus."

The bishop put his paw on his head. "Be at peace and be blessed my son."

Gabriel felt peace flow through him.

He walked out to the transport almost dazed.

Ben smiled. "It is alright Gabriel, you get used to it after a while."

"Sir, I . . ." Gabriel tried to say.

"I have lived around them for three, almost four years. Their faith is strong. Their ability to love is even stronger. So is their ability to hate. Beary's family is over powering." Ben said.

Kat had walked into the old book store. An older boar was setting behind the counter. He looked like a college professor.

"Young lady, what can I do for you?" He asked.

Kat replied. "Sire, I am looking for an instructional manual for a dumb young 2nd Lieutenant Boar. That is about to get married. He even admits he is totally clueless."

The old boar raised his eyebrow. "Are you the . . ."

"No, my husband is adequate in that department. Thank you." Kat said. "It is for my adopted daughter."

He thought. "Well, I have an old two volume set of books that was written by a young neurologist. Let's see oh, here it is, *The Neurological and Physical Benefits of Various Cultural Love Making Practices with Illustrations, By Dr. Angelina Maria Maxumus, Volumes 1 and 2.* I have a few copies."

Kat smiled as she looked through a copy. She turned the book sideways then read the page. "How many sets do you have?"

He looked at her, "My lady, that book is very rare. It caused quite a stir when it came out. It was banded in some systems."

Kat replied. "How many do you have and how much?"

He looked at her. "I have six sets, my lady."

"Good, wrap five up as presents. I'll take this one for myself." Kat said.

"But, we didn't settle on a price?" He said.

Kat looked at him. "Well how much?"

"Fifty credits a set." He said.

Kat handed him three hundred credits. "You will wrap them in front of me. I will inspect each volume."

The old boar nodded. He would not try and cheat this one. She seemed dangerous. He wrapped the volumes in beautiful paper.

Kat smiled and took her bag across to the dress shop.

Paulette was trying on another dress. This one fit her like a glove. Kat smiled.

Paulette twirled in the mirror. She seemed to radiate.

Kat looked at the shop owner. "My daughter will take that one."

Paulette looked at her. "Kat, are you sure?"

Kat nodded. "It is perfect Paulette."

The older female looked at them. "You said your daughter?"

Kat looked at her. "Yes, Mayotte is my adopted daughter. I am her or was her legal guardian till she came of age."

Paulette went and changed out of the wedding dress. So it could be packed. She came out to show Kat a few other things. When she saw Kat reading a book, "Kat, what is that?"

Kat explained. "A book, the Boss's Mom wrote."

Paulette looked over her shoulder. She felt her face go flush. "Kat, is that even possible?"

Kat shrugged. "She says it is. Apparently, it causes very interesting sensations. The boss will die when he reads the foreword."

They had gathered up their packages, as Ben and Gabriel pulled up. Ben lowered the window. "You feel like lunch?"

Paulette looked at Kat. "Mommy, I am hungry aren't you?"

Ben heard her. "Kat, have you already adopted Mayotte?"

Kat nodded. "Eight years ago. Why?"

"The church has asked me to adopt her, as her father- at-litem. I guess I need your permission." Ben said.

Paulette looked at Ben. "Captain, you understand you would legally be my father."

Ben grinned. "I have already married your mother."

Paulette got in the car and kissed his cheek. 'I get a husband and a father all on the same day!"

Ben kissed Kat and whispered. "See, you already have brought me honor."

Kat looked at him, *oh, how she loved this gentle, loving, and cad of a boar. Whose heart was so big, that it must contain half, the love in the universe?* "Let's go eat"

CHARLES & IRENE NICKERSON

Admiral Astrid arrived. He was brought in through the admin shuttle landing bay. Flannigan met him.

"Admiral, welcome aboard the *Empress Angelina's Quest*. It is my honor to escort you to the Captain's Wardroom. He is in a scheduled meeting." Flannigan said.

The Admiral looked at him. "Who was the idiot that reinstated you?"

Flannigan reported. "President Coldbear and Admiral Starpaw signed the orders Admiral."

Astrid looked at him, as a female passed him with a young cub. She was wearing a bathing suit as was the young male cub. "Is that a proper uniform on this ship? What is that cub doing in this area?!"

Flannigan answered. "Lady Jessica is special branch, Admiral, a civilian. So is Sir Nikolaos."

The Admiral looked at him. "That cub was special branch? That is preposterous."

Flannigan responded. "Sir, he is a highly skilled protector. This way Admiral, if you please, we will take this lift."

"Where are Maritinus and Katimai?" Astrid demanded.

Flannigan shrugged. "Sir, as you should know, MSD units are separate commands. As such, all I know is that he was reported as being on medical leave. Ensign Maritinus is a pilot. She belongs to the air wing, also a separate command."

"What do you mean separate commands?" Astrid demanded.

"Oh, look Sir, we are here." Flannigan knocked on the door "Captain Gracchus, Admiral Astrid is here."

"Show him in Chief." Gracchus said as he looked at the young female Maxmimus in the gold and silver gown.

Shoshana nodded. "I am here Captain. I will protect you." Gracchus heard in his mind.

Admiral Astrid burst into the room. "Gracchus what kind of messed up ship, are you running here! Where are Maritinus and Katimai?"

Gracchus looked at him, "Who?"

Shoshana replied. "Captain Gracchus, this over grown blow hard, is asking about Captain Ben Maritinus, commander, of the 981st MSD and Ensign Lady Kat Maritinus my uncle's wingbear."

"Oh, thank you for clarifying it, your highness." Gracchus said.

The Admiral was livid. "Do you think this is a joke?! I'll have you court marshaled Gracchus! Who is this female child to talk to me the way she did!" Astrid fumed.

Shoshana stood up. Her voice seemed to boom in his head. "Set down you pompous pig. I will tell you who I am. I am High Princess Shoshanna Maxumus, granddaughter of Empress Angelina Maxumus and Vice President Octavious Maxumus. I am also the niece of Lieutenant Beary Maxumus, commander of the air wing. I am also the Official Ambassador of the Government of Andreas Prime to the Bearilian Astrofleet on the EAQ!

I would also like to point out, you over rated pompous worm, that this is a civilian mission, supported by the military. It also does not fall under your chain of command. Neither does Captain Maritinus, Ensign Maritinus, nor Captain Gracchus for that matter. So unless this is a courtesy call, to thank us for doing your job, I suggest you keep a civil tong, or you may lose it."

Astrid had tried to penetrate her mind. Only to have his mind pushed back, hard. He had never felt so much mental strength. She had brushed him aside like he was a gnat. That was when he heard her voice in his mind. *Try that again and I will crush your mind like a ripe grape. Astrid, you are a child compared to me.*

Astrid looked at her as she sat down. "What are you?"

Shoshana smoothed her dress. Then she sat down, very prim and proper. "I told you Admiral, your worst nightmare. A female you cannot scare or control. I am someone, who could easily destroy you, if I wanted to. You will not threaten any member of this crew. Also Admiral Astrid, I have questioned the prisoners. I have promised them proper treatment." She turned and looked into his eyes "They will receive it or I will hold you responsible. Do we understand each other?"

Astrid could feel her force open his mind. She placed pictures of unbearable pain in his mind. Though he didn't feel the pain, he understood that it was only because she blocked it. "Yes," he said weakly "we understand."

"Also tell your cousin, if he wishes to challenge the rights of the Red Paw to the honor he threw away. That my handmaiden, Ice Song Artemus, would be happy to challenge him, to defend Kat's honor. Unless, he is a coward and is afraid to face a female warrior or the Red Paw and Maxumus Clan." Shoshanna stated.

Astrid stood up and bowed. "I will relay your message. Goodbye Gracchus." He started to leave when two young cubs meet him at the door.

"I am Nikolaos and this is Andreios. We will escort you off the ship." Nikolaos said.

He went to push them out of his way. "Out of my way . . ."

Nikolaos took him down. Andreios put a phaser to his head. Nikolaos whispered. "The paper work might be messy, Admiral. However, after what Benedict and the others did . . . killing an obnoxious overbearing Admiral might only slightly be frowned on. Especially, after you failed to follow the lawful orders, which were given, by two Special Agents."

Jessica came up. "Nikolaos let him up. You also Andreios, nice take down."

The Admiral looked at her. "Who are you?"

"Their senior field agent Admiral, come with me. Just so you know Admiral, if you had tried that with me. I would have killed you. The paper work isn't that hard." She smiled when she got him back to his shuttle. "They have a license to kill, so do I." Jessica said.

Astrid was really mad. He didn't know what to do. He knew he couldn't call Starpaw or Zantoran. They had threatened to put him in a desk. The Maxumus girl really scared him.

Augustus Henderson smiled when Paulette and Kat came in. "My, you two, are lovely young females. You are absolutely, breath taking."

Paulette blushed, "Thank you, Father."

Kat asked. "Are you married Father Augustus?"

"Oh, yes my dear, have been for a long time. My Anna is an artist. Well really an illustrator. She is fixing our tea." Augustus said.

Gabriel sat next to Paulette. Ben sat next to Kat. Kat handed the Bishop a piece of paper.

"Oh, I see Kat. However, you changed your name and clan. So let's have you sign the new form and attach the old form to it. That way it will all be legal. Also Ben, will have parental responsibilities." Augustus said.

Kat signed the form. "Thank you, Bishop."

Augustus turned to Paulette. "The church gave you the name Mayotte. You may take the name Maritinus, if you wish?"

Paulette looked at Ben and Kat. "I will soon be Archangel. Would it offend my parents, if I kept the name the church gave me, just three more cycles?"

Ben kissed her. "Paulette, you will have your whole life to be my daughter. Your children will be my grandchildren. It is enough."

Paulette hugged him. "Thank you Daddy. I have never had a daddy, Kat!"

Anna brought out the tea and sat it down. Then she saw the books in Kat's bag. "Oh, what is this?" She pulled it out.

Kat almost fainted.

"Oh my, look Augustus! Where did you find this my dear?" Anna asked with glee.

Augustus got up and looked. "Those were some of your best work?"

Anna sighed, "Would have been better if Octavious wasn't such a prude. He was wearing a body suit. I had to guess on some of the proportions."

Augustus nodded. "Not on Angelina."

Anna smiled. "No, she never minded modeling for me in the nude. She had such a nice tight body. What about you two? Just a few quick sketches for your husbands or maybe you two for your wives?"

Ben and Gabriel just shook their heads.

Kat and Paulette looked at each other. "Yes, please!"

Anna beamed. "Well come on follow me."

Ben looked at the Bishop. "Father I . . ."

"Son why do you think we have fifteen cubs." Augustus laughed.

"When the scout ship that crashed on Earth returned, it had with it the Book that contained the stories of the Creators involvement with the sons of Adam and the daughters of Eve. It had a book in it called the *Song of Songs*. The next time you see Angelina. Ask her for a copy of her father's translation. It is beautiful. The Creator is a creator of love. Does he not tell all of Creation to go forth and be fruitful?" The Bishop said.

Ben nodded. "I wouldn't mind a sketch in my uniform for her."

Gabriel nodded "Me either."

Augustus replied, "A nice compromise Gentlebears. She'll like that."

Ben looked at the book. He was afraid to open it "Angelina wrote that?"

"Sure did. She and Octavious had just got married. She was told she had to publish or else. So she did this book. It is well researched. Medically it is brilliant. Sanitized copies are still used for some treatment procedures. By that I mean no illustrations. It caused quite an uproar. It was band in some systems. Some tried to get the church to denounce it. There was a fat chance of that happening. Not with her maiden name. Besides her old man was very proud of her for writing it and proud of my Anna for her work drawing it. True art is true art. Besides he knew what a prude Octavious was. He knew it caused him a lot of grief." Augustus said.

Gabriel was taking it all in.

Ben was trying hard not to laugh. Thinking of the private joke he now knew Kat was going to drop on Beary. He also knew she was safe because Pompey would love it. So would Snow Flower and Jessica. Oh, crap he was a dead bear walking. "Bishop, are you good at funerals?"

The bishop looked at him. "Why, Ben is there a problem?"

"If Kat does what I think she is going to do. My best friends, including Beary, are going to kill me." Ben said.

Augustus laughed. "Then, may I suggest page twenty-five before they do. It is my personal favorite."

He looked at Gabriel who looked confused. "You better stick to page ten through twelve tonight. At least till you, get the hang of it."

Anna sketched them quickly. "You have done this before Kat?"

"No Anna. I am just comfortable in my own skin. Ben does not seem to be. Though, he is totally delicious." Kat said.

Paulette had felt nervous at first. She watched Kat. Kat was Mommy; she had cared for the runaway orphan two years younger than her and convinced a priest to let her adopt her. Had gotten her through school, flight training, and had kept them together. Now she had given her a daddy, a husband, and a family. Even if her daddy was what a year older, he was her daddy.

She walked over. She was stunned by Kat's picture. It caught Kat perfectly, all the pain, the strength, the over powering love, and the tenderness. It wasn't a nude bear it was a picture of an angelic being. Tears flowed from her eyes "Oh, Anna, oh, Mommy it is to wondrous for words."

Anna beamed. "It is your turn Paulette."

Anna positioned Paulette, "Oh, to be that young again."

Anna smiled, Kat stood behind her as Paulette's image took shape on the paper. Tears flowed as Paulette was revealed, the scared little girl, confused young female, bright student, brilliant WTO, and the loving daughter. Then at last the blushing bride.

Kat turned away to wipe the tears. Then she saw her, own picture. She fell on her knees and wept.

Anna touched her shoulder. "Kat, are you alright?"

"Oh, Anna that picture cannot be of me, it is too wondrous. You captured Paulette perfectly. I am not that creature." Kat said.

Paulette wrapped her arms around her. "Mommy you are. That is how I have always seen you."

Paulette looked at her finished picture. "Is that me?"

Anna nodded. "Yes dear, that beautiful young female is you."

Paulette kissed Anna. "May I give it to Gabriel after we are married?"

"That was the idea sweet heart." Anna said.

Kat kissed Anna. "Ben will not be able to take his eyes off of it."

Anna smiled. "He already can't. It is the image he sees all the time."

Kat thought. "You should sketch Pompey, Erin, and maybe Sho-Sho for Beary. Pompey is pregnant with twins."

Anna thought, "An oil painting of them, for Angelina. You must tell him to bring them down."

Kat thought. "I'll ask Ben."

"Well come, I will show you were you can get ready. Maria, help them please." Anna said.

"Yes, my Lady." Maria said with a smile.

Anna went out. "Alright you two, I never take no for an answer."

Augustus explained. "In uniform dear, you know how Beary feels about the rug painting."

"He was two months old. He was adorable." Anna said.

Ben adjusted his uniform as Anna sketched him. "You are a hard one Ben Maritinus. So many layers, then it is there the true you. I now see why Kat loves you."

Ben got up and looked at the picture. "You are a dangerous female Anna. Even when someone is clothed you lay them bare."

Anna sighed. "Thank you Ben. It is what she sees."

"Your turn Gabriel have a seat." Anna said.

She started drawing, as she did tears started to fall from her eyes. Then she smiled. "You have suffered so much, walked through the fires. But you have been reborn, found truth, and love. Come Gabriel look at the face of love."

Gabriel looked at the drawing. He wept. It was all there the pain, the burning hate. It also radiated the almost consuming burning love he felt for Paulette.

Anna told him. "That is a love to last an eternity, Gabriel Archangel."

Gabriel kissed her paw. "Thank you, Lady Anna."

At 18:00 Cycles Ben and Gabriel was waiting in the Chapel. Kat signaled for Ben. Ben walked down the aisle and joined her.

"Walk your daughter down the aisle Ben." Kat said.

Ben looked at Paulette. "Daughter you are breath taking."

Paulette bit her lip. "Thank you Daddy, for the gown. Mommy said it was a gift. It was so expensive."

Ben whispered. "And worth it, I can't wait to see Gabriel's face. He won't be able to breathe."

Paulette kissed him and smiled. "I'll give you lots of grand cubs Daddy."

Ben squeezed her Paw. "Just, be happy Paulette. That is all any father wants."

Ben led her down the aisle. Gabriel saw her and felt like his knees were going to buckle.

Bishop Augustus asked. "Who gives this female to this boar in marriage?"

"I, Ben Maritinus her father and Kat Maritinus, her mother, give her paw to this boar."

Bishop Augustus performed a simple ceremony and a brief sermon on the Creators love. Then he invited the two couples for a light dinner.

Gifts were exchanged. Paulette asked Anna to sign her copies of Angelina's books. Then Kat did the same.

The wives cried over their husbands drawings.

Ben and Gabriel sat in awe of their wives drawings.

Soon the two couples made their way back to the Green Horn. Ben stopped the young couple. "Gabriel, we need to call my family first, come in."

Soon, Aleut and Lunara came on. "Son, is everything alright?" Aleut asked.

"Yes father . . ." he then explained everything.

Aleut smiled, "Paulette Mayotte Maritinus Archangel you have brought great honor to my son granddaughter. I look forward to teaching my great grand cubs to fish with their aunts and uncles. Your name will be added to our family roles under, your fathers and mothers name."

Lunara beamed. "Bring honor to your father tonight granddaughter. I hope your mother has told you a little of our ways."

Paulette dropped her head and smiled. "Yes Grandmother."

"Then we will celebrate your wedding tonight and hold a feast when you return home.

Gabriel Archangel, treat her well." Lunara said.

"Yes, Lady Maritinus." Gabriel said.

"None of that you are now my grandchild also." Lunara said.

Aleut ordered. "Ben, follow our customs."

"Yes father, she is my daughter." Ben said.

Aleut's chest swelled. "You have spoken well my son."

With that the com unit turned off.

Paulette led Gabriel into their room. She smiled "Get undressed husband. I'll return."

Gabriel took off his shoes and socks but stopped. He looked up. She was wearing a loose fitting robe.

Paulette came over, undid his shirt, hung it up, and then his pants. Gabriel was frozen in fear.

"Come husband. I will bathe you, as a wife should, as is the custom." Paulette lowered him into the water. Undid her rob, climbed in, and bathed him. She then started kissing him. "Gabriel, give me your paws like this very gently . . ."

Gabriel carried the now sleeping Paulette to the bed. He fell on his knees. He had hurt her. He was sure he had failed.

Paulette, reach out and touched his face. "What are you doing get in bed. I need your heat silly."

"But, I hurt you! I did it wrong." Gabriel said.

Paulette laughed. "Gabriel you are silly. It was my first time. Of course it hurt a little. It is supposed to. You were gentle you did fine. Now hold me close to you."

Gabriel, did as he was told. She hooked his leg and pressed her body against his chest, and fell asleep.

Kat was purring away. Ben couldn't sleep. He should be exhausted the female wore him out. But he couldn't take his eyes off the drawing of his wife. When he looked at her he saw every detail Anna caught and his desire grew.

Ben final gave up, reached down, grabbed the book, and turned to page twenty-five.

Kat stirred. "Ben, are you alright?"

Ben looked at her. "I know what is in those packages. I am a dead bear walking. My friends will kill me."

Kat looked at him. "Ben they . . ."

Ben looked at her, "Before I die, I want page twenty-five!"

Kat looked at page twenty-five. "Oh well, if that is what my husband desires. Then by all means, I will comply."

A cycle later, Ben was fast asleep, with a smile on his face. Kat was humming to herself. Page twenty-five is a keeper. I think I will tab it with a blue marker. She then slid down and snuggled in.

The next morning Gabriel slowly woke up. He felt funny. "Paulette what . . ."

"Good morning husband, umm you are awake. Good." Paulette smiled.

He gasped "Paulette . . . what is going on?"

Paulette told him. "Just relax Gabriel. I did some reading. This is page thirteen. You are doing just fine."

Gabriel felt real strange. Then Paulette smiled, leaned over, and kissed him. "You did real fine husband. I will certify you are celibate no more."

Gabriel looked at her. "You are not hurting"

Paulette purred. "Gabriel, it may hurt a little at first, which is normal. It also brings pleasure that too is normal.

Come we have to dress. Kat says there is another ceremony. Then there is shopping to be done."

Gabriel put his arms around his wife, kissed her neck, and touched her belly. "I love you Paulette. Will you teach me more?"

She turned in his arms. "We will learn together."

When they came out Ben looked at Paulette she was glowing. "Gabriel did you bring honor to my daughter?"

Gabriel whispered. "Finally, yes Sir, I did."

Paulette smiled. "He is being too hard on himself Daddy."

Kat placed a wreath of flowers on Paulette's head. Then she put a garland around Gabriel's neck.

Then Ben tied their paws. "You are now married, by your Clan's custom Paulette Mayotte Maritinus Archangel. May, the Creator bless you with many cubs, and may, they sing of their parents love."

Paulette' eyes filled with tears as she hugged Ben. "Oh, Daddy, I am so blessed to have you for a father. My children will sing about the greatness of the power of their grandfather's love."

Ben kissed her. Then he turned away. It was unseemly for a warrior to cry, even in joy.

Kat sighed. "Great, now I will have to bed him again. I want to go shopping."

Ben retorted. "I just had a piece of dust in my eye female. It could happen to anyone. Do not shame my daughter."

Kat laughed. "Typical boar, you raise them and they take all the credit."

Paulette laughed and grabbed Archangels paw. She said a silent prayer. "Dear Creator, please protect us. Let us live like this a long time, let our cubs grow. But if our time is short, thank you for the love you have sent us."

They walked down the streets and looked in the various shop windows.

Gabriel was a little nervous. He pulled Ben aside "Skipper I didn't plan on shopping for furniture. I don't think I have . . . Skipper, she doesn't have a ring. She is using my OTS . . ."

Ben thought. "You think you have enough to get her a ring?"

Gabriel nodded. "Yes a small one."

Ben announced. "Ladies, my son-in-law, and I have something to take care of."

Kat smiled and pointed to a furniture store.

Ben steered Archangel into the jewelry store. Archangel went over and started looking at rings. That is when Ben saw something. It was small almost unnoticeable. He smiled.

He walked over to the young lady, at the counter. "May I speak to the owner please?"

The young lady smiled. She led Ben to a small back office. "Mr. Aiden, this gentlebear would like to speak to you."

The older Ursa Americanus stood up and smiled. "Yes, how may I help you?"

Ben smiled and handed him a card. "I was hoping you could offer me your wares at the family rate."

The older bear stiffened and held his ring under the card. The Symbol of the Dragon appeared. "How may the Red Dagger, serve a Knight of our Empress?"

Ben felt embarrassed and explained the situation. The old boar laughed.

"Linus Aiden, Sire Maritinus it is a pleasure to meet you. I will be happy to help the young 2nd Lieutenant, get an appropriate ring set for the Daughter of a Knight of the Clan. Also, it will be at the family rate." The old boar chuckled.

"Janice, don't show the young boar those pieces of junk." Mr. Aiden said.

Janice looked at him. "But, Sir he said . . ."

"Janice, these bears are receiving, the family discount." Mr. Aiden said.

Janice looked at Ben and bowed. Then she went into a back room.

Mr. Aiden set out some extremely exquisite ring sets. Gabriel looked at the prices. "Sire, I can't afford these."

"Non-sense, this is the tourist markup son. You are getting the family discount. Just tell me what you like." Mr. Aiden said.

Gabriel couldn't get the sketch out of his mind. He looked at the strange diamond with the pink huge to it, surrounded by light blue stones, held up by angel wings. "Sir, this set please. This is Paulette."

Mr. Aiden whispered. "Λοϖεσ Ωιvγσ."

Gabriel looked at him. "What Sire?"

"That is the name of the ring in the ancient language. It means Love's Wings. You have chosen well." Mr. Aiden said.

"Mr. Aiden what do these words inside the bands mean?" Gabriel asked.

Mr. Aiden explained. "They are a blessing, Charity, Love, and Grace. These are dragon blessed rings. They are very old."

Gabriel looked at him. "Sire, I know I can't afford them."

Mr. Aiden answered. "You told Janice you could spend up to five hundred credits. I will take four hundred."

Gabriel paid him. "Sire, I don't know how . . ."

Mr. Aiden told him. "Love your wife and pass these on to your children's children."

Janice came out and handed Ben a set of data crystals. "This is a copy of all the intelligence we have gathered. I tried to break into your fighter to use its com system. It was cloaked. By the way, the lock you put on the Hanger Number Three, I picked it in less than two micro SubSTUs."

Ben nodded. "I'll tell fleet security that they need better."

Gabriel looked like an excited little cub. He held his purchase close to his chest. "Skipper, why did he sell me this ring set? It is worth five hundred times what he charged me. You didn't . . ."

Ben shook his head, "No Gabriel, you truly bought that yourself. All I, did was get you the family discount."

Gabriel looked at him, "Skipper that is a huge family discount!"

Ben explained, "It is a remarkable family Gabriel. You haven't even been touched by it completely yet."

When they got to the furniture store Kat was lying on a big wooden bed. Ben just shook his head. "Kat, it is too big."

Kat sighed. "I know, but someday, I want one this size. That way all of our cubs will be able to snuggle in bed, with us."

Paulette added, "And grand cubs also."

Ben just sighed all of a sudden he felt old.

Archangel laughed. "It is alright Dad. I will keep the fire lit in the fire pit for you."

Ben looked at him and laughed. "What with your walking stick?"

Kat finally decided on the furniture that would fit in their space on the EAQ. She also orders some for Paulette.

Gabriel was nervous. "Skipper, it will take me years to pay you back."

Ben responded. "Gabriel, this is a gift to my daughter. I can afford it. Kat knows that. Yet she has haggled, wheeled, and deal over every piece. The poor merchant is ready to pull his hair out. Yet, this will be a good sells day for him."

When Kat was done she exited the store in triumph. "I outfitted both suits for less than ten thousand credits. It's all high quality furniture also."

Ben pointed to a restaurant, "Food is that way, let's go."

Kat took his paw and whispered, "Where did you two go?"

"Gabriel needed to go shopping. You'll see. I got him a great deal." Ben smiled.

At the table after they were seated and a bottle of Cherry nectar was brought to the table. Gabriel took hold gently of Paulette's left paw.

"Dad that OTS ring doesn't look right." Gabriel took it off her ring digit.

Paulette looked like she was about to cry. Until, he opened the box.

Gabriel gentle pulled out first the engagement ring, with its pink hue diamond and light blue stones, held up by Angel wings. He then put on the wedding band. He then handed her his band. So she could put on his.

Paulette looked at the rings on her paw then at her husband she kissed him. "Mommy, look isn't it wonderful?"

Gabriel lowered his head. "Its name is Love's Wings it is a dragon blessed set."

Kat responded. "Yes, Paulette it is."

They talked through lunch. Then Paulette's eyes shined. She whispered into Kat's ear.

Kat nodded. "I think he deserves a reward."

Paulette grabbed Gabriel's paw and dragged him out of the restaurant.

Ben looked at Kat. "Where are they going?"

Kat grinned. "The same place we would be going, if we didn't have to figure out how to get our purchases up to the ship. Also, Beary, Pompey, and Erin down here so Anna can paint them."

Ben got an evil grin on his face. "Kat, you are a bad influence on me. It is going to cost you."

Kat cooed. "Oh, I like the sound of that?"

Ben pointed, "First, new underwear for me. Then my second request." He smiled. "I'll make the calls. Go shop."

Kat smiled and walked over to the boar's store. Some he would like and maybe a few she liked.

Ben called the bishop and explained his diabolical plan.

"Ben, as a Bishop in the Church, I cannot condone such an act of deviousness. However, as a loving husband, who wants to not sleep in the Canus house tonight. I'll do it. I'll even fabricate some forms. She will love to do Lady Artemus and her children also."

Anna laughed. "Ben is a good bear, an imp, but good."

Ben hung up. Then he called Captain Gracchus. "Sir, it is Captain Maritinus."

"How are you feeling son? I am sorry; I wasn't much help to you after you were wounded." Gracchus said.

Ben replied. "Sir, the medicine I have received has returned me to good health."

Gracchus warned. "Ben, Admiral Astrid was after your head. I think Shoshana scared him off, at least temporarily. I believe your, father- in- law plans on causing trouble for you, Ben.

Also, I need to know about our situation with Archangel?"

Ben responded. "My daughter will, be happy to certify that he is definitely not a celibate priest. I believe she is trying to beat her mother at becoming pregnant."

Gracchus was confused. "Captain, we must have a bad connection. It sounded like you said that Ensign Mayotte was your daughter."

Ben explained. "That is correct Captain Gracchus. Actually Kat had adopted her years ago. But for her to be married the church, who was her guardian, required that a boar also adopt her. Kat and I redid the paper work. However, I need Beary, Artemus, their families, and dragons to come down and validate the paper work.

Could you have them bring an empty ROSE? We bought furniture."

Gracchus sighed. "Ben you are up to something. 99% of what you told me was true. The other 1% I imagine you have fabricated something plausible. So it isn't a lie. Ben I know excrement when I hear it."

Ben laughed and came clean and told the other part of the situation.

Gracchus thought. "You think I could send Jeanne down also? I would love a drawing of her like that."

Ben replied. "Sir, I am sure Anna would love it."

Jeanne came in and looked at her husband. He was smiling ear to ear.

"Argus, what are you up to?" Jeanne asked.

Argus explained Ben's call. "I would love a drawing of you."

Jeanne sat down and felt her belly, "A nude? Argus you would never have . . ." Then she smiled. "Ben said she is real good?"

Argus nodded. "They're not obscene. He said there ethereal."

Jeanne replied. "Well, I could get the drawing done with my clothes on."

Argus kissed her, "Or off, which ever you prefer." As he bent down and kissed her belly.

Jeanne asked. "Are you going to tell Beary and Artemus the truth?"

Argus shook his head, "Nope, Beary, and Artemus are a little up tight."

Pathfinder found Beary in the gym. "I see you are still in good shape."

Beary sighed. "Hi Jane, I have to exercise just to keep up with Pompey's energy. Being pregnant seems to increase her energy level."

Pathfinder laughed, "Captain Gracchus, was looking for you and Artemus. I called Savato. He said he would meet you there. Also, Caesar says you are due for your flight physical."

Beary asked. "How did Artemus do?"

"He said he passed. Caesar wants him to lose five SWU." Pathfinder said.

Beary nodded. "That is why I am working out."

Beary and Artemus came in, sat down. Gracchus smiled. "I need you two to take your families to Kalian. To this village and fix a paper work problem for our dear Ben. It seems he picked up a daughter and a son-in-law on this trip. Also take a ROSE or two. Apparently, Kat bought out half the village's furniture stores. Jeanne wants to go with you to see if she can buy out the other half."

Beary dropped his head. "Mayotte was a ward of the church."

Gracchus nodded. "I should have known you understood ecclesiastic laws."

"My grandfather is a great teacher. His favorite subject is what he calls *The Troublesome Protective Laws to Govern Females and Cubs*. That neither protects nor governs either." Beary said.

Artemus responded. "Tell the Commander, we'll get the family together, and be ready in about a cycle."

"Take Sho-Sho and Ice Song also. Oh, Ben also transmitted some intelligence he gathered. It might be important." Gracchus added.

Caesar met them coming into the family section. "Gracchus just called. There are too many pregnant passengers. One is his wife. I go also."

Artemus said. "Beary, you fly *The Star*, I'll handle the ROSES."

Pompey thought. "Maybe, we can do some shopping while we are at it."

Ben and Kat walked slowly back to the hotel. That is when he saw the jewelry shop. "Come on Kat."

Mr. Aiden saw him coming and smiled. "Sire Maritinus, what a pleasant surprise, did the young lady like her wedding set?"

Kat replied. "Our daughter was very pleased. I think her young boar is being pleased as we speak."

Mr. Aiden laughed. "My Lady, how may I serve a Lady of the clan?"

Ben retorted, "She does fit in doesn't she. I want something special for both my bride and my new daughter."

Mr. Aiden nodded. "If I am correct, yesterday was both her wedding day and, under ecclesiastic law, her new birthday as your daughter. So yes I think I have just the thing.

Janise, bring some honey nectar for the good Knight and his Lady."

Janise smiled as she brought it out, "Sire Maritinus and my lady, may I pour for you?"

Kat smiled. "Thank you, my dear."

"Ah, here they are!" He laid two identical necklaces on the counter. Each had a green diamond with a rainbow of other precious colored stones in a circle around it. The links of the chain were made to look like a mother holding a child. One necklace said a mother's love. The other said a daughter's devotion.

Kat looked at them "Oh, Ben . . ."

Ben told him. "Well, Mr. Aiden that is your answer. We will take them."

Mr. Aiden smiled "My Lady, my sources say you and your daughter are a fighter crew."

Kat stiffened.

Until Ben, smiled and nodded.

"Yes, Sire, Paulette is my WTO." Kat said.

"Then I will throw these in also. You will not find better blades anywhere. They were forged by Drop Wing the Bold. They are special." Mr. Aiden said.

The blades had a blue hue to them. Beautiful stones in the, carved handles, which were in the shape of dragons. She picked them up. The balance was perfect. The sheaths were also blue and seemed to shimmer.

"What are the sheaths made of?" Kat whispered almost reverently.

Mr. Aiden explained. "Dragon scales, my lady. Those daggers are two thousand years old. You must promise to carry them as part of your uniform and your daughter also. The Prince will agree when he sees them."

Kat looked at him, "But Sire, these have to be priceless!"

Mr. Aiden explained. "My lady, these are a wedding gift from the Red Dagger."

Ben bowed. "Thank you, Sire. They will cherish them and bring honor to the clan. By the way, how much do I owe for those?"

Mr. Aiden wrote out a number.

Ben looked at it. Shook his head doubled it, wrote that number down, and showed it to Mr. Aiden. Who smiled and nodded.

Ben counted out the bills and handed them to him.

Janise wrapped two separate packages and labeled them.

Kat fitted one dagger on her belt. It seemed to have no weight at all. The other was placed in a gift box for Paulette.

Kat kissed Mr. Aiden and Janise.

Ben smiled and thanked them.

As they walked Kat took Ben's paw. She had questions, but was afraid to ask.

"Kat, I can't explain. You have been greatly honored and been made privy to one of the most carefully guarded secrets of our adoptive clan." Ben said in a whisper.

Kat closed her eyes. "Then it will be locked in my heart and soul."

Kat looked at him. "I need you Ben." She whispered.

Ben shrugged. "I think there is time."

As they past suite four they heard uproarious laughter and giggling.

Ben looked at Kat. "What do you think that is about?"

Kat replied. "I don't know, but let's not bother them. I have my own needs."

Paulette finally caught her breath. "I don't think that it is possible!"

Gabriel smiled, as he pulled her over, and kissed her. "Not at our level of expertise. But, it was fun trying."

Paulette kissed him. "I think I have created a monster."

"No, Paulette, a bear. You have brought me back to life. While all this is fun. Just seeing you, holding your paw, or hearing that musical voice is enough." Gabriel said.

Paulette kissed him and laid her head against his chest. "Gabriel, I need a promise from you."

"What Paulette?" Gabriel asked.

"If I am killed, you must not return to hate." Paulette said. "I love what I do. However, we die Gabriel. On average 50% of all fighter crews die. Kat and I have made the cut, twice. The odds will someday catch up with us."

Gabriel looked at her. "That's bull, Paulette. You're veterans that increase your odds. Newbies are always the first to get it and dumb 2nd lieutenants.

Paulette, I dodged mine. I survived. My chances just increased 60 %. You're right we live with the risk of death every day. So what? There is no point fearing death. If the Creator is going to take us then he takes us. Still, Paulette don't you ever give up on me, yourself, or the Creator. I have had one female do that to me. Don't, you ever do it!"

Paulette saw the tears in his eyes. "I won't Gabriel. I will live unless the Creator takes me himself. I will never give up, I promise!" She kissed him. He kissed her and started to caress her.

A cycle latter she woke up, went in, and took a shower. Gabriel came in.

"Paulette, are you alright? Did I do, something wrong?" Gabriel asked.

Paulette smiled and pulled him in. "Wash my back, would you?"

He gentle wrapped his arm around her waist. "You didn't answer me."

"No silly, I . . . put my fears on you. Which opened your fears, some help mate I am . . ." She started to cry.

Gabriel kissed her eyes, "You are a great help mate. You have saved me, in more ways than one. You sacrificed yourself unselfishly to protect my secret. Offered me your love, then taught me how to love. What more could I ask?"

Paulette looked at him. "You keep talking with honey sweet words like that then you are going to be very worn out."

"Come on get dressed. We should go find your parents. Kat has probable bought out half the village." Gabriel said.

Gabriel knocked on Ben's door.

Kat came to the door with a robe wrapped around her. "Oh, children, could you just give us a moment, to a get dressed." Kat said as she said smiling and biting her lip.

Paulette replied. "We'll wait in the small restaurant downstairs. Mommy, ah take your time." she giggled.

Gabriel smiled as they walked away. "Page forty-three?"

Paulette laughed. "It was definitely page forty-three."

Gabriel swatted her tail. "I enjoyed page forty-three."

Paulette smiled. 'I figured you would."

Ben looked at Kat. "Female, you are going to be the death of me."

Kat leaned against him. "Ah, but what away to go, we better get dressed."

Ben asked. "Did she look happy?"

Kat nodded. "Yes Ben, happier than in years. She has her demons too. We both do. Too many friends dead, too many close escapes. If you're not careful you start thinking that your luck will run out. You know the drill."

Ben nodded, "It doesn't matter combat, illness, or accident. Death comes when the Creator sends it. You have to live, that is the hard part. That is a lesson a Kat has taught me."

Kat kissed him "You have taught me, the more love you give, the more it multiplies. For Ben Maritinus, no bear has a greater capacity for love."

Paulette was lost in Gabriel's eyes. When she heard "So this is where my gold bricking S5 has been hiding. She was lost in a goldbricking Marine."

Paulette stood at attention as did Gabriel.

"Caesar, he looks to have recovered real well under her medical attention." Beary said "At ease you two."

"Boss, we . . . Commander . . ." Paulette stammered.

Jeanne came over and kissed both of them. "Congratulations, on your marriage, Lieutenant Archangel, and you Ensign. Would you mind if I sat down. Walking causes my legs to swell a little."

Caesar came over, checked them, and frowned. "You have skipped the pool for at least two days!"

Jeanne held up her paws. "Doctor, I have been . . ."

"Commander you are going on report." He then looked at Pompey. "You set, let me see yours also; ok you are both on report."

He looked at Paulette. "When you get pregnant, you will follow my staffs directions or else."

"Yes Doctor." Paulette said.

Jessica hit Caesar. "You'll scare her."

Caesar looked at her. "Don't get me started."

Jessica scowled. "I wish you would. I am not getting any younger."

Beary and Artemus just turned away. That is when they saw Ben and Kat. "Well they call us down here and keep us waiting." Artemus said.

Ben responded. "I'll call the church, give me a moment."

Beary saw the dagger on Kat's hip. "Where did you get that?"

Kat knelt, pulled it, and offered it to Beary "It was a gift Sire, given so, I may serve you. There is one for my daughter also."

Beary lifted her up. "Kat, no Red Paw Warrior kneels to anyone but the Creator and his Word. Neither, does any member of my clan or family. You are to never be without that dagger. Give Paulette hers now please."

"Paulette, come here please. This was a gift, it is special. You're never to be without it." Kat said

Paulette put the sheath on her belt.

All of a sudden, Star Fire appeared in Beary's paw, a thin flame covered its blade. The daggers glowed. A thin band near the top with a blue stone glowed.

"Ladies, if you please pull out your daggers. Remove those golden bands and place them on your right paw." Beary ordered.

The bands slid off, then tightened on their paws. Kat and Paulette looked at the rings.

Star Fire disappeared. Beary looked at Kat and Paulette. Then he looked at Ben. "We are going to have to talk."

Everyone else looked stunned. No one had ever seen anything like it.

Shoshanna and Ice Song, both in bear form, came over and kissed Kat and Paulette. "We will explain everything. You have been chosen. Uncle, we will explain later. This is not the time or place."

Beary nodded, "Ben, are they ready for us?"

Ben nodded, "Ya Boss, they are ready." He said absent mindedly. Oh, but first may, I give my daughter a late birthday present?"

Beary nodded, "Sure Ben, what is another moment or two."

Ben handed Paulette the box, with the daughter necklace. Then he handed Kat, her box.

Kat opened hers and slipped the necklace on.

Paulette was shaking as she opened the box. Tears fell as she read the inscription. Then saw the one on Kat's neck. Gabriel put it on her neck. She looked at Ben. Then threw her arms around his neck and cried. "Oh, Daddy thank you, I . . . Oh, Daddy!"

Erin smiled. "Ben is a good daddy, isn't he Mommy."

Pompey whispered, "Yes, dear."

Nikolaos walked over and kissed Kat's paw.

"Sir Nikolaos, thank you, but why?" Kat asked.

Nikolaos explained. "You and Ben did for her, what father and mother did for the three of us. I can't kiss Ben. You can share your kiss."

Kat bent down and kissed him gentle on his lips. "I will share this kiss and keep the other for myself."

Nikolaos smiled.

Jessica just shook her head. He was defiantly a lady killer. Just like Ti, innocent but not too much.

They all walked up to the church. Jessica and Alexis were on the wings watching. Nikolaos and Andreios bring up the rear. Maryam skipping out front like a little girl without a care, with two throwing knives hidden in her sleeves. Behind her was Sho-Sho and Ice Song.

Beary smiled. *An assassin might get them from long range but not up close. He had seen Maryam practice this little dance. He had even acted as a target with practice knives. She had hit him with twenty before he closed on her. Then she shot him with a training phaser. In real life he would have got through. Well, maybe a phaser blast to the head might even stop him permanently.*

Beary looked around some more at his little parade: Artemus was walking with Snow Flower, who was carrying Agathag, Pompey was holding Erin's paw, and Ben was walking quietly paw in paw with Kat.

Gabriel and Paulette were clinging together for life. Caesar was taking it all in. Commander Gracchus was humming to herself.

It seemed unreal to Beary, as all moments of peace did lately. He was afraid the universe would step in and throw things out of kilter again soon.

They reached the church. Ben opened the door and ushered them all inside.

Beary gasped when he saw them. "Augustus, Anna what are you doing here?" Then it hit him. He had been had. As Anna came over and kissed him.

"Beary my boy oh how you have grown, would you introduce us?" Anna said with glee.

"Now Anna none of that, we . . ." Beary tried to say.

"Lieutenant Maxumus stop being rude and introduce us." Jeanne ordered.

Beary nodded in defeat. "Commander Gracchus this is my Cousins Anna Henderson and Bishop Augustus Henderson."

Jeanne exclaimed. "Please call me Jeanne. Oh, you're not that Anna Henderson the famous artist!"

Beary shook his head and sat down. *Oh Lord here we go.*

Augustus came over. "No point fighting it Beary. She'll have them all drawn, painted, and smiling before you know what happened. Plus, I do have some papers you and Artemus need to sign. Come on or she'll have you on the rug again."

Pompey's eyes lit up. "You painted that wonderful painting in Angelina's study?"

Beary turned. "NO!"

Anna shook her head. "He is as bad as his father. Caesar, you will pose for me won't you? After all you are a Doctor."

"Anna I don't . . ." Caesar started to say when Jessica squeezed his tail.

"Would you do a couples portrait Anna?" Jessica asked.

"Oh, Jessica, you mean you two finally got married. I would love it!" Anna said with glee.

"Pompey you must let me paint you, Erin and Sho-Sho together. Sho-Sho dear, could I paint you as a dragon though? Also, sweet heart, while you and Ice Song are lovely in this form, you may change here in the house we are family." Anna said

Ice Song didn't wait she changed then stretched. "Thank you my lady."

Sho–Sho changed more slowly, "As you wish, Lady Anna."

Anna looked at the two young dragons. "You both are so magnificent.

Lady Snow Flower, I would like to do one with all your children. Then just one with your daughters, perhaps, one with Artemus, and the boys." Anna concluded.

Then she looked at Jeanne, "A special one for your husband."

Jeanne nodded. "Yes, please."

Then she turned to Alexis. "I haven't forgotten one of my favorite models either."

"Anna!" Alexis said.

"So who is first?" Anna asked.

Jeanne smiled.

"Come on Commander." Anna said.

Jeanne looked at her. "It is silly. Argus wants a nude of me but . . ."

"Commander, I think I know what he wants. Go behind the screen and get undressed. There is a robe, put it on, then come out." Anna instructed.

Jeanne came out. Anna positioned her on a coach with her paws rubbing her cub bump. She then positioned the shear rob to cover her modestly yet revealingly.

Anna hummed. "Oil, I feel like painting you in oil."

She quickly went to work capturing all the hopes; disappointments, lost loves, found loves, fears, and now new joys that made up the Commanders life. When she was done she hummed. "I really like this painting. I thing I will take a copy of it. Then put it in my collection."

She brought over a machine and after she signed the original. She copied it. "Here you are Commander, the original."

Jeanne looked at it and tears flowed from her eyes. "Oh, Anna it is too beautiful. That cannot be me? What do I owe you?"

Anna laughed, "Just love the cub and the boar that gives you that glow when you think of him."

She painted Caesar and Jessica. She compromised a little with Caesar, as he said to save his dignity. They both were stunned by the painting.

She did Alexis next as a Valkyrie Warrior. As Anna said it finished a collection she was working on. She gave Alexis a copy.

Alexis sighed. "Well at least the important parts were covered."

Nikolaos walked over, "You will have to be careful where you hang that my lady. Or Andreios and I will be busy defending your honor." Then he smiled. "Of course, if we were older we would have to fight each other."

Alexis smiled. "Nikolaos Artemus, shame on you." Then she kissed him. If he or Andreios were older I might not mind.

Andreios shook his head. "Brother, you are shameless."

"You were thinking the same thing." Nikolaos said.

"True, but I am not as bold." Andreios said.

"No just more devious." Maryam said.

Anna came and got Pompey, Erin, and Sho-Sho.

Anna smiled "You don't mind doing a nude do you Pompey?"

"Not at all, I am daughter of the Southern Continent. Wild and free, I am not a shamed of my body." Pompey said with an impish smile. "Beary should not be ashamed of his either, believe me."

Anna grinned. "I see why Angelina loves you so much. This painting is for her."

She positioned Pompey with Erin on her lap and slightly turned them so her cub bump showed. She positioned Erin's arm across Pompey's chest at just the right point. Then had Sho-Sho curl around them as if she was protecting them. She adjusted Pompey left arm slightly around Erin's bottom.

She then started painting. "Shoshana, you must open your heart to me. Do not fear me. I will not hurt you." Anna said.

Sho-Sho blinked. Because, she didn't see her speak, then she realized she had spoken directly to her mind. "Yes, Lady Anna."

She painted quickly. Anna captured all the love and strengths of each of her subjects. She captured the bond of love, which exists between a dragon and the girl cub. Most of all she captured the intense burning love and desire in Pompey's heart for her family. She also captured the hidden pain, joy, and burden in a young dragon's heart. She sighed when she was done. "Pompey, why, don't you, two get dressed, while I finish this up."

Sho-Sho came around and looked. "It is amassing Lady Anna! Grandmother will cry."

Anna nodded. "She will, at that."

"Lady Anna, would you . . . could you paint the two forms of me for my father?" Shoshana asked.

"I would love to dear." Anna said.

Sho-Sho changed into Maximus form.

Anna smiled. "Is the gown part of you?'

Sho-Sho smiled "It is my wings. I have only learned to form them in two ways the gown and this way. Sho-Sho formed them into a cape that hooked at the neck. I can open the cape but you see the problem."

Anna marveled at the perfectly formed tight body. "I think both your uncle and father would have heart attacks. Dear, we better stay with the gown. You are to over powering in this form, my dear."

She painted this form. Then she had Sho-Sho change forms. She then painted her again fading and blending the two forms. When Anna finished she copied both pictures. "One, for Angelina also, but the original is for your father."

Sho-Sho cried, when she saw the painting. She had been laid bare. Yet it was wonderful. "Lady Anna, accept a dragon's love." She kissed Anna power flowed into Anna.

Anna replied. "Sho-Sho, you are so young and so powerful. Thank you for your blessing. I will use it for someone who needs to be blessed.

That is when Sho-Sho realized "Lady Anna you . . ."

Anna shrugged. "My grandmother was Katherine of Hazelwood. Dark Wing, may he rest in peace was her companion. He gave my mother his Heart of Hearts, before the transport left. He had been mortally wounded by a traitor dragon. I need to return it to Andreas Prime but he does not wish to leave me."

Sho-Sho kissed her. "Let him be. He is happy. He is still watching over you. I could free him, but he would refuse. I understand that kind of love."

Next came, the Artemus family portrait. She positioned Artemus and Snow Flower on the couch holding Agathag. She then positioned Nikolaos and Andreios on either side of their parents and slightly behind. With Maryam setting on a chair on one side next to Snow flower. Ice Song in dragon form was setting next to Artemus.

Again her brush captured it, all the fear, and determination in each cub. The uncertainty and fear the parents, felt at almost losing a child. She captured the fear and triumph of a young dragon, torn from her home and thrown into a new family. Mostly, she painted the enormous bond of love that bound them all together.

Tears flowed from Artemus eyes as he looked at the painting. "It is so over powering."

Nikolaos said. "Ice Song, do not cry. I love you sister."

"I know silly. These are tears of joy!" Ice Song sang.

Snow Flower told them, "Now, for a picture of me and my girls. Boys, go get a snack, goodbye for now."

"Maria, give milk and cookies to the young men, if you would please." Anna said.

"Yes, my lady." Maria said.

Ice Song asked. "Lady Anna, could you paint me with mother, Maryam, and Agathag in my other form."

"Yes dear, but Sho-Sho had a problem . . . Oh I see!" Anna smiled the creature standing before her looked almost like an Angel.

"I am a Frigorific Dragon my lady. We have smaller wings. We are ice and water dragons." Ice Song said.

Anna smiled. Maryam took off her dress. "Come on Mommy. I saw Erin's painting. This should be fun?"

Snow Flower sighed. "Oh well."

Anna positioned them so the painting would be appropriate. It was a picture of a mother with her daughters, enjoying a bath, in a hot spring. Maryam laughed a hooligan's laugh, as she looked over her shoulder at Anna. In just the pose Anna wanted. Ice Songs wings were visible but hidden in a spray of water from the water fall. That she tilted her head into. Snow Flower bathed Agathag on the edge of the spring.

This painting captured only pure love, joy of daughters, and mother.

When they were done, dried off, and Ice Song had changed back, she looked at Anna. "Do, I really look like that?"

"Yes, dear you do." Anna said.

Snow Flower looked at the painting, "Oh, poor Gisfrid! Daughter, we need to talk."

Then she looked at Maryam. "No boys for you, young lady!"

"Don't worry mother. I live with brothers, boys are gross," Maryam said. "At least for now they are anyway."

After, Anna finished painting a sea scape, with Artemus and the boys, in swim suits, playing in the surf. She went to find Beary.

"Beary you are coming with me now." Anna ordered.

"Anna . . ." Beary said.

"Beary Augustus Maxumus it is for your wife and maybe your mother!" Anna demanded.

Beary looked at Anna, "I am not lying on a rug without my cloths."

"Oh no, I have a better Idea." Anna said.

She handed Beary a pair of swimming trunks. "Put these on, in there, and come out."

She had Beary set straddled backwards over an old wooden chair. "Yes, that makes you look like a young Pirate Captain, trying to decide what he wants to do with his conquest."

Then she turned the picture of Pompey, Erin, and Sho-Sho around so he could see it. Then she turned the others.

Beary's eyes went from one to the next. Then his eyes returned to the picture of his family.

That's when Anna started painting. Her brush flew over the canvas. Red swirls seemed to form around Beary. In her mind a Fiery Red sword was in his paws. A blue star was over his shoulder and standing behind him a fire red dragon with her talon on his shoulder smiling wide. Anna felt exhausted when she finished. Then she looked at the painting. Tears started flowing, "Oh, Beary!"

Beary got up and looked at the painting. "Anna, how is it possible? Star Fire never came into my paw."

Beary heard a voice, "Anna, stop being silly. You painted what she wanted you to paint. See, she is in the painting. She, who is allowed to walk between here, and there, he is her love. Just, as you are mine.

Guardian, I am Dark Wing, at least what is left of the one that once was the companion of Katharina of Hazelwood. Tell Princess Shoshanna, the Great, that she is correct. I choose to stay with my Anna. I am free to do as I please. This is what I please."

Beary kissed Anna. "I want two copies. Send one to Gamey for the hall and a small one for Pompey. Your right, mom will want the original."

Anna bowed, "My Prince . . ."

"Anna, cut that out. I am just, Beary nothing more. I love you." Beary said.

Beary went in and started getting dressed.

Anna looked at the painting. "So much power, he doesn't realize does, he?"

Dark Wing appeared next to her. "Yes, Anna he does, but he is afraid of the power. That is why she is so proud of him. He is humble and good. Look at his eyes. Those are not the eyes of a conqueror, but of someone with an unlimited capacity for love." With that Dark Wing disappeared.

Maria brought out dinner. No one had noticed Kat had slipped out and had returned.

"I have a gift for all of the wives here." She handed out the packages. Ben tried to find an escape but he was stuck between Artemus and his Son-in-Law.

Gabriel looked at him. "Sorry, Skipper. If you take off. I'll be the one they kill."

The commander opened hers first, read the title, and the name of the author. Then she opened it. "Oh my, what interesting drawings, Anna you did these didn't you?"

Anna nodded. "Yes. Beary's parents were the models. Of course Octavious wore a body suite. Angelina had no such problems; she had such a fine body."

Beary looked over Pompey's shoulder and turned crimson, "Oh my!"

Caesar opened up Volume Two and leafed through it "I have seen the sanitized versions, but never the originals. They are quite good. You know Beary, Pompey would benefit from the message techniques on page six hundred eight-five and seven hundred ninety. So would you Commander."

Jeanne jotted those pages down. Then she looked at Anna. "Will you sign my copies please?"

The other all said. "Mine also please?"

Anna beamed.

Beary was dying.

Artemus nudged Ben. "You know, you're dead."

Ben smiled. "Try page twenty-five, then decide what you think."

"Don't forget page forty-three." Gabriel whispered.

Ben looked at him "How did you know . . ."

Gabriel just smiled "They are mother and daughter."

Then Gabriel looked at Artemus. "Don't try page eighty-six. It isn't possible."

Augustus laughed. "Octavious threw out his back on that one. That is, till he learned the secret, zero gravity."

"Oh, that makes since." Both Gabriel and Paulette said as the other ladies turned to page eighty-six.

Beary just got up and walked outside. Maryam joined him.

"You are embarrassed Beary. Yet you will enjoy the gift will you not for Lady Pompey's sake?" Maryam asked. "Do not boars have fantasies about their wives?"

"Maryam, aren't you a little young for us to have this discussion?" Beary asked.

Maryam sighed, "Physically Beary yes. But dragon blessings have consequences. Mentally all three of us are advanced beyond our ages. It causes some confusion, especially for the boys. Partly because we are surrounded by so much love, it has become as natural to us as killing."

Beary looked at her. "I am sorry Maryam."

"Why Beary? Do you not remember, I asked for this life? I love protecting Erin and Lady Pompey. It is all I live for. I am good at what I do and my skills are only getting better. So is my speed. When Erin is ready to date, I will be of age.

Sho–Sho will resist. However, dragons come of age younger than we do. Ice Song has already set her heart on poor Gisfrid. They have been communicating.

Do not be angry at Kat. She knows we are heading into danger. Mother cries when father does not know. She will not tell him. She says it would dishonor him if he knew of her fears.

Ben, getting hurt affected Pompey also. They will not tell you. This book, while you see it as a personal embarrassment, they see as a gift of life."

Beary looked at Maryam, "Squire Maryam, thank you."

"I love you Beary." Maryam said.

"I love you too Maryam." Beary said.

She looked up at him and smiled. "I know that silly."

After dinner the families made their way back to the hotel. The girls and boys were put to bed in adjoining rooms. Then the adults went into their rooms. Jeanne decided to bunk with the little girls. Sho-Sho, still in Maxmimus form, changed her gown into a night gown. Then she lay down on the couch. Ice Song lay down on the bed with the three small girls. Erin got up and crawled in with Shoshanna.

Sho-Sho looked at her. "What is it my love?"

Erin looked at her. "Evil, is looking for us." she whispered.

A mysterious figure moved through the back streets of the village. He was having trouble locating his target. No one had seen the Polarian all day. The inn keeper had hinted that they had checked out.

The jewelry store owner had told him about a small cottage, that a couple had rented. It was at the end of this lane but it was so dark. That was when he saw a lantern in the window of the cottage. He saw a white figure in the window. He fired his seeker. It penetrated the window and exploded into a shower of feathers.

He felt a sharp pain in his back "That was one of my best pillows." A voice said as the pain increased as the dagger was twisted in his back. It was pulled out and slammed back in.

The assassin thought, "*How? He was supposed to be one of the best.*" as darkness closed around him.

Janise pulled the hood off her head. Then she wiped her dagger. She took out a camera, took his picture, then took his paw print, and sent it in. Then Janise called a number and left the scene.

The next morning even Beary, had to admit that maybe his mom knew what she was talking about. It might, also explain why his dad always seemed hungry for her.

He had messaged Pompey as volume two had instructed to do for prenatal care of females. Pompey seemed too purr, then she fell fast to sleep. She woke up feeling better than she had in days. In fact he noticed everyone seemed to be in a better mood.

Jeanne told him. "Kat's gift, she gave them won't last. Beary you know it. So do I. Although, I am looking forward to the doctor's prescription, Maryam did a sanitized version of the lower back message and my back is better. The paintings and the books, they all proved that we are alive. We need that."

Beary looked at her. "You're expecting trouble Commander?"

Jeanne replied. "Beary, I always expect trouble. So are you. You have been looking over your shoulder since we got here."

As they went into the hotel restaurant, Ben pointed out an older bear. He was standing at the counter talking to the owner. "Beary that is Zeck Hammerhead."

Beary looked, "Zeck the Hammer, where do you see him?" Beary exclaimed.

Zeck looked up. He looked confused, "Cub?"

Beary went over and hugged him. Then he remembered himself. "Lieutenant Maxumus Sir." Beary saluted.

Zeck laughed. "Hi Cub, boy you grew up good. We need to talk."

"Let me buy you breakfast." Beary offered.

Zeck nodded. "May I invite my friend, Mr. Radcliff?"

Beary replied, "Of course Sir."

Vern Radcliff smiled. "Well if you're buying, let's go somewhere we can get a good breakfast."

They went across to another restaurant. The dragons and cubs sat at one table. While the others sat at a large round table.

Zeck looked around the table, then at the children's table. The restaurant had three doors. He noticed that the two teenage cubs were watching him and Vern. While the next oldest girl cub watched the front door and the two boys watched the two side doors. All while acting like young cubs.

"Cub . . . Beary I have been a friend of your family along time. I need some answers to some delicate questions. You see, I am not only the Air Field Manager, but Vern and I are the law here."

Beary nodded. "Sir, have we broken the law?"

Zeck shook his head. "Not that I am aware of. Although, I am not sure it is wise to let cubs carry weapons."

Maryam, Nikolaos, and Andreios just laid their badges on the table. Jessica and Alexis did also.

Zeck shook his head. "The teenagers, what are they?"

Shoshana explained. "I am my Grandmothers, Ambassador to the Bearilian Fleet on the *EAQ*, Sir.

Ice Song responded. "I am her handmaiden and bodyguard."

Jeanne finally spoke up. "Sir, with all due respect, what is this about?"

Zeck sighed and dropped two pictures on the table. One was of Ben the other of Kat. "A bear by the name of Dresden Stixks, a professional killer, had them in his pocket. I was wondering if Sir and Lady Maritinus knew why?"

Ben asked. "Why don't you ask him?"

Zeck shrugged. "Wish, I could, someone I know, with a deep cover, and one of those shiny badges put a knife in him. After, he tried to kill you. Now, do you know why?"

Ben shook his head. "If it was Beary . . . wow, I can think of a whole bunch of systems that want him dead. Me, no, especially . . . not when you throw in Kat."

Kat looked at him. "You don't think . . . as cruel as he is . . . he wouldn't go that far . . . would he?"

Ben shook his head. "No Kat. This must stem from some other incident."

Zeck looked at them. "He also had this number in his pocket." He showed them a card 25-97-788-676-8787.

Ben and Kat looked at it and shook their heads.

Jessica spoke up, "It is a communication exchange on the planet DeVaan owned by the ComStar company. 25- Is DeVaan prefix. The 97- is a company owned reference. The 788- is the Archduchy of Averroes. The 676- is the town of Sason. The 8787 is the drop location."

Zeck said. "So if we went to this location we could find out something?"

Jessica shook her head. "Nope, you might find a secretary handling mail or just twenty computers redirecting calls. None of which have any record of it being made."

Zeck asked. "The Bearilian Government allows this?"

"DeVaan is a privately owned planet, ComStar a privately owned company. That has very tight security and discretion. They protect all their clients equally." Jessica said.

Zeck looked at her. "So, in case of an emergency, you have one of those cards?"

Jessica nodded. "Fourth level back up, but yes it is a resource and it has saved lives."

Zeck looked at her. "How many lives has it cost?"

Kat was wide eyed. "DeVaan is a major shipping and market for Quartzite Médaille. It is a type of ore that is mined on my home planet of Polarian. It is Quartz with liquid gold inside. The magma of our planet is pure gold.

We also ship canned fish and other products from our ocean, from their warehouses."

Zeck looked at Kat. "Why not directly from your own ports?"

Kat shrugged. "Our system is not on any major trade routes. DeVaan is at the junction of many."

Zeck said. "So, who were you two talking about?"

Kat looked him. "My biological father . . . he wouldn't have done this . . . It is too dishonorable . . . He is a chief of a powerful clan . . . He would not risk bringing . . . dishonor on . . . his clan."

Zeck tilted his head. "Why would you even suspect him?"

Ben took a deep breath, "Her father disowned her and dishonored her. My father Aleut Maritinus has restored her honor and given her a clan. Beary's Mother, has also, since I am a Knight of the Dragon of the Caesar/Maxumus Clan. In doing so he has been marginalized as chief. I also challenged him and told him I would kill him, for the slurs he threw at her."

Zeck looked at him. "Do you plan to do this?"

Ben shrugged. "If the opportunity presented itself, then yes. I would not seek him out. There would really be no honor in killing him. He is a bully of females not much more."

"Do you think he is afraid of you enough, to hire someone to kill you?" Zeck asked.

Ben and Kat both laughed. "Sir, he is the High Chief of the Seventy Tribes of the Red Circle Clan. He wouldn't hire an outsider. He could have sent warriors of his own clan."

Zeck looked at him. "Wouldn't that have risked a Clan War?"

Ben shrugged, "Not very likely today. Even the death of a chief's son and his wife, would not move a council to such a war."

Beary nodded. "There would be retaliation from my clan. It would fall on those that committed the act. It would be swift and silent."

Zeck just nodded. He knew about the Red Dagger, by accident. A team had saved his life years ago, at the loss of one of their own. "Well just be careful. I don't want to explain to Octavious or Angelina, why I let one of their kin get hurt in my town."

They all finished their breakfast and head out to shop. Beary barely felt the female brush past him. Hardly noticed the container dropped into his pants pocket, till she was gone.

He fished it out, saw the seal, and put it back in his pocket. He found a boar's room and excused himself. Once inside a stall he opened the canister. Inside was a small data crystal and a note it read; ***Aiden Jewelry 10 STUs***.

Beary smiled and looked down the street. "Sho-Sho, take Erin to the toy store. Here are some credits. I want to take Pompey to the jewelry store."

Sho-Sho gave him a look. "Alright, Uncle Beary, come Erin. You, come too Maryam."

Ice Song took Agathag and Andreios with her. Nickolas tagged along to the toy store.

Beary, guided Pompey into the jewelry store. While everyone else, went into the nearest furniture store to shop.

Beary looked around. He didn't see the young woman that bumped into him.

An older boar came out and smiled. "Hello, Sire and my dear Lady, may I help you?"

Pompey replied. "Kind Sir, I just wanted look at some of your lovely things."

Aiden bowed. "Of course, I will be pleased to offer my wares to The Star at the family rate." He lifted up his lapel to show a family crest of the Red Dagger.

Beary nodded. "We will be happy to except."

The young female came out. "Lieutenant Maxumus and Lady Maxumus, I am Janise Copland of Special Branch. My code name is Song Bird.

I am an Augustine, Sire. I am related to Mrs. Maro, we are third cousins."

Beary looked at her. "I don't remember the name Copland among the Augustine clan names."

"No, it was my husband's name. He was killed aboard the Rip Claw in the battle against the Arcrilians."

Beary nodded. "I am so sorry."

Janise shrugged. "You, The Star, and your friends held them at the drift. He and his shipmates didn't die in vain. We are taking back territory thanks to the *EAQ*. However, I wanted to warn you about two things. First, I have been picking up signals from the Andapos System. No one lives in the system. The fifth planet has an oxygen nitrogen atmosphere. The star is unstable. It does however have a stable wormhole that leads to the Pratis system."

Beary looked at her. "It isn't on any of the fleet maps."

Janise nodded. "No sir it isn't. I cannot discuss the reason why. Or tell you anything about the other two worm holes in that system. Only *AND557*, I am authorized to give you this information. I also have to again tell you, we have received signals from that area. We shouldn't have received.

Also, Admiral Astrid has been making inquiries about the clans and Captain Maritinus. He called DeVaan. It was not the same number the killer had on him.

Do you wish me to pursue this?"

Beary shook his head. "No, you risked your cover as it is. It is alright. I have someone who can take care of it."

Janise nodded. "Alright sire, this is the intelligence on the signals coming from the Andapos System."

Beary looked at it. "Do you have any ideas as to whom or what is sending these signals?"

Janise shook her head. "They do not match the wave frequency or modulation that was used by the enemies you just faced. They are someone different."

"Ok, thank you Janise. Thank you for eliminating the threat to Ben and Kat also." Beary said.

Janise shrugged, "He was on our watch list. He had escaped from Braden Penal Colony. He killed five guards in the process. He had a *KOS* order on him."

Beary nodded *kill on sight orders were rare. He was a bad one.* "Thank you anyway Janise and thanks for the signal intelligence."

Pompey was looking at a couple of necklaces. "Beary, I want this one for me. This necklace is for Erin and this one for Sho-Sho. Oh, and these daggers for Maryam. This necklace for Ice Song would be perfect. These watches would be good for the boys."

Beary just smiled. "What about wedding presents?"

Pompey thought. "Not jewelry. We will look across the street. What do we owe you Mr. Aiden?"

Mr. Aiden looked into her eyes, "My Lady, you are The Star; you may have anything you want."

Pompey kissed him. "Nonsense." She opened her purse and handed him eighty thousand credits."

Mr. Aiden looked at her. "My Lady, please at least except the family discount."

"Mr. Aiden, your mission here has served our family well. Allow me to honor that service." Pompey said. Then she gave him that devastating smile.

Mr. Aiden just smiled. "It will be as you wish, my dear lady."

Nikolaos was looking around at the toys. An older female came over. "Can I help you, young boar?"

Nikolaos bowed. "My lady, I am looking for something for my canus. She is a new pup."

"Then you want a training aid of some type?" The lady asked.

"No, those I have. Something personal, just for her, I cannot explain. More of a, token of affection for her." Nikolaos said.

The old Female nodded. "These are brushes; they will allow you to comb her coat. To touch her gentle as you do."

Nikolaos thought. "Can you put her name on it?"

The Female nodded. "Yes, it will only take a moment."

Nikolaos explained. "She is Ghost Wind."

Beary and Pompey joined the others. Jeanne was haggling with the owner over a new bed.

Beary walked over to Kat and Paulette. "My wife has told me, we need to buy you a wedding present. So pick out something you both want."

Paulette dropped her head. "Boss, we have the furniture. Daddy got that for us. We need linens."

"Ok, go get what you need, here," Beary handed her six thousand credits, "if you need more just let me know."

Paulette just stared at him "Boss this . . ."

"Is a gift Paulette, now go, shop." Beary ordered.

Paulette grabbed Gabriel and headed to a linen store.

Kat had tears in her eyes, "Thank you, Boss. She is not use to so much kindness."

Beary replied. "Kat you are family now, which doesn't change things, Kat I might . . ."

"Beary, I am your wingbear. We are one of the few deep recon certified crews you have. I would be insulted if you failed to put us in harm's way. When you knew we were the best choice. Ben and I have already discussed it, so have Paulette and Gabriel. Risk is part of our life. You can't just take off and do it. You have a new job." Kat said.

Beary kissed her cheek. "Ok Kat, what do you want?"

Kat thought. "Well, I didn't buy it. Ben said I could . . . well it was expensive and I outfitted the kid's rooms. Do you see that desk over there? Ben and I could both work at it."

Beary looked at the price and called over a sales bear.

Ben walked over. "You had him buy it for us?"

Beary told him. "It was Pompey's idea. You can argue with her."

Ben held up his paws. "No, Thanks Beary it is a nice desk."

Paulette and Gabriel returned. "Here Boss. I got everything we need. You have money coming back."

Beary shook his head. "Paulette a gift is a gift. Whatever is left is yours." He kissed her forehead and went to find Jessica and Caesar."

Paulette looked at Ben. "But Daddy, it is two thousand credits."

Ben shrugged. "Paulette he designed the APU's and the warp engines the fleet is using along with Dr. Vallen. He will not miss the credits."

Kat hugged her husband. "Ben, Beary is worried I told him he had to use us."

Ben nodded. "It will be hard on all of us Kat. It will be hardest on him. Family is important to him. The Maxumus are not afraid to die. They will throw themselves in harm's way. Especially Beary, but he always fears for his family."

Kat nodded. "He fears for everyone Ben, not just family. He has seen something that has scared his soul."

Ben squeezed her paw and whispered. "I was with him when he destroyed *The Eye*."

Kat whirled and looked at him. "It has been destroyed and he was the one. That means that those that depended on it will be coming for him and his . . ."

Ben kissed her, "Yes, they already have."

She felt her ring glow. "That is why we were chosen for these. So we could help protect the boss?"

Ben shrugged. "Kat, I don't know."

Astrid read the report about a dead fugitive on Kalian. He called a number. "Tell me, you didn't send someone to kill a Marine Captain and his wife?"

Chief Katimai said. "Then I won't. Tell me did he succeed?"

Astrid looked at the com unit. "You idiot, lucky for you he got killed by a local cop, before he could. Do you know what would have happened to me? Why didn't you tell me he was connected to the Maxumus clan? My career could be ended, over just the noise I have made, not to mention my life."

Katimai looked at him. "What did you find out?"

Astrid looked at him. "Nothing, the Maxumus are clean squeaky clean. Beary Maxumus is a cub scout, *Bearilian Star* and a ton of other awards for bravery. He has two PHD's and very rich without his parents or his wife's money.

Pompey Maxumus is the daughter of Vegus Pompey. He is a wealthy business bear. Her personal wealth is close to one point six trillion credits, from what I can tell."

Katimai laughed. "You make it sound like they could buy a small system."

Astrid looked at him. "The Maxumus Clan is wealthy enough to buy several if they choose. Do not make them angry. Half of Special Branch is members of their clan. So are several members of the fleet."

Katimai laughed. "You are an old female. I will deal with Maritinus, that dog, and the Maxumus pig if he gets in my way."

Astrid looked at him. "You are mad. I wash my paws of you and this whole situation."

Astrid turned off the com and insured he securely erased the contact.

The figure was lurking around the stores. He had known something had gone wrong when Dresden hadn't made the rendezvous. Then he had seen the news. Dresden had been killed by a local cop.

His targets were surrounded in the store. He would wait till they came outside. He moved into the shadows of a stair well.

Maryam watched him as he turned from the window. She saw the weapon. "Andreios stay with Erin and Agathag. Nikolaos across the street in the alley, a bear 6' 1", dark fur, gray coat, blue pants, and folded rifle, I think."

Nikolaos nodded. "Give me a few moments to get in position."

Maryam watched Nikolaos cross the street and disappear.

Sho-Sho nodded.

Maryam skipped across the street. "Hello, Mister, are you lost? May I help you?"

"No Cub, just get lost. I am waiting for someone." The boar said.

From behind him Nikolaos said. "We know. The question is why? If you are planning on hurting him, we will not allow it."

Grim Darks was a harden criminal. These two young cubs made him laugh. "What are you going to do?"

Maryam shrugged. "Arrest you or kill you, your choice."

He went to grab her as he said. "Why you I'll . . ."

But he found himself flying through the air and hitting the ground. He reached for his weapon when a knife buried itself into his wrist. He found his digits no longer worked. The boy cub was on him with a phaser pistol to his head.

Nikolaos spoke very calmly. "If you move, I will kill you. You are under arrest."

Maryam came up behind him and cuffed him. Then she bandaged his wrist. Jessica came running as did Zeck.

Nikolaos cleared Grim's weapon and started searching him. Nikolaos found Ben and Kat's pictures, along with some cash, and a card with a phone number.

Jessica looked at him. "How did you spot him?"

Maryam shrugged. "He was acting weird. Then I saw his weapon."

Sho-Sho came over. "Sire Hammerhead, can we take him to your office and let me question him."

They led Grim Darks over to a small office. She threw him into a chair.

Sho-Sho sat across from him in her Maxumus form. She smoothed her gown. "Now Mr. Darks, we are going to talk and you are going to tell me everything you know."

Grim looked at this teenaged Maxumus, "You can't break my mind little girl. Older bears than you have tried."

"Oh, Mr. Darks, you are wrong on two counts. I will break you and I am not a bear." Sho-Sho smiled as she penetrated his first level of defense. His eyes got wide. "Now, we can do this the easy way or the hard way. The easy way you survive with your mind intact. The hard way I take all the information and leave you brain damaged. Which will it be?" As she started to peel away his second level of defense.

"Stop!" he screamed. "I'll talk, just ask your questions?" Grim was scared.

"Who hired you?" Sho-Sho asked.

"Look, I don't know. Dresden was the main shooter. I was transport and back up. I have never made a hit before. If the primary is caught or killed the backup is supposed to make the hit. I was just trying to fill the contract. Dresden had all the information. All he gave me was a phone number and those pictures." Grim pleaded.

Sho-Sho nodded. Then she peered into him. She made him look at all the evil he had ever done.

"No . . . Stop . . . Please no . . . just kill me but . . . don't do this to me . . ." Grim pleaded.

Sho-Sho looked at him. "You will feel all the pain you have caused others. Your body will not allow you to hurt yourself or anyone else. If you then truly ask for grace, then this blessing will cease. Then you will have a new chance at life. If you try and go back to your old ways it will start over."

Grim looked at her. "What are you?" He screamed.

Sho-Sho smiled and put a picture in his mind.

Grim screamed. "Help me!"

Zeck looked at her. "What have you done?"

Sho-Sho shrugged. "I have given him a chance at redemption Admiral. Keep him safe. Then release him. He will never hurt anyone ever again."

Grim crawled into a cell. The cuffs fell off as he closed the door and lay on the bed shaking. "Please make it stop." He said as tears flowed from his eyes.

Beary looked at Sho-Sho. "What did you learn?"

Sho-Sho sighed "He told the truth. He was a backup and was not trusted by the primary. He was small time wanting to go big time. I cured him. He had undergone Psychological-Op Training. He was good but not that good."

Beary looked at her, "Military training?"

"No private syndicate of some type. Omega group was the name he remembered. It was a planted memory." Sho-Sho said.

Beary nodded. "Ok, Sweet heart, I am sorry. I have been asking you to use your abilities questionably."

Sho-Sho kissed him. "Beary, my sins, if that is what they are . . . are my own. I will protect my family that includes Ben and Kat. Ice Song agrees. Sire, Admiral Astrid is ours."

Beary just nodded.

That evening everyone returned to the *EAQ*. Two ROSES were full of furniture. Each labeled with the rooms that they belonged to.

Caesar looked at Gabriel. "Lieutenant you can return to light duty tomorrow i.e. paper work. Ben, that goes for you also, no training or heavy workouts. I want you both swimming starting tomorrow."

Both just nodded.

Jeanne just held up her paw. "I know messages and swim."

"Plus, five laps around the track walking, both you and Pompey start tomorrow. Do it together." Caesar ordered.

Pompey and Jeanne just pouted.

Argus looked at his new bed. Then saw the two books. He opened volume one. "Jeanne, what is this?"

Jeanne came over and kissed him. "It is a gift, from Kat. We will have to wait on some of these but, some are still safe husband. Also volume two has some message techniques that would benefit me and the cub, doctor's orders."

Argus looked at the drawing, "Who were the models?"

Jeanne laughed, "The Author and her husband."

"Beary must have about died." Gracchus said. Then he turned around and saw the painting of his wife.

"Well, what do you think?" Jeanne asked biting her lip.

Gracchus sat down and pulled her close. Tears were flowing from his eyes. "Oh Jeanne, how much I love you, I have always loved you. I was such an idiot. I wasted all those years . . ."

Jeanne kissed him. "We both were." Then she smiled. "Just relax Argus." She said with a twinkle in her eyes and an impish smile.

Argus looked at her. "Jeanne what . . . Jeanne?"

A little while later, he laid his now sleeping wife on her new bed. *This book was trouble.* He smiled. He looked at the painting. *She was worth the trouble.* He finished dressing and went into his office.

"Lieutenant Maxumus, do you have a moment?" Argus said into a communication unit.

"Yes Captain. I'll be right up." Beary said.

Beary came in, Gracchus waved him to a chair, and put a cup of tea in front of him.

"Your Mom wrote quite a book." Gracchus said.

Beary nodded. "That is what I have been told sir."

Gracchus looked over his cup. "You read it?"

Beary thought, "Pompey has been explaining it to me. I can't bring myself to actually read it."

Gracchus nodded, "Well, thank her for me.

Beary, what do you think about this other Intel?"

Beary thought. "We have to check it out. I could go . . ."

Gracchus shook his head. "Not your job, Artemus', your squadron commanders', or executives'."

Beary shrugged. "I only have two other crews that are deep space scout certified."

"Pick one and send them out." Gracchus said.

Beary nodded. "Sho-Sho wants to handle this other situation."

"Beary, he is an Admiral." Gracchus said.

"True but Sho-Sho isn't fleet. She can get in and out unnoticed." Beary said.

"The security cameras what will they see?" Gracchus asked.

Beary told him. "Two fleet officers. That is it, nothing clear."

Gracchus nodded, "I know nothing about this.

Supplies will be here tomorrow. Well, I'll let you get back to work."

Beary got up and walked back to his office. Kat was waiting for him.

"When do we leave Boss?" Kat asked.

"Kat what are . . .?" Beary started to ask.

"Boss, I have been acting as your intelligence officer. I saw the Signal Intel and the wormhole data. Franklin in Valkyrie 6 and my crew are the only two qualified to do the mission. He is in sick bay with the flue. Besides, Paulette and I are the best at this. It is our primary mission." Kat pointed out.

Beary sighed. "Making the decision for me, Kat?"

"No, Sir, but we are volunteering. Beary, you send someone else out there. They . . . Look boss we know this job and its risks. We are good." Kat said.

Beary looked at her. "Alright Kat, but you make it back. Or I will come after you and spank your tail. You leave in forty-six cycles."

Kat smiled and kissed him on the cheek, "Thanks boss." With that she took off to talk to the crew chief and Paulette.

Artemus asked. "What was that about?"

Beary looked at him. "I might have just sent them to their death. She volunteered. She was right she was the best choice but . . ."

Artemus sat down. "Beary, we face this situation every day. Kat is right, you know it. Besides you have to go after her, I go too."

That night a shuttle arrived at the *Castles Gate*. It landed cloaked. No one seemed to notice.

Chief MacIntosh looked at Sho-Sho and Ice Song. "My ladies, I won't even ask where you got those codes."

Sho-Sho responded, "It is best chief, if you don't know. We will be back. Stay locked and cloaked."

"Yes, Lady Maxumus." The chief said. He knew he could be court marshaled but he didn't care. *This Admiral was a pain. He had threatened too many of his bears.*

Sho-Sho and Ice Song were in bear form. They were dressed in fleet uniforms, walked quickly and quietly towards the Admirals suite. While crew members saw them, no one would remember them. The security cameras turned briefly, as they walked by, never showing their faces. When they walked up to the Admiral's door they confused the guard's memory. Then they walked in.

Astrid was sleeping.

Ice Song looked at him. "I could kill him. It would be easy."

Sho-Sho shook her head. "It has become too easy, all of it. Wake up Admiral. I wish to talk with you."

Astrid looked into her face. Then saw Ice Song. "What are you doing here!" he started to reach for his alarm.

Ice Song placed the tip of her sword in front of the button. "No Admiral. She said she wants to talk. Personally, I would just kill you. I believe you are involved and guilty. She thinks otherwise."

Astrid was scared. "What are you talking about?"

Sho-Sho answered him, "The attempted murder of two of my clan members, Admiral Astrid. You might not have been involved. However, you know who ordered the hit."

Astrid felt pain sweep his body. "NO! Stop . . . I didn't know. I only heard about it on the news. I called him he gloated about it. I washed my paws of the whole mess. Please stop."

"I will spare your life Admiral, this time. If you ever cause problems for my family again, I or my handmaiden will find you and take your life. However, I promise, you will take days if not months to die." Sho-Sho said as she prepared to leave. "Do not bother calling your security bears they cannot see us."

With that they left. The Admiral sat stunned. He watched as they walked out. His guard never moved. He hit his panic button.

The guard flew in. "Admiral, are you alright?"

"Why didn't you stop them?" The Admiral screamed.

"Stop who Admiral?" the guard asked.

"The two females that was just in my room. They walked right past you!" Astrid screamed.

"Sir, no one opened your door. Neither did anyone come in or out, till I did." The guard said.

Astrid looked at him. "It must have been a bad dream." The gash on his night stand told him it wasn't.

MacIntosh returned them to the *EAQ*. "Lady Maxumus you didn't kill . . ."

Sho-Sho shook her head. "Not this time Chief."

Ice Song sighed, "I wanted to. She wouldn't let me."

Mac smiled. "Goodnight, my ladies."

Sho-Sho looked at Beary. "It was Kat's father, but why?"

Beary shrugged. "He is evil and cruel that is all. Don't worry I'll take care of it."

Sho-Sho paused. "You have to send Kat and Paulette into danger?"

Beary sat down. "They are the best for the job. They volunteered. I couldn't say no."

Sho-Sho kissed her Uncle. "Be at peace Beary. All you can do is trust the Creator."

Beary thought. "It is easier being the tip of the spear than the one that has to throw it."

Ben looked at her. "You didn't have to volunteer!"

Kat moved over to him in the hot tub and sat on his lap. "Yes, I did. Franklin is sick. Plus his crew isn't good enough. If they ran into trouble alone, they would end up dead."

Ben looked at her. "What about you and Paulette?"

Kat shrugged. "We have done this before. We know the odds. We can handle anything and get the job done."

Ben lowered his head. "I don't want to lose my girls."

Kat kissed him. "Make love to me."

Ben looked at her. "Kat, is that your answer for everything?"

Kat shook her head. "No, but it is a silly argument. It will solve nothing. I want you and need you. Is it not better if this is our last night together, for it to be a night of love and passion? Instead of a night filled with anger and harsh words."

Ben looked at her with tears in his eyes. "I do love you Kat Maritinus."

Kat kissed him. "Not nearly as much as I love you or need you."

Paulette lay on Gabriel's chest. "Celibate priest, ha, you sure are a fast learner."

Gabriel kissed her shoulder, "Good teacher is all. When do you take off?"

Paulette looked at the clock. "Eight cycles, I have to be in the briefing room in six cycles."

Gabriel looked at her. "Shouldn't you sleep?"

Paulette kissed him. "I will have time to sleep later. Just fill me with your love Gabriel, before we go."

Gabriel looked at her, "Don't forget your promise to me Paulette!"

"I won't. Now please hold me, love me." She whispered in almost a pleading voice that broke his heart.

Beary was lying awake. Pompey looked at him. "Staring at the ceiling isn't going to change anything."

Beary looked at her. "They just got married. It isn't fair."

Pompey looked at him. "Life never is husband. Do you think I would be happy, if it was you going? I wouldn't. I know it is your job. This is Kat's and Paulette's. They are good at it. I read their files.

Would you hesitate to go?"

Beary shook his head. "No, I would go in a SubSTU."

Pompey nodded. "Then why do you think they feel any different?"

Beary kissed her and felt her growing midsection. "Have I told you I love you?"

Pompey smiled, "Not nearly enough lately. I kind of know it. I absolutely adore and cherish you my lover."

The next morning MacIntosh and Beary crawled all over Valkyrie 38. Every system was checked. New sensor pods and repeaters were loaded. All defensive and offensive weapon systems were triple checked.

Beary looked at MacIntosh. "Well Chief, is there anything else we can do?"

MacIntosh shook his head. "Sir, 38 is ready as I can make it. It is the third best fighter in the wing. That difference is minute."

Kat and Paulette looked over all the Intel and received their mission brief.

Caesar gave them a quick physical. "Kat, you two come home safe."

Kat nodded, "Take care of Ben, until we get back. His back is still a little sore."

Caesar thought. "I am not sure that was from his wound, but I'll check it out."

Paulette said, "Gabriel's breathing is improving."

Caesar replied, "Aerobic exercise is good for that."

Paulette blushed and smiled.

Kat looked at her. "Ok, Paulette, time to go to work. Saddle up."

Paulette responded. "Yes mommy."

Beary, Ben, and Gabriel saluted as the 38, was raised to the launch area.

"Red Talon Control, Valkyrie 38 ready to launch."

"Valkyrie 38, Creators speed, hot launch."

Kat shot out of the launch bay. Then they headed for the Andapos System.

Nikolaos quietly brushed Ghost Wind. Who, was growing. "I love you Ghost Wind. You are to be my partner."

The small pup looked at him. "Love I, Niko." She snuggled in his arms.

Nikolaos smiled, and then sang to her as he brushed her.

CHAPTER 8

Andapos System

KAT AND PAULETTE flew on. "Paulette, go down and check the com status. We should be coming up on the first repeaters drop point."

"Alright Kat," She rode down to the lower deck and pushed her chair over to the communication station. "Coming up on first relay drop point in five . . . four . . . three . . . two . . . one . . . drop; repeater away. I have signal."

Paulette rode back up to the flight deck. "You should get some rest Mommy."

Kat scanned the instruments. "Alright, Paulette, she is all yours. Give me four cycles." Kat lowered her pilot's seat and unstrapped. Then she pulled down the hot cot. She strapped in and went to sleep.

Paulette checked over her equipment. They were still sixteen cycles from the Andapos System. They would drop another relay repeater in twelve cycles. They should start picking up some information in six to eight cycles.

Artemus was at home. He loved the painting of his daughters. Ice Song looked at him. "Father, do you prefer me as a bear?"

Artemus looked at her, "Ice Song, I love you. You are a beautiful young dragon. The only reason that illusion is beautiful is because the real Ice Song is beautiful. I will say that Gisfrid will have a hard time taking his eyes off my daughter."

Ice Song blushed and kissed him. "Thank you, Daddy. You have been so good to me. I should be ashamed. I almost forget my other father."

Artemus held her. "I am just blessed to share you with him."

Ice Song laid her head on his lap. "You say the nicest things Daddy."

Snow Flower came in. "Come on young lady you have work to do. Your father needs sleep also."

Ice Song kissed Artemus and went out.

Snow Flower kissed him. "I'll wake you in five cycles, now sleep."

Artemus looked at her. "I love you Snow Flower."

"I love you too, Savato. I have to go to work." Snow Flower said.

Beary kept walking in and out of the Flight Control Center.

Finally Romanov came over. "Boss, they dropped the repeater on schedule. They drop another in twelve cycles. There is no point in you coming in here every five SUBSTU."

"Sorry Gloria. I know you and the ladies have this covered." Beary said.

Romanov smiled. She couldn't help it, she loved him. So did her crew. Respectively of course, Lady Maxumus looked, like she could be mean, if she wanted to be. "It is not a problem, Boss. We even understand. You just distract the crew."

"Ok Gloria, I'll go back and do my own work. Let me know if there is any news." Beary said.

He walked out to the hall and down towards his office.

"He is fearful." Reuben said.

"Yes, but not for himself, he never fears for himself. Always the fear is for everyone else." Romanov said.

Paulette hit a button. It set off a buzzer near the hot cot.

"Alright daughter, I am up!" Kat said "This hot cot would be better with your father in it."

Paulette smiled. "You can't get enough of him can you?"

"No, I can't. How about you, when it comes to Gabriel?" Kat asked.

"Mommy, should you ask that?" Paulette asked laughing. "No not really. He is so gentle and tender. So sweet and loving, Mommy, I am happy."

Kat smiled. "Good now go and dream about your Marine."

"Yes Mommy." Paulette lowered her chair, checked the sensor and communication systems. Then she hit the hot bunk.

They dropped the second repeater on time and proceeded. Paulette started recording the strange signal coming from the Andapos System.

Paulette looked at Kat, as she checked to insure cloak and shields were on maximum. "It is a communication system of some kind. A *Quadninary System*, four coded sequences wrapped around each other. There are smaller signals also."

"Ok, Paulette, weapons up. We're going in." Kat said.

They moved into the system. The signal seemed to be coming from something orbiting near the sun.

The wormhole started to form. Kat fired a cloaked sensor pod. About that time twenty sleek Black fighters poured out. Kat fired another toward the sun. That was when a powerful sensor beam passed near their cloaked fighter.

Kat fired four missiles down the path of the sensor beam. Then she peeled the 38 to the right. The twenty fighters, that had exited the wormhole, fanned out in their direction.

Her missiles struck just as the sensor beam found the 38. It burned through the 38's cloak. They saw the shield flair on a space station.

The black fighters raced for them. Kat turned and launched the sixteen missiles in her internal rotary launcher. Three of the black fighters exploded. Two started drifting. Fifteen launched missiles in her direction.

Thirty missiles seemed to be almost tracking 38. Kat threw it through a series of high risk maneuvers. Paulette release decoys and tried to strengthen the cloak and shields. She also fired off four more Mark 4s.

Three missiles exploded near the left rear shield. They rocked the 38, but the shields held.

Two more black fighters exploded.

But this time six missiles exploded close enough to 38 to defeat its shield. The left wing took shrapnel damage. Pieces of shrapnel hit Paulette in the side and leg.

"Mommy, I think I am hurt." Paulette said.

"Stay with me Paulette!" Kat said. Kat headed for the fifth planet. She launched the remaining eight missiles.

"Red Talon, this is Valkyrie 38, mission failure. We are transmitting data. Sorry boss . . . Tell Ben and Gabriel we love them. Multiple Bandits . . . not safe . . . do not attempt rescue."

A black fighter headed straight for her. She hit her rail guns. It exploded. She dived the 38 through the atmosphere of the fifth planet.

The 38 was falling apart. Somehow it still was flying. She found a place to set it down. It hit like a rock. Paulette groaned."

She lowered her seat. Then Paulette's seat was lowered. She wanted to scream. Paulette was covered with blood. She had two six SubSMU pieces of metal sticking out of her side and her leg.

Kat with tears flowing prayed. "Dear Creator, help me!"

Her ring glowed. A voice seemed to fill the 38. "Kat Maritinus, pull out the metal. Then lay her dagger on the wounds."

Kat pulled them out. Paulette screamed and the blood flowed even more. Kat took Paulette's dragon dagger out and placed it on her side wound. It glowed blue. The blood stopped and the wound sealed.

She then placed it on the leg wound which also sealed.

The voice then said. "Put it back and get the med kit. Give her a unit of blood. Her type is in it."

Kat did as she was told. Color started to return to Paulette's face.

"Mommy, why are you still here? They will be coming. You have to run. Just leave me. I am done. I'll just be a burden and slow you down." Paulette said.

Kat looked at her. "Did you forget your promise to Gabriel?! If you die, I die daughter. I stopped the bleeding. I have you bandaged. I have replaced some of the blood you lost. We are going to have to move."

Kat camouflaged the 38. Set an APU, and turned on the cloak, which, was still working.

She put some equipment, weapon packages, and Paulette on an equipment sled. Then they took off.

Paulette whispered. "Mommy please, I am slowing you down."

Kat moved beside her. "Paulette you will not die on me. Gabriel would not forgive you or me. I stopped the bleeding. Your pulse is stronger. Now rest. I think I have found a place for us to hide, until help comes."

Paulette with tears flowing said. "Help, isn't coming. You told them not to."

Kat nodded. "If they are smart they won't. It is too dangerous. The Boss, however will come Paulette. He won't listen to reason. It isn't in him."

Artemus was on the com unit. Beary sat up in bed. "What is it Savato?"

"The girls went down Beary. Kat said not to try and rescue them." Artemus said.

"I'll be right there." Beary said.

Pompey started getting dressed.

"Where are you going?" Beary asked.

"Ben is going to need me. Especially, when you tell him he can't go." Pompey said.

Beary nodded, sighed, and then kissed her, "Thanks, my lady."

Caesar met him as they started for the flight office. "I don't want to hear it. I am going."

Gracchus was waiting for them. "You read her message. She said not to attempt rescue. Yet you are going."

Beary looked at him. "Do you want my commission now or when I get back? I am going."

"What and have a mutiny on my hands. Just bring them back alive, Beary, if you can." Gracchus said.

Ben and Gabriel were standing there as Beary walked up. "You two are not going." Beary said.

Ben looked at him. "They are my Family!"

"That is right Ben. If it was Pompey and Erin would you let me go?" Beary asked softly.

Ben dropped his head. "No, I would stun you, if I had to."

Blackpaw and Nighthunter brushed past them "It is alright Skipper; we'll bring them back for you and the Lt."

Night Wind moved past. "I will track them, do not worry. I will find them."

We and Akhiok danced past with tools and equipment.

Beary looked at them. "What are you two doing?"

Akhiok responded "Valkyrie 38 might be salvageable. Besides you two aren't leaving us behind."

MacIntosh threw his gear on and smiled. "I can't let them be unsupervised."

Artemus looked at Ben. "Come on Boss, a Marine Captain and Lieutenant's ladies, are waiting."

Beary looked at them. "I'll bring them home. I promise." With that he was gone.

Ben looked at Pompey.

Pompey reached out and hugged them. "He will bring them home or die trying."

Tears weld in Ben's eyes. "Pricilla, I am sorry."

"Don't be, you both are family now. You, Gabriel, Kat, and Paulette, he would gladly die for any of you." Pompey said as she held them in her arms. Snow Flower joined her.

Romanov came into the control room. "Ok second shift you work for me now, also. You better be good."

Lieutenant Bushnell looked at her. "You heard her. We have a ship down. The Bosses are going after them."

Barbarossa and Pathfinder opened their sealed orders. They almost ran into each other. Pathfinder looked at his slip. "Yours says the same thing no second attempt."

Barbarossa nodded angrily. "I guess they were thinking the same thing."

Gracchus looked at them. "They are willing to throw away their careers to do it. One insertion team strictly volunteers. You two have an important job, to protect this ship and his family."

Jane sat down. "Ok Captain, we understand."

Gracchus looked at them. "Don't bet against him, I wouldn't."

Beary looked at his team. "We don't know what we are up against. From the information Kat sent, they used a sensor beam to burn through our cloaking ability."

"Do you think they followed them down?" Blackpaw asked.

"We would. I bet they did. A cornered Kat could be dangerous." Beary said.

Artemus was red lining the Purple's engines. He finally backed them down to warp four. "They can't maintain six, for more than two cycles, Beary."

Beary nodded. "Let them stabilize then push them again for a cycle."

Artemus looked at him. "I hope you brought your fang sticks and some chewing gum."

Kat fortified the cave she found. Paulette was running a temperature. She gave her some antibiotic and some anti-inflammatory."

She then went out and planted claymores, along the approaches to the cave.

Kat wrapped Paulette in a blanket. Then she gave her some water.

Paulette looked at her. "Kat, for the Creator's sake, why don't you leave me? I am holding you back. I'll get you killed!"

Kat came over and held her. "Daughter, don't you love your husband?"

Paulette cried. "It was a beautiful dream Kat. I don't want you to die because of me."

Kat kissed her. "Daughters are supposed to outlive their parents. Paulette you have to live for Gabriel, you promised. Besides, I do not plan to die. I have a Marine Captain to ravage when we get home."

The two rings glowed again. The voice spoke. "Enemies searching from the air, stay still. I'll shield you."

Paulette whispered. "Who is that voice and where is it coming from?"

Kat shook her head. "I don't know. It helped me heal your wounds and stop the bleeding. Just trust it."

The voice spoke again. "Paulette, stop trying to die. You must live."

Paulette was frightened now. "I will keep my promise to Gabriel."

The rings took on a warm glow.

Six black crafts landed. Reptilian troopers jumped out. They looked like frilled lizards standing on their back legs. The Commander called his troops together "We want these Pilots alive. They might be able to tell us where we can find the one we seek the destroyer of the eye."

One spoke up. "They killed some of our fellows. Why can we not kill them?"

The Commander scowled. "After they are questioned, they will be killed. Not until then. Now fan out and find them"

The lizards spread out one thought he smelled blood. However, he couldn't pinpoint where it was coming from. They passed close to the 38 several times, but the cloak held.

Their aerial survey also failed to show were the two Bearilians were. The commander looked at his map. "They have gone underground. We should look for caves that they could hide in."

One of his captains looked at him. "Commander, there are hundreds of caves in this area! These mountains are riddled with them."

The Commander looked at him. "So, split up your teams and search them."

Kat was resting when the voice called to her. "Kat wake up. You must leave now. Get Paulette and go deeper into the cave. Take the passage to the right. Remember to the right. Leave your traps just go."

Kat woke Paulette up. "Come on let's go Paulette."

"Mommy, why don't you just . . ." Paulette tried to say.

"Paulette Mayotte Maritinus Archangel, stop it. I will not, cannot leave you! Now get up, get on the sled, and let's go!" Kat ordered.

Paulette pulled herself up onto the sled. Kat got it going. She guided it deeper into the cave, and then took the passage to the right.

After about what seemed like forever. She saw a light ahead. Soon they were standing at another cave opening, overlooking a valley.

The voice appeared again. "Follow the trail. Stay near the cliff, about one KSMU to another cave. Go in and hide. Help is coming."

A lizard patrol was starting up a trail leading toward a series of caves. One hit a trip wire. Four claymores went off.

The mines killed the trooper that tripped the wire and the three behind him. The six other members of the patrol slowly rose from the ground.

A communications sergeant came forward. "Should I report contact?"

The Lieutenant shook his head. "Report, possible direction of travel, and that we have run into bobby traps."

The sergeant nodded and made his report.

They slowly moved up the trail. One of the lizards saw movement and fired. A beam shot past him, just missing him.

Then another fired a grenade. The beam reached out and struck him in the throat, killing him. The grenade arched out and exploded right where the beam had come from.

The Lieutenant ran up only to find the remote device and small phaser. "How many ways do these bears have to kill you?" He screamed in frustration. "Spread out, move carefully,"

They cleared four caves. Then they started to move towards a larger one. That was when the ground seemed to erupt around them. When it was over the lieutenant looked around him. His uniform seemed shredded, but he was untouched. He sat down in shock.

His Senior NCO came over his arm bleeding. He tied a bandage off. "Lieutenant, are you alive?"

"I am untouched, except my uniform seems damaged. You and I are all that is left alive?" the Lieutenant asked.

"Yes Sir, I was lucky. I caught two in my arm but they didn't hit anything vital. I was on the edge, but you were in the middle of the blast." The sergeant said.

Kat put the remote detonator away. She steered the sled into the new cave. She camouflaged the entrance. Then she placed her last two claymores on the trail on either side of the entrance.

"Valkyrie 38, Spirit 6 on guard, click twice if you are receiving. Help is on the way."

Kat hit her mike twice and smiled, "Paulette, I told you he would not listen."

Paulette nodded. "What if they are after him?"

Kat shrugged. "Then they die. The Boss did not come here to die. He came to take us home and spank my tail."

Joshua grinned. "Boss, I got two distinct clicks on guard."

We looked up. "There are a lot of enemy down there Boss. They're spread out but they are looking."

Blackpaw and Nighthunter checked their equipment over. "Skipper, we're ready when you are."

Beary just nodded.

Night Wind slipped on his vest. "I too am ready to hunt, my Prince."

"Artemus get us close. We will halo in while you try and locate 38." Beary said.

We looked up. "We have six fighters heading this way."

Beary nodded. "Take them; we might as well give them something to think about."

Twelve Mark 4s' cloaked and with shield emitters headed for the enemy fighters. Unfortunately, for the enemy, for some reason the enemy fighters were running without shields. Two Mark 4s can ruin your whole day. The six black fighters just disintegrated without knowing what hit them.

Joshua just smiled. "Shields must have been down."

Artemus nodded. "They won't make that mistake again."

Kat heard a series of explosions in the sky south of her position.

Paulette sat up. "Those were Mark 4's warheads going off."

"I think the Bosses are here Paulette." Kat said.

"Spirit 6 on guard to Valkyrie 38, do not reply. We are on our way. Stay hidden, we will come to you."

Night Wind looked at Beary. "Sire, I do not have wings!"

"It is alright I do. You will be attached to me." Beary said.

Night Wind gulped but nodded. "Yes Sire."

Beary picked him up and locked him into the harness "Ok, let's do it."

Blackpaw and Nighthunter dived out.

Beary stepped forward slipped the goggles down over Night Wind's eyes, adjusted his, and stepped out.

Night Wind watched as the ground started to race toward them. He screamed over the wind. "I thought you said you had wings!"

Beary replied over the sound of the wind. "I do, it just isn't time to use them yet."

Night Wind looked at the ground. "I hope it will be time soon!"

Then he saw Blackpaw's and Nighthunter's parachutes open. Then he felt his and Beary's descent slowed. He looked up to see the canopy over their heads. "They don't look like very good wings."

Beary laughed. "They do the job."

Blackpaw and Nighthunter landed and retracted their parachutes.

Beary lowered Night Wind, gently set him down, and released him. Then set down and retracted his chute.

Night Wind rolled in the grass and kissed the ground. "Sorry, I forgot myself."

Blackpaw laughed. "Felt like doing the same thing my first jump."

Nighthunter responded. "If I remember right, you did, wrapped in your lines."

"Hay any jump you walk away from . . ." Blackpaw was saying.

"Is a good jump," Beary finished. "Let's find them."

"I have their scent about half of a KSMU north of us and up. There are twenty Reptilians between us and them." Night Wind said.

Beary nodded, "Eliminate the threat, get the ladies, and get back to the rendezvous point."

This group was a little too curious. Others had passed by. This one was coming straight for her. Two were racing up on the right and three on the left. She hit the two remaining claymores. These five were ripped to shreds. The others dropped back.

One tried to climb a tree. She waited till he almost reached the top. Then she used her sniper rail gun and fired. The Reptilian was tossed from the tree.

A grenade bounced in front of the cave and exploded. Kat ducked behind some big rocks. Luckily all the shrapnel was stopped by the rocks.

Paulette was propped behind two large boulders and the sled set along her side. "Mommy, are you alright?" She whispered.

"I am fine. Now stay quiet, while I kill a few more of these reptiles." Kat said.

Kat saw another one rise up. She shot him in the head. She knew she had killed seven so far. She didn't know how many there were. Then she heard a scream come from down the hill. It was cut short then another explosion Three Reptiles ran for her cave. She shot two. The third fell as something took it from behind. The large canus tore the back of its neck clear out.

Night Wind then ran and dove into the cave. He smiled at Kat. "They are not worth eating, they taste bad. Where is your pup?"

Kat pointed behind the boulders. "She was hurt, lost some blood. I replaced some. She has had a fever and some infection. I gave her anti-biotic."

Night Wind nodded. "The others will be here soon." He walked over to Paulette. "How are you, Lady Paulette?"

"I am alive, Sir Night Wind." Paulette said.

He nodded. "The Prince will take you home to your mate, my Lady."

He then turned and crouched beside her.

Blackpaw, Nighthunter, and Beary slipped into the cave.

Nighthunter went over to Paulette. "Lady Archangel, how are you?"

"I think I will live Gunny. Is Gabriel alright?" Paulette asked.

Nighthunter took her paw and looked at her wounds. They had been bad. He checked her fever. It was elevated, but not too bad. "Is she due anti-biotic?"

Kat nodded. "Yes, it is about a cycle late. Our friends showed up."

Nighthunter gave her the pills and some water. Then he loaded Paulette on the sled. "Lady Maritinus, you did well, as good as any Marine. I'll take care of my Lt.'s lady."

Beary nodded. "Alright Kat, let's get out of here. Night Wind, take the point. Let's go."

They followed the trail back toward the first cave. Then Kat heard a voice. "Take the trail down to the stream. Follow it quickly."

Kat turned to Beary. "This way, down to the stream, trouble is coming the other way."

Night Wind had already stopped and silently moved parallel with them. He headed down towards the stream.

He joined up with them. "I smelled a large force coming this way. It is good we diverted down here."

Kat took the point. "This way boss quickly."

They traveled for two cycles. Then they stopped to rest.

"Spirit Blade 2 to Spirit 6 on guard."

"Spirit 6 recovered package. Go Spirit Blade 2."

"Spirit Blade 2, found object. Some repairs possible will need to tow home."

"Understood, one WIA, in our group, we should be there in five cycles. Spirit 6 out."

Artemus looked at Caesar. "It looks like we are going to need you after all."

Caesar lowered his head. "Thank the Creator . . . when I saw all that blood . . . I was afraid we had lost one."

MacIntosh and the two ensigns worked on fixing what they could. Mac considered the option of just blowing up the 38. Still if the crew survived, then perhaps the ship was worth repairing.

We looked at him. "Kat expended most of her munitions. No missiles, half a load of rail gun ammo and the phaser power is low."

Joshua chimed in. "Phaser power coupler was damaged. I can repair it. It probably won't hold up to more than one or two shots."

MacIntosh shook his head, "Ensigns, we just want to get it home. Not fight a protracted battle."

We laughed. "Sorry, chief, we're both WTO's. It's what we do."

Artemus saw a column of troopers heading their way. "We have a few Mark 8's, with Anti-ground forces munitions. I think I'll slow this group down." He launched three Mark 8's cloaked.

The Reptilian Captain was mad. He was losing contact with some of his patrols, only to find out latter that the patrols were dead. It was hard to believe two pilots had caused so much damage. Also a flight of fighters had been blotted out of the sky.

He walked ahead of the column, to talk to a scout sergeant. He heard something fly over. He grabbed the sergeant and threw him into the gully beside the trail. Then he dove in after him.

The sixty troopers felt and heard what sounded like small rocks falling around them. A few older NCOs dove for the gully, as the bomblets went off. The trail seemed to turn into a cloud of dust.

When the dust finally settled, forty-nine reptilian troopers, laid ripped apart around the trail. Five were wounded and six NCO's had escaped unscathed.

The Reptilian Captain looked at his seven NCO's. "Look to the wounded, do what you can. Someone find me a working communicator!"

Artemus thought. "I love the jamming ability we put into the Purples."

They had traveled for four cycles. Beary called a halt to rest. The forest was getting dense. Night Wind was getting nervous.

Night Wind came over. "I smell enemy near. I am not sure where. I should hunt."

Beary answered. "Be careful, I think it is a trap. That is why I stopped here. We can defend from here. A little farther up and we would be caught in the open."

Night Wind nodded and disappeared into the brush.

Beary signaled everyone to disperse.

Nighthunter placed Paulette against a rock. Then he placed the sled on one side and him on the other. "Rest my lady. I'll protect you."

"Gunny, you do not . . ." Paulette tried to say.

"Yes, my lady, I do. The Lt. saved my life on Falian. That is how he got hurt. I am going to repay the debt." Nighthunter said.

Kat was the first to spot one of the Lizards. He had climbed a tree and was trying to line up a shot. She brought up her rail gun and fired. Her fifty caliber slug smashed into his phaser rifle and continued on into his head. He slid from the branch and hung suspended from the tree. "Snipers, be careful."

Beary saw another one. He fired a bolt from his crossbow. It hit the limb the lizard was setting on and exploded.

The lizard trooper dropped to the end of his safety harness. That is when Blackpaw put one in his head.

Three jumped out of the trees at Nighthunter. He shot the first one, the second one grabbed him. All of a sudden a blue flame seemed to cut him in half. The third was raising his weapon when Paulette's dagger flew from her paw. It struck the third Reptilian in the throat severing his head. It then flew back to her paw. Her ring glowed bright blue.

Nighthunter came over. "Are you alright, Lady Archangel?"

"Yes Gunny, are you?" Paulette asked.

"Thanks to you, yes." Nighthunter said.

Then they heard a gurgling scream, then another. Kat saw three lizards, trying to scamper up trees. She shot them. Then there was quiet.

Night Wind limped into the group. Two knifes were sticking out of his vest. He had a cut on his front leg. "There was an eleventh one. He is now dead."

Blackpaw checked the vest and smiled. He then pulled the knives out. "They didn't penetrate the vest. Here let me fix your leg."

Blackpaw poured in an anti-biotic powder. Then he sutured the cut shut and bandaged it.

Beary looked at him. He studied the small tight sutures as he finished bandaging Night Wind's leg. "Where did you learn to do that?"

"I grew up on a farm, you learn to do minor repairs." Blackpaw said.

Night Wind nodded, "Thank you, Blackpaw. It feels much better."

Blackpaw told him. "Be easy on it, it could tear open. It wasn't very deep, but you don't want to make it worse."

Night Wind tucked it up. "We train to run on three legs and still hunt."

Beary signaled everyone to head out.

A cycle later they arrived back at the rendezvous point. This was the 38. They loaded Kat and Paulette into the *Star of Vandar*.

Caesar looked at Kat. "You hurt?"

"No, Paulette was. She took two pieces of shrapnel, lower right abdomen, and leg. She lost a lot of blood. I had to give her a bag." Kat said. "I also gave her Anti-biotic."

Caesar scanned Paulette. "Beary, when we get off planet, I am going to need to operate. Kat you saved her life. There is some damage I need to fix. Do you understand Paulette?"

Paulette nodded. "Will I live doctor?"

Caesar replied. "Yes, Paulette, you are going to live."

He then looked at Night Wind's cut. He gave him another shot. "I don't like knife cuts."

Beary checked over the 38. "You three, sure you want to do this? We can fly it by remote, from the dagger."

Joshua shook his head. "I can fly it boss. We can act as WTO, and Mac can keep everything working below. You'll have to tow us to orbit. The 38 should be able to make warp two or better."

We smiled. "I have phasers and half a load of rail gun ammo. We can't protect ourselves, but we can protect you."

Beary nodded. "Mutual defense, alright. All three of you wear transporter transponders. If I need to pull you out, I want to be able too."

All three nodded.

Beary looked at them. "We all take off in three STU's." With that he sprinted back to the Purple and explained the plan to Artemus.

Kat looked at him. "I could fly it."

Caesar shook his head. "Sorry Kat, mandatory seventy two cycle grounding, until I can do a physical."

Kat saw an empty crate setting in the corner. It said Mark 4's on it. Artemus explained. "I brought a few extras. I replaced a few I used. I still have six, Mark 8's, I am not taking home. I think their drop ships will make a good target."

Mac had wired two APUs into the shields and cloak emitters on the 38. They helped take the strain off the engines. This ability hadn't been in the original design. However, when the shipyard rebuilt them, they added this ability.

Beary slowly lifted off and started to tractor the 38 off the surface. They slowly headed for outer space.

Artemus located the Reptilian drop ships then launched the Mark 8's.

The Reptilian Commander was furious. He was getting reports that his patrols had been slaughtered. That, a strange creature, had been attacking his troopers. One of his commands had been whipped out by bomblets.

He walked to the edge of the trees. The sun was hot. He decided to set down. He heard the sound of hail falling on metal. He turned around, and then flipped behind the rock, as thousands of small explosions shook the ground.

When he looked up all his drop ships were burning. Their support equipment and crews lay destroyed and dead around them.

Beary watched his power output carefully. As they put a shield around the 38 and helped coxes her out of the atmosphere.

Once they were clear of the planet. They started up the warp engines of the 38. Chief MacIntosh closely monitored the power output of the engine as they pushed it to warp one and left the system.

It took six cycles before a Reptilian patrol found the communication jammer. That Savato had left behind. When they went to disable it they set off a booby trap. That killed another three troopers.

The Reptilian Commander reported what had happened. He also reported that he believed that the Bearilian pilots had been rescued by forces unknown. The Star Base Commander was less than pleased.

The 38, was able to maintain warp three point nine but couldn't make warp four. Still the fact that it was holding together at all was amazing everyone. The six cycle head start had given them plenty of space between them and the Reptilians. They still had thirty seven cycles of flying before they made it home at this speed.

Beary knew Ben and Gabriel would be beside themselves. Still he still wanted to give it some more time before he called it in.

For the last cycle, Caesar had been operating on Paulette, as Blackpaw assisted. Kat just sat with tears in her eyes. She was too tired to cry. Too afraid to even look at what Caesar was doing.

Night Wind put his head on her knee. "She is doing fine. He is just cleaning her injury. She will heal quicker. You will see."

Kat scratched his head. He grinned. "It feels good."

Kat sighed, "I am sorry. You are not a pet, but a canus."

Night Wind shrugged his massive shoulder, "My lady, I appreciate the affection none the less. Does not everyone?"

Kat smiled, "Sir Night Wind, you are very wise. Night Song is a very lucky female."

"No my lady, I am the one who is lucky, to have her for a mate. She is a great hunter, a good mother. She makes life worth living." Night Wind said.

Kat kissed him. "May the Creator, bless you and her."

"Also you my lady and Ben the Slayer," Night Wind responded.

Beary looked at Artemus. "Can you spare me a moment? I need to stretch."

Artemus nodded Nighthunter slid into his seat.

Beary sat down next to Kat. "You did a good job back there. You didn't panic. Didn't destroy your ship . . ."

Kat shook her head. "I knew they wouldn't find it. If they would have . . . it would have blown up. I had it rigged with a remote. We disconnected it when he entered. He put the receiver on safe. Only one of ours knows how to do that."

Beary nodded. "You saved Paulette . . ."

"Sir, she is my daughter . . . It wasn't me. I didn't know what to do . . . there was so much blood. The Voice told me what to do . . . Beary you're going to think I am crazy. A voice was talking to me and Paulette the whole time protecting us. Encouraging us . . ." Kat searched Beary's face.

Beary nodded. "Sounds reasonable, you are wearing the rings and wearing Drop Wings' daggers. Kat, you, and Paulette have been coopted into my family. Those daggers were made by a dragon of the Augustine Family. He was a priest, a warrior and a forger of weapons. His Spirit chose you and Paulette to carry them. The rings connect you to the daggers. Normally only Valkyrie could handle such weapons. Females like my Erin. However in rare cases other were chosen."

Kat looked at him. "You mean I did hear a Voice?"

Beary nodded. "Yes Kat, but a word of advice. Dragons give blessing out of love. Sometimes they have unintended side effects."

"Like wings and a dragon's tail." Night Wind said.

Beary smiled, "Yes and that is dealing with a normal dragon. Spirit dragons can be even a little harder to deal with."

"Tell me about it!" Artemus said over his shoulder.

Kat seemed nervous. "Should I be scared?"

Beary shook his head. "No, Kat, but you have been blessed. So has Paulette. I do not know how far Drop Wing plans to take his blessing. Talk to Sho-Sho if you need to. She is wiser than you might realize."

Kat just nodded.

"Now to other business, bend over." Beary ordered.

Kat looked at him. "You are serious aren't you?"

"Kat, I have to keep my word. You made me come and get you." Beary said.

Kat bent over his knee. Beary lightly swatted her tail.

She stood up saluted then kissed him. "I love you my Prince. It is hard to belong to a loving family. I know how to love; being loved is new to me."

Beary told her. "Kat, I would have come after any of our pilots."

Kat nodded. "I know that! But, you wouldn't have swatted their tail with love, like you promised. Beary, you realize now every pilot in this unit, will double their effort. Even though we were technically family, they know I said not to come, yet you did. They know you will come for them also."

"We don't leave anybody behind, Kat." Beary said.

"Kat smiled. "Spoken like a true Marine Sir."

"HURA!" both Blackpaw and Nighthunter chanted.

Artemus laughed. "She just smoked you that time Boss. I tell you she is as good a pilot as you are."

Kat shook her head. "No, but I will be."

Ben looked at Jessica and Pompey. "Shouldn't they have called in by now?"

Pompey shook her head. "Ben, you know better. Beary won't contact the ship till he knows they are clear."

Ben looked at her. "But what if . . ."

Pricilla looked at him and smiled, "Then Ben, Snow Flower, Jessica, and I are widows. You will have to take care of us and our children. Because, you know our husbands will not return alive without them, one way, or another."

Ben started to shake. Snow Flower put her arms around him "Beary and Artemus would never leave a pilot behind. No matter whom they were. Kat and Paulette are family. They will move space itself to bring them home."

Ben looked at her. "I would give my life for either one of them."

Snow Flower kissed him. "They would rather you live for them Ben Maritinus, a long happy and honorable life, with Kat."

Gabriel came in. "Boss, I don't know what it means. The traffic we are starting to receive from the Andapos System is heavy and seems angry. We still haven't broken their language or code. It is evident someone was getting reamed."

Ben sighed. "Well, I guess it's alright. Only Beary could upset someone that bad."

Ten more cycles passed the 38 was still holding together. We, was piloting it, while Joshua napped. MacIntosh was resting while keeping one eye on the gauges.

Beary looked at Artemus. "Is there anything showing up on either the long, or short range scanners?"

Artemus shook his head, "No, Beary, we are not being followed."

Beary looked at the clock twenty seven more cycles they would make it back.

Gracchus looked at the message in his paw. Then he looked at Jeanne. "They're sending the *Castles Gate* and its task force, minus the medical ship, and a destroyer task force, after the Reptilian Star Base."

Jeanne shook her head. "What about us?"

Gracchus shook his head. "Precede, as ordered survey Pratis System, safest possible route, best possible speed."

Rubin came in. "Captain I might be able to help?"

"How" Jeanne asked?

"As I understand it, the problem is that a ship, going through a wormhole, doesn't have shields or weapons for approximately one STU." Rubin said.

Gracchus nodded.

"What if, you formed a shield in front of the opening of the wormhole with shield generators?" Rubin asked. "It might not hold for more than two STUs, but, that is all the longer you need it."

Gracchus looked at him. "Rubin, if you can pull this off, I will get you a civilian medal!"

Rubin shrugged. "I can do it. I just need five more days to make it work."

"You have three." Gracchus said "Which means I know you only need two."

Rubin nodded. "Three is better."

Rubin left to make it happen. Of course his people were already working on it.

Jeanne looked at her husband, "So much talent in one clan. It doesn't seem fair."

Gracchus thought. "They nurture it, feed it, and allow it to grow. That is the difference between them and others. I have watched it. They even did it with us. They gave us a second chance at love and life."

Jeanne sat on his lap. "This is really improper behavior for a first officer."

Gracchus smiled at her. "I'll report you to the Ship's Captain."

Beary looked at the scope. There was a lot of activity in the Lesser Anzico System.

"Red Talon Control, Spirit 6, lost lambs recovered. One *WIA* but she is alright. Package recovered, will need to be tractor beamed in. Three cycles out."

"Spirit 6, Red Talon Control, understood, standing by, praise, be to the Creator."

"Captain Maritinus and Lt. Archangel, this is flight control lost lambs coming home one *WIA* but alright."

A cheer went up around the ship.

Ben just collapsed at his desk and said a prayer.

Gabriel smiled and kissed the emblem of the Creator the old dragon priest had given him.

Pompey kissed Erin and Sho-Sho. Then she went into her bedroom and cried.

Jessica and Alexis held each other and laughed till they cried.

Snow Flower sat down and wept with her children around her.

Night Song sat and gently hummed to her pups. "Dad is coming home."

Three cycles later, Valkyrie 38 was tractor beamed into the landing bay. Then it was lowered into the repair bay. Chen and Joshua got out and smiled.

MacIntosh gathered his gear and stepped out looked at his maintenance team. "Treat her gently, lads. She is a grand lady. Get her fixed and do it right."

Beary landed *The Star of Vandar*. It was lowered into its ready bay.

Caesar opened the door and signaled two medics to bring in a stretcher. "Paulette, I want to keep you in sick bay for a couple of days. Just to make sure the infection is taken care of.

Kat you are going also. You are having a complete physical now.

Night Wind, I want you to see the Vet now, also. No arguments."

Night Wind bowed. "Yes, Doctor."

Kat looked at him. "But, can't I go see Ben . . ."

Caesar told her. "He'll be waiting. The only reason he hasn't charged in here is because he knows I would deck him and throw him out."

Beary and Artemus just smiled.

Caesar turned to the medics. "Come on. Let's get going."

Gabriel and Ben were waiting. Ben gasped as he saw Paulette, being carried out on the stretcher. He and Gabriel ran over to her.

"I am alright Daddy. It was just a little scratch. Mommy and Doctor Caesar took good care of me. Mommy needs you. She is so tired." Paulette said as she took Gabriel's paw.

Ben went to Kat.

Paulette looked at Gabriel. "I am sorry. I almost broke my promise . . . I was afraid for mommy . . ."

Gabriel bent down and kissed her. "I understand, but you didn't you came home to me. I love you."

Paulette kissed his paw. "I love you so much Gabriel. Stay with me please."

Gabriel nodded. "I can for a little while. Then I'll be back."

"Nighthunter protected me." Paulette said, "He said he owed you for saving his life."

Gabriel shrugged. "I don't remember. Everything happened so fast. I don't know what happened."

Ben put his arm around Kat, as she came off, and kissed her.

"Oh, Captain Maritinus, Sir, that was a nice kiss." Kat said. "Doc says I have to go straight to sick bay, for a physical. Can you walk with me?"

Ben nodded. "I think I can do that Ensign Maritinus. Were you hurt?"

Kat shook her head. "Paulette was hurt bad, two pieces of shrapnel, one was in her lower abdomen. The other was in her upper right leg. There was so much blood. A voice told me what to do. I sealed her wound with her dagger and gave her a bag of blood.

Caesar had to operate on the way home, to repair some damage and clean out some infection."

Ben nodded, "I am glad your home. Beary and Artemus . . ."

Kat touched his face. "They were right. You would have done the same for them."

Ben looked at her. "Then you don't think me a coward because . . ."

"Oh Ben, it took more courage to stay behind. My dear sweet husband, I know the pain it caused you." Kat said with tears in her eyes.

Ben kissed her eyes, "None of that. You are home and safe. Let's get your physical done. So I can take you home."

Kat melted into his arms as they walked to sick bay.

Blackpaw and Nighthunter finished gathering their gear. When Beary came over, "I don't know how to thank you."

The two Gunnies saluted. "Skipper, we would follow you anywhere anytime. Also, we like Captain Maritinus and the Lt. Their ladies are fine officers. We can't afford to lose the good ones.

If you need us again, Skipper, you know where to find us." With that they headed out.

Artemus smiled. "Boss, to them your still a Marine and always will be."

Beary sighed. "Yah, I can live with that. We better check in."

Romanov was waiting. "Welcome back Bosses. Hotel is flying CAP. Third shift is coming on duty. With your permission, I am going to bed."

Beary looked at her. "Gloria how many hours since you got any sleep?"

Romanov just shrugged. "I have slept here and there."

Beary nodded. "Twenty four Cycles down time for you and my ladies no arguments. Gloria, thank you. Tell the others thank you also. Also thank you to second and third shifts."

A cheer went up from the crew members of both second and third shift in the flight control center.

Romanov just smiled *Ok he was just too darn good. He had her and the rest wrapped around his paw. Funny thing she didn't care.*

"Goodnight Boss. You better check in with Captain Gracchus. Then go see your ladies." Romanov said, as she headed to bed and to tell the others to sleep in.

Beary and Artemus walked into Gracchus office. "Hi Captain."

Gracchus smiled, "Took your sweet time making it back."

Artemus shrugged, "Had trouble finding a service station for the 38."

Gracchus nodded, "Glad you got it home. How are the ladies?"

"Kat is fine. Paulette will be soon. Give it a week, she is healing well. Caesar says he had to clean out the wound a little. She is healing fast." Beary said.

Gracchus nodded. "Astrid's Task Force is being sent after that Reptilian Star Base. We are to proceed to the Pratis System. Rubin has a trick up his sleeve that might help. I'll have him brief you tomorrow. Go be with your families."

Beary and Artemus nodded they stopped in and checked with Barbarossa and Pathfinder. Then they went home.

Gabriel went and found Nighthunter and Blackpaw. "Gunnies I don't know how to thank you. Especially you Gunny Nighthunter, Paulette said you took care of her."

Nighthunter shook his head. "Skipper, she saved my life twice. Now, I owe both of you. She is a remarkable lady and officer, Skipper."

Blackpaw nodded. "They both are, Lt. we were honored to help."

Gabriel nodded, "I better get back to her. Thank you again."

After Archangel left, Blackpaw looked at Nighthunter. "You, have done good with that one. He is turning out to be a good officer."

Nighthunter nodded, "If he survives. He might make general someday."

Blackpaw put his gear in his locker. "What about the Skipper?"

Nighthunter grinned, "He was born for greatness. Just like the Ghost, Lieutenant Artemus, and Dr. Vantanus."

Blackpaw sighed. "I hope we are around to see it."

Nighthunter nodded, "Me too."

Gabriel returned to Paulette. He pulled a chair over to her bed and held her paw. They talked for several cycles. Then he fell asleep with his head resting on the edge of her bed. Nurse Blaze put a blanket over his shoulders and sighed.

Beary and Artemus found their families waiting for them, as did Night Wind. There were kisses, tears, and a lot of thankful prayers offered up to the Creator and his Word.

Caesar quietly slipped into his room. Jessica was waiting. "Hi Sailor, I have some cherry nectar for you and some honey cheese."

Caesar looked at her. "Looks like that might not be the only thing you have waiting for me."

Jessica smiled, "Oh, you can nibble on anything you like."

Ben looked at Kat. She looked so tired. He turned on the mineral bath and helped her take off her uniform.

"Tonight my dear Kat, you get pampered." Ben said as he led her to the bath and lowered her in. He then climbed in and started washing her.

"Ben, this is not done. It is the wife's duty . . ." Kat tried to say.

Ben kissed her. "You are a warrior equal to any boar. You are also my wife. If it brings me pleasure to honor you, who would dare to say it is wrong."

Kat looked at him. "Ben, what did I do to be so blessed as to be loved by you?"

Ben looked at her. "Kat, you loved me first, and saved me. How could I not love you?"

Kat started crying and clung to him. "I am sorry Ben, I am being silly. I just keep expecting you to be like him. You keep proving me wrong."

Ben shook his head. "Kat, I will never be like him. If I am you may kill me with my own knife, for I will have dishonored my clan."

Kat kissed him. "No, you are the most honorable and loving boar I know. It is I who must never dishonor you."

Ben gently washed her stomach. "Now relax and let me do my job."

Kat's eyes got big "Oh, Ben!"

Pompey was setting in a chair in their room. "I am so glad you found them. Ben was almost out of his mind."

"Did he blame me for sending them out?" Beary asked."

Pompey looked at him. Then she got mad. "Beary Augustus Maxumus, I thought we were past this type of self-incrimination. You know Kat and Paulette were the best for this job. Another crew would have ended up dead. We got valuable intelligence. Which, Astrid is going to need. You are so quick to put your life on the line. Do you ever wonder what others feel?"

Beary looked at her "Pricilla I . . ."

"Don't Pricilla me! Don't you know that there isn't a pilot on this crew that wouldn't die for you? Romanov and her ladies are in love with you. One maintenance bear made a comment and Ensign Reuben almost beat him to a pulp, before he could say that she had misunderstood him. Ben is family. He loves you. He would die for you also. Just as I know you would for him. So how can you even ask such a selfish question?" Pompey said near to tears now.

Beary dropped his head. "Your right, I don't understand it."

Pompey dropped her head and walked over to him "For such a brilliant soldier, engineer, and scientist, my husband you are stupid. They can't help falling in love with you. Because, they know you love them. They trust you. They know you won't throw away their lives. They know the risks. It goes with the job. None of them are afraid to die. They just don't want to let you down."

Beary placed his head on her protruding stomach. "I love you."

Pompey kissed the top of his head. "I love you my Guardian, and husband."

Beary whispered. "Yes, my lady and how may, your servant serve his lady?"

Pompey smiled "I guess there is an advantage to being the Star."

Beary responded, "I told you, you were nobody's property."

Pompey nodded, "You did, but you forgot to tell me the other half. But mom did."

Beary nodded, "I figured she would. However, you don't need a ring to control me."

Pompey laughed, "No one can control you Beary. All they can do is love and be loved by you."

The next morning Caesar checked Paulette's injuries. He told her she could go back to her quarters, as long as she took it easy.

Ice Song visited her and healed the wounds completely. She even erased the scares. She also explained about the dagger and the ring. She again emphasized that Paulette was never to take the ring off.

Kat had talked to Sho-Sho. Sho-Sho explained the ring and dagger to Kat. She also told her to never take the ring off. She also explained that as far as Sho-Sho and the other dragons were concerned, Kat and Paulette had been elevated to the status of *Valkyrie of the Dragon*.

Kat was perplexed she didn't understand. Sho-Sho smiled and just kissed her. Then told her they would talk more.

That evening Paulette and Gabriel were visiting Kat and Ben. They had just finished eating when there was a knock at the door.

Master Sgt. Red Wing and three other dragons stood at the door.

Ben answered the door. "Master Chief, what can I do for you?"

Red Wing bowed. "Sir, I am here, well we are here, to represent the dragons on the crew. Is Lady Maritinus and Lady Archangel here?"

Ben nodded. "Please, come in all of you."

Red Wing bowed. "My ladies, we are here as representatives of the Dragons of Andreas Prime and the *EAQ*. We wish to acknowledge your selection as ςαλκυψριε οφ τηε Δραγον. By the rings you wear, we acknowledge you, Daughters of the Red Paw and Caesar/Maxumus Clan. Corporal, if you please."

Corporal Dew Fang stepped forward, held out two small boxes, and bowed "The gold box is for Lady Maritinus, the silver for Lady Archangel, please wear them with our gratitude and love."

Kat opened the box. Inside were two golden bracelets and a golden band with a blue stones. "These are beautiful."

Paulette's were silver. "They are exquisite." She said.

Red Wing said. "Please put them on."

Kat and Paulette did. They fit perfectly.

Red Wing ordered. "Now, touch the stone on the right bracelet."

They did. All of a sudden, Kat and Paulette were wearing what appeared to be full armor.

Red Wing explained. "It is called, Λιγητ Αρμορ, or light armor. It will stop any blade or projectile. It is also good against phasers. It was worn by the Valkyrie of Andreas Prime. It can be over powered but we have improved it, my ladies."

Kat looked at him. "You honor us too highly."

Red Wing kissed her. "No, my Lady, you, and your daughter were chosen. May you, be blessed by the Creator and his Word, *Valkyrie of the Dragon*. Sir Knight, we will take our leave. Good night."

Ben shook their talons. "Thank you, for the honor you paid my ladies."

Red Wing saluted. "Captain, we are always at your service." With that they departed very pleased with themselves.

Kat and Paulette looked at each other. "What does this mean?"

Ben sat stunned and smiled. "It means we call home, now!"

Ben's fathers face appeared. "Hail son, do you bring honor to your family and clan."

"No, father, not I, but your daughter and granddaughter have brought great honor to your house and clan. They were shot down by superior enemy forces, after destroying six of the enemy. Then landing her damaged fighter, she hid it from the enemy. Kat then saved Paulette and killed many of the enemy single handedly." Ben said.

Kat shook her head. "Father, he is not correct. I had help. A Spirit Dragon guided me in saving Paulette. He led us out of danger."

Aleut's eyes grew wide. "Go on, tell me the rest."

Ben continued. "She and Paulette have been declared *Valkyrie of the Dragon* in their tongue, by the dragons on board the *EAQ*, as representatives of the Dragons of Andreas Prime. They gave them each a set of light armor."

Aleut dropped his head, tears fell to the ground. He then let out an ear shattering roar. Five young warriors appeared. "Get the *Book of Warriors.*"

They brought in the book. A scribe stood before it. "Place in the book, Kat Maritinus, *Valkyrie of the Dragon*, wife of Ben Maritinus, daughter of Aleut, and Lunara Maritinus, *Warrior of the Red Paw*.

Add Paulette Mayotte Maritinus Archangel, *Valkyrie of the Dragon*, wife of Gabriel Archangel, daughter of Ben and Kat Maritinus, granddaughter of Aleut and Lunara Maritinus, *Warrior of the Red Paw*. Ben, give my granddaughter the *Mark of the Clan*."

Ben bowed. "Yes, father."

Aleut thumped his chest. "We Celebrate! My joy overflows. I love you my children." With that he cut off the com link.

Ben called Ice Song. She came over then blessed Paulette. She then gave her, the *Mark of the Red Paw*, with a dragon heart.

Pompey was sleeping peacefully. When, her private com unit went off. Beary answered it. "Hello."

A young Maxumus replied, "Sorry, Beary. I had a message for Lady Maxumus."

"What is it, Mr. Vance?" Beary asked.

"We have information, as to the individual, that ordered the hit on Captain Maritinus and Ensign Maritinus. We wanted instructions from Starburst. As to whether she wanted us to apprehend him."

Beary shook his head. *Dad!* "No Ed, it would cause embarrassment to Ben's people. I take it, Sho-Sho was correct. It was her father Chief Katimai?"

Vance nodded. "Yes, Beary, it was."

"Look Ed, let me take care of it. You might have to cover up the mess, to protect a friend of mine." Beary said.

Ed shrugged. "Beary, I work for your dad. I could see to it that he has an accident."

"No Ed, for the Red Paw, this is personal." Beary explained.

Ed Vance nodded, "No problem. We'll quietly watch the back of whoever they send. Without them knowing we are there."

"Thanks Ed. Give Debra my love." Beary said.

Pompey rolled over. "Taking my private calls?"

"When did you become Starburst?" Beary asked.

Pompey told him. "I do work for father, after all."

Beary nodded. He then called Aleut.

Aleut was deep in celebration, when Beary called. He listened quietly. "They did not tell me."

"Ben does not know the truth. He suspects, but I have not told him." Beary said.

Aleut nodded. "You have acted wisely Beary. I know your people would and could have killed him. I take it; you have called, to see if I prefer to have that honor."

Beary nodded. "Or if, you wish to give me permission to act as your agent."

Aleut nodded, "You honor, our ways, like one of my own. For that you are always in my heart. This I must do, Beary."

Beary nodded. "May the Creator, protect your hunt."

Aleut replied. "May, his Living Word be in your heart."

CHAPTER 9

Effect

"RED TALON 2 to White Dragon 6."

Cathy Ellis came on her private com unit. "Jeanne, what happened over there? Astrid was really shaken, when he got back here."

Jeanne shrugged. "He ran into Princess Maxumus. Shoshana was not pleased with his attitude and slapped him down. That is all."

"Who is she?" Cathy asked.

"Oh, she is the Ambassador from Andreas Prime and her grandmother's representative. Our Sho-Sho is a remarkable young lady." Jeanne said.

"She must have been. Anyway what do you need?" Cathy asked.

"Nothing, I just wanted to make sure, you saw all the intelligence we gathered, on the Reptilians and their systems." Jeanne said.

Cathy shook her head. "It hasn't filtered down to us yet."

Jeanne nodded. "Look Cathy, they broke through our fighter's cloak. It might have been compromised, by one of several wormholes. It is a Class VI base station. I am sending you your own copy of our latest intelligence estimate."

Cathy Ellis shook her head. "Thanks Jeanne, I'll share this with my captain. We weren't told half of this."

"Cathy, they will try and board you. You, have to be ready for them." Jeanne told her.

Commander Cathy Ellis nodded, "Understood Jeanne, Frasier will listen to me. Astrid runs things. We'll do what we can."

Astrid looked at the information in front of him. Plus, the steady stream of information, the probes the pilot from *The EAQ,* had planted, were still sending. He was facing a Class VI Star Base and at least six first line warships. Plus a hand full of destroyers. Sixteen total enemy ships plus fighters.

He had a dreadnought, six heavy, and twelve light cruisers. Plus twenty destroyers, of course five were staying to protect the hospital ship, and the system.

So that left him fifteen destroyers. Of course he had two hundred seventy-five Red Daggers, four Green, and thirty-eight Blue Daggers and thirty-six Fighters.

He checked his figures again. Yes he had the upper paw.

Beary listened to Ruben's plan. He then looked over the simulation.

Romanov asked a dozen questions then nodded.

Beary leaned back. "Ok, you two figure out the fine points. If it works it will save our tails."

With that Beary went back to his office.

That night Kat and Paulette were sleeping. In a dream a large blue dragon appeared, "My daughters, I am Drop Wing the Bold. It is time I talk to you. Leave your husbands and go to the maintenance bay. So we may talk."

Kat and Paulette woke up, put on their alert shorts, and a top. Then they headed for the deserted Maintenance Bay.

Honey was there looking at the 38. "Kat, did you call me here?"

Kat shook her head, "No, Honey I didn't."

Ensign Honey Tajima looked at her. "I have a strong urge to paint something on the noise of your fighter. I feel I have to do it."

A voice boomed out. "Then paint it. That is why you were summoned after all."

Honey looked around, as a blue dragon materialized. "Well go ahead, young one, and paint the picture in your mind."

Kat and Paulette looked at the dragon. "What is it daughters? Do you not recognize me from your dreams? I am Drop Wing and you are my chosen ones."

Kat stood up. "Sir, what do you require of us?"

Drop Wing ordered, "Serve the Guardian. You are now his Valkyries. His personal guard, that is why I gave you twin lightning as your blades. I also give you this blessing." He touched them, and then peered into them made some minor adjustments.

"There now you are somewhat Maxmimus. No blade will penetrate your skin. You need to let the good doctor examine you. But don't worry. I am not like Agathag. I know what I am doing." Drop Wing said.

Kat looked at him. "What of our cubs?"

Drop Wing said, "They will be great warriors all, if you live. Which, I plan for you to. Erin will need Valkyrie to lead. Maryam will be at her side as will Agathag. Your Cubs will be her Captains."

Honey looked at the large blue dragon painted on the 38.

Then Drop Wing walked over to the 38. "Be blessed Honey Tajima." Then he placed his talons on the 38 "You are damaged no more." All of a sudden the 38 looked brand new. "I always was good with metal."

Drop Wing looked at Honey. "Go sleep my child, know your father is at peace in the arms of the Creator."

He then looked at his two Valkyrie. "Present yourselves to your Prince. Show him these crests." He handed them each a small shield.

Ben woke up he couldn't find Kat.

Then Gabriel called. Paulette was missing also.

Then Kat called. She told him to grab Caesar and Gabriel then to meet them at Beary's office.

Kat and Paulette came in. Beary was finishing a report.

"Kat what are you and Paulette doing here at this time of night." Beary asked.

Kat and Paulette handed him their shields.

Beary looked at them. "Kat, I don't understand?"

Kat bowed. "Guardian of Vandar, we are your Valkyries, your bodyguards. We are not to leave your side except in death."

Caesar stormed in and scanned both of them. "What the . . . Beary when are these darn spirit dragons going to stop messing with bears DNA!"

Star Firerena appeared. "Doctor, really are they not more protected."

Ben and Gabriel looked at her and bowed.

Caesar looked at her. "My Lady, Firerena that is not the point!"

Star Firerena nodded, "True Caesar, my child it is not. The point is that Beary is facing great evil. He needs all of you to defeat that evil, in the battles to come. You and your help mates are vital."

Ben looked at her, "My lady I . . ."

Star Firerena kissed him. "Ben Maritinus, know that you are blessed by one greater than any dragon.

Gabriel Archangel, serve your father-in-law well and you will be blessed this I promise." Then she kissed him.

She turned to Beary. "Drop Wing is with them. I am with you. I love you my child." With that she left.

Beary shook his head. "I am sorry Kat, and Paulette. I don't know what I can do."

Kat and Paulette both smiled, "Don't ever leave us behind."

Beary looked at the report on the 38. "It says the 38, is going to take a while to fix."

Paulette laughed. "Oh, I don't know. I think she looks good. Care to look Boss?"

Beary followed them out to the ready area. Maintenance crews were crawling all over the 38.

Beary saw the dragon painted on the nose. "I see he fixed it."

"Yes Sir." Kat said.

Task Force 5 left. Pompey and Jeanne watched as each warship went to warp. "I am afraid."

Jeanne looked at her. "You are worried?"

Pompey just looked at her with tears in her eyes.

The next morning she kissed Beary "When do we leave?"

Beary looked at her. "Tomorrow, the shield emitters are ready; we send a few through followed by *Storm Cloud* and eight fighters. We extend the perimeter and the *EAQ* comes through. If it all works we are through in two STUs."

Pompey looked at him. "If it doesn't work, then what happens?"

Beary shrugged, "If the enemy is out there we die."

Pompey shook her head. "Not this time, others are going to do the dying this time."

Gracchus looked at Beary. "Astrid, will be launching his attack about the same time we go through the wormhole. Are you and your bears ready?"

Beary nodded. "Strictly A-team Captain, Artemus in *Storm Cloud* with the ladies, me, Barbarossa, O'Haggerty, and Kat. Then once you get near the end of the wormhole you launch Alfa flight. They clear thirty SubSTU after us. Then you come out one STU later. We make it work."

Artemus came in. "Briefing time let's go Boss."

Beary nodded. "See you on the other side Sir."

Romanov looked at the pilots. "Alfa Flight, you will launch into the wormhole. Don't fight it. Use your thruster. Just let it spit you out. Follow the beacons we lay out for you.

Command flight, put up your blast shields before you launch. Launch order is Spirit 6, Valkyrie 38, Harbinger 2, and Elf 4. Follow our orders without question and we will get you through."

Senna smiled. *These four WTO were the only ones that had passed. The only four other pilots that passed were all in Alfa flight. That is why they got the short hop.*

"A ROSE will lead off. It will launch the first shield emitters, one STU before we exit the wormhole." Romanov concluded.

Beary stood up. "The lives of our families depend on us making this work. Let's get it done."

Storm Cloud launched. Then they sent the ROSE into the wormhole. Then they gathered their ducklings. "Command Flight stay centered on the beam we are going in."

One by one the fighters followed the *Storm Cloud* in. Then one STU later so did the EAQ.

Tennyson smiled, as he adjusted the lateral thrusters. *This was fun all he had to do was keep them centered on the beam while Barbarossa flew it. It was like playing his piano gentle touches always produced sweet music.*

Romanov looked at Artemus. "Sir, we are at the release point."

Artemus nodded.

Ensign Fa Lo typed in the commands. The ROSE opened up and the emitters launched. The ROSE closed and continued on.

Artemus looked at Ensign Chen We, who was looking over some manuals. "What's wrong Chen?"

"Boss, I am worse than useless. They won't even let me touch anything in here." We said.

Rueben replied. "You are not qualified, to touch anything. At least the Boss can fly it."

Artemus nodded. "But I am smart enough to know when to let a better pilot do the flying."

Romanov just laughed. "Two STU warning, Start laying beacons."

Beary checked his scope. The *EAQ* was right where she should be. The first of the emitters had exited the wormhole as had the ROSE. One STU to go, the time seemed to pass so slowly. Then he felt it the kick of being spit out. He lowered his blast shield.

"Storm Cloud, to Command, all shield emitters, are operational. Launch additional emitters."

The fighters turned to a predetermined axis and launched their shield emitters. Then cleared the area thirty SubSTU later Alfa flight emerged and did the same thing.

Romanov reported. "Additional shield emitters are coming on line. *Storm Cloud* cloaking weapons free."

Beary came on, "Spirit 6, to all command units, cloak and weapons free."

Thirty SubSTU later Alfa flight reported, all units were cloaked and weapons free. Then the *EAQ* emerged from the wormhole.

Every one held their breath but no attack occurred. Then Ensign Re picked up something on her long range scan. "Sir there is a battle raging at mark 256 range four hundred ninety thousand KSMU, near the first Asteroid Belt.

Artemus reported it to the *EAQ*. Then he ordered Hotel and Golf launched as CAP.

Beary ordered an Alfa strike, consisting of Gem Flight1, Bravo, and Charlie Flights to join Command and Alfa.

With *Storm Cloud* leading the way, the *EAQ* quietly cloaked.

On the bridge Argus ordered battle stations.

The Polarians of the **Red Star Clans Home Defense Force** had ambushed these devils this time. Fifteen of the black fighters had been destroyed in the first wave.

Then a second and third wave appeared. Now, they were in trouble. They were running low on missiles and rail gun ammo. The old Mark 2's could destroy these black fighters, but it took several.

Now, their surprise attack had turned into a slugging match. Which, they were starting to lose.

The Commander of the Polarian Flight was in trouble. He had two black fighters on his tail and he couldn't shake them. His threat receiver went off. He knew they had gained lock on him. Then he saw them explode.

He watched as more of the enemy fighters started exploding.

"*Red Star Home Defense Force* this is *The Empress's Valkyries* and *Gem Flight1*, we hope we can be of assistance."

"This is Frostbear, praise the Creator."

"Frostbear, this is Spirit 6, we are picking up a large warship starting to come through a wormhole at coordinates 320 755 210.

"Spirit 6 that would be their mother ship, Frostbear, over."

Captain Gracchus launched, four hundred, Mark 4's, against the Lizard ship. Even with its shield s down, the warship seemed to absorb the damage without much difficulty.

The *EAQ* was now in range to fire its rail guns and phasers. The Reptilian Warship was almost clear of the wormhole, when the rail gun shells and phasers smashed into its armor. Fifteen large and thirty smaller projectiles smashed into its armor plating. The phasers also did some damage. Another four hundred, Mark 4's, raced toward the large Reptilian Cruiser.

One of the four warp nacelles were ripped off. But then the Reptilian Ship's shields started to form and weapons started to come on line.

It responded by launching three hundred missiles at the *EAQ*, firing its own rail guns and phasers.

Gracchus responded by launching defensive missiles and a third wave of offensive weapons.

The defensive systems intercepted most of the missiles the shields deflected the rail gun shells and phasers.

Still, this wasn't a slugging match Gracchus wanted to get into. Then much to his surprise, over a thousand; older Mark 2's appeared and slammed into the other side of the Reptilian Warship. Then fifty very large caliber rail gun shells followed.

He immediately launched another volley of Mark 4's and his own rail gun shells.

The strain on the Reptilians shields was too much. The Mark 4's had finally got dial into the right frequency and smashed the three remaining warp nacelles. The armor plating on the Reptilian ship started buckling and internal damage was being scored. That was when they launched boarding pods against the *EAQ*.

Gracchus just sneered. "Sorry, we have seen this one before."

The CAP had been ordered to land. They were now begging to launch. Gracchus said no, and launched defensive missiles. Several pods were destroyed. Over a hundred hit the outer shields. Their troopers tried to beam in, only to hit a secondary force field closer to the ship. They all died.

Gracchus ordered his rail gunners to rake the other ship. With its shield down and power failing the Reptilian Ship started coming apart. Then it happened, its engines lost containment and it exploded.

"Bearilian ship please identify"

"This is the *BAFRSV Empress Angelina's Quest.* Can we be of assistance?"

"This is *Red Star Clan Home Guard Forward Command,* I think you already have. I do have wounded pilots. Can you assist in recovery and treatment?"

White Daggers and Gem Flight 2 launched, as did Delta and Echo Flights.

Soon, twenty life pods were picked up. Some of the Polarian pilots were hurt, bad. Others were just shook up.

Ten others were recovered with *KIAs* inside. These were taken to the ships morgue.

Romanov relayed the news to Beary.

"Spirit 6 to Frostbear, we have recovered thirty of your pilots. Twenty are *WIA* and ten were *KIA.* Would you like to join us on the *EAQ?*"

"Frostbear to Spirit 6, yes, thank you. I started out with sixty warriors this morning. It seems I lost half my fighters and one sixth of my command. It would have been more, had you not arrived when you did."

Frostbear landed on the *EAQ.* In the landing bay his fighter was directed to an elevator and lowered to a spare loading bay. Maintenance bears started servicing his fighter.

A NCO looked at him. "Sir, we don't have any Mark 2's. However, the Mark 4's, use the same rail system. We'll give you a fresh load."

Frostbear nodded. "Thank you, sergeant."

Beary walked over. He was followed by Kat and Paulette. Joshua was finishing shutting down the Ghost and talking to the crew chiefs of the Ghost and the 38.

Beary introduced his team. "I am Lieutenant Beary Maximus, the CAG of the *EAQ.* This is my wingbear Ensign Maritinus and her daughter and WTO Ensign Archangel."

Frostbear looked disappointed. "Such gorgeous creatures and they are married?"

Ben spoke up from behind him, "To a better bear, than you Franz Frostbear."

Frostbear turned around and looked at Ben. "No, it cannot be! You are already a Marine Captain. You are hardly a cub! Don't tell me that ravishing female is your wife!"

Ben nodded. "Yes and Paulette is my daughter. She is married to one of my 2nd Lieutenants. They are also both full *Warriors of the Red Paw.*"

Frostbear whistled. "Well she helped save my tail today, if she is the one that flies the fighter with the blue dragon on it."

Beary nodded. "She does and I fly the Ghost."

"So, it was you two that shot them off of me. Thank you." Frostbear said. "So Ben, how did you score such a fine lady?"

Kat walked over to her husband, "He is a superior Marine and extremely talented in bed."

Ben turned pink as Kat walked off. "Sir, I will start gathering the intelligence we gathered. Come Archangel."

Paulette stopped and kissed Ben's cheek. "He is also a wonderful daddy. He made sure I got a good lover for a husband. He arranged the whole thing."

Ben was almost red as they left. Beary, was struggling not to laugh.

Frostbear's mouth was hanging open. "Dag gum Ben, I didn't know you had it in you!"

Ben just smiled. "Kat can be a little hard to handle at times."

Beary spoke up. "Commander Frostbear, why don't you let me show you to your bears?"

"Call me Franz. Sir, I am just a local school teacher, who happens to know how to fly a fighter." Frostbear said.

Beary held out his paw. "Call me Beary. How do you know our Ben?"

"Oh, our tribes are related. His great grandfather was married to my great grandfather's sister. So we are loosely cousins. My oldest brother is now, *Chief of the Red Star Clan.* Aleut helped us greatly when my father died five years ago." Frostbear said.

"The Arcrilians never bothered our planet, like they did the others in the Pratis System. It was too cold for them.

The Reptilians tried to land troops. They are cold blooded. Even in the summer it rarely gets above ten degrees. It is winter in the Northern Hemisphere were the land masses are. Needless to say we slaughtered them." Frostbear explained.

First they went to the morgue. Frostbear looked at each face. One was a young bear he shook his head. "It was his first mission. He just finished training. He was a bright student. Now he is gone. Out of the ten that were killed, eight were new to the defense force. I only knew two of them, this one, and one of the veterans that were killed. The others came from a different village, on the other side of the continent.

It seems we always loose the new pilots first."

Beary nodded. "If you survive, that first encounter, your chances go up. We will aid in seeing your warriors are properly sent home."

Frostbear nodded. "I should see to my wounded."

Beary led off. "This way please."

Frostbear dropped back to talk with Ben. "So, cousin what is his story? I mean he is young to be a CAG, isn't he?"

Ben responded. "No, my wife says he is the best pilot she has ever seen. Coming from Kat, that means something. Also, I would follow him to the *Halls of the Moons of Bantine*. I would give my life for him, without hesitation and considerate it only a small repayment of my debt to him. Everyone he touches feels that way. Still, he doesn't see it that way. He feels it is he who owes the debt."

Frostbear looked at his cousin. "You sound like he is family to you."

Ben shrugged. "He is. Our Clans have been joined. Snow Flower married into his clan. I was made a Knight by his mother.

Why don't you have dinner with Kat, the children, and me tonight? Kat is a great cook."

Frostbear nodded. "Alright Ben, I would like that."

At the sick bay, Frostbear was introduced to Doctor Greenbrier, then Caesar. He saw how well his bears were being treated. He also saw Ben slip into a room.

Nurse Blaze nodded. "He is stronger today Captain. Some of the tissue is regenerating."

Dr. Cooper came in. "He is better Ben. We will be able to start waking him in a few days. His days as a combat Marine are over. I am sure you understood that."

Ben nodded.

"But," She continued, "He should be able to live a normal life after rehabilitation. I have already talked to Angelina. We will transfer him to Andreas Prime, and she will take over his case."

"Tell Angelina I will pay . . ." Ben started to say.

Dr. Cooper held up her paw, "She said to tell you, that if you even spoke such non-sense, she would have you spar with her. You are her Knight. He was one of your Marines. His care is on her."

Ben just sighed. "Thank you, Janise."

Dr. Cooper touched his face. "It is ok Ben; you know Angelina really loves you. I think she is as proud of you as she is the others, even Beary."

Ben leaned against the door. "Janise, you have known them longer. Do they overpower everyone with their love?"

Janise thought about it, then smiled. "Yes Ben, then you, except it and you, start living that way too. Scary, isn't it?"

Ben just smiled, "I guess all blessing have side effects."

Nurse Blaze stepped out and ran right into Frostbear, "Franz!"

"Aurora what are you doing here?" Frostbear asked.

"I am a nurse, assigned to Doctor Vantanus' staff." Nurse Blaze said.

Frostbear called Ben over. "Hey cousin, do you know Aurora?"

Ben laughed, "Franz, we are on the same ship. The *EAQ* is big but not that big."

Frostbear looked at Aurora. "Could she join us for dinner?"

Aurora dropped her head. "I am not sure; Lady Maritinus would want me there."

Ben made a call.

Kat smiled "Tell Aurora, I am a good winner, if, she can be a good loser."

Ben walked over and whispered into Aurora's ear.

Nurse Blaze laughed. "Well, that is telling the snob isn't it. Thank you, Ben. Tell Kat I would love to escort Franz to dinner.

Ben nodded. "I need to get back to work. Nurse Blaze, if you could take care of my cousin, I would appreciate it."

Beary and Kat looked over the intelligence.

Kat looked up. "Did we jump the gun? Or was this Reptilian Ship hiding in the wormhole?"

Beary looked at her. "I have never heard of that. It would take an enormous amount of power to fight the tidal currents in a wormhole."

Paulette looked at him. "Why four warp nacelles? It was just a heavy cruiser. What if two served another purpose?"

Beary looked at her. "Go on Paulette."

"Boss, I am not a warp engineer." Paulette said.

Beary shrugged. "We have one. He seems pretty useless at the moment. So, what do you got?"

Paulette sighed, "How much pressure does a rock exert on a stream?

What if two of the engines, create a null field in the stream. A rock, so to speak, the flow of the wormhole would flow around it. Wouldn't it? Unless, something collides with the ship, like another ship or a meteorite, in which case it would be dislodged."

Beary pulled out a tablet and did some figuring. "Paulette, you are brilliant. I'll have Dr. Vallen check these figures. It could be done. I wouldn't want to do it, but it could be done.

Paulette, you just earned a pay raise."

"Beary, I just wish fleet would get my pay straightened out." Paulette said.

Beary looked at her, "What?"

Kat shrugged. "We're still not getting paid Boss. It is not a big deal for me. Ben is taking care . . ."

Beary shook his head. "Here Paulette, take this." He handed her forty thousand credits. He turned and handed Kat the same.

Paulette looked at him "Sir this is more than a year's pay!"

"Paulette, you work for me and you are family. That means you have a share, in the various industries we own. You and Kat are also *Valkyrie of the Dragon,* which gives you title to some land on Andreas Prime. Beany will get your finances straightened out. However, you are not without means. That is just a small gift to help hold you over." Beary said.

Kat kissed him. "Beary, I don't need it."

Beary shrugged. "No, however, a female needs mad money, Kat."

"With this I could . . . never mind Boss." Kat said.

That evening Nurse Blaze led Commander Frostbear to the Maxumus family section.

Nikolaos meet them. "Hello, Nurse Blaze."

"Sir Nikolaos, this is Commander Franz Frostbear. He is Ben's cousin."

Nikolaos bowed. "Then you are family sire. I am Snow Flowers' son. Still sire, I must ask you to check your weapons."

Frostbear looked into his eyes. "You are young for a warrior. I see you have already survived your first hunt."

Nikolaos replied. "Yes sire, all of my siblings, but my youngest sister Agathag, have completed many hunts."

He complied and smiled. "Hunt well Nikolaos, of the Red Paw."

"Hunt true, Franz of the Red Star." Nikolaos replied.

After they entered, he whispered to Blaze. "He seems dangerous."

"He killed an intruder, with his bare paws, when we were boarded." Blaze told him.

Ice Song saw him. "Welcome cousin. I am Ice Song Artemus. Ben's rooms are the third door on the left."

Franz looked at her. "You are a dragon?"

"Yes, I am. I am Agathag's companion and Princess Shoshanna's handmaiden. I have also been adopted by Sir Artemus and Lady Snow Flower. So, I am their daughter also." Ice Song stated.

Kat opened the door. "Please come in. Paulette, get our guests a glass of honey nectar."

Paulette smiled. "Yes Mommy."

Ben and Gabriel looked up and walked over.

Gabriel bowed, "Nurse Blaze, good evening."

"Lieutenant you look all healed up." Blaze said.

"I have been well cared for." Gabriel said, with a wink.

Paulette handed them a glass of nectar. "Not nearly as well as I have."

Ben shook his head. "Do I need to turn on the fire hose?"

"Only, if you turn it on you and mom first. You weren't even dressed when we got here." Paulette said.

"I . . . was taking a shower." Ben said.

"Oh, page seventy-two, dad." Gabriel said, with a smile.

Ben shot him a look. "Gabriel is my First Platoon Commander. He started out rough, but a great Gunny has turned him around."

"He still wasn't satisfied so he married me off to an angel. She then turned out to be his daughter. Now, I have to live up to his expectations." Gabriel said.

Franz couldn't get his head around it. How could this be the Ben he knew? Then he looked through the bed room door and saw Kat's picture. He turned a shade of pink.

Ben whispered. "Overpowering isn't it. It was painted by Anna Henderson a very famous artist. She is also Beary's cousin.

Aurora looked at it. "Oh, Kat may I."

Kat went in with her.

"Kat, I have seen some of her work before, but this is exquisite! You look like an angel. No wonder he loves you so much. I am sorry sister. The best female did win." Aurora said.

Kat kissed her. "He broke down in tears as I walked in. To his clan, if I would have acted different, he would have been dishonored. I fell in love with him the first day I saw him. I did not know anyone else might . . ."

"No Kat. I didn't till you showed up. Then it was like . . . Oh, it is silly." Blaze said.

"Come Ben, will get nervous." Kat said.

Nurse blaze smiled. "Your picture, in your uniform is stunning. Still you should have posed for Kat, as she did for you."

Ben shook his head, "No, too ugly."

Kat just shook her head. "Not at all, he is delicious."

Kat went and served dinner; roast lamb, cold fish, and salad. She then served a cherry tart for dessert.

Ben was laughing and enjoying this lively evening. Then his com unit went off.

"Ben, I am sorry." Beary said "Have Kat and Paulette report to the flight line. We are scrambling soon. You are needed in ops."

"Kat," Ben said.

"Come on Paulette the Boss needs us." Kat said.

"Aurora, I think you are also needed or will be." Ben said.

Gabriel handed Ben a bag, "On your six, Skipper."

Aurora took Franz paw. "Come on."

Beary, Artemus, and Ben with Gabriel in tow arrived in the Captains office.

Commander Cathy Ellis was on the view screen. She was heavily bandaged. "Argus, it's bad. I have three operational Red Daggers left. The *Light Sword* is just, gone. Four hundred bears, just gone. So are the *Sea Hammer* and the *Knife Claw.*

The *Hanover* is badly damaged, so is the *Gunderson.*

The *Castles Gate* is damaged, but we are still operational. Admiral Astrid is dead, along with most of his staff. We got boarded. The Marines cleared the boarders. We lost half of our Marine detachment.

Oh, Captain James has taken operational command. Did I tell you, Captain Lansin on the *Half Sword* was killed? It was boarded also."

Argus looked at her. "Cathy, I am sending help."

"I can't figure it, two hundred seventy-one Red Daggers, four Greens, and thirty-eight Blues Daggers just gone, along with thirty-six fighters. Some have to still be alive. Don't they?" Cathy Ellis asked.

Caesar shook his head. "Team 12, teams 2, and 4 prepare to launch for rescue missions."

Artemus looked at Beary. "Gem Flights 3 and 2 load rescue pods."

"*Storm Cloud*, prepare to launch to coordinate rescue mission. Echo, Foxtrot, and Golf launch, prepare to form up on *Storm Cloud*.

Kat, and Joshua, let's get going it is time to go to work." Beary said.

"Ben can you coordinate with Mountain and take care of the CAP and the *EAQ*." Beary asked.

Ben nodded. "I can handle it."

Third Squad boarded the Purples and the Whites.

Pathfinder and Barbarossa walked up. "It is about time they put you in charge, while they take off. Come on Ben. We'll help you learn about controlling air power."

Ben sighed. "I figured you two were my teachers, along with Dan."

Pathfinder smiled. "Danny boy and his crew are good, at what they do, but they need some training up also."

This wormhole was extremely stable. It quickly opened up into the Andapos System. What waited for them was devastating.

"Spirit 6 to White Dragon, we are beginning rescue and recovery operations."

"White Dragon 5 to Spirit 6, understood. Destroyers are trying to stabilize and help larger ships."

"Spirit 6 to all Valkyrie, Gem, and Medical Flights, coordinate, with *Storm Cloud*. Spirit 6 passing control, to *Storm Cloud*."

Romanov shook her head. "Ok ladies, you heard the Boss. We are in control. Set up search patterns let's get it done."

"Valkyrie 38 to Spirit 6, I have a life pod bearing 270, mark 320."

"Spirit 6 to Valkyrie 38, let's go get it."

Kat picked up a faint life signal. She could also tell power in the pod was failing. She fired a power line across and reeled the pod in.

All of a sudden she heard the rail guns fire. A black fighter that was drifting nearby exploded.

"38 Sword to all units' enemy fighters are not all dead. We just had one try and target us, as we picked up survivor."

"Spirit 6 to all units, no chances, flame them."

Soon small explosions could be seen. Every enemy fighter, that was still in a large enough pieces, to be a threat, was turned into smaller pieces.

They delivered this pilot to a White Dagger. He was a young Red Pandarian. He was suffering from lack of oxygen and shock.

Artemus and We found a Red dagger. We and a Marine entered. A Reptilian tried to rise up. The young Marine shot him twice and then put a round in the other two Reptilians' heads. We checked the WTO. He was dead. The pilot had lost a lot of blood. However, he was still alive. They placed his body on the *Star,* along with his dead WTO's. The young Marine started working on him as they went to find a White."

Garnet was turned into a morgue ship and collected the recovered bodies. They returned them to the Heavy Cruiser *Hammerhead.* It had suffered some damage, but as the Captain said nothing critical. Also, the so-in-so didn't succeed in boarding his ship.

The wounded, once stabilized, were taken to the *Castles Gate* and the Heavy Cruiser *Hero's Song.*

After sixteen cycles, they had recovered twelve fighter pilots alive and the bodies of ten. This left fourteen pilots unaccounted for. Unfortunately, in their business that was the norm, not the exception. An exploding fighter doesn't leave much to find.

Of the two hundred seventy-one Red Daggers, they recovered sixty crew members alive and the bodies of the rest. One Green Dagger crew was rescued and part of two Blue Daggers. The others were lost. Most of the bodies were recovered. One Green had been blown in half, its crew lost to space.

Over two hundred eleven Red Dagger crews were lost in one battle. Most do to enemy troops beaming in.

Beary stood in front of Captain James. "Sir, there wasn't any Marines, on board the Daggers?"

"The Admiral said it was unnecessary use of Marines." Captain James said.

Beary looked at him. "But, it was part of the design. We proved it on the *Saber Claw!*"

Captain James nodded. "Yes, but Astrid was a . . . Look Lieutenant Maxumus, he is going to be remembered as a hero, because we won. I lost seventy crew members. Not to mention, the Admirals staff was wiped out. Two Destroyers and a new Light Cruiser are gone. Not to mention, the fighter crews and dagger crews who died. That doesn't include the dead on the other ships, which were severely damaged.

It was his fault. He was too darn arrogant. He disregarded the intelligence you sent. It is what got him killed. Still, they will say he was brilliant.

You know why we won? A young destroyer Captain, knowing his destroyer was going to explode, rammed the Base Station, as his core exploded. Pushing the Base Station into the Star as its shields collapsed. We watched it melt from the heat.

Fleet won't even remember his name. Yet, the Great Astrid will live on as a great hero."

Beary lowered his head. "Sire, if my family can be of service to the families, of the fallen, please let us know. Father, mother, and I would be honored to assist them."

Captain James looked at Beary. "I am sorry Lieutenant Maxumus. Thank you."

"No sir. It is an honor to serve." Beary said.

Back on the *EAQ,* Beary wrote a confidential report to his father. According to Captain Frasier James of the *Castles Gate,* the battle was still in doubt. Till Captain William Fulbright of the *Knife Claw,* knowing his destroyer was doomed rammed it into the Base Station, as his warp core lost containment. The resulting explosion and impact pushed the Reptilian Space Station into the star. This collapsed its shield causing it to melt and explode. He claims that the heavy losses were caused by Admiral Astrid disregarding fleet procedures. This was told to me during a time of grief and anger. So please weigh this information properly. Also father, please protect Captain James and see that the crew of the *Knife Claw* are not forgotten.

With the message finished he sent it securely to his father.

Octavious read the message. "Dee, I have a job for you."

Deloris came in. "What do you need Octavious?"

He showed her the message.

"No problem, I'll take care of it." Deloris Maxumus said.

The *Torcida Corazón* was your typical back water port bar. Where creatures with no name go to hangout and to look for companionship, anonymity, or work from other creatures with no name.

No one approached the large Polarian, in the gray cloak, after the first night. Kassem had tried to shake the new comer down. Kassem was a large bear, everyone was afraid of him. This older Polarian had picked him up and thrown him out the door, as if he was a rag doll. Then sat back down and went back to drinking his tea.

Tonight, he was again at his table with a pot of tea. He was watching the door.

The young waitress came over. "Sire, please, can I get you anything?"

He smiled a gentle smile. "More tea," Then gave her three gold coins.

She looked at them. "Yes Sire."

The owner started to take all three coins, till he looked over at the Polarian. Who, held up one digit. "These two are for you. Take him his tea and see to his privacy."

Two cycles later, Alakanuk Katimai came in. He had already been drinking. He was trying to find another hit bear to go after his daughter and Maritinus. It was becoming difficult. He staggered to a table and sat down.

The Waitress came over and took his order. When she returned he took a sip and grabbed her arm. "This isn't what I ordered. It is watered down. You are trying to cheat me!"

He went to hit her. A paw grabbed his arm and spun him around. He was sent sprawling on the floor. "Here Miss, take this money and leave this cull to me." The other Polarian said.

Alakanuk stood up. "You, how dare you?"

"I have come for you, Katimai." Aleut said.

Alakanuk charged him. Aleut side stepped him and sent him crashing into a table.

Alakanuk drew a knife and charged Aleut. Aleut grabbed his paw and twisted it. He then drove the knife into Katimai's own chest.

Aleut whispered into his ear. "How dare you send killers after my children you low life, you have no honor. You are an abuser of females and a coward. Now die by your own knife."

Aleut pushed the knife deeper and angled it up.

Alakanuk Katimai gasped. He tried to pull out the knife. Aleut kept pressing it in. Katimai felt his strength leave him. Then he died.

Aleut pulled out his own knife. Cut open the back of Katimai's shirt and cut the symbol of a warrior from his shoulder. He then spit on it, and shoved it in a pouch. "This bear was a criminal to his own kind. Do with him as you will."

With that Aleut left, after he took Katimai's purse and threw it to the young waitress. "This is for his disgraceful actions towards you."

A few moments later bears entered the bar. Mr. Vance surveyed the room. "Looks like someone got to him first. We are taking the body."

The owner looked at him. "We called the local police."

Mr. Vance held out his badge. "Tell them Special Branch is taking care of this. This one was wanted by us. He tried to hire someone to kill one of ours."

The owner gulped. "Yes Sir, I guess, they will understand."

Half a cycle later the local police arrived. "What do you mean they took the body and cleaned up the evidence?"

The owner looked at the police sergeant. "They were Special Branch. I wasn't going to argue with them."

Task Force 8 was sent to replace Task Force 5. Construction of a Bearilian Battle Star was begun, near the fifth planet. It was to help secure the region.

The *EAQ* started its survey of Pratis V.

Beary stood on a hill overlooking a small valley. Ben and Gabriel were with him.

Ben looked at him. "They were holding them down there?"

Beary nodded, "I never thought I would see this valley again."

Halberd came over. "Skipper, Third Platoon is checking in. No sign of enemy presence."

Ben replied, "Thank you private. By the way it should be corporal tomorrow."

Halberd nodded, "Yes Sir, thanks to you."

Ben waved his paw. "You earned the promotion son not me."

Nighthunter said. "Lt. we're ready."

"Ok Gunny, tell the bears I want them to do this by the book. Just because no one else has found any enemy troops doesn't mean there isn't a division down there. I don't like writing letters and my wife doesn't look good in black." Archangel said.

Nighthunter barked. "You heard the Skipper you maggots. We do it right so everyone goes home in one piece. Our Lady doesn't want to wear black."

Everyone turned and looked at Paulette standing there in her flight suit. Then they went to work with deadly seriousness.

Ben just shook his head, and smiled at Beary. "Those two are worth an extra company. They're better than flying the flag."

Beary nodded, "They are a symbol they can understand."

Joshua walked over. "Ghost is secured boss."

Beary nodded. "Ok, ladies and gentlebear let's go, stay sharp."

They stated down a different trail. Joshua was edgy. "We should have brought Night Wind along."

Kat nodded. "I feel them also. Stay sharp."

That's when they heard the first shots off to the right.

Gabriel called Ben. "We are taking fire. Two marines down. Ok they're hit but moving to cover. We're advancing. Captain there is more than a company of Lizards down here, in those buildings." Then there was a burst of phaser fire. "Ok they are falling back. Sir, I do have a few wounded. Medics say nothing serious yet."

"Ok, Gabriel, I'll get you some help." Ben said.

"Halberd, get second and fourth platoon over here." Ben ordered.

Sergeant Whitepaw and two dragons moved to cover Ben.

Kat saw the first sniper, as he tried to line up on Joshua. She snapshot her rifle. The fifty caliber slug caught the lizard in the chest, throwing him from the tree.

Joshua launched a grenade into a thicket. Two more reptilians were thrown out burning.

One fired a phaser rifle at Beary. It hit him in the shoulder. His fur sizzled, as Paulette dispatched the Reptilian with a shot through his head. She then ran over to see how bad he was hit.

Beary waved her off, "I am fine Paulette. It just burned a little fur."

She looked at the wound, "Alright, my Prince."

Kat and Joshua scanned the trees. Each killed two more snipers.

Kat and Paulette put on their bracelets and head bands. "Boss we're going to clear the woods. Joshua, protect the Boss."

With their armor on Kat and Paulette took off into the trees. Blue flames appeared like lightning. The air cracked with what sounded like thunder. Then it was deathly quiet. Then a large Reptilian charged Beary. Joshua was busy fighting two others. He shot one then the other was on him.

Beary threw the Reptilian. Then Star Fire was in his paw. The Reptilian drew his own sword and charged. Quick blows were exchanged. Then he stopped and turned. "How, no one can defeat me." Then he fell to his knees and toppled over.

Joshua pushed the other Reptilian off of him. He then pulled the knife out of his vest. "Boss, are you alright?"

Beary opened his vest and sighed, "You're going to have a nasty bruise Joshua. Maybe a broken rib but it didn't penetrate the vest."

Kat and Paulette returned. They were breathing heavily. "We cleared out the area Boss. Three got away from us. I guess you and Joshua found them."

Sergeant Whitepaw saw the blue lighting off to the left. "Sir, what is going on over there?"

Ben looked at him. "Kat and Paulette got upset."

Gabriel called in. "Captain we have Reptilians trying to flank us on the right."

That is when they heard. "Slayer1 this is Valkyrie 1 with Alfa flight we'll take care of the problem, lay smoke."

Gabriel had his Marines lay down purple smoke. About that time the forest was ripped apart by a steady stream of forty SubSMU rail gun shells. The Reptilian Troopers were torn to pieces.

One that was hiding in a tree fired a hand held rocket it exploded against Valkyrie 4's shield. Valkyrie 3 then shredded the tree.

Sapphire arrived and fired two, Mark 8's at a cluster of Reptilian Troopers. The anti-troop munitions opened up over them, then exploded just above the ground. The effect mowed everything down for one hundred SMU around where they went off.

Andropov and Blackpaw arrived. Ben sent them to secure the right side.

Dancer and Fourth platoon arrived. Ben sent a squad with Killinger to make contact with Beary and secure the left flank.

Dancer set up his heavy weapons.

"RPD3 this is Valkyrie 1 we will loiter. If you need us we are here."

"Valkyrie 1, RPD4 is on line to the right. Spirit 6 is on the left. RPD 3 out."

Beary stood by a tree. The Reptilians had retreated into the concrete bunkers. That the Arcrilians had used as their base. Killinger joined up with him.

"Sir, you been wounded!" Killinger said as he called for a Medic.

Beary waved him off. "It is nothing, have him look at Akhiok he took a knife in the vest."

The medic gave Joshua a small white pill. "Ah, it is an Arachnid Gallbladder."

"Doctor Vantanus, orders anytime a knife is involved." The Medic said.

"I know what they are for. My people use them just like the captain's do." Joshua said.

The Reptilian Commander realized he was isolated. Plus his command had just been decimated from the air, and by a strange weapon that had hit his troops north of his location.

"How many troops do we have left?" He asked.

"We have one hundred troopers still in this bunker. We cannot maneuver outside, they control the air. We cannot contact the Base Station or the *Raptors Revenge*." The Captain responded.

"After all the searching, we finally find what we were searching for. Now, we are trapped." The Commander said.

"But Sir, they thought they had killed him a dozen times. Yet they said he destroyed this outpost." The Captain said.

"Yes, but he must be the one. His picture matches the last image of the eye!" the Commander said.

Beary called to them. "Reptilians, surrender. Your base station and fleet have been destroyed. You are isolated."

The Commander hit a *PA* button. "Who demands our surrender?"

Beary shrugged. "Lieutenant Beary Maxumus, Bearilian Fleet."

The Commander looked up. "You are the Ghost, the accursed Destroyer of the Eye!"

Beary said. "Yes, I am he."

The Commanders blood boiled. "We will kill you! Attack now!" The Captain tried to stem the tide, as one hundred Reptilian Troopers tried to pour out of the bunkers.

Ben gave the order "Fire!"

The mortars of the 4th Platoon coughed. Then Alfa Flight came in on a strafing run. The exploding mortar shells, the exploding forty SubSMU shells, the deadly fire from the First and Second Platoons, and Killinger's squad quickly decimated the Reptilians.

A few reached Beary's, location. Kat and Paulette killed six of them. The Reptilian Commander stood in front of Beary.

Beary looked at him, "Is your hate so blind that you were willing to waste your command, just to get a chance to kill me?"

"Yes!" The Commander said, "A thousand times that number, just to end your life!"

Beary shook his head, "Not today."

The Commander charged Beary with a blade. Beary twirled out of his way. Star Fire appeared in his paw. He swung it true, severing the Commander's head from his body.

Star Fire disappeared.

Killinger looked at Beary, "You alright Skipper?"

Beary nodded. "Yes Gunny."

The Captain knew he was dying. He put the phaser rifle up to his shoulder and fired. The beam hit Beary, square in the chest knocking him back. He smiled as five grenades landed around him and exploded.

Kat and Paulette were kneeling over Beary, taking off his vest. It had deflected 80 % of the beam. Still he had been hit hard. The fur on his chest was burnt. Tears were welling up in their eyes.

Ben ran up. He saw the rock. He pulled an ammonia capsule and snapped it. Ben put it under Beary's nose.

Beary coughed.

Ben shook his head. "You're going to have to stop hitting your head. You scared my girls, to death.

Kat and Paulette don't waste your tears. He has been hit harder than that without a vest."

Beary sat up gingerly. "Your concern is overwhelming."

Ben sighed. "Come on you big baby, we have work to do."

Beary looked at the vest and put it back on. As long as he didn't get hit in the same spot it would be alright.

The medic looked at him and gawked. Joshua got up. "You get used to it." With that he grabbed his gear and followed them.

The medic looked at Killinger. "Gunny, he shouldn't have been able to get up. I am not sure he should even be alive?"

Killinger shrugged. "That is why they call him, *The Ghost.*"

Beary, Ben, Kat, and Paulette entered the bunker. Gabriel, Joshua, and Nighthunter followed. They found a bunch of data crystals and files. Most were about Beary.

Ben ordered all the files put in a vault room. Nighthunter grabbed six Marines. The boxes were piled in. He smashed the new data crystals the Reptilians had made. He threw these into a metal barrel along with the older Arcrilian ones. "Is that everything?"

Nighthunter nodded. "Yes Skipper."

Beary looked at him. "Ben, what are you doing?"

"I am protecting my family and yours. Nighthunter put in four thermite grenades; one in the barrel, the rest in amongst the pile. Make sure it all burns to ashes." Ben ordered.

Nighthunter saluted and went in. He dropped the grenades, came out, and shut the vault door. The heat was so high it almost melted the metal vault door.

Ben went in, everything had turned to dust. He came out. "Blow the tunnel, seal it."

Nighthunter nodded. "No problem Skipper, I have enough plastic to do it right."

When they came out, they walked up to a small hill.

"Beary, there was nothing in there that was valuable to fleet. There was a lot that could put Erin and Pompey at risk. Not to mention Kat and Paulette." Ben said. "I was with you when you destroyed *The Eye*. I will die to protect you, Pompey, and Erin. I will do whatever it takes. Even, if I have to fight you to protect you." Ben said.

Beary put his arm around his friend. "I love you to Ben."

Ben nodded. "Just so we understand each other."

They walked back to the hill top. Six marines were being treated for injuries. Andropov came over. "We have six wounded none critical. The new inserts really helped."

Dr. Kroller came over. "Lieutenant Maxumus, what are you doing? I was told you were hit!"

Beary shrugged. "No big deal."

Kroller had him take off his vest. He looked at the burn mark on his chest and shoulder. "How can you still be moving?"

Ben laughed. "You might check his head he knocked himself out."

Kroller scanned his head. "He has a small bump nothing to worry about. But this chest wound . . ."

"Will be healed in a day or two, doctor, just give me some salve, it will be fine." Beary said.

Kroller looked at his scan. "This can't be right. He has no internal damage at all."

Ben nodded. "Don't worry Doc, you get used to it after a while."

CHAPTER 10

Results

BEARY AND MOST of the Marines had returned to the *EAQ*. Third Platoon and 2Lt. Nepos, were providing security for the scientists. They had set up a base camp on Pratis V, near one of the old cities. The soil survey showed that the planet had recovered well from the damage caused by the Arcrilians. It would be easy to reestablish farms. The buildings were another problem.

Most of the cities would have to be raised. In fact the Pratis civilization would have to start over. Some of the culture would survive; part of it would be lost. However, that would be the bears' choice. The scientists were only there to see if the planet was ready to be reoccupied.

Beary was setting in his front room. Pompey had looked at him and left the room crying. Erin told him mommy has been doing that a lot lately.

Beary got up and went into the bed room. "Pricilla, what is it?"

She looked at him. "You could have been killed!"

Beary shook his head. "Not from a little tickle like this. Look Pricilla, you know this job can get me killed . . ."

"I know. I am just being silly. Still they were after you. Don't you see they want you dead?" Pricilla said.

Beary nodded, "Yes."

Pricilla fell into his arms. "You know it's the hormones. They must be boys. I didn't have this type of mood swings with Erin."

"Well, not as bad, but it is alright. I love you and you are devastatingly beautiful." Beary said

"Even with me as big as I am? I really am a star." Pricilla said.

Beary kissed her. "You are still the most beautiful star in the universe. Come on let's try one of those back rubs."

When Beary got done Pompey sighed. "Oh, that felt so good, but what can I do for my husband? Oh, I have an idea. The girls say page forty-three is fun. Oh, I see husband. I have been a terrible wife. This is a technique our mothers tell us about. Well, I am a daughter of the Southern continent, wild and free. You husband will enjoy this gift."

Beary looked at her. "Pompey, what are you doing?"

A while later Pompey looked at Beary. He was smiling in his sleep. She traced the burn mark on his chest. The hair was already growing in thicker and more metallic. Page forty-three had been fun. Especially for Beary, she smiled.

She could feel the twins moving around. *Yes, death was stalking them. It had been for a long time. Then she thought no, not death, pure evil. She didn't need to fear death. Evil was after her family. Evil could be destroyed. Had not the Guardian proven that already? Evil hide from the light. Was she not The Star? Then she would burn bright and shine. So her light left nowhere for evil to hide from the Guardian.* With that thought Pompey fell asleep.

Star Firerena appeared and kissed Pompey's head. "Fear no more my love. I will protect you and him."

Drop Wing appeared next to her. "You are too attached to them Star."

"Constance agrees with me. I need to help them." Star Firerena said.

"I do not disagree, but what if he isn't the one?" Drop Wing said.

"I care not about that! He is my love as is she." Star Firerena said.

"Love the most powerful force in the universe." Drop Wing said as he faded out.

"Yes, it is!" Star Firerena said.

The next morning Aleut called Beary. Pompey answered "Good morning Aleut"

"Pompey, I see you are bringing great honor to your husband!" Aleut said.

"Twins Sire, Maryam insists they are males." Pompey said.

"Do they kick strong?" Aleut asked.

"Yes, Aleut, I think they also wrestle." Pompey said "I will call Beary."

Beary looked at him. "Was your hunt successful Sire?"

Aleut nodded. "Yes, Beary, it was a very successful hunt."

Beary bowed, "Thank you Aleut. The Clan Maxumus is indebted to you."

"No Beary. He was my enemy. But, your words bring honor to your mother. I look forward to you joining us for a feast to celebrate Kat and Paulette and of course their husbands. He said with a wink."

Beary asked. "Perhaps Erin can go fishing with you?"

Aleuts chest swelled. "I would be honored."

With that he broke the connection. It wouldn't be good for Beary to see the tears of joy.

Kat looked at the com unit. "Yes, Ensign Reuben?"

"Sorry Kat, but you have an incoming call from a Star Glow Katimai. She said that she was once your mother."

Kat woke Ben up, told him what was happening.

Ben said. "Put it through Hannah, please."

A very haggard female came on the screen. She lowered her head. "Please Sire; do not be angry with my daughter."

Ben asked. "Why would I be angry with my Kat?"

Kat popped up behind him. "Good morning. I am not dressed. We were playing."

Kat's mother looked at her. "You were what?"

Kat smiled, "I was seducing my husband, taking pleasure in his delicious body."

Star Glow Katimai looked faint. "Please sire, do not beat her."

Ben looked at her. "My Lady, I am a Warrior of the Red Paw as is my wife; I would not dare to dishonor my clan by doing such a thing."

Star Glow looked stunned. "I need to tell you, Alakanuk is dead."

Kat looked at her. "Are you alright?"

"He left instructions that I was to be set out if he died along with any of his daughters that were unmarried. I understand Lady Maritinus that it is not your concern. However, I thought you should know he will no longer torment you." Star Glow said.

"That cull dishonored you even in death?" Ben stood up.

Kat's mom stared, and then turned away. Ben grabbed a robe.

"Forgive me my Lady." Ben said embarrassed.

"No child, but I understand Kat's meaning." Star Glow said.

Kat beamed with pride, "He is all mine!"

"Star Glow, you are to call a Sir Gamey on Andreas Prime. We have land there. I also have a small hunting lodge in Port Aleut. You may make it your home. Sir Gamey will arrange transport for you and your unmarried daughters. If you need any credits he will arrange for your needs." Ben said.

"Why would you do this?" Star Glow asked.

"Do you love my Kat?" Ben asked.

"I have always loved my daughter Sire." Star Glow said.

"Then I ask only one thing and you may refuse. Your late husband's name is distasteful to me. Would you change your last name?" Ben asked.

Star Glow bowed. "I and my three unmarried daughters will be Newdawn."

"Tell your new names to Sir Gamey and he will have new travel documents made for you. I claim you Star Glow as my mother–in- law and your daughters as sisters. You are now under protection of The Red Paw and the Caesar/Maxumus clans as my family." Ben said.

Star Glow bowed even lower. "Sire, how can I repay you?"

Ben told her. "You gave me Kat."

She hung up and called her three daughters. All four then cried. They were free. But, they were also scared. What kind of bear had Kat married? No one could be that kind.

Ben called Gamey who smiled. "You know you and Kat, well Kat, has a small castle. Her mother and sisters could make a nice staff."

Kat looked at him, "Castle?"

Gamey replied. "Yes, you and Paulette each have a small hundred room castle in the woods north of the Maxumus Castle. There both in two joining valleys called Golden Woods. They are actually in the Augustine lands. But, they are deeded to you and Paulette. About thousand hectares each, good mount country; a couple of old mines also, plus lumber if you do it properly."

"Gamey, that can't be possible?" Kat said.

"Oh, I almost forgot you have thirty dragons, which are part of the house of each castle. They are anxious to serve their ladies.

Oh, and a treasure of what did Beany say. Sixty five million credits, we are investing some of it. I did need to spend five million each to fix the castles up, especially the plumbing." Gamey said.

Kat sat down. "Thank you, Sire Gamey."

"Well, I and Mrs. Morrow will take care of your mom and sisters." Gamey said then signed off.

Ben laughed. "Well, I married a female of means."

Kat sat down, "Small castle?"

She called Paulette and explained what Sir Gamey said.

"Mommy, you must be dreaming. What do you mean a small Castle? . . . Only hundred rooms? What do these bears consider large?" Paulette asked.

Kat shook her head "Daddy says Beary's is around six hundred rooms they think. There might be a few they haven't found yet."

Gabriel just shook his head.

Paulette mouth fell open. "No, I don't mind that they invested some of it for us. You sure you heard right. I guess we could pay Beary back. No, he probably wouldn't take it."

Gabriel looked at her.

She mouthed. "I have sixty five million credits."

Gabriel just fell back on the bed.

Gabriel looked at her. "I guess it will make a nice vacation home."

Paulette told him. "If they try and take us away from Beary. Kat and I will resign from the fleet."

Gabriel looked at her. "So, you plan to stay on his wing."

"Till death," Paulette said "it is our destiny."

Gabriel kissed her. "Then I stay with dad till they put me in the ground."

"Ben, I need to call father. I would like to do it alone." Kat said.

"Alright Kat, I'll go check on some things." Ben said.

Kat called Aleut, "Greetings Father."

Aleut looked at her. "Daughter I . . ."

"I just called to thank you, father for protecting us. I know you destroyed that dishonorable cull." Kat said.

Aleut dropped his head. "I was concerned daughter that you would be angry."

"Oh no, father, I knew it was him that had ordered Ben's and my death. I didn't want to believe it, but I knew it. I also knew that Pompey was looking into the attacks. If you hadn't killed him, Beary would have had it done." Kat said.

Aleut sighed. "He offered, but I told him it was my responsibility, my daughter. I want you to know it was a fair fight. He pulled a weapon and truly died by his own paw."

She dropped her head. "He was a coward even at the end. Father he disowned and disinherited my mother and three of my sisters at his death. He left them with nothing. Ben has claimed them. I have a home for them. And the means to care for them . . ."

Aleut asked "What new name did Ben have them take?"

"My mother's name was Star Glow Newdawn before she married. She has reclaimed the name Newdawn for her and my sisters." Kat said.

Aleut nodded. "Then my daughter they will be entered in the family book. Your mother will be my sister. Your sisters my daughters, if your mother allows."

Kat looked at him. "Oh, Father, now I know how Ben has become the bear he is. He has learned to love, from the greatest chief of all Polarians."

"Thank you daughter, but no, I am still learning from he, who I cannot even approach, the true Father of all, our Creator, and His Word." Aleut said.

Kat told him. "I love you Aleut Maritinus. I will bring you honor I swear."

Aleut nodded. "You daughter, already have. I love you." With that he signed off.

Lunara looked at him. "Come and lay in my arms and hide your tears. Though tears of joy should not bring dishonor to a warrior."

Aleut looked at her. "Or love."

After several more months the survey of Pratis V was complete and they moved to Pratis IV and III.

Both Jeanne and Pompey were getting close to their delivery date.

For the Marines and pilots life had got almost monotonous. Ben had decided to pick up the pace of the training. He also set teams on working on fixing some of the inadequacies of their equipment.

Kat and Paulette both woke up one morning went in and ate breakfast. Then they went in and threw up. They both dragged into sick bay and looked at each other.

Kat looked at Paulette, "Oh no, Paulette, not you too."

Paulette looked at her. "It must be the flu. I hope Gabriel and Ben don't get it?"

Caesar looked at them. "Why don't you both come in? I'll do you both. Renee, can you help me?"

Nurse Apell answered, "Alright Doctor Vantanus."

Apell led them into a room with two exam tables and had them put on a gown. "Alright Ensigns let me take your vitals." She made several notes.

"He will want a blood draw also to see if we have elevated white blood cells."

Caesar came in and examined them. "Ok, get dressed. I'll see you in my office in a few moments." He walked out, smiled, and looked at the blood test and shook his head.

Then he saw Jessica walk in. Nikolaos looked worried. "She threw up after she ate."

Caesar looked at Dr. Golden. "Dr. Golden, could you please see to my wife. I think we have an epidemic."

Jessica looked at him. She noticed he was smiling. "Caesar, you don't think . . ."

He turned and shrugged with a smile. "Renee, call Captain Maritinus and 2Lt Archangel for me. Tell them I need them here now. Just in case, Dr. Golden needs to talk to me about Jess."

Renee Apell nodded and made the calls.

Ben, Gabriel, Kat, and Paulette sat nervously in Caesar's office.

Caesar came in. "I am sorry. Dr. Golden needed to see me about Jessica. It seems we have an epidemic. Kat you are to blame."

Kat looked at him. "But, I always follow proper procedures!"

Caesar laughed. "I think page twenty-five is the culprit, but it could be others."

Ben looked at him. "Caesar, Kat is with . . ."

"Yes Ben, you are going to be a Father and Grandfather at about the same time." Caesar said.

Ben let out a war hoop. Gabriel fainted. Kat and Paulette hugged each other.

Then Ben looked at Caesar, "Jessica also!"

Caesar smiled. "Yah, she couldn't decide whether she was going to cry or laugh. Nikolaos was all smiles."

Then Caesar got serious. "Young ladies, you can continue to fly for a few more months, and then you are grounded. Also, you will follow Dr. Golden's directions or you will wish you had."

Both of them looked at Caesar. "Yes Caesar."

That night the family held a dinner. Beary toasted all three couples.

The talk and the food were lively. The Artemus children said that they would be happy to train the new arrivals when the time came.

Snow Flower looked at Artemus. She had been afraid to give him another cub, not that she had prevented it. But she also had not been as attentive as she could be either. Not that he seemed to notice.

Pompey was very uncomfortable. She finally asked to be excused and went to lie down. Beary followed soon after.

Slowly everyone left for their own rooms.

Artemus was getting ready for bed when Snow Flower knelt in front of him. She wrapped her arms around his knees. "Am I losing you?" she asked.

Savato looked at her. "Snow Flower, what are you talking about?"

She looked up at him. "It is a simple question. Do you still love me Savato? Does your heart still burn for me?"

He picked her up. "How can you ask that question? Do you not know you consume and own my heart?"

Snow Flower turned from him. "Then, why have you not asked me to give you another cub?"

Savato looked at her and turned her towards him. "I am afraid. I almost lost you and Agathag the last time. Also, I do not know what effect these changes will have. I am not the bear you married. I could not stand to lose you."

Snow Flower fell into his arms and wept. Then she looked into his eyes. "Savato give me another cub. I am selfish, five children are not enough. We have three daughter and only two sons. I want an even number of each."

Savato looked at her. "But, what if we have another girl?"

Snow Flower cooed. "Then you will just have to keep trying till you get it right. I think you should get started."

Captain Gracchus looked at Jeanne. "Are you alright?"

"Argus, I just feel . . . oh my . . . Argus!" Jeanne exclaimed below her was a large puddle of water. "I think my water broke!"

Argus looked at her "DON'T PANIC!" He hit a com unit "MEDIC TO CAPTAIN'S QUARTERS NOW!" Just set down Jeanne."

A medic team and Nurse Apell arrived. She sized up the situation. "It is alright Captain. It is just time for us to take her to delivery. You should come also.

Commander, if I remember right this is your first cub?"

"Yes Captain Apell it is." Jeanne said.

"Well, no problem. We will let Dr. Golden have a look." Apell checked her and the cubs vitals "Good the cub is in no distress and you are doing fine.

Ok, Corp bears let's go. Captain, I'll have someone come and clean this up for you."

Pompey was so uncomfortable. She tried to adjust again. Then all of a sudden she felt the bed and her night gown become very wet.

Beary woke up. "Pricilla, I think your water broke."

"Beary . . . Oh, no . . . not the new sheets!" She wailed.

"They will wash. Let's get you to medical." He got up and handed her a clean night gown.

Then Beary walked to the girls' room. "Sho-Sho and Maryam" he whispered. Both woke up and looked at him. "Pricilla is going into labor. I am taking her to medical. It could be a while. I'll call when the time gets closer."

Sho-Sho nodded as did Maryam.

Beary then helped Pompey on with her robe. "Do you want me to get you a wheelchair?"

Pompey looked at him. "My Grandmother gave birth while watching her flock. I think I can walk to medical."

When they arrived Nurse Blaze saw her. "Oh my, two in one night! Commander Gracchus is in delivery room one. We will put you in delivery room two."

Caesar came through the door, "Not you too!"

Pricilla asked. "Is it a full moon?"

Caesar shrugged. "We are in orbit around a planet with three moons take your pick."

Beary said. "You go with Nurse Blaze. I know the drill."

Beary followed Caesar to get washed up and put on a gown. Captain Gracchus was just setting there half dressed.

"Captain, Beary will help you. He is an old hand at this. Dr. Golden wants to see me." Caesar said.

Dr. Golden was talking to Jeanne. "I want Caesar opinion, but you are not a young female Commander."

Caesar looked at him. "You want to do a cesarean section?"

Dr. Golden nodded. "It would, I believe, be safer for the cub and her, in this case."

"Commander, it will not affect your ability to have more cubs. However, they will more than likely need to be delivered by cesarean also." Caesar explained. "Also, we will use a local, as with any surgery there are risks. They may not be as great as going through natural birth for you."

Jeanne looked at the two doctors. "Just do what is best for my cub."

Caesar nodded and went to prep the operating room. "Renee, we are doing a C-section in operating room one. Set it up. I'll talk to the good Captain."

Caesar explained the situation to Captain Gracchus. He told him he could be in the room as long as he behaved himself. Gracchus agreed and went to join his wife.

Beary slipped into the delivery room and held Pompey's paw.

Doctor Golden and Caesar gave Jeanne a local. Then he made a small incision. Doctor Golden worked quickly. Soon a brown furry cub was brought into the world with an ear shattering cry.

Nurse Apell took her over to a small tub shaped table and weighed the cub. "Well Captain, come over and help me clean up your new daughter."

Gracchus tentatively walked over. He looked at the small girl cub. "She is so small."

"Small, she was almost twelve SWUs and twenty-seven SubSMU long. She is a healthy young lady." Nurse Apell said. She finished cleaning her up.

Dr. Golden walked over and gave her the once over. He kissed her and wrapped her in a diaper, a pink blanket, and handed her to Captain Gracchus. "Take her over to your wife so she may eat her first meal. Caesar is done closing her up. I have blessed the surgery."

Jeanne looked at her daughter and showed her where to attach. The little cub started suckling immediately. "What will we name your daughter, Argus?"

Argus sat down. "I don't know Jeanne. I don't understand the grace that has given her to us."

Jeanne looked at him. "Then that shall be her name Grace Hope Gracchus."

Doctor Golden filled out the birth certificate and smiled.

Renee came out and made a ship wide announcement. That Grace Hope Gracchus was the newest member of the *EAQ*.

Dragon song broke out. A stone cradle was delivered to the Captains quarters. It was lined in very soft dear hide. A relief of a dragon and the *EAQ* was engraved into the stone.

Pompey smiled as the first real contraction hit. She squeezed Beary's paw and breathed through it.

Nurse Apell came in and checked in on her. "You still have a ways to go you are only dilated about half way lady Maxumus."

"Pompey, Nurse Apell, I think we can drop the formalities. I really am just a shepherd's daughter."

When morning came, Sho-Sho and Maryam brought Erin to see her mother.

"Brothers, have not come out yet?" Erin asked.

Pompey smiled as another contraction hit. "Not yet, but they are getting anxious. Oh, Beary that one really hurt."

Caesar checked the monitors. "You're doing fine. No sign of distress the cubs are just lining up. It shouldn't be much longer."

Dr. Golden placed his talon on her stomach. "There that should help my lady. It will ease the pain a little."

The next contraction was strong but not as painful. Pompey smiled. "Thank you, Doctor Golden."

Maryam came over and kissed Pompey. "My Lady, I will take Erin out and we will wait with the rest of the family."

Beary nodded. "Thank you, Lady Maryam."

Sho-Sho smiled. "I love you both."

Pompey replied. "We love you Sho-Sho."

Sergeant Red Wing and two other dragons were pacing the halls when Sho-Sho walked out. "Princess, may we sing for our lady?"

Sho-Sho smiled. "Keep it soft, but I believe she would like that."

Soon the trio broke out in soft dragon song. The soothing melody floated through medical.

Pompey relaxed. "It is just like with Erin. The music is so wonderful."

On Andreas Prime, Widja was worried. She had known she had been carrying an egg. Still, it had been hard, to lay. It was larger than normal. Tonight it acted as if it would hatch.

She called Gamey. He had come home. Soon the egg stared to crack two heads broke through the shell. Then two small dragons emerged one Purple, one Emerald Green.

Gamey looked at Widja, "Twin dragons?"

Star Firerena appeared behind them. "For the Twin Hammers of Corson, Beary's sons will be born tonight. These will be their companions. Oh, the little purple is a girl and the emerald green a boy. Congratulations, Sir Gamey, and my dear Widja." With that she left.

"Busy body," Gamey grumbled then smiled. "What do we name them?"

Widja thought. "Let's call the little girl Roseanna."

Gamey whispered. "She will end up being called Rosie. I like that also."

Widja feed them some deer. "What of our new son?"

"What about the name, Shamus?" Gamey asked.

"They will probably call him Shay." Widja said.

On the *EAQ* Pompey was finally starting to deliver the first of her cubs. The first male cub came out into the world. Caesar handed him to Nurse Apell. She then, took him over to clean up.

She no sooner gave birth to the first than the second cub started to come. Caesar eased him out and handed him to Nurse Blaze. He then cleared the afterbirth and fixed a small tear.

Dr. Golden checked Pompey over. Then he went to check over the two cubs.

He blinked as he checked them over. Tears weld in his eyes. "Sire, your cubs are perfect." He then diapered them and wrapped them in blue blankets. Then he brought them over to Pompey. She showed them where to attach and they took their first meal.

Pompey looked at her two sons. Even though they were identical twins, she could already tell them apart. "Beary, I made a promise before we were wed. I would like to keep it."

Beary nodded.

"Caesar, would you announce the births of Caesar Ben Maxumus and Savato Horatio Maxumus." Pompey said.

Caesar bowed. "It would be my honor, my Princess."

Pompey scolded, "None of that."

Caesar replied, "You cannot deign a Knight his devotion for his Lady."

Beary nodded. "He is correct, My Lady."

Caesar went out and smiled. "I am to announce the birth of Prince Caesar Ben Maxumus and Prince Savato Horatio Maxumus.

Ben smiled and slapped both Savato and Caesar on the back. "Pompey has honored us greatly!"

"You don't mind having only the middle name?" Caesar asked.

"No, besides is not Benjamin a family name. She shortened it to honor me." Ben said.

Beary called Gamey. "Gamey, Pompey just gave birth to two male cubs, Caesar Ben and Savato Horatio."

"That is good. When you return, I will present my new twins to them as companions, Roseanna and Shamus." Gamey said.

Beary smiled. "Congratulations Brother!"

"Thank you." Gamey said with pride. "You should call your mother."

"I'll do that next." Beary promised.

Beary called the Caesar/Maxumus castle. Mrs. Maro answered. "Hello Beary, She is in with an Ambassador from the Gorn Federation. I think she wouldn't mind the interruption."

"Thanks Bec." Beary said.

Angelina smiled. "I hope this is good news."

"Pompey had the twins, two male cubs, Caesar Ben and Savato Horatio." Beary said.

"Oh, how wonderful, I'll let your father know. He is on Bearilia Prime at the moment. Give all my loves a kiss." Angelina said.

"I will mother. We love you." Beary said.

The Gorn Ambassador smiled. "*The Son of She Who Kills in Silence* seems to have grown into a great bear."

"Oh, he has, the Arcrilians called him the Ghost." Angelina said.

The Gorn smiled. "I see he takes after the mother as much as the father."

"Yes, old friend, but he does not know of our past." Angelina said.

He sighed. "Ti's a shame, but no one would believe the stories anyway."

Ben called his father. "Hail Aleut it is I your son."

Aleut smiled, when he saw Kat, Paulette, and Gabriel. "Have you brought honor to your family?"

"Beary's sons have been born. They are Caesar Ben and Savato Horatio." Ben said.

Aleut smiled. "Good names. Our clan is twice honored."

Ben then got a bigger smile. "Your daughter and granddaughter also have brought honor to you."

Aleut grinned. "Kat and Paulette are you by chance with cubs?"

"Yes, Father." Kat said.

"Lunara, Kat, and Paulette are with cubs!" Aleut bellowed with joy.

Lunara came in. "My children how wonderful! I will have another grandchild and a great grandchild, at the same time! I will be the envy of all the ladies of the village. I know Ben, it is wrong, but it pleases me."

Kat told her. "I am happy we can please you mother."

Paulette smiled. "We love you both."

Lunara swelled. "We love you child."

Aleut thumped his chest. "Hunt well children." He turned off the com unit.

Lunara looked at him. "Tears Aleut?!"

"Yes Lunara, my joy is so over whelming I cannot stem them." Aleut said.

Lunara wrapped her arms around him "Then it is honorable tears my husband."

CHAPTER 11

Immigrants and a New Start

GRACCHUS LOOKED AT the message. Fifty transports were coming filled with families. They were coming to reestablish the colony on Pratis V. He shook his head. "Don't they know there is no infrastructure down there. Most of the buildings need to be torn down.

We are looking at almost one hundred thousand bears. How do they purpose to take care of that size of a population?"

Jeanne was feeding Grace, "I am sure fleet has thought it through."

Argus looked at her. "Grace has mellowed you out."

"No, but it won't do any good getting upset about something we can't do anything about. It isn't our job. We just need to finish our survey and move on to the next system.

Isn't that right Gracie? Oh, look isn't she so pretty?" Jeanne said.

Argus looked at his wife and daughter. "Ya, my girls are beautiful."

Pompey smiled, at the double stone cradle. Then she kissed the two dragons that delivered it. "Thank you, it is wonderful."

The two dragons almost turned pink. "My Lady, it is a small thing. We just wanted to give the young Princes something to sleep in."

Pompey beamed. "It is a grand gift. I am truly touched by all of your kindness."

They beamed and backed out they were floating down the hall as they left.

Beary shook his head, "You are a witch. They were ready to swear a bond to you."

Pompey smiled. "All I did was thank them for this wonderful gift."

A small transport arrived. First, a dignified older bear requested to meet with Captain Gracchus.

When he arrived he was shown to Captain Gracchus office.

"Captain, I am Jeremy Tailorson. I was the Governor of Pratis V. I have been appointed by our bears to lead the rebuilding of our planet."

Gracchus looked at him. "Sir, while the planet has healed. There is no infrastructure. All of the buildings need to be raised."

"Yes Captain, we read the report. We have equipment coming in to do that. We will recycle the building materials, so we do not have to waste anything." Governor Tailorson said.

Gracchus nodded. "Still Sir, I am concerned that one hundred thousand bears . . ."

"Yes, I understand, but we will be splitting that up into work teams, throughout the planet. We are also bringing supplies to sustain us." The Governor said.

"Now to more pleasant topics, I understand that one of the Marines, that pulled Captain Maritinus and his Marines off of Pratis V, is a member of your crew." The Governor said.

Gracchus nodded. "Lieutenant Maxumus is the CAG. Major Maritinus' younger brother, Captain Ben Maritinus is the Commander of our MSD unit."

The Governor grinned. "Is he anything like his brother?"

Gracchus answered. "I wasn't there, but it is said he killed over one hundred Arcrilians on Dryden, all by himself. He helped rescue the stranded Marines. Maxumus lead that rescue also."

"Could you call both of them for me and have them, join us?" Governor Tailorson asked.

Beary and Ben both reported to Captain Gracchus' office.

Gracchus smiled. "Governor Tailorson, this is Lieutenant Beary Maxumus and Captain Ben Maritinus."

Tailorson looked at them they were so young; "I just wanted to thank you on behalf of the Pratis V population. These medals were designed by a famous artist known as *The Rose*."

Beary replied. "Thank you, Sire, they are beautiful."

The Governor beamed. "No, it was your actions that have allowed us to return home. It is we who are grateful."

They talked a few moments then Ben and Beary left.

Ben looked at Beary. "You know this Rose?"

"Yes, Annabelle Rosa, she is my Aunt or Cousin . . . Anyway she is family Ben. I am still confused how it all lines up." Beary said.

A few more weeks past the work on Pratis V continued. The old cities were slowly being torn down. As one area was cleared construction on new shelters were started.

A few pioneers had started new farms and ranches in the lush grass lands.

It would take decades, but Pratis V would thrive again.

The survey work on Pratis III and IV were completed. Both planets were in about the same condition as Pratis V.

Teams from their populations were being put together to try and recover their planets.

For the crew of the *EAQ* excitement was starting to build as they looked towards their next system.

"Red Talon Control this is Blue Dragon Control we will be arriving. Commodore Atilus sends his complements to Captain Gracchus."

"Blue Dragon Control, please authenticate, BBV."

"Red Talon, we authenticate HHJ."

"Blue Dragon, welcome to the Pratis system you and all your friends, Red Talon out."

Captain Centaures looked at Grizlarge. "How do you think the Cub is going to take the news?"

Grizlarge looked at him. "Captain, they get to go home for what a year, maybe two. They get to build a new warship. Plus they get to stay together. Gracchus might not want the job."

Atilus looked at them. "No, he will take it. Jeanne gets her command. They stay together. Besides they know what is going on, we don't."

Gracchus looked at the large transport that was with the *Saber Claw.*

"Beary, you, Artemus, and Ben better come to my office. I think trouble is coming." Gracchus said.

Beary looked at Artemus and called Ben. Then they headed up.

When they got there they looked at the Captain. "What is going on?"

Jeanne looked at them. "Argus thinks trouble. I think he might be right. Atilus is coming over."

A cycle later Atilus arrived with Centaures and Grizlarge in tow. "Well Gracchus, it is a heck of a ship the Cub built for you. *Eleven* and *Twelve* have launched. *Thirteen* and *Fourteen* are being built."

"So, Commodore, why are you here?" Jeanne asked.

"Well, my Goddaughter did just give birth to twins. The Master Chief was begging to see the one named for him." Atilus said "Also, I was asked to deliver these orders and a new military crew for the *EAQ*."

"What!?" Everyone asked at the same time.

"It is simple the military crew, the intelligence crew, and Maxumus family members are being reassigned to new construction. That includes Doctor Vallen and most of the medical crew. Except a Doctor Hendrix, he has been requested by the new chief medical officer. Also Doctor Janise Cooper is now military. She will be going with you." Atilus said.

Beary looked at him. "Commodore, I know for a fact Janise isn't military."

Atilus smiled. "She signed a reserve commitment, which she never served. She just got called up."

Beary looked at him. "What about my air crews?"

Atilus looked at him. "I thought I made that clear. You are being transferred as a unit. Your Valkyrie III will be staying for the new air unit as will your purples. Your two Green Daggers go with you. The new air unit brought their own. So did the new MSD unit. Also Caesars Command White goes. The new Chief Surgeon has one also. Clean off the nose art on your crafts."

Beary looked at Atilus. "Why are we being replaced Sir?"

"You know more than I do Son. All I know is promotions are being given. Oh, that reminds me. Argus you are now a Commodore. Jeanne you are the Captain of this new warship. You will have to find a First.

Beary you and Artemus are now Lt. Commanders as is Caesar. Ben you just made Major. Your MSD unit is being rolled into a new command. You will be working with a Major George Ironpaw and MSD 567. The Commander is a Lt. Colonel Lance Maverick. He is a so in so, Ben. He is tough as nails. But he has a good record. He has been at Marine Headquarters for two years."

Ben replied. "It will be good to have someone to answer to other than a Five Star General."

"Anyway," Atilus continued, "here is the promotion list. You leave in two days right after the transfer. Oh, you're going back to Andreas Prime. You need a secluded place for the Marines to train and set up a headquarters"

Ben asked, "Is fleet paying?"

Atilus nodded.

"My wife and daughter have the perfect location. I think arrangements can be made to bivouac the Marine units." Ben said.

Beary nodded. "Arrangements will be made for all of our current crews, Commodore Atilus."

"Well now. I want to see my Goddaughter, Erin, and the new little ones." Atilus said.

Gracchus gave Beary a look, "Artemus could you, and Ben, escort them down. I'll catch up."

Artemus nodded and led them off, with Ben following.

Gracchus looked at him. "What by *The Moons of Bantine* is going on?"

Beary shrugged. "I am as blindsided as you are Commodore. You and the Captain will of course stay at the House of Maxumus."

"Thank you Beary, but only because we will be working there on the new ship. Atilus told us nothing and everything. I don't like it."

"Neither, do I Sir. I need to tell my maintenance bears to get to work." Beary said.

Atilus fawned over Erin and the two boy cubs. So did Grizlarge and Centaures.

Sho-Sho was troubled. She was glad to be going home. Still she felt trouble was going to follow them. She also couldn't shake the guilt she felt, at the death of Admiral Astrid. Ice Song had pointed out he had died honorably. This was better than he deserved. Yet, it still bothered her.

The *Change of Command* went well, except, for the tension that existed, between, Captain Apell and the new Chief Surgeon. They exchanged a few words. Then Nurse Apell picked up her bags and left for the shuttle.

Caesar joined her. "You alright Renee?"

"Yes Caesar. Those were the kindest words we have exchanged in ten years. The old goat must be getting soft. Still, Dad is a great doctor. He told me you were lucky to have me. I told him, you darn well knew it too." Renee said.

Caesar nodded. "Darn straight, no one would have taken my head nurse."

Jessica joined them. "I would have to kill them. I would never have gotten pregnant, if you hadn't made him come home at night."

Renee Apell laughed.

Kat looked at the crew from the transport. "Gentlebears, I am a trained fighter pilot. I have killed several enemies. Some up close and personal. If you put one scratch on any of my furniture, I will personally cut off your hides."

The older of them looked into her eyes, "She means it and I think she could do it. We will be very careful Ensign."

One was wrapping her picture. He looked at it. Then he looked at her.

Kat replied. "Yes, my husband is a lucky boar. He gets to do more than look at the painting. Sometimes four or five times a day."

With that she walked out the door.

The older one shook his head. "Don't even think about it. Any boar that can handle that could kill all of you without breaking a sweat."

Janise Cooper was livid, as they helped her on to the shuttle. "I am not military!"

Caesar looked at her. "Janise according to this you are Lieutenant Janise Cooper BAF Medical Corp Res. You work for me. Whether, you like it or not doctor."

Janise looked at Caesar. "Well, as long as I am working for you. But don't expect me to put up with all that military crap."

Caesar shook his head. "Janise you signed the papers."

She dropped her head. "You get drunk one time with a good looking boar. Does he take advantage of me no . . . he has me sign that blasted piece of paper."

Renee laughed.

Beary called Admiral Starpaw. "Sir, can you tell us what is going on."

"Sorry son, not at this time. Everyone gets one month of leave when you get to Andreas Prime. Then you get to work. Ruben and Teddy work for you. The ship is a new concept. We need you, Doctor Vallen, and your team to make it work. We need new fighters, and daggers, the works, son. You know what were up against better than anyone. Someone was selling our secrets to the Reptilians. We don't know what else has been compromised. Build something new and outside the box." Starpaw said.

"Yes Sir." Beary said.

Gracchus looked at Beary. "Well, what did you find out?"

Beary shrugged. "We get a month of leave. Then we get to work. The rest Atilus told us, you?"

"Fleet was really shaken by what happened to Task Force 5. No one wants to blame Astrid. Plus the problems with Darius V and the fact that classified information got lost going through there. The Base Commander and a few others already were forced to retire. A few enlisted are facing Dragons Breath. They were found with locator tags.

They pulled us because we are still alive. They think we know something no one else does." Argus said.

Beary dropped his head. "We do. We are the targets."

Argus looked at him. "That is the one thing we don't tell Fleet. Besides Golden Dragon 1 and your Mom are on the hit parade also."

"I am sorry Sir. I seem to have dragged your family into this." Beary said.

"Beary, let's just say Jeanne and I are in. We wouldn't have it any other way." Argus said.

Gamey was busy preparing for guess. Mrs. Morrow shook her head. "I can't believe Ben got fleet to pay them for leasing the land up there."

Gamey asked. "How is Kat's mom and sisters doing?"

"They are frantic. The dragon staff is helping. Still she wants to please Kat.

The oldest of the three went to Paulette's to run that Castle. The mom was driving her crazy. The dragons like her.

I have hired additional family staff and a couple Polarians to work for them as security." Mrs. Morrow said.

"Shari, don't spread yourself to thin." Gamey said.

"Don't worry you over grown lizard. I have it under control. Besides my babies are coming home including Sho-Sho." Mrs. Morrow said.

"Gisfrid is anxious and nervous. Ice Song has him beside himself." Gamey laughed.

"What about our Sho-Sho?" Mrs. Morrow asked.

"You saw her picture. She is breath taking but she is guarding her heart. Beary and I would have been like our children, if we could have been together when we were young." Gamey said.

Mrs. Morrow laughed. "You two would have been a paw full."

After about three months the Military Transport *Long Train* went into orbit around Andreas Prime.

CHAPTER 12

A Quiet Home Coming

THE SHUTTLES LANDED at a nearly deserted landing field. Transports with covers over them met the Marines. General Flame heart greeted Beary. "Welcome home my prince. Sergeant Marcus is waiting for you and your family. Transports are also available for the other families."

Beary said. "Sir, Ben was going to ask if the Dragoon Detachment could be assigned to his unit."

Flame Heart responded. "If Sire Maritinus and the Valkyrie wish them to join them, then by all means they are part of the *Red Paw Dragons*."

Beary replied. "Thank you, Sir."

"My Prince, here you are my Commander." Flame Heart said

Beary turned to Master Sergeant Red Wing. "Master Chief, you, and your team are now *Red Paw Dragons* report to Major Maritinus."

Red Wing saluted, "You heard the Prince. Dragoons report to the Major we belong to him, Lady Kat, and Paulette."

Ben just smiled and waved. Kat jumped into a truck next to a driver. "Ok, Sergeant we are full. Take me to my castle. I am looking forward to seeing it."

Paulette grabbed another with First Platoon and Gunny Nighthunter. "Ok, driver let's go see my new home. Gabriel will follow with the rest of First Platoon."

Ben smiled, as he grabbed a transport for the headquarters group. First and Third were going to Paulette's Castle. Second and Forth Platoons were going to Kat's, with the headquarters group.

It took almost two and a half cycles to reach the *Golden Woods*. Then they turned up a Green Valley. The driver looked at Kat "This is *Dragons' Love Glen* my lady. It is your land. Your daughter's land is *Dragons' Grace Glen*."

Kat looked at the lush green pastures. Then they turned a bend. On the hill side was a watch tower with two walls angling from it. Behind it was a keep, with two wings that seemed to be built into the living rock.

"Welcome home Lady Maritinus." The driver said.

Blackpaw just stared. "It is a fine home my lady."

Kat jumped out and looked around. She saw a chapel off to one side. Then she saw a few other buildings. Then standing in the door of the watch tower was a large blue green dragon and her mother. Kat walked forward.

The dragon bowed. "Lady Valkyrie, I am Augustinus the Wrath. I am the *Guardian of your Keep*."

Kat asked. "So, you are the boss dragon here?"

He replied. "Yes my lady and your companion my lady."

Kat looked at him. "That you will have to discuss with my husband, but you are cute."

Augustinus blushed. Then a laugh bellowed behind him.

"I knew I would like our new lady!" A crimson dragon came out. She was stately and beautiful. "Lady Kat, I am Fire Heart his wife. He is a little stiff but he is good where it counts."

Kat glanced at Ben. "Reminds me of a Marine Major I know."

Ben had just got out of the transport to have his wife and a crimson female dragon laugh at him.

Augustinus came over. "Sire, I am Augustinus, I am your wife's companion. That is my wife. I think we are in trouble."

Ben looked at him. "They are peas of a pod. Well, Augustinus they have their good points."

Augustinus looked at his wife. "Yes Ben Maritinus, that is true. We are ready for your Marines, Sire."

"Augustinus, we are family, are we not. Are you not now my wife's brother, by custom?" Ben asked.

"Something like that, yes Sire." Augustine said.

"Then it is just Ben, to family." Ben said.

Then Ben saw her and two of her daughters. "You must be Star Glow. Come mother and introduce yourself and my sisters."

They all three fell at his feet and started to kiss them.

Ben shook his head and lifted them up. "On Andreas Prime, no one kneels to anyone, but the Creator and His Word. Mother here you are family. You are not a slave or a servant. Gamey, hired you to help run our home, because that is what family does here. Kat and I have other duties. You, Augustinus, and his staff will run this home for us. Now, please introduce me to my sisters."

Kat walked over quietly and watched her husband.

Star Glow turned to the first. "This is Ice Shine and this is Flow."

Kat looked at her. "Where is Eloisa?"

Star Glow answered. "She is at the other castle, as its house keeper."

Kat then kissed her mother and sisters. "Flow is a great cook Ben, better than me."

"Well Flow, do you think you can keep my Marines feed?" Ben asked.

Flow bowed. "For you Brother, I will do it right."

Star Glow looked at Kat and whispered. "Is he for real daughter?"

Kat whispered. "He had a good teacher. You are invited to come also to the celebration. Oh, by the way Paulette and I are with cub."

Augustinus let out a howl, "My lady what great news!"

Fire Heart told him. "You better get busy mister he or she will need a dragon."

Augustinus looked at Ben. "I am the Wrath. I strike terror in my enemies. If, I have any energy after she is done with me."

Ben sighed. "Tell me about it. Pregnancy hasn't slowed her down."

Meanwhile Paulette was enjoying the ride and the scenery. The driver turned down a valley. "My Lady this is *Dragon's Grace Glen* your home."

Paulette looked out the window. "This is my land?"

The driver nodded "Yes, my lady."

He turned a bend up on the hill were two watch towers connected by a wall with buildings out front. Behind the wall was a keep that seemed built into the face of the hill.

"My lady welcome to your home." The Driver said.

Nighthunter said. "Nice house my lady."

Paulette sighed "This is a small castle?"

Nighthunter nodded. "The House of Maxumus is much bigger."

"The Caesar/Maxumus Castle is bigger still." The driver said.

Paulette got out and ran up to the door. Two young dragons met her.

"My lady, I am Brigonos the Lancer. This is my wife Bright Sky." The Silver Dragon said.

"It is a pleasure to serve you my lady." The light blue dragon said.

Paulette beamed. "It is my honor to meet you."

Brigonos bowed "My Lady, I am your head dragon. If, it pleases you, your companion, but if you prefer a female, my wife is an excellent warrior."

Paulette looked at them. "Brigonos and Bright Sky I am new at this. Drop Wing came to my mother and me. He said you are now Valkyrie and changed us. I don't know how this works. So, why don't we figure it out together? Besides from what I understand we are brother and sister now, correct or something like that? Anyway we are now family."

Brigonos nodded. "Yes my lady."

Paulette shook her head. "I am the adopted daughter of a bear with an endless capacity for love and a hellion who gives love. Call me Paulette. I am not sure I will ever be a real lady."

Gabriel walked up. "The Senate said you were an officer and a lady."

"Brigonos and Bright Sky, this is Gabriel Archangel my husband and in about four months daddy to my cub."

Bright Sky beamed. "Then we need to get busy so he or she has a companion.

Oh, Eloisa come meet your niece."

Eloisa started to kneel.

"Aunt Eloisa family does not do that here. They hug and kiss." Paulette said.

"I am here to be your house keeper, my lady." Eloisa said.

"Eloisa, I am grateful, especially with a house this big and all these Marines to care for. However, you are not a servant. You're family with an important job. Brigonos and Bright Sky and the other family members also have important jobs. Beary our Prince says, we all serve the family and the family serves us all. Do you understand?"

"No, Paulette, I do not." Eloisa said.

"Well, I am just starting to; maybe we can figure it out together later. I need a nap." Paulette said.

Bright Sky laughed. "Gabriel, go with your wife we will see to your Marines.

Gunny Nighthunter here are your room assignments for First Platoon."

Nighthunter saluted. "Thank you Lady Bright Sky. Ok you maggots let's get you bedded down."

2Lt. Nepos came over. "My lady, where do you want my Platoon?"

"Third Platoon is in the west wing Lieutenant. If your men need anything, they can call the kitchen and food will be served in their rooms tonight." Bright Sky said.

Nepos bowed. "Thank you my lady. Gunny Killinger, let's get it done."

"Third Platoon, you heard the Skipper move!" Killinger barked.

At the Maxumus castle the transports pulled into the gate. Gamey and Widja was waiting for them. So was Gisfrid, who seemed nervous.

Beary got out of the transport. He was swept off the ground as two strong dragon arms enfolded him. "It is so good to have you home Brother." Gamey said.

Beary hugged him too. "I missed you also Gamey."

Gamey sat him down. Then Widja hugged him.

The process was repeated with each member of the family.

Even Commodore and Captain Gracchus were hugged. A staff member was assigned to Grace Hope. They were told that after all she was an honored guest.

Mrs. Morrow kissed Pricilla, then Beary. Then she took Erin to her room. Miss Morrow and another staffer took the boys to the nursery.

Sho-Sho looked at her father and mother. "I am home."

Gamey wrapped his wings around her. "I love you Shoshanna."

Sho-Sho clung to her father. Tears flowed from her eyes.

Gamey held her tighter. "It is alright Sho-Sho. Come and meet your new brother and sister."

Widja looked at Beary. "It was hard for her?"

Beary nodded. "She had to grow up too fast Widja, too much power, too much responsibility. Yet, she handled it very well."

Widja smiled. "Thank you Beary."

Ice Song looked at Gisfrid. "Hello Gisfrid."

Gisfrid smiled nervously, "Ice Song, I had a whole speech, but I can't think of what I wanted to say."

Ice Song dropped her head. "Do you not have anything to say?" She said as a tear fell to the ground.

Gisfrid bathed her in blue flame. Then took her in his arms and kissed her gently but firmly."

Ice Song looked at him as she pulled away. She bathed him in white fire, wrapped her tail around him, and kissed him even harder.

Artemus came over. "Do I need to get a fire hose? Gisfrid what is your intentions towards my daughter."

Ice Song backed away and smiled. "Yes Gisfrid. What are your intentions?"

Gisfrid looked at Artemus, "Sire, I wish to court your daughter."

Artemus looked at him. "You will discuss it with Ballard."

Gisfrid nodded. "I have Sire Artemus. He said he is now second father you are first. I must have your permission."

"Then Gisfrid Maxumus I will discuss it with your parents. To see if they feel you are worthy of my daughter. If they agree then you may properly court her." Artemus said.

Gisfrid bowed. "Yes, Sire. Please know I love Ice Song."

"That is a good start Gisfrid. I know she loves you." Artemus said. "Ice Song go see Ballard then come home, Gisfrid you should accompany her. However, if you are going to kiss do it properly. No little ones till after you are married."

Ice Song dropped her head. "Really, Daddy I am a good girl."

Artemus just raised an eyebrow. "I'll wait up."

Ballard greeted his daughter. He played several of his new songs for her and Gisfrid. He told her he loved his new job. He was very proud of her. Artemus had sent him a copy of the painting of the family. It hung in his parlor. He was so glad that Sir Artemus was so kind to him.

Gisfrid was confused. So he asked, "Ice Song your father Ballard?"

Ice Song explained. "Are ways are different. He dishonored himself. The Prince spared his life and is protecting him. Beary gave him a job. He offered me up as Agathag protector. Then Artemus and I were changed as were you. I adopted Artemus as my father. Ballard became my second father and part of the Artemus family. He is now a brother to my new father.

Savato is my true father now. To be honest since my first mother died. Savato has been the only real father I have had."

Gisfrid kissed her. "Then I will make sure I court you by his rules. So you can be my mate."

Sho-Sho shook her head. "So, you really are going to marry this low life."

Ice Song replied. "It is the only way I get you as a sister."

Sho-Sho nodded. "Well that is true."

Sho-Sho kissed Gisfrid. "Hi big brother."

Gisfrid kissed her. "You see the twins."

"Yes, they are cute." Shoshanna said.

It took a couple of days to get everyone settled in. Most of the air crews were put up in an old hunting lodge that belonged to the Maxumus clan. Gamey had planned to reopen it as a hotel resort. It was located a few KSMU outside *Saint Elaina's*. It had its own secluded beach and fifteen hundred hectares of forest land around it. It had swimming pools, tennis courts, and a fine stable with trained mounts.

When the crews were told they could go on leave, most chose to stay where they were.

Beary, Pompey and clan joined Ben's family for a quick trip to Bearilia Prime. They took a large private transport that the clan owned. Beary looked around. If the families grew much more, they would have to buy a bigger one.

They arrived outside of Ben's village. Aleut came over to meet them. Beary had sixteen casts of Gold Label nectar unloaded plus twenty meat lambs. Caesar added twelve boxes of medical supplies.

Aleut looked at the gifts. "Beary, Caesar such fine gifts are not necessary. They are appreciated." He added with a wink.

Ben and Kat came out. Kat flew into his arms and kissed him. Then she handed him a bracelet of fine gold. "This is from my mine. I helped make it. It isn't very good."

Aleut looked at it and hugged her. "It is wonderful daughter. Look at the honor you bring your husband!"

Kat beamed. "I am carrying the cub well."

Paulette came out next. She kissed Aleut and gave him a wooden box. "This is made from a tree that grows in the woods near my castle. I helped make it."

"Granddaughter it is a fine gift. You also bring honor to your husband and father." Aleut said.

"Thank you, Grandfather." Paulette said.

Erin came out and smiled. "Hello great Aleut."

Aleut smiled. "Welcome to my village Princess Erin."

She squealed then hugged and kissed him "I have baby brothers."

Aleut nodded. "So I have been told. Do you like them?"

"Oh yes, but they mostly eat, cry, and make dirty diapers. Mommy says that is normal at their age." Erin said.

Artemus and family said their hellos as did Sho-Sho.

Kat had to almost drag her mother and three sisters off the transport. Two large warriors gently escorted Star Glow to a place of honor. While three strapping young warriors gently escorted her sisters to the fire pit.

Aleut and Lunara greeted them. "Sister and daughters, welcome to our village. Please make yourselves at home. These warriors are here to serve you."

Lunara summoned a warrior. "Bring our sister and daughters refreshments."

The warrior bowed. "Yes Lunara."

Star Glow looked confused the warrior obeyed Lunara as if her word carried as much weight as did Aleuts.

Aleut explained. "Lunara is Clan Mother. Her word is law as is mine. Only the council can overrule it, as they can me."

Lunara responded. "No clan mother has ever been over ruled. The same cannot be said about a chief."

Aleut retorted. "It has only happened twice in the history of the clan wife."

Lunara took over from here. "Tonight we relax. Tomorrow we start the celebration of the weddings and the coming cubs. We will celebrate the good doctors wedding also and their coming cub. Of course, the birth of the twins must be celebrated also. Oh, ten days I think should do it. We will feast, sing, and dance. When you are tired you may sleep and join in again."

Beary looked at Kat. She seemed to be enjoying the water. "Your mother seemed nervous."

Kat sighed. "This is strange to her. I was strange a strong female. My father hated me because I wouldn't break or give in. She comes here and meets Lunara, a chief in her own right."

Ben kisses her neck. "Clan Mother." He corrects her.

Kat responded "It is the same thing."

"No, she has more power than father does." Ben told her.

Pompey smiled as she washed Beary's back. "My husband seems to enjoy some of your customs Ben."

Beary smiled. "Who doesn't enjoy being pampered?"

Jessica laughed. "I know I do."

Caesar sighed, "We're on vacation. So maybe I can do that a little more."

Snow Flower watched Ghost Wind play with Nikolaos. "She is growing fast and is very jealous of Nikolaos."

Several young Polarian girls came and sat to watch them. Ghost Wind growled in her throat.

"Ghost Wind, do not be impolite." Nikolaos said.

"But Niko, they look at you hungry like." Ghost Wind said pouting.

"Ghost Wind, young male canus will look at you that way also someday. You will not want me to chase them away." Nikolaos said.

"Well, but you are my Niko. What if they try and separate us?" Ghost Wind asked.

"You are my love and my partner. Even when we take mates we will not be separated." Nikolaos said.

"Ok Niko, I will try and be good, for you." Ghost Wind said.

One of the Polarian females approached. "She is beautiful. Is she a good hunter?"

Nikolaos replied. "She is learning the skills of a huntress; Ghost Wind is too young for her first hunt. She is my partner and love."

"I am Night Breeze Bearing. May I touch her?" Night Breeze asked.

Nikolaos said. "She is not my property. You will have to ask her."

Ghost Wind told her. "I will permit it, as long as you are gentle."

Night Breeze looked at Ghost Wind. "You can talk?"

"Yes, I can." Ghost Wind said.

Night Breeze gentle stroked her fur. "You are beautiful Lady Ghost Wind. I also understand why you are jealous of your partner. He is very handsome."

Ghost Wind looked at her. "You are brave Night Breeze. You know I am jealous of him. Of all the young females you alone approached and you approached me. I like you. You may talk with Nikolaos. Only I may call him Niko."

Night Breeze kissed her. "Thank you Ghost Wind. Sir Nikolaos, I have been given permission to talk with you."

Nikolaos looked at Ghost Wind. "I don't belong to you either."

Ghost Wind huffed. "That Niko is a matter of opinion. I marked you."

"You were a little puppy. You couldn't help it." Nikolaos said.

Ghost Wind smiled. "That is his story."

Night Breeze took Nikolaos paw. The three went for a walk and talk. The other young girls were upset.

Maryam saw some boys throwing knives at a target. "May I compete with you?"

One of the older boys looked at her. He tried to push her away, as he said. "This is only for warriors in . . ."

Maryam smiled, as she threw him to the ground. She pinned him on his stomach and put a blade to his throat. "I have completed my first hunt and have slain several enemies. Do you doubt me?"

"Please, Lady Maryam Artemus, forgive him." An older warrior said.

Maryam let him up. "No harm done."

The older boy bowed to her. "Forgive me Death Dancer. I did not know you were real."

The other boys pleaded with her to compete with them.

Maryam smiled. She even offered to have them pick weapons for her to use.

After two cycles the competition came down to her and one other young Polarian Warrior candidate.

"Maryam Artemus, I am David Maritinus, Nephew of Aleut Maritinus, and cousin to Ben Maritinus." David said.

Maryam shrugged. "It is a pleasure to meet you."

"When, I beat you. You will agree to become my betrothed." David said.

Maryam looked at him. "I am too young for such non-sense."

"Are you afraid of a challenge?" David asked.

Maryam glared at him. "I fear no one."

An advanced course was setup; warriors from throughout the village come to watch. Aleut arrived too late to stop it.

They both started at the same time; knife for knife, spear for spear, and arrow for arrow. Each target was a perfect bull's eye. The last target was a double handed axe throw.

Maryam's two struck dead center.

One of David's hit dead center the other slightly below.

He dropped to his knees. Maryam walked over and lifted him up. Then she gave him a very passionate kiss. "Let's try again in oh, say nine years. When, we are old enough, for me to consider losing the contest. Or you get a little bit stronger with your left wrist."

"Maryam," he said as she walked away, "will you accept this necklace, after all you won."

Maryam laughed. "David Maritinus you are a charlatan. All right, I will wear your necklace. In nine years you better be able to back it up or I will give it back."

David put it on her and kissed her. "You still will not be old enough to marry."

"No, but I believe in a long courtship." Maryam said.

Aleut looked at David. "Cub, you will not be able to handle her when she is older."

David shrugged. "I cannot handle her now. I am two years older. But, I will have her as my wife Aleut."

Andreios was looking at an interesting object. He was trying to figure out its purpose.

"Don't touch that!" A young female Polarian yelled.

Andreios bowed. "It is a solar water purification system is it not?"

The young Polarian nodded. "It would be if I could get it to work. It is a school project."

Andreios smiled. "Maybe I could help."

She looked at him. "You know something about these?"

Andreios shrugged. "Maybe, I do just a little. Your design is good. Do you have another jar?"

Andreios made a few modifications and it started working.

She looked at him. "You are kidding me. That is all it took!"

Andreios nodded. "I am Andreios Artemus."

"I am Ruth Chukchi. Would you like to come in for some tea?" Ruth asked.

"Thank you." Andreios said.

"Father this is Andreios Artemus. He helped me fix my class project." Ruth said.

"Well young Andreios, are you a young engineer?" Sire Chukchi asked.

"I have been training under Dr. Vallen and Dr. Beary Maxumus and a few others." Andreios said.

"Have you worked in metal?" Sire Chukchi asked.

"Yes, Sire. I make jewelry and weapons." Andreios said.

"Come here show me. Can you make a ring from this piece of gold?" Sire Chukchi asked.

Andreios prayed over the gold and started heating it. He formed a ring but drew off some of the gold. He formed a rope bracelet. Then returned to the ring and reheated it and reformed it putting a similar design into it. Then he pulled three blue stones from a pouch in his pocket and placed them on the ring. Then Andreios prayed over it again and presented them to Sire Chukchi. "Sire, will these serve your needs."

Sire Chukchi looked at him. "I don't understand."

"You wished a gift for Ruth. Tomorrow it is her birthday is it not." Andreios asked.

"But, how did you know?" Sire Chukchi asked.

"You imprinted it on the metal. It told me when I formed it." Andreios said.

Sire Chukchi looked at the ring and the bracelet. They had been formed by a master craftsbear, not a cub. Yet, he had watched them being made. "Yes, Sir Artemus, but what do I owe you?"

"A cup of tea and perhaps if you don't mind a few cookies." Andreios said.

"Ruth these are for you. They were made by a Master Craftsbear. Would you give him some tea and cookies? He says that is his payment for his work." Sire Chukchi said with a smile.

She looked at the stones. "Andreios these stones are worth a fortune! Your parents will not want you to give them away!"

"Why? I picked them up from a stream near home, cut, and polished them myself. I may do with them as I please." Andreios said.

"But they are worth a lot of credits!" Ruth exclaimed.

Andreios shrugged. "I want for nothing Ruth. I have my duties and my shop. I have a family and two clans. The Creator has blessed me."

She gave him his tea and cookies. Then she kissed him.

Andreios told her. "The cookies are wonderful. You baked them? The kiss was also nice."

Ruth beamed. "Yes, I baked them."

Sire Chukchi went into the other room. He looked at his late wife's picture and smiled. Then a tear fell to the ground.

That night Snow Flower noticed the necklace on Maryam. "Maryam, what is that you are wearing?"

Maryam shrugged. "It is a gift from a David Maritinus. He challenged me. He said if he won I was his betrothed. He lost of course. I still took the betrothal necklace. I told him he had nine years to get good enough to beat me or I would give it back. He is cute in nine years I might let him win."

"Young lady, we need to talk!" Snow Flower said.

Ghost Wind looked at Nikolaos, "Yes, she is nice. Still did you have to invite her to join us for the celebration tomorrow?"

Snow Flower looked at Nikolaos "Not you also!"

Andreios walked in.

"Where have you been young boar?" Snow Flower asked.

"Well, there was this young female . . . Her dad has a metal shop and she helps . . ." Andreios tried to explain.

"Savato come and talk to your sons!" Snow Flower said.

Savato took her paw. "Behave properly."

"Yes, father." Andreios and Nikolaos said.

Snow Flower looked at him as he led her into their room. "That is all you're going to say?"

Savato looked at her as he undressed her. "Yes, that is all I need to say. Except that you are gorgeous and I want you."

Snow Flower sighed. "Oh well."

The celebration started at 8:00 cycles the next morning. Ruth came for Andreios and asked if she could take him to the hot springs. Night Breeze was with her so was David. Ice Song explained that she was the older sister, and she would go with them. Ghost Wind start to complain. Night Breeze said that she had brought a treat for her and of course she was expected to come.

Erin, Agathag, and Sho-Sho went and found a place to set so they could watch the dancers. Beary and Pompey with the twins joined the other adults in the circle. Soon they saw Erin out dancing with the other children. It was like she had been taught the dance from birth.

Aleut said. "Erin is remarkable she only watched it once."

Beary explained. "But, she saw it twice with her and Sho-Sho's eyes."

Aleut nodded "The bonding and she is a true *Royal Valkyrie* of your people."

Beary sighed. "It appears possible."

Aleut laughed. "Oh, it is more than possible. She got up early and joined me for coffee. She showed me her new trick. I told her she should keep it secret. She said she would, but I was special."

Beary dropped his head "Thank you, Aleut."

Star Glow and her daughters started to relax. They even started having fun.

That night there was dancing and eating. Slowly Beary and Pompey took their children to bed.

Sho-Sho and Ice Song serenaded Aleut and Lunara with a song that Ballard had written called *Song of Winter Love*. Several couples drifted away after they were done. Lunara kissed both of them and said that they had given a great gift to the village.

Nikolaos and Ghost Wind walked Night Breeze home. Four young boars confronted them.

"What are you doing with one of our female's outsider?" One of the boys said.

"I am Nikolaos Artemus of the Red Paw, Grandson of Nord Polard." Nikolaos said.

"I say you are nothing." The largest boy said.

Ghost Wind growled.

Nikolaos told her. "There is only four. Look after Night Breeze Ghost Wind. They are not worthy of you my love."

Another one laughed. "He talks to the dumb beast."

"Who, are you calling a dumb beast? You, ignorant blow-hard." Ghost Wind asked.

"It can talk!" Another one said.

The largest one looked at Night Breeze. "I told you what would happen, if you went out with an outsider, to you and him."

Nikolaos's eyes turned red. "You dishonorable pig, you would threatened a female. Come and dance if you dare."

The larger one swung at Nikolaos. But Nikolaos wasn't there. He felt Nikolaos hit him lightly. He started to laugh till his legs stopped working and he fell on his face. The three others charged in. Nikolaos hit them before they knew what happened. They were falling. Then a large paw grabbed Nikolaos from behind. Nikolaos hit the wrist. Then hit the older warrior two blows to the chest. Then he heard Night Breeze yell, "No!"

Nikolaos dropped his arm walked around to the older warrior's back and hit him in the back. Then bowed his head, "I apologies Sire, forgive me."

Another warrior looked at him. "What happened here?"

Night Breeze spoke up. "They attacked us."

"Are they dead?" The first warrior asked as he slowly rose up.

"No Sire. I only incapacitated them long enough to get Night Breeze home." Nikolaos said.

The other one looked at him. "Can you wake them?"

Nikolaos nodded. He then went and hit all four in the center of the back.

They all four slowly sat up. "He tried to kill us!" They wailed.

Ghost Wind huffed. "If he wanted you dead, you would be dead."

"Come all of you. You will go before Sire Maritinus he will determine the truth." The older warrior said.

Aleut looked at Nikolaos, after he had listened to the statements of the other four boys. Night Breeze had not been allowed to speak yet, nor had Ghost Wind.

"Nikolaos, they make bold charges." Aleut said.

"Yes Sire, they do." Nikolaos said.

"What do you say?" Aleut asked.

"They are cowards and liars, Sire." Nikolaos said.

Aleut sighed. "It pains me to agree. Do you cubs know why I know you are liars? No, *Warrior of the Red Paw* can lie once they receive the Mark."

The father of the oldest boy laughed. "He is a cub, how can he have the Mark?"

Aleut looked at Nikolaos. "Show them!"

Nikolaos took off his shirt. On his right shoulder was the *Mark of the Red Paw,* with a dragon heart.

Aleut turned to them. "Tell them how you earned The Mark Nikolaos of the Red Paw."

Nikolaos looked at the four boys then at the father. "I earned it in single combat, against creatures that would harm members of my clan and family."

Aleut looked at them. "He is a true warrior. As is his brother and sisters; Andreios, Maryam, and Ice Song have received The Mark. They all earned it in combat. Do you wish to say anything Nikolaos?"

Nikolaos bowed to Aleut. "My first mother was killed by pirate scum. I took an oath that no female under my protection would ever be harmed again. If I could prevent it and if not . . . I would see she was avenged. You four threatened Night Breeze. I will be leaving soon. You might think to harm her. Know this, if you harass her, if you hurt her in any way. I will return and take your life. This I swear. Sire if you wish to punish me, I will accept your judgment."

Aleut smiled. He looked at the four boys. "This is how a warrior acts. Not a coward or a cull. Crawl home, in your shame and dishonor, then mend, your ways."

Three of the boys dropped their heads and left. The older boy refused to leave.

"No, he used a trick!" The oldest boy screamed.

Maryam walked in. "Oh, it is the boy who likes to pick on girls."

The father scowled. "This is a hall for warriors not little girl cubs."

Maryam lowered the right shoulder of her shirt for all to see. "I Qualify, Sire."

Aleut tried not to laugh. "Maryam, you are not helping."

"Sire, he wants a rematch against Nikolaos. That would not be wise. Nikolaos' blood now boils. He would not stop in time. This one would die. Then his father would demand revenge and he would die. It would be a waste." Maryam said.

Aleut nodded. "You are wise Maryam. What do you suggest?"

Maryam shrugged. "He likes to bully females. Let him fight one. Me!"

The father started to say something. Aleut held up his paw.

"What say you cub?" Aleut asked.

"Bare paws no weapons." The older cub said.

Maryam nodded, "Fine with me."

Artemus wasn't happy about it. But Snow Flower was. She was even taking bets on how long the cub would last.

Nikolaos went over to Maryam. "Why did you interfere?"

Maryam kissed him. "Because, my brother killing has become too easy for us, and I love you."

Nikolaos sighed, "Alright Maryam."

Nikolaos went and stood with Night Breeze.

Maryam smiled and motioned for him to come on.

The cub charged. He swung his paw. He knew he hit her. Her head snapped to the right then her feet caught him in the side of the head.

He stumbled back. He tried to tackle her. She slide through his arms and hit him in the stomach, as she slide between his legs.

He was hurting. He straightened up and went at her again.

This time Maryam jumped up, wrapped her legs around his head, and threw him to the ground. He tried to rise up, but then lay down.

Maryam looked at Aleut. "It is done."

Aleut nodded.

She turned and walked away. At that point a knife was in the air. She flicked a blade it hit the knife and deflected it into the ground. Then she was on the cub. She knocked him back down, pinned him to the ground, and placed a knife on either side of his throat.

"You said no weapons. Then you try and kill me from behind, like a coward. Where is your honor? I could take your life and not even your father could complain. But you are not worthy of a warriors death." Maryam said then she stood up.

The father ran to his son. "Aleut, he is not right!"

Aleut looked at the boy. "Maryam, by our law he can be put to death. What say you?"

Maryam looked at Aleut. "Death does not lead to redemption. Give him a chance to regain his honor."

Aleut looked at the boy. "She spared your life twice do not waste it. It shall not be spared thrice."

The boy cowered in fear, as his father rushed him home. The father packed their belonging. His wife helped him. They would have to leave till their son could regain his honor.

When it came time to leave, Aleut presented the Artemus Cubs with gifts.

Night Breeze had made a vest for carrying things for Ghost Wind. It was made of soft seal hide and was water proof. She also made a pouch for Nikolaos to carry dreams in.

David Maritinus told Maryam that he would look forward to seeing her soon.

Maryam told him he better practice more if he wanted her.

Ruth kissed Andreios and told him to stay in touch. She said she would cherish her gifts.

Aleut kissed Kat and Paulette. Then he said that he and Lunara would visit soon.

Star Glow kissed Lunara and thanked her for her kindness. The daughters did likewise. The years of abuse had not been washed away but healing had started.

The trip back to Andreas Prime was quiet each couple pondering the future. Ben looked at Gabriel who was now a 1st Lieutenant. Kat and Paulette had made Lieutenant Jg. Life seemed to be spinning out of control.

Artemus looked at his children and worried about the innocence that was lost. Maryam smiled at him. "Daddy, the Pirates took that away from us. You gave us love and purpose."

Artemus got up and kissed her. Then he smiled at Agathag who was playing with Erin. No, none of his children would have normal lives, but they would have lives filled with love.

Beary looked at his two sleeping cubs, both had a metallic shine to their coats. He wondered if they had the gene. Caesar told him that Erin did but like Ti it was more subtle.

When they got back the friends went home.

Star Glow took Ben by the arm. "Sire how, can I ever thank you?"

Ben looked at her, "Mother, I am Ben your Son-in-Law, the one that loves Kat."

"But why do you show us this kindness? You have to know what my husband did to me and my other daughters. He never touched Kat. He feared her." Ben held his anger. The cull was dead.

"Star Glow you are blameless. You lived in fear at least to a point. I grew up in a home of strong females, like Kat and strong males, like my father. You probably never considered ending you and your daughters torment. If I treated Kat like he did you, my mother would kill me, if Kat didn't." Ben said.

Star Glow started to cry. "Then why forgive me? If you know I was weak!"

Ben shrugged. "It is not my place to judge you Star Glow. Is not love, and grace simple gifts to give mother? They cost me nothing. Yet, they are what you need."

Star Glow kissed him. "My daughter has done well. I will serve you well son. I swear."

Ben kissed her. "Just forgive yourself and be happy. You have a new life."

Beary looked at the two young dragons that Widja brought into the new nursery. "What are their names?"

"The purple one is Roseanna. The emerald green is Shamus." Widja said.

"How do . . . I mean . . ." Beary tried to ask.

Widja just said. "Watch they will call to one another. Did you not feel Gamey's presence your whole life?"

Beary thought. "I don't know, but I do miss him when we are not together."

Widja nodded. "Your bond is not as strong as it would have been. You and he are too old now. He hatched too early because his father was ill. Still the bond is there."

Beary looked at Widja, "What about you? Were you destined to be bonded?"

Widja laughed. "But, Beary I am. She hatched too soon or me too late but the bond is stronger than she knows. Now, watch as they choose."

Without hesitation Roseanna walked over and curled up near Caesar Ben. Shamus did the same with Savato Horatio.

Widja smiled. "They chose each other."

Erin asked. "Sho-Sho your brother and sister have chosen. Are you going to teach them your secret?"

Sho-Sho thought. "Erin, I will discuss it with Great Grandmother. Perhaps it should be her decision."

Erin sighed, "They will grow strong. Do you fear their strength?"

Sho-Sho looked at Erin, "Yes, mine, Ice Song's, and yours Erin."

Erin replied, "Don't be my love. We will not abuse our power. No, Sho-Sho you did not! You did what you had to do."

Sho-Sho looked at Erin this was the first time she had ever spoken harshly to her. "Erin?"

Erin dropped her head. "You have been tearing out your heart. Do you really believe you can hide your pain from me? It makes me mad that you even tried! I know I am only a little cub, but I share all your memories. Plus the blessings have had their side effects. My abilities are growing as fast as yours my love."

Sho-Sho looked at her. "Oh, my poor love!"

Erin shrugged. "Sho-Sho it is who we are. We need to play the game. I need to be a little girl cub. Even if my mind is growing faster, did not the same thing happen to Daddy? Look at Maryam and Nikolaos and Andreios. Even Agathag is starting to become like us."

Sho-Sho looked at her. "But, how is that possible?"

Erin replied. "She was touched twice by Fire and Ice."

CHAPTER 13

Epilogue

THE PRATIS SYSTEM is being resettled and the friends have been recalled to start construction on a new Warship.

Sinister forces are trying to infiltrate Bearilian Society. Even after the fall of the Gang of Seven. Decent bears are wondering if some of their leaders aren't still for sell.

Beary's family has grown, so has the number of bears connected to his life. With each addition his quiet fears grow.

Octavious is now Vice President of the Bearilian Federation.

Angelina has started a new medical institute on Andreas Prime. She and Octavious past have threatened to surface. New threats face the Federation and their family.

Tiberius and Babs have returned home to the *Palisades* with a cub on the way.

Private Harpeth's family was brought to *Andreas Prime* to be near him, as he goes through rehabilitation. Angelina has personally taken over his case.

The entire *307th Aces Marine Division* was transferred to *Andreas Prime*. This became their new home base.

Alpine City was quickly becoming a major military shipyard. While *St Elaina's*, was becoming a major commercial port, much to Justinian's pleasure.

The *EAQ*, with its new crew moved on, with, a destroyer escort, towards its next system.

Soon others would be joining the team.